In Peace Lies Havoc

USA Today & *Wall Street Journal* Bestselling Author

AMO JONES

Editing: Paige Smith.
Proofreading: Rebecca Fairest Reviews.
Betas: Sarah Grim Sentz, Tijuana Turner.
Book Cover: Hang Le.
Formatting: Champagne Book Design.

To my Koro, who I lost earlier this year. Who stole me from my mother when I was nine-years-old, booked us flights to Christchurch, New Zealand, and took me to my first ever circus.
I get my rebellious soul partially from him.

"Welcome to Midnight Mayem. We are not a circus, we are not a carnival, and the only thing that you should be afraid of losing tonight, is your sanity…"

Introduction

Thirteen years ago, I felt evil. It penetrated my flesh and imprinted its scent into my soul to create a haunting concoction of poison, also known as The Shadow. I would further use this scent to draw out other evil because The Shadow was the worst of the worst. He wasn't just dark or evil; he was deranged. There was no good in his soul, no droplets of light. He tormented me. Everywhere I turned, he was there to make sure I knew that I'd never be free.

In every dark corner, he would be there. Watching me, waiting. For what? I never knew. But I was about to find out...

Prologue

Dove Noctem Hendry. Cheer captain and most popular girl at Charlston Academy, apparently. People were astounded that I became so popular so quickly in Eureka Springs, Arkansas, even as a small child. We moved here when I was just short of eleven, right after—the incident. The incident was something we didn't talk about. I mean, my parents and highly paid shrinks could only bring it down to me suffering from PTSD and suppressed memory. It's all I'd known, which was not much at all. But according to this yearbook, I was the most popular girl at school and a modern-day ballerina. Yearbooks are weird. Like, hey! Here's a reminder of what might have been the worst years of your life. Mine weren't bad; they were actually pretty great. I just didn't like reminders in general.

A knock on the door pulled me out of nostalgia. "Come in!" I yelled, closing the book.

My dad was standing at the threshold, his collar loosened around his neck and a smile on his face. "We're thinking of getting takeout for dinner. What do you want?"

I fluttered my eyelashes. "Thai!"

Dad nodded his head toward the hallway. "Thai it is. Come on, before your mom starts yelling about your ballerina slippers being left out in the foyer." Mom complained about everything, but she liked to pick even more when it came to me. I was used to it. When you'd been cultivated by the neglect of your own mother, it's easy to acclimatize to the callousness of the world.

Her emotional desertion only somewhat stabilized me in a way, making me stronger, and anyway, I was one hundred percent a daddy's girl.

Climbing off the covers, I dashed into my closet to pull on my Ugg boots. My mom did nothing but stay at home and work on her garden beds, and my father was into political science. He wanted to run for office one day, probably sooner rather than later.

I treaded down the marble stairs, an extra bounce in my step. I had been reciting the cheer that would no doubt take home Nationals, so every single step was a dance step.

"Come on, kiddo." Dad pulled me under his arm, kissing the top of my head, just as my mom smiled at me, opening the door.

It happened fast.

Pop! Pop! Pop!

I remembered my dad shoving me behind him, and the desperate screams coming from my mom. We all dropped to the ground, my father lying on top of me, his back to my front, shielding me from harm.

"You need to run, Dove. Run."

I—words were caught in my throat, threatening to choke me.

The door swung open, and four men stood still, all with their guns raised. They were wearing plain black bandanas, and on any other day, I would have thought they were street thugs, maybe wanting money. Until I noticed a couple of them were wearing suits.

The main one tilted his head, and just when I thought he was about to say something, my dad opened his mouth. "Dove is going to leave before you do anything…"

They seemed to think over their next move. Words being silently spoken between the distance of each breath.

"Dove…" My father leaned up onto his elbow, his eyes coming to mine. A dark blue pool that's deep enough to spill over his cheeks. "You're going to leave." His voice was slow. Hushed, but forceful.

I shook my head, not wanting to leave my dad. Not like this. Not ever.

"Little Bird…" he pleaded, tears finally leaking over the edges. "Please."

He shoved me back, and the first thing I felt was the warm liquid seep through my clothes and stick to my belly. The first thing I smelled was the strong metal slosh of blood. The first thing I heard was the dying screams of my mother. But the last thing I heard before everything went black was his voice.

"We'll be back, Dovey. I'll hear you when you speak. I'll see you where you dance. I'll always be watching you…" His voice sounded juvenile. Not as old as what I would think they all were due to their size and shadows.

Another man stepped into the pact. This one I felt was older. He was wearing a fedora that shaded his mouth and a cigar was hanging between his lips. "Leave."

I felt him in places that I shouldn't have felt. Through foster home after foster home, he was there, existing between the furnishings and oxygen. I could sense him when I thought I was all alone. The Shadow was everywhere I was. It existed between what was real and what was in my mind. It tormented me for what felt like all of my life, and the worst part about being tormented by something you didn't know, was that you never knew when that torment would end.

Present

I was fourteen years old when I stopped expecting the world to soften its edges for me and learned to roughen mine instead. I learned that if you find yourself in a dark day, it only means that the sun is about to rise. Well, it was a mantra that I became accustomed to as I was growing up. I had to bring it down to that simple paragraph to strengthen my mind and remind it that I was going to survive. Bouncing from foster home to foster home until you hit eighteen isn't ideal, but I'm an optimist, so the way I see it, I never had to really rely on anyone.

Not. At. All.

And besides, I've managed to keep a fairly positive outlook on life, despite my current circumstances. Once I hit eighteen, I emptied my bank account and hitched a ride way the hell away from where anyone would know me, or where most people like to call Miami Beach. Okay, so it's not a terrible place to live, and it's probably one of my favorite places to be, but eventually, I want to bail. Maybe settle in the PNW or somewhere with a little more frost in the air. I prefer cold to the heat.

"Dove!" Richard calls out from behind the bar. I work in a bar right on the outskirts of the city. It draws in the right crowd for good tips. Rich folk who just want to splash some cash.

I raise my eyebrows at him in question, so he continues to jog toward me, his hands shoved into his pockets. "Sorry. I always forget about the speech thing."

They always assume that because I don't talk much that I'm incapable of doing so. Humans are so quick to slap a label on someone who doesn't conform to the norm. I do talk, but I don't talk much *here* where I'm scared and shackled to the reality of always being watched. I knew it wasn't safe. I wasn't safe. *"I'll hear you when you speak."* I shiver, zipping my leather jacket up farther while slipping my hands into my pockets to keep them warm. "Are you able to work at the bar tomorrow? Jules called in sick, and we usually have a backup, but we can't get ahold of any of the temp girls."

I shrug, nodding my head. "Sure!"

"Good!" Richard murmurs. "I appreciate it, Dove." I watch as his back disappears into the dark room, strobe lights flicking and flashing, cutting through the obscurity like light sabers during a *Star Wars* movie.

I quickly slip through the thin crowd of people, heading straight for backstage.

"Dove! Hey, girl!" Natasha waves at me from her makeup cubicle.

I nod my head at her, slipping off my clothes until I'm standing in nothing but panties and a bra.

"You up second tonight, boo!" Tash further says, swiping blood red lipstick over her soft lips.

I smile, gathering up my belongings and placing them in my cubicle. I begin on my makeup and hair, making sure I go extra on both. Peering back at myself in the mirror, my lips curl between my teeth. My skin is silky smooth with a natural tan, and my hair is a deep red. Girls used to be envious of my skin because it's never seen one freckle or imperfection, and unlike most redheads, I don't burn in the sun; I tan.

I pile my hair onto the top of my head and get started on my makeup. Lining my dark green eyes with black liner, I giggle as Tash begins rapping beside me. It's what she does to warm up every night. I love Tash, but I feel sorry for her. She has a five-year-old daughter and a shit excuse of a husband. I know that if she could, she wouldn't work here. I've asked a couple of times why she does, but she shrugs me off as if she's made peace with her fate.

It makes me uncomfortable, and we're not that close, so I leave it.

Thirty minutes later and I'm ready.

I step out onto the stage, all lights cutting out as a single spotlight flashes on me. Clutching the pole in my hand, "Voyeur Girl" by Stephen starts playing. It's the song I always open to. Now it's almost as though the beat and lyrics are inscribed into my bones, orchestrating my fluid movements as I dance around the stage. I lose myself in the music and let my body be taken over by the trance-like sound. I don't have to look around to know that people are watching. Tash says that men come every night when they know I'm dancing. I don't know how much

3

truth there is to that because I never pay attention. I know I'm above average. My mom and dad had paid good money all my life to make sure my footing, my temperament, and body remained in sync with whatever music was playing, but aside from that, I have always had a natural wave for dance.

I continue to float around, my body rolling against the pole. I skim my hand down my belly, toward my upper thighs as I bend down, spreading my knees wide and bringing them back together. I slowly open my eyes, but I don't know why because I never open them. My eyes are always closed, fixed on splashing art against a dark canvas by the waves of my body. But I open them, and they land on a man seated by the bar. I can't make out his face because he's wearing a dark hoodie that's covering most of it. His knees are spread wide as he lounges back against the bar. I may not be able to see him, but I feel him on me. With every thrust of my hips, I feel as though his eyes are caressing the curves of my body. Chills creep over my flesh as I squash the thoughts that are invading my mental space. The song winds down, and sweat pours out from me as I flick my long red hair all around. Gazing back to where the man was, I find him still there, watching me carefully. Everyone fades into the background as the energy surrounding us crackles in the air. I watch as the tip of his cigarette burns like a lit match, calling me to him with every inhale. Smoke clouds gather around him as he exhales. *Why can't I look away?*

Even though I can only make out the outline of his eyes, I feel them on me. Eye contact is the language that no one can speak, but chemistry is fluent with; it's the language of fate. It's two souls catching on fire without a single word being spoken. I continue dancing to the song until the very last strum before making my way backstage, wanting to see if I can get a closer look at him. *Him*. There's an air of familiarity that hovers over his body, enticing me. Or maybe it's the language that no one speaks, and I've suddenly decided to take classes.

"Hey, Dove!" Rich interrupts my thoughts, nudging his head toward me as I make my way to the bar. "The usual?" Rich is a middle-aged man with a full beard. He has two little girls who he raises alone since his wife died in a car accident when they were babies. Richard also owns this bar. Most people would think that some guy who owns a strip joint must be desperate and sleazy, but that's just not the case. He has three girls who he kept on since he purchased the place from the previous owner a couple of years ago, and that's not by his choice, because he kicked all the rest of the girls out, wanting to turn this into more of a biker bar—since that's what he also does—but he knew Tash and I needed the work and the tips. We could have taken on the bar by bartending, but he had already promised the barmaids that they would keep their positions. So he kept Tash, Vane, and me, which worked out perfectly since the three of us get along quite well.

"Yes, please," I say, my eyes flying around the room to see if Mystery Guy is still here.

He's not.

My heart sinks a little, so I pick up my vodka, lime and soda and shoot it back, running the cushion of my thumb over my lip to swipe off the residue.

"I'll see you tomorrow." I slide my empty glass over toward Rich, who runs his hand over his long, scruffy beard.

"Yeah, all right, baby girl."

I slip to the back of the bar toward the staffing area, grabbing may long coat that drops to my knees, and buttoning it up. I pull my phone and headphones out of my pocket, swiping through

Spotify to find a new song. Something I can maybe sweat out to when I go back to my run-down apartment. I love to dance. It's something that keeps my soul alive and my limbs on fire. Music is the cure to all of my troubles for the exact minutes that it plays. After a while, I push on any song as I'm shoving through the back exit of the bar.

The door slams closed, and I fidget with my phone, ready to walk to the bus stop.

A hand slams over my mouth, shocking me into fight-or-flight. I tear out my earphones, kicking and screaming to turn around, but the thick body that's behind me holds too tight, unwilling to let go.

I feel soft lips brush against the lobe of my ear, warmth slithering over my skin. "If you want to break free, Little Dovey, I would advise you not to scream." His other hand comes up to the front of my throat, and he clenches. "It gets my dick hard, and you don't want that."

Two

Dove

I lie on pristine marble flooring, my body jerking with every breath. The room is clean, almost sterile. It's one large square with cell bars as a door. There's a diamond chandelier that dangles lavishly from the center of the roof and a single toilet and basin to the back of the room. A ball of fire has sparked inside my chest, its grip refusing to let go. I'm cold. So cold. Goosebumps scatter over my skin in colossal welts, my once tanned skin has now fallen to a sepia white. Grazing my finger over the leftover crumbs from my cookie on the ground, I draw the number twenty-one.

Twenty-one is how long I've been here.

The men who visit me usually arrive in fours, but this

morning, the man who is seated opposite me is alone. He's not someone I have seen before now and something tells me there's a reason why. He's wearing a black party mask with neon lights attached to it: both eyes are blue crosses. He tilts his head, but doesn't speak, almost like he's examining me.

I crawl backward, not wanting to be near him. I can feel him. I felt it when he walked down the corridor. His anger. His antagonism. He picks up the knife that's beside him, blood dripping off the blade and falling to the once spotless floor. I watch as his finger runs over the red liquid, tainting his skin. Then he suddenly flies to his feet, and I jump, horrified by what might be to come.

One.

Two.

Three.

Four.

Four steps and he's in front of me. *I don't want to be here.* My body shakes, and my head pounds. They keep us fed and hydrated, so I know it's from fear.

I squeeze my eyes closed as the sound of his zipper slashes through the empty room. The smell of blood is stronger the closer he gets.

I picture myself dancing. *Happy.* Pointe shoes tied around my ankles, my hands flailing above my head as I begin the steps to execute a perfectly elegant arabesque. Smooth flesh comes to my mouth, and I don't have to open my eyes to know what it is. I bite down, not wanting to spread my lips, but his hand comes to the back of my hair, and he yanks my head back, my eyes flying open. The man picks up his knife and presses it to my throat. I can feel the blood dripping down my collarbone. Either from me or from whomever else he had just killed.

I continue to refuse, so he presses the blade harder while his cock jerks against my soft lips.

Tears pour down my face as my resilience kicks in. My mouth parts, and his cock slips in. I've never been raped before. Never felt forced. Something happens when you've been taken advantage of. It's as though they take some of your humanity and replace it with their odor. His dick slides in and out fast, forcing himself down my throat. When I bite down on it roughly, he leaves it lodged down my airway, cutting off my breathing. Once he's had enough of me fighting him, he shoves me backward and crawls up my body, his hand cupping my pussy. He shoves through two fingers then three, before tearing off my shirt with his other hand.

With every thrust of his fingers, he takes a part of my soul, and I don't want it back. He didn't need to put his dick inside of me to rape me, but I'm still thankful that he didn't. This was something else. There was a reason to why he exhorted himself into me by using his fingers only. He had a message to send, and unfortunately, I was going to be the deliverer.

Once he leaves, I fall asleep with tears crusted over my cheeks and memories flashing through my head of my father and the Thai food that I never got to eat with him.

Soft sobbing echoes around the room, along with snuffling and shuffling of a body.

"Do you know why they took us?" the voice asks, but I don't pay it any attention. She is one of many, one of twenty-one, making her twenty-two. She starts crying again, and I have to fight the urge to tell her to be quiet. The tears only enforce their sick games, I am sure. "Do you talk?"

Actually, I do, but I don't want to reply to your pathetic cries for help. Twenty-one girls have cried. Nothing I do or say can comfort you.

I remain still, going over the number, until I can see the grey marble that sits beneath the old crumbs. *Twenty-two.* I write.

I finally sit up, resting my back against the wall.

The girl's eyes come to mine. They're brown, the same color as the floor on which we sit. Her wrists are bruised by the shackles that keep us locked to the walls. Water drips down my back from the crack in the concrete above us. She's pretty. But they all are.

"You're pretty," she whispers, swiping her long brown hair away from her face. Tears have left cleaned streaks down each of her cheeks.

I don't speak.

She tilts her head. "I gather we're probably going to die in here." She leans her head against the wall, drawing her long legs to her chest. I want to be nice to her. Tell her that maybe they won't kill her. Tell her that I don't know what happens after this. But I don't know. *I never know.* They come and they go, and I stay. For twenty-one girls. Some girls are in here for longer, some only a short time. *Time.* Something I've lost track of. The sun sets and the sun rises, but my world remains still, confined to these walls that keep me locked inside.

I examine the new girl closely. I've noticed how all girls are similar in one way. Age. That's as far as I have gotten.

"I take it you don't speak." She exhales, her head bowing. "It's fine. I guess it makes sense in a way. My name is Rose; I'm twenty years old, and up until yesterday, I was a dancer at—" I jerk forward, my eyes narrowing. "Wow!" she murmurs, flinching backward. I don't blame her. I probably looked crazy. But all the girls who have been in here, none of them have spoken much to me. Mainly, they all cry. Scream. Then there was the one who tried to claw her way out of the bars on the door, her fingernails detaching from her flesh as blood seeped down her hands. None of them directly blurted their story to me. Were they all dancers? Like me? Maybe.

Rose searches my eyes, her face morphing. "You understand me?" She must think, because I don't speak right now, that I don't speak English.

I nod.

She licks her dry, cracked lips. "Why did you jump? Are you the same age as me?"

I shake my head.

"No?" she mutters.

I nod.

"You are?"

I roll my eyes, getting tired of this. I want to speak. I open my mouth, the words teasing the tip of my tongue gently, but like always when faced with something I don't want to deal with, I choke, and my mouth slams closed.

"You're broken, Dove. You will always be broken." I shiver, The Shadow's voice echoing over my flesh. He followed me everywhere. I woke during the night and swore I saw him lurking in the dark corner of my room. Everywhere I went, I could sense him. *Is he here, too?*

"Wait!" Rose interrupts my internal meltdown, inching forward. "Dancer? You were a dancer, too?"

My head snaps up, my eyes eating up the distance between

us. I nod, my long red hair falling over my shoulders. I lick my swollen lips, wanting to force words out, but they don't come. They never do. But then—"Yes."

"Wait!" Her hand comes up to silence herself. "You do speak?"

I chew on my lip. "Yes. I just don't like to, and I have issues when I'm faced with unfamiliar trauma. It's a defense mechanism that happens when I'm scared." I shake my head, forcing myself to be quiet. I don't want to sound weak.

Rose seems to understand, without understanding. My chest begins to flutter. Can I like her? I don't like anyone. "Well, I danced at a hip-hop club. For money. Having no family and being broke as shit isn't always fun, but fun doesn't pay the bills." Rose is beautiful. Her skin is a few shades darker than mine, but more on the lighter scale. She's clearly part African American. When she smiles, her straight white teeth beam. "I'll go through the dance styles, and you tell me what yours was?"

I nod, excited with the new lead.

She eyes me up and down. "Hmmm, ballet?"

I freeze.

"Ballet?" she asks, smiling. "I was right!?"

I shake my head. "No." She was right, in a sense, but it has been a long time since I hung up my slippers. Now, I don't dance for pleasure. I dance to live. Literally.

"Damn. I was sure you looked like a ballet girl."

I roll my eyes at her judgment. "Okay."

She laughs. "All right, all right, I know, that was bad. Okay, how about hip-hop?"

I shake my head. "No."

"Jazz?"

Shake.

She raises one perfectly manicured eyebrow. "...stripper?"

I gulp, my lips curling under my teeth. I nod.

"Damn!" She laughs. "Little preppy princess is a stripper. I mean, I see it. You got that whole my son's girlfriend thing going on."

I glare at her.

She chuckles again. "I'm sorry. I don't have a filter."

Clearly.

"Well, how long have you been here for?"

I bring my finger to the ground and write twenty-two. "Twenty-two girls later..."

"And they've all left?" she asks, fear glassing over her eyes briefly.

With good reason.

I offer her a sympathetic smile. "They just disappeared. I don't know where to. I never spoke to any of them like I am you."

"To where?" Roses whispers.

Heavy boots slap against the ground as metal keys clink together, interrupting my answer.

"Twenty-two!" one of them hollers, a skull bandana covering the lower half of their faces.

Four of them. The same four who always come to collect. They're all heavily garmented in black clothes. Black jeans, shirt, hoodie, and black beanie. It's obvious they're hiding their identity. Since the night that one of them took me, I've not seen anything of what they look like. I wince internally from the memories of the intruder, the stranger in the neon mask. *Was it one of the four?* But even as I think it, my eyes falling over their bodies, I know that all four of them are too tall, too large. The rapist—because that's exactly what he is—was skinny. Too short.

I relax. For now.

Reaching for Rose, I catch onto her arm. I don't want them to take her. *I like Rose* for some reason, and I don't like anyone. Something inside of me has latched itself to her. My soul recognized hers like an old friend, as if they'd been friends for lifetimes before ours.

One of the guys snorts, tilting his head back to look at the other, who is watching me carefully. His dark green eyes peer into mine. He's death draped in sin, tormenting me to come out and meet my maker.

I blink, breaking the eye contact. They never speak much. Silence, like the calm that washes over an angry sky just before it opens up and rains down on you.

Two step inside of the room this time.

Something is wrong. It's usually only one who comes in while the others wait outside. The one with devil eyes comes closer to me. I crawl backward until my back clashes with the cold wall, drawing my knees to my chest. The glistening chandelier that hangs from the room swings like a timer, counting down the days, the hours to my death. *Tick, tock, tick, tock.*

He begins to kneel in front of me, and Rose's cries die out behind me as I get lost in the trance of his eyes. The world is sucked into a dark vortex, and I'm surrounded by just him.

And those eyes.

They drop to my mouth and then come back to mine. I can see up close that he's young. The skin beneath his eyes is smooth, his eyelashes thick, fanning out every time he blinks.

His hand comes to my arm, and he yanks me up to my feet. His eyes stay on mine as his hand curls around my upper thigh, beneath the short skirt that I'm still wearing from the night I was taken. Short skirt and fishnet tights.

All class.

Someone laughs behind him.

I momentarily falter. *Will he try to rape me, too?*

He sinks back down in front of me as his eyes focus on mine. My heart thunders in my chest, thrashing around like an angry ocean. His rough palm glides down the back of my thigh and then calf, setting off electricity with every touch. I don't mind his touch; it feels familiar. My eyes flutter closed; my chest heavy as I suck in each breath. His skin against mine is surreal, like a blue flame pirouetting around a mold of snow. Everything is quiet. *Why is everything quiet?*

The sound of metal falling against the ground shakes me back into real time, and I know that he has unlocked the final shackle that was around my ankle from the night they took me. I flinch, opening my eyes to find another man dressed in the same attire standing beside the one who grabbed Rose. Rose is smirking at me, one perfectly arched eyebrow cocked.

My cheeks flare to life, embarrassed by how effortless this stranger could stimulate my emotions.

In an instant, he's standing back in front me, leaning forward until I smell his inimitable cologne—leather and cigarette doused in honey and then set alight to burn. "That'll be the only time I ever get on my knees for you, Little Dove."

His voice is like silk, soft enough to coax, but strong enough to wrap around my throat and choke me. Before I can think of anything else, his grip around my arm tightens, and he yanks me forward, out toward the open cell door. The four men who are with him quiet, all watching carefully, while we pass them. The one who has Rose, shoulder barges the man who has me in his grip. "You spoke!"

The one with his hand around my arm glares at him as

we all start walking down the long corridor. Room after room. Opulent marble flooring against vicious combat boots. With each step we take, the smell of saltwater becomes aggressively stronger. Some rooms have people in them, not just girls, guys too, and some are empty. Before I can map any of them to memory, we've reached the end, and the guy with me yanks open a heavy metal door. Another long corridor, only this one is narrow and lined with multiple hanging light bulbs, all surging as we reach the end. I can smell mildew vaporizing off the walls, the dampness manifesting from the affluent rooms I came from. We push through yet another door, this corridor shorter.

Cold.

I'm so cold.

I shiver. It seems to drop in temperature the deeper we go. He yanks open another door, and instantly, we're in the middle of a large room. Engines are firing furiously, the glacial temperature now doing a complete 180, hitting scorching heights as sweat throbs from my flesh. It's then that the smell hits me. Fish mixed with oil. Then the ground starts to swerve more.

"I don't remember coming onto a boat..." Rose murmurs underneath her breath. I want to agree with her. I don't remember this either. I don't remember getting onto the boat, only waking here.

Rose's question falls on deaf ears as they continue to lead us forward, up metal steps and onto the main platform. I freeze when the wind whips across my face, my teeth chattering. The vast size of the ocean stretches wide around the large yacht, rocking in the middle of the ocean.

My eyes travel up to my captor and then to Rose.

Just as Rose is about to open her mouth, the loud sound of helicopter blades cutting through the air interrupts her.

16

"What's going on?" Rose yells. The chopper begins to slowly lower to the helipad on the front of the yacht, the wind rushing around us in a frenzy. There's a black seven-point star that's on the helipad, with lights flashing on every point.

I slowly step back, just as the doors open. I watch as all of them, one by one, remove their bandanas.

Four guys.

Four very young guys, probably around my age—maybe a bit older. I scan them closely.

The edgy one who has taken it upon himself to attach himself to me has thick brown hair that looks naturally ruffled, as if he doesn't give a shit what it looks like. His eyes are as green as tainted jade and his skin is so annoyingly flawless that it bothers me. His shoulders and arms are a vivid display of how hard he trains at the gym, and he must stand at least a foot taller than my five-foot-four inches. I've decided I'll call him *One* until I know his name. *Two*, who I gather is the big mouth in the group, judging by his smirking face pointed directly at *One*, has dark brown messy hair and bright blue eyes that dance in mischief. His eyes remind me of Atlantic ice. I'm not sure how to take him for now, but I shall call him *Two*. The third, now named *Three*, has black hair, is brooding, and looks almost bored with everyone's existence. Like us breathing the same air as he is, is an insult. He has a sharp jaw, a straight nose, and a little cleft that's indented into his chin. The final boy is glaring right at me. His eyes are like whiskey, and every girl is probably parched. He has a square jaw and larger lips, with tattoos sneaking out from beneath his collar and up his neck. It's obvious that he's beautiful, they all are, especially *One*. One pushes buttons inside of me that I didn't know I had. Without saying a word, he's saying a lot.

One tugs on my arm, leading me toward the helicopter and

17

rudely interrupting me from my observations. They're all tall, with One being the tallest. They're all lean, with Four being the biggest.

"Get in!" One points up the little steps to the sleek black chopper, and I abide. It's not like I have any other choice. "If you haven't figured out yet, this is your lifeline." I try not to look at him for too long, because—well—because he's pretty. If you can even call someone like him pretty. There's a fine line between pretty and scary, and One uses that line as a tightrope. It's not just his appearance either. It's the way he carries himself and takes charge. You just know a true alpha when you see one. They don't need to bite because their bark is more like a roar, terrifying enough to scare away anyone who comes near.

Rose glares at One as she takes her seat opposite me. "And if you haven't figured out, she doesn't speak much."

One kicks his foot out. "You assume I don't already know that." His fingers hover over his phone as his attention comes to me. As soon as the chopper begins to lift off the ground and the other three guys are seated, One opens up his phone and the rest of us fall into a long stretched silence.

We descend onto a helipad that's in the middle of a large field. This helipad has the same seven-point star as the one that was on the yacht. *Interesting.* There are large green shrubs that surround the helipad in one circle, blocking every view of the giant mansion I noticed on our way down. As soon as we land, One opens up the door, and I follow closely behind him.

He looks between Rose and me, his face placid. "Will you follow my instructions carefully?"

Two chuckles, licking his lips and standing beside One. "You think they've got it in them?"

One glares at me. "No."

Rose's hand comes to mine, and I give it a little squeeze. Doesn't do much for reassurance, but at least I know she's beside me. A stranger can fill the void of a gaping hole that panic punched into, so for that, I'm thankful I have her beside me.

Three and Four remain behind Rose and me.

"Answer me…" One demands, his eyes strong as steel. "Will you follow instructions?"

"Yes," Rose hisses.

One steps forward, and it's then that I realize he's coming closer. His dark shadow expands like an umbrella around me. "Dovey, if you don't abide by the rules that will be set out for you, there will consequences."

I don't answer, my eyes flying across the grass, as if I'm in search of something. *Anything.* Maybe what I'm searching for are the words that flutter over the tip of my tongue, threatening to slice him across the neck.

I flinch when his finger wraps around my chin, tilting my head up to his. I don't like to be touched. He towers over me, so my neck has to bend for my eyes to meet his. Green on green, only different shades. Both human, only different souls.

"Do you understand?"

I don't, but I nod my head anyway. One and Two begin walking in front of Rose and me, with Three and Four following behind us. We exit out of a clearing that surrounds the helipad, the sun now setting in the distance, burning the sky to a crisp orange.

"What is going on…" Rose mutters, and I squeeze her even more.

One and Two continue through the thick clearing until

they part out of an exit. Music is pulsing loudly, throwing my mind back into The Club. As soon as we exit the same clearing, my footing falters. Eminem is vibrating around the place and the entire backyard of the mansion is filled with equipment I haven't seen. People are shuffling around the area—workers, I think. One and Two pause, turning to face me. Delicately manicured hedges line the gardens and a large swimming pool sits to the left of the yard. To the right is where all of the different equipment is laid: poles, a large square cage that's big enough to fit a group of humans, and a black, silver, and lilac styled tent that has been dismantled. The mansion spills out onto the large patio area where a boulder is carved into a naked woman and man, curled up together. There's a fountain surrounding them, and table and chairs neatly stacked around the patio. The home is something straight from Europe, with its Victorian style architecture. The moss that is growing between the stones faintly reminds me of a certain person's eyes.

"What's going on?" Rose repeats, her attention shifting directly to One. Even she knows who the alpha of the pack is.

"Ahhh, Rose Kinnish and Dove Hendry. I've been waiting so long to meet you…" A soft voice beckons from behind us, and I turn to quickly face the intruder.

Long legs meet a long torso and a small face. She has short black hair and beady little eyes. That doesn't take away the fact that she could be beautiful. I say *could* because there's something about her that taints her beauty. Something dark and sinister. She also has a small scar that is indented into her upper lip, which is curved like a half-moon.

She studies me closely. "You've met The Brothers of Kiznitch." She gestures to the four who stand around us before putting a cigarette between her tiny lips and lighting the end.

20

She inhales and then points toward One. "Kingston." *Kingston.* She then points to Two. "Killian." To Three. "Kyrin." Finally, to Four. "Keaton. Tell me," she blows out more smoke, "why do you think you're here?" She drops her smoke onto the grass, and I watch as her red bottom pump squashes it into the blades. She steps forward. I have to fight the urge to retreat back. When we don't answer, a small smirk glistens over her mouth. "Interesting for you." She points to Rose. "Not so interesting for you." She comes back to me.

"Why are you telling us this?" Rose interrupts.

Her eyes clip to Rose. "Wouldn't you love to know." She continues. "I run a show, and I only have the best of the best, but the art in which we gather our performers is different to how others do. I like my performers broken and unamendable, but of the purest construction." Her eyes shift to Kingston. "Or, just emotionless. I gather machines, not humans, and I orchestrate them in becoming moneymaking puppets." I want to say that I'm not a puppet. I want to say so much. Sweat trickles down the side of my head as words threaten to spill from my mouth, but before I can formulate enough fire to spit them out, my teeth clamp closed like a bear trap. "You don't get an option. Neither of you. You will come with us. You will dance." She looks between the two of us. "I will pay you. In return, you're not to tell anyone about what goes on from this point forward. You sign on the dotted line, and Midnight Mayhem owns you. You never walk away. You'll never have that option." Her eyes, once again, fly between us. "Do you understand? You cannot have a life outside of Midnight Mayhem."

Rose sucks in a deep breath. Midnight Mayhem? What is Midnight Mayhem. "I know who you are."

The woman looks directly at Rose now and brings her

perfectly manicured coffin-shaped acrylic nail to Rose's cheek. "Sweet girl. You don't know me. I am Delila Patrova, and I can either be your worst nightmare or your best friend. The decision is yours. The decision is always yours."

Kingston's hand wraps around Delila as he pulls her into him and leans in to whisper into her ear. Delila's eyes zone in on me as interest sparks in the deep depths of her empty pupils. "Really." She stands, running her hands over her perfectly steamed slacks. "Dove Noctem. You can sit out for a while. Observe. Your training will begin at a later date. Now!" She snaps, clicking her fingers. "Do either of you object?"

"What happens if we do?" Rose raises a challenging eyebrow at Delila.

The air shifts around us, the wind stirring black magic into the cool winter air. Delila smiles sweetly. "Well, I'm afraid you are of no use to us..." She pretends to ponder over her words. "Or to anyone, really..."

Rose squeezes my hand.

I squeeze her back. *Shut up and stop talking before you get us both killed.*

"Now I'm going to ask..." Kingston steps in front of Delila, and I watch in fascination as she backs up, allowing him to dominate the conversation. "Do you agree to surrender your life to Midnight Mayhem? I don't feel like getting blood on my hands today, but will if I need to."

I chew on my lower lip, contemplating my options.

I have none.

I nod, squeezing Rose so she agrees.

Rose groans. "How do we know that you won't kill us?"

Kingston glares at her. "Never said we wouldn't, but you don't have many options, do you?"

"Right—enough of this. We hit the road in four days. You girls will need to…" Her eyes drag up and down both Rose and me. "…go shopping. I'll give you an advance. Midnight will eat you alive otherwise." She tsks. "Kill, show them to their room."

Three

Dove

Soft pink cotton stretches over the large king-sized bed as Killian opens the door and gestures for us both to enter. There are two beds, and the room itself is bigger than what most people would call a living room.

"We usually put new initiates in separate rooms to stop them from trying to escape," Killian speaks for the first time, drawing my attention to where he's standing against the doorframe. His eyes darken on me. "But something tells me, Little Dovey here lost her wings."

My jaw clenches at his tone and arrogance. *Bastard.* He kicks up from the doorframe and gestures down the hallway. "Some of us come back here when we're not on the road. There are twenty-seven bedrooms, an indoor and outdoor pool, a private spa, basketball court, gymnasium, theater, garage, and I'm sure I've missed some shit. The property is on a few hundred acres of land, where all of the crew live in their own homes. In other words…" Killian smirks. "Don't wander too far. You never know where you might end up." He disappears back out the door, leaving both Rose and I gobsmacked.

"Shit," Rose gasps, taking a seat on the bed that's opposite mine. She blows out a breath of air, her eyes traveling to mine. "We're so fucked."

I lick my lips, making my way to the bed that Killian said was mine. Sinking into the soft covers, I replay everything that happened up to this point.

"What do you think of this?" Rose asks, kicking off her shoes and running her fingers through her dirty hair. Caged humans in diamond chandelier rooms and scary men who wear bandanas. "I'm not really sure yet." *Lie.* I know how I feel about this. I feel like we could have ended up murdered or being sold to human traffickers. I remember my father always saying to me, *"You won't always get what you want in life, Dovey. Sometimes things are going to happen that will make you wish you could change the course of your destination, but you can't. You just have to keep driving and switch gears."* I need to switch gears.

"I need a bath," Rose answers, disappearing through one of the many doors in the room. I take this time to evaluate the area. I need a bath, too. I haven't had one in—I've lost count. Twenty-two girls—but I find my body cemented to the bed, unable to move. I'm free physically (or am I?), but mentally the shackles have only tightened.

My eyes close.

The Jordans were the third foster family I had been invited into. I appreciated them because they allowed me to do the things I still loved to do—like dance. There was an old studio on the corner of Beacon Street in downtown Phoenix. I'd dance there every Friday. It was run-down and aged, but that wasn't because of the owner's negligence, it was simply because she couldn't afford to maintain the upkeep. The passion still burned in her eyes whenever she would watch me dance, and you could see that that was why she kept the studio open--to simply admire the art of dance.

I was walking to the bus stop after a late-night session, flicking through the music on my iPod, when I felt the familiar wave of his presence. My footing halted. My fingers flexed over my iPod as sweat slipped down my temples. Slowly, I brought my eyes up, tearing the earphones out of my ears.

I stopped breathing when I felt him behind me, his breathing on my nape. "We'll be back for you, Little Bird." The Shadow pressed into me from behind, his hard chest to my back. "I'll always be back."

I suck in a breath at the familiarity of the voice. *Do I know The Shadow?*

The more the voice replays in my head, the stronger the familiarity. Or maybe I've just heard his voice and words so much that I've started to think that I know him.

Once Rose is out of the bath, I slip in and remove my soiled clothes. Clothes that I never thought I'd be rid of because they were stuck to me like a second skin, rotting into my pores and leaving their stale stench embedded into my bones. I give the tub a quick wash before filling it up. There are delicate soaps sitting on a small table that's beside it, a copper bowl filled with bath bombs and salts, and a monstrous size glass Chanel Chance perfume bottle sitting on the bathroom counter. The walls are a clean white, a complete contrast to the people who live here. The tiles are a deep mahogany red. An interesting color choice, I think, but it only intensifies the opulent ambiance of the overall house. I drop one of the bath bombs into the water and watch as it fizzes, filling the room with sweet aromas that have me sighing in release. I quickly dip into the bath, wincing as the hot water drowns my sins away. Stings pinch at my skin from the temperature, biting me all over my flesh. I duck beneath it, my hair floating in the water as the world silences. Everything is so quiet when you're under water. Like you can block out the world and be alone with your thoughts.

Thoughts I don't necessarily want to be alone with.

I pop back up, brushing the hot water away from my face. Scrubbing away the excess from my eyes, I jerk up when I see Kingston at the end of my bath, glaring at me.

I should scream.

I want to scream.

I *can't* scream. Instead, I sink farther into the water in hopes that the purple dye from the bath bomb hides all of the parts I would rather he didn't see right now.

"Ah…" I clear my throat, trying to find another word for *what the fuck are you doing in here* that won't get me killed.

His jaw tenses. I can see the muscles on either side flexing with every clench. His eyes are dark, moody and brooding, and I'm every bit intimidated by this man. "Can I help you?"

Can I help you… The first words I speak to him, and they're *can I help you.*

His top lip curls slightly, his eyes dropping to my lower body. "Undecided."

"What are you doing in here?" I clench my thighs closed further, in pure paranoia that he can see beneath the dyed water.

He stares at me, dropping all of the dead expressions that he had on his face just seconds earlier. "What's your name?"

"What?" I exhale, puzzled by his question.

"What's your name?" He repeats, his expression remaining the same.

"Dove?"

There's a long stretch of silence before he kicks up from the tub. Everything slows as he passes by me, his smell drowning the sweet scent of my bath.

"I'm confused."

He pauses right beside me, and I look up at him from my position. He's studying me, but I can't understand the method in which he's learning. "Good. Oh, and Dove, lock your fucking bathroom door."

Then he disappears, and I sink farther into the warm water, watching as it caves over my skin.

I don't know if I'm reading too far into things, or if I'm right in the way I feel about Kingston. I don't know if it's from my past terrors that are threatening to rise to the surface. You see, when I was a little girl, a shadow chased me. An entity. Instead of stepping out from behind it to feel the sun against my skin, this shadow ruined every expectation I had of seeing the light.

four

Dove

After a long day shopping with Rose on the "advance" Delila gave us and exploring the mall that's nearest to her mansion, we've found ourselves in the tent, stretching out our bodies and warming up. I've noticed we've had a guard beside us today, guiding us where we are to be without telling us where we need to be. Every now and then, he'll speak into a little headpiece and then direct us to where we are going next. It works for me because, otherwise, we would both be wandering around aimlessly, but hopefully, it's not going to be a forever thing.

After Delila said that I wouldn't have to perform yet and that I'd sit out for a bit, I thought that meant training, too.

Judging by the grey sports bra and grey sweats that I'm now wearing, I was clearly wrong.

"You good?" Rose asks, lathering her body with scented coconut oil, one eyebrow quirked.

I lick my lips and brush my long red hair into a high ponytail. "Yes."

The door slams open behind us, and I turn quickly to see who's entering. Three girls waltz in, and I don't even get a chance to inspect any of the others because the blonde ringleader snatches my attention first. Her long, wavy blonde hair hangs to her tiny waist, and her tattoos float up the side of her ribs, up her left breast, and come down her left arm. She has tight, tanned skin and a bitch face that makes you want to either punch it or sit on it.

She stares me up and down. "Ew."

Punch it.

My eyebrows immediately shoot up, surprised by her obvious hostility. Just as I open my mouth, Rose steps in front of me, her arms pushing me back. "We got a problem, princess?"

I tap Rose's arm to move her. I can fight my own battles. I don't need her to do that for me, but blonde one and her minions slide past us and make their way behind the makeshift curtain. From my understanding, Delila has something set up in the back of her mansion. A tent dipped in black with the softest lilac trimmings. No signage on this one. I got the feeling that this was purely for practice or training.

"Hey." Rose's hand comes to my chin, tilting my face up to hers. I like Rose's eyes. They're gentle, soft. Just like her soul. She has a small heart-shaped face and a petite body to match. Over the past twenty-four hours, I've been asking myself how I would have lasted these past couple days if it weren't for her.

"You okay?" Resilience is absolute when you've had your life ripped away from you at such a young age, but finding a person who takes some of the tension that the world has given you and slaps on some armor, ready to square up against your enemies, is an irreplaceable friend.

"Yes." I nod, smiling. "I'm fine."

"I will beat that bitch straight in the mouth if she becomes an issue, and I don't give a shit who she is..."

I stretch my neck, letting Rose's ranting drift into white noise, as I try to focus on the task at hand: *getting through tonight alive.* And not messing up my steps.

I roll out my shoulders, inhaling and exhaling through each stretch. "What do you think they'll have us dance?"

Rose shrugs, brushing the wand of her lip gloss over her lips. "Not sure. Anything they give us, I'm sure we can do."

As if on cue, Delila shoves through the curtain, clapping her hands. Below rock bottom is a place called hell, and I'm pretty sure Delila was the interior decorator. "Come on. Both of you on stage. I want to see a duology first. Freestyle with each other." She mumbles under her breath, "Let me see what the fuss is about."

Butterflies quiver in my belly. I'm not really a freestyle dancer. I'm more of a choreograph type of girl, but I find my legs moving and following Rose to the other side of the curtain.

It's bright. As in, pure daylight. I was expecting a gloomy shade, so I at least didn't have to see who was sitting out in the crowd. My eyes catch what props I can see from here.

A clear tank. I think I've seen that on some Criss Angel TV show.

A gymnastics balance beam.

The trapeze equipment.

Three massive rings connected by long metal bars. I can imagine what that's for. I've seen it before. At least I've seen something similar to it, but this one looks different.

A couple large hula hoops.

Four black dirt bikes with a Harley Davidson emblem on them.

"—Dove?" Delila snaps from the front seats. Ringside. "When you're ready." I ignore the crowd that's seated a few rows behind Delila because I know that The Brothers are behind her, and I see another pack to the left, who I'm guessing is the bitch and her pack from earlier. There are other people scattered around who I don't know yet.

I lick my lips and give a quick, reassuring smile to Rose. Her eyes peer back at me with cocky reassurance, a small wink in passing. As if we've done this before, as if we've shared the same floor. I instantly feel a little more at ease as the music starts.

It's not what I expect, and my eyes close as the soft melody of the piano taps through my eardrums. I sway from side to side at the haunting melody, allowing the music to seep into my pores and take the reins of my body. *Possess me.* The notes continue as I float around the room, my eyes closed. I reach one hand out in an eagle float, and my fingertips touch Rose's gently. My eyes blaze open onto her as I twirl into her body. The music drops and a light electric guitar starts playing. I pulse my body softly until I'm on my knees in front of her, rolling onto my back and arching off the floor, my hands pressed behind my head, bringing myself up into bridge position. The song changes to "Lovely" By Billie Eilish, and my eyes connect with Kingston from upside down. He keeps me anchored to the spot, his palm covering the bottom of his mouth. I push up from the ground and lose myself in the song, never looking away from Kingston. I don't know where Rose is, and I can't find it in myself to care. The music has taken over, and my blood is pulsing to the rhythm. It's hypnotic and poisonous, but I want to swallow it all and then feed it to King. When the chorus kicks in, I snake my hips while my hands come beneath my shirt; I slowly remove it from above my head, so I'm standing in nothing but a sports bra and my sweatpants. Kingston kicks someone beside him, his eyes remaining on mine. It's just him and me as the energy we both exude sucks everyone into a dark vortex. It could almost be intimate, if he didn't want to kill me. Intimacy is just like murder; they both make your heart race and your palms sweat while leaving your thoughts in disarray, but then when you're done, you're left with the remnants of someone else's soul or blood on your hands. When the song comes to a close, he removes his hand, and instead of finding an expression I thought he was giving me, he's scowling.

He pushes up from his seat and storms out of the tent.

The music cuts, and I freeze, that vortex we sucked everyone into now cracked open. I didn't realize Delila had stood up until she says, "Wow." She's almost directly in front of me, her head tilted.

I step back, searching for Rose. "Where's Rose?"

Delila waves me off. "Don't worry about her. She's going to a more suited position." Delila grabs my arm and yanks me toward the exit. The very same exit that Kingston left through.

"Suited position?" I ask, confused. "She's a dancer."

Delila laughs. "You are a dancer and an artist, my love."

I yank my arm out of her grip.

She sighs, turning to face me. I feel like a sour child, but Rose is my friend. "Look, she's going to work with a couple of the other girls—all right? She is *fated* to be there. You, Dovey, you are something else. You captivate the room by using your body. It's art. We haven't seen that in—well…" I don't miss the pause. "…in quite some time."

She starts tugging me along again, and this time, I let her, seemingly satisfied with my answer about Rose. "Okay. Will I see her a lot?"

"Yes, yes." She waves me off. "Now, I know just where to put you…" She's muttering to herself, and I can't care enough to ask her what she's saying, so I go with it. She stops outside of a large RV. It's pure black with black windows and wheels and looks more expensive than the average style home. There are a few cars parked outside of it. A red Ferrari, a black Aston Martin and a Ford Raptor. I tilt my head at the emblem that stretches out over the side of the RV. It's faded to a soft grey, but I can see the same seven-point triangle with the number IV in the middle. There's wording in the lines, but I can't make out what it says.

Delila bangs on the door. "Open up, King!"

I freeze, yanking my arm away from her once again. "*What?*"

Delila ignores me, banging again. "—you know it's right."

"Um, what's right?" I ask frantically.

The door slams open, and King is standing at the threshold with a cigarette hanging from his soft lips, his hair messy and his chest on full display. My mouth dries as I catch the same triangle that's on the RV tattooed over his thick chest, with another tattoo near his hip. Calvin Klein briefs sneak out of his jeans—that are un-fucking-buttoned—with perfect cut lines tucking below.

He blows out a cloud of smoke, his dark eyes on mine. "What?" he answers her, but never removes his eyes from me. If he caught me staring, he didn't mention it. Which I appreciate. I can admire that he looks like a fucking god, but that doesn't make me one of his disciples.

He's trapped me with his gaze again, and I can't break free.

"You saw what we all saw. *You know.*" Delila softens her tone.

King finally looks down to her, blowing smoke rings out from between his lips. They hit her square in the face. "Yeah, so?"

"Well," Delila reaches back for my arm, "she can stay with you, too, and be your fifth, then we just need Kyrin to find his fifth."

There's a long pause. Infinite. I can't even see the ending of this pause that's how long it is, and then Kingston laughs, his head tilting back. I watch as his throat bobs and the veins in his neck flex with the movement. Why is that sexy? *You are not a disciple.* "Yeah, no, that's not happening. Good one." The door begins to close on Delila, but her hand flies out to stop it.

"I wasn't joking, King. She's your fifth." When King doesn't answer, Delila takes the first step up, blocking the door from closing a second time. "You saw her dance. *You know.* Don't try to deny it."

Kingston leans to the side, his abs clenching at the movement. I try to ignore the tattoo on his left peck, but it's difficult, considering it's the same shape as the one on the RV. I want to study it as hard as he studies me. "Nope. I mean, she's good, but not *that* good, and I don't give a fuck *what I know.*" His tone is laced with acid dripping from his sharp teeth. He carries on his insult. "And we don't let hoes into our routine."

Delila's eyes slant. "You let them into your RV."

Kingston grins. "We aren't talking about my cock, Delila." His smirk darkens as he takes a final suck on his cigarette before exhaling. "But if we are, she can't get on that either."

I snort, shaking my head. I probably shouldn't have, and I

probably should have kept my mouth shut, but the feminist in me is choking on my rage, and well, she's a powerful bitch.

I tilt my head. "Right, of course, you think because I'm a stripper that I open my legs to every man that shoves a hundred-dollar bill beneath my panties."

"Well, don't you?" he retorts, and his quick wit makes my eyes snap to his. He's baiting me, his smug face proof of that.

"Open my legs?" I ask, and I'm well aware that this is probably the most words I've spoken to anyone in one whole sentence, at least in a very long time, but what can I say? He's a siren to my voice box. "Of course, I do. But in the fashion that you're implying? No." I want to say unfortunately.

He rolls his eyes, glaring straight at Delila. "Not happening."

"King…"

"What makes you think she can handle the cage?" he asks.

Delila leans forward and whispers something into his ear. Kingston freezes, and then all humor on his face is gone as he brings his eyes back to mine. "Fine." He leans backward and whistles to someone inside the RV.

Delila steps backward, rolling her eyes. "Sorry you have to see this."

"See what?" I ask, just as movement catches my eye and a half-naked girl struts down the stairs, shoving a bra over her head. I quickly look away, mainly because she's had her tits out, and she's not getting paid for it.

Kingston takes a seat on the step and shoves some combat boots over his feet. "Well, come on then, Little Bird, let's see if you can fly."

five

Dove

I't's different this time. Lights are out, and it's darker, the sun long since burning to ash. All I hear is my breathing, the heavy exhales and inhales from my chest. I run my palm over my legs in an attempt to swipe the sweat, but that's all just an inner ploy to distract myself from the fact that I'm standing in the middle of a makeshift stage, in the pitch black night, with no idea on what is about to happen to me next.

I close my eyes and lick my lips, focused on my breathing. *If they wanted to kill you, Dove, you'd be dead. Chill.*

The first thing I feel is the sand beneath my shoes vibrate. The first thing I hear is the clinking of metal, and the first thing I think to myself is...*what the fuck have I gotten myself into?*

"Breathe, Little Bird," a voice whispers over the nape of my neck, sending chills down my spine. Something covers my eyes and is being tied to the back of my head. "We're not going to hurt you—*much.*" That was a different voice, and I turn in an attempt to chase the owner, but I'm met with darkness everywhere. I can see a spotlight through the blindfold, but it's not clear enough to make out who is around me.

Fingers drag up my arm, setting off goosebumps.

I flinch away.

Someone chuckles, only this chuckle I recognize. "What's the matter, Little Dovey…" Kingston starts, and then he leans forward, his lips skating over the back of my ear. "Don't like shadows much?"

I still, my blood turning cold. "*What?*" I whisper, reaching for the blindfold, but someone halts my movements by forcing my arms to my back. Cold metal from the handcuffs latch around each wrist. "What did you just say?"

He ignores me, and I'm being pushed down to my knees. Did he just say The Shadow, or did I imagine it? It wouldn't be the first time I've imagined myself into thinking The Shadow is present or has whispered something into my ear. It usually comes during a nightmare, but I'm almost certain Kingston just said what I think he did. Regardless, he's obviously meaning the shadows that I see through the blindfold. My paranoia will kill me one day.

"Stop!" Delila yells out from somewhere. "I didn't say perform one of your acts on her. I said incorporate her into the act."

"First of all—" I think that's Killian. "How are we supposed to incorporate her into it without showing her what it is that we do, D?"

Silence.

"Because we can save that for her first night. We don't give swimming lessons; we throw people into the deep end and hope they can swim."

I pull on the cuffs. "Can someone take the blindfold off?"

"No," Kingston growls out. Goosebumps stand to the surface of my skin.

"Well, can you remove the handcuffs? I need my arms to dance."

My wrists are set free as quick as they were locked.

"You're right," Delila finishes, and just like that, the blindfold is torn off my eyes. "We can't have her in there without knowing what to expect." She eyes me up and down, and I squirm. I don't like Delila, nor do I trust her. "We will wait until we're on the road. For now," she says to me, a smirk on her mouth, "make yourself at home. Get to know people without getting to know them too well, and for the love of God, Dove—" Her fingers wrap around my chin, directing my face up to hers. "Don't get yourself killed." She pats my cheek and smiles sweetly before stepping back and looking out to the audience of performers. "We leave tomorrow night. First stop is here, New York." She starts walking away when she grumbles, "Hopefully, we can find another Beatrice while we're at it."

When Delila is out of earshot, I turn to face Kingston and the other four. "Want to explain to me what it is that you do so that I can at least get a feel for it?"

"No," Keaton says, turning to leave behind Delila.

Six

King

"She can't be your fifth. That's too close." Keaton kicks out his legs, lighting up a cigarette. My finger continues to caress my upper lip as I watch all three of them. I see where they're coming from, but at the same time, it makes my task easier.

"He's right. She can't. I mean, she's good, but you haven't had a fifth. Ever." Kyrin argues.

"What the fuck? How can none of you see what I see? Y'all need some glasses or have something to tell me? That girl dominates the room when she dances. You're telling me that that's not his fifth?" Killian, being himself, is fighting for the girl. Good for her. She'll need all the fans that she can get, but that still doesn't argue the fact that I'm going to destroy her.

I clench my jaw. Their bickering is balancing on my last nerve, and I know it's my last because I used up all the rest of them when Dove walked up in here.

Once.

Twice.

"And have you ever seen someone as fucking hot as her? The doe eyes and dark red hair. I'm fucking digging it. It's the same color as my Ferrari." Killian still won't shut the fuck up, and he's managed to now introduce his pride and joy.

"Enough," I growl, glaring at Killian. The fact that he's the first one to have his balls in the palm of his hands over this chick isn't surprising. "I don't want her in my space any more than any of you, only for obviously different reasons."

Keaton shakes his head, his fingers diving into his thick mane. "Why didn't Delila put her in Midnight? They could do with another."

"Because Midnight has Rose, and Dove is too advanced for them," I answer fluidly, needing either a joint or a glass of something strong to take the edge off.

I kick off my bed and make my way to the front of the RV where Justice is sitting in the driver's seat. "Why are you on the chair already? We don't leave until tomorrow." Justice is our driver, and when we're on the road, he bunks with us. Our RV is the biggest one out of the Mayhem family, so he fits into our dynamic easily. He's older than the rest of us, hovering in his late thirties. There have been rumors going around about him and Delila for years, but he denies it all. I'm not a dumb motherfucker, though. I can smell the pussy on him some nights when he rolls into bed.

We have four bedrooms in here with a small fifth should we need it. And by fifth, I mean it's the room at the very back of the

RV with nothing but a bed inside and a curtain to keep it separated from the rest of the RV—which is where Justice sleeps.

"Didn't you hear?" Justice teases boldly.

"Why the fuck are you smirking?" I narrow my eyes at him. Just as he opens his mouth, there's a loud knock on the door.

I'm still glaring at him as I back up and pull it open. "What?" I snap, finally dragging my venomous glare away from Justice and to—"What the fuck do you want now?"

Dove flinches. If I were a better man, I would feel a little guilty about it, but I'm not. I'm not even in the vicinity of a better man, and aside from that, why does she always look so broken? *You fucking know why.*

"Sorry," she murmurs, licking her lips. "Ah... I have to—" Her voice drifts into the background as I take in what's in her hands. A small suitcase.

Justice chuckles from behind me, squeezing my shoulder. "Good luck. You're going to need it."

I watch as Justice disappears into the distance with his bags before I bring my eyes back to Dove. "You're fucking kidding me." I slam the door wide open and step aside to let her in.

She takes the steps up, and when her feet land on the final one, I tower over her and lean into her ear as she passes. "Well, well, well, look who's going to be sleeping with monsters."

She pulls away from me just as Killian walks his overconfident ass down the stairs that lead to our rooms and bathrooms. "Hey!" He smiles at her, his arrogant face lighting up when he spots her.

She ignores him, turning to me. If I gave a fuck, I'd be a smug bastard over that, but I don't. My fucks are with my last nerves.

I point to the back of the RV. "Your room is down at the end.

Bathroom is to the right, and the kitchen is to the left. Seating is here, and there's a bar, but that's upstairs—where you are *not* welcome."

She nods. "Sure." Then she turns her back on me and makes her way to the back. I tilt my head, watching her ass sway as she walks, then I notice the fucking iPhone she has shoved into the back pocket of her jeans. Fucking Delila. She obviously feels a certain way about Dove. That much I picked up. Delila doesn't feel a way about anyone unless it's hate.

Once Dove is out of earshot, Killian turns to me. "Try not to be too much of an asshole. Remember all the shit we put her through on The Cannon."

"Be good for you to remember your fucking place before you start barking orders at me, Kill. I'm not in the mood for your dick tricks." I shove past him and head straight for the door. I need to fucking talk to Delila and see what the fuck it is she's thinking.

I make my way to Midnight's RV—almost as big as ours, just with more glitter. I'm almost certain she was heading here after dropping her bomb.

I yank open the door and step inside, instantly engulfed in the rich scent of strong ass perfumes. Think I'd be used to this shit by now, but I'm fucking not.

"King! Hey!" Val purrs, pushing off the white sofa and taking the next few steps toward me.

I whack her hand out of the way. "Where's Delila? She in here?"

"Nope!" Maya murmurs from the daybed. My eyes drop down her body. Loose boyfriend jeans and a sports bra, earbuds hanging from her ears. "She left about five minutes ago. Why, what's up?"

43

"Nothing," I snap, turning to leave.

"King?" Val reaches for my arm.

I pull it away. "What, Valdis?" She hates her full name, but it fucking suits her. *Goddess of Death*—she was named appropriately.

"Never mind," she mutters, sulking. I slam the door once I'm back out in the open. She should know better than to try any bullshit with me. I care about very little, and I like it that way. Usually we would be all in our houses, but because we have an early departure in the morning, we're already in our RVs. All of us have homes built here, in our suburb, but we also own houses in other places. Aspen, LA, Australia, Rome. We always have a place to go when and if we ever need it.

I go straight for Delila's RV, bypassing everyone else's. Pure white crystal chandeliers hanging from her roof—all of that type of shit. Swinging her door open without knocking, I catch her mid-walk, a silk robe on with white and pink lace panties and bra. She leans back on the counter, her robe spreading open wider while tilting her head. "What have I done now?"

"You know what the fuck you've done. This isn't part of the deal, Delila. You don't run boss bitch on The Brothers, and you damn well know it. Get rid of her."

Delila's eyes slant. "It's interesting that you want her gone so bad, King. Considering who she is..."

I chuckle, licking my bottom lip. "I don't give a fuck who she is. We don't need another fifth. She can do *one* show with us. One. Put her on the fucking Chinese poles for all I care."

Delila's eyebrows raise. "Really? Interesting." She brushes me out, closing the door slightly. "I'll take that show, King, but mark my words. You'll find that she is the missing piece you've needed."

I slam the door myself, frustrated with how things have slightly altered. Pulling out my phone, I dial my old man.

"I'm calling a huddle. Your brothers will all meet us there," My father said, loosening the tie that was around his neck. He tossed it onto the kitchen counter. "My office in an hour, and King?" He muttered, gaining my attention. "Get rid of the sad fucking face." He disappeared out of the kitchen, and I silently flipped him off, spooning another serving of granola into my mouth. Dad calling a huddle wasn't unheard of. Midnight Mayhem was back in New Orleans, so that meant pack huddle. Most kids would be fucking ecstatic to be home to see family, nope, not fucking me. I wanted back in my RV and back with my brothers faster than anyone. I hated this time of year. Three days before Halloween. It brought back heavy reminders of bullshit that I didn't need reminding of.

I emptied my bowl into the sink and put it into the washer before making my way down to my dad's office. It dripped in opulence and power. You walked into my father's office, and you knew a bad motherfucker owned this joint.

And he was.

The worst.

My father was the head of the Romanian Mafia, and so was my grandfather and his father and his grandfather and so on. We had tight alliances, but our strongest was and always would be with the Russians, or more importantly, the Romanov's. Vladimir Pakhan Romanov is the Krestnii Otets of the Russian Bratva; he's also my father's oldest friend.

I kicked the door closed as I entered, surprised that Kill, Ky, and Keaton were already seated with their fathers behind them.

"What's going on? Do we have another task?" I asked, looking pointedly at my dad. "I fucking hope so, because I'm in the killing kind of mood."

Dad leaned over, pressing the palms of his hands against his executive style mahogany desk. "Just a quick one before you're back on the road." I watch as he reaches for a Brazilian cigar from the humidor and places it between his teeth. "Figured you might need the distraction."

Seven

Dove

After folding all of my new clothes and putting them away in the small dresser that's hidden in the closet, I flop back onto the bed and look around the small room. There's nothing to it but a bed and a marble door that leads to the closet. I'm at the back of the RV, though, so the entire back wall is glass. I'm guessing it's tinted, so people can't see in; only, I can see out. The bed is my favorite—wide enough to fit five people comfortably and plush enough to liquefy your day into dreams. I have to admit, even being around all of the extravagance of the mansion and the riches of the atmosphere, I'm still taken aback by this RV. I originally came from money, so I know wealth when I see it, and this is wealth. These boys are rich, and every single person who performs in Midnight Mayhem oozes lavishness. I see it. This isn't a normal carnival type vibe. There are no ex-cons or drunks. These people aren't on the road to run away from something or someone; they're on the road to chase people for the fuck of it. They're here to make the mundane feel exotic, if only for a couple hours.

Sighing, I pick up the new phone Delila bought and set up for me and open up a Google search. I've been thinking about Delila and how I feel about her and Rose. Whether or not I should confide in them with what happened back on the yacht with the neon masked rapist. I want to. I feel dirty and violated from what he did to me, while knowing it could have been much worse. But another part of me doesn't really know if I can trust anyone to confide in yet. No matter how close Rose and I are becoming, I'm still not comfortable enough to talk about it. I'll deal with it in on my own, and then allow people in when I'm ready.

I type the club into my iPhone and grab the number from the search results before dialing Rich. Like both Delila and King said, I have agreed to be a part of this now, so there's no going back.

"Rich, it's me, Dove."

Rich sighs. "Jesus, Dove. I've aged fifty years since you've been gone."

"Well, we can't have that. You're already old as shit," I joke, chuckling at myself.

He grunts. "I see you've expanded your vocabulary a little more."

I lie back on my bed, my hand resting over my belly. I want to know how long I've been gone, but I don't want to freak him out by openly asking it. "So, how's the bar been since I've been gone?"

"Too busy. This last week has been busy. When are you coming back?"

48

One week. Okay, so twenty-two girls only equaled one week. Hearing Rich's voice has calmed me to an extent. I feel like my life is twisting and turning, and I can't quite grasp onto the things that are happening. Now I have to give him the news. "Ah, not anytime soon. I have been dragged into some..." I freeze, racking my brain for an excuse. "Family drama..." That's the best I got.

"Family?" he asks, shocked. "Thought you didn't have any."

"Oh, I don't, not really. This is *not* my birth family. One of my foster homes." I know he wants to ask more questions, so I quickly cut him off. "I'm going to try to come home for a visit soon, but can you do me a favor?" I chew on my lip nervously. He doesn't answer, but that's nothing new with Rich. "Can you empty my room and sell everything?"

"What!" he yells. "What do you mean?"

I sigh, rolling to my belly. I loved living with Rich and helping him out with his girls, but I know that this is the right thing to do. I can't be living there to help pay the rent, and I can't go back to empty my room anytime soon. I know he will want someone in there soon to help pay the mortgage and take care of the girls. "I'm living here now. I can't explain much, but can you please do this for me? Let the girls choose whatever they want. I know Angela wanted my iPad. She can have that. Sell the rest and donate the money to..." I pause, thinking over my next words. "Survivors of sexual abuse."

Rich sighs. "All right, little lady. Whatever you need."

"Thanks, Rich!" I spend the next five minutes going back and forth with him, catching up on the drama. He finally lets me go, and I hang up, rubbing my warm ear.

My phone vibrates on the bed beside me again, and I half-think it's Rich with a change of heart, but it's a text from Rose.

I can't believe I'm being made tonight.

I read over her words. When Delila gave me the phone this morning, she said that Rose has one, too, with both our numbers saved into each other's device. I send her a text back.

What do you mean made?

She texts back instantly. **My initiation into Midnight is tonight before we leave. Tell me you'll be there.**

Initiation? They have an actual initiation? When will mine be then? Will they even have one for me?

What time?

Midnight.

My fingers hover over the words. **I'll be there.**

I set my alarm for eleven-thirty, kick off my jeans, and remove my bra before diving beneath the covers of my bed. I watch the sun setting through the glass window, warming my skin, before falling into a deep sleep.

The ringing of my alarm blares through the quiet night. I shoot up from the bed, swiping the sleep from my eyes. "Shit."

"Going somewhere?" Kyrin asks, leaning against the frame where my curtain hangs.

"Holy shit!" I shove my shirt down to cover myself more, but it's no use. My shirt is too short, and Kyrin is already eyeing me up and down.

"Don't flatter yourself, Little Bird. I've seen better."

I force myself not to let it bother me so much. I was a stripper. Why the fuck should I care anyway?

I drop down onto the bed, reach for my black jeans and shove my feet through them. "Yes. I'm going to watch Rose's initiation."

Kyrin grins. "Really?"

"Yes," I snap, doing up my button. I rake my fingers through my long hair in an attempt to brush it. "Why?"

He shrugs, nodding his head. "I'll walk you."

Shoving my feet into my Chucks, I eye him skeptically. "Why would you do that?"

His tongue sneaks out and runs across his bottom lip. They're all very good-looking. Annoyingly so. Kyrin and Keaton are the quiet ones; they're the monsters who sit in the corner and watch everyone kill each other before they come in and feast on people's battered souls. Killian is the jokester. He's the one I feel somewhat comfortable with. Mainly because he has nice eyes. They're smiling eyes. The kind of eyes that he doesn't have to smile for them to smile, unlike Keaton's, whose are more serious and intense and fanned with dark eyelashes. Kyrin has jet-black hair and cognac honey eyes. The kind that you don't trust because he looks a little deranged.

Kingston. Well, King is something else entirely. He has chocolate hair, that's the perfect length to run your fingers through, tanned skin, and vivid green eyes. There are my color green eyes, and then there are Kingston's green. They almost look alien-like. His eyelashes are as thick as his hair, and his cheekbones sit high. They're all gorgeous guys and all athletically built, with King being the biggest. Kingston has the triangle tattoo over his left pec and a vine of roses over the right side of his stomach that slips down beneath his pants, but other than that, I don't think he has any other tattoos. Keaton is covered in ink from head to toe. They're all over his neck, head, arms, and even some on his face. Kyrin has a sleeve, but that's all I've seen so far, and Killian, as far as I've seen, is clean.

"Why would you want to walk me?" I ask again, standing and shoving my phone into my back pocket.

Kyrin shrugs, glaring at me. "Because."

I pause for a few seconds, attempting to find the energy to further question him on his answer. "Fine. Will I get an initiation?"

He waves ahead, stepping aside for me to shuffle past him. "No. We don't do one for The Brothers."

I ignore how uncomfortable I feel around him and make my way out of their RV, shivering when the cold air hits my arms. I am somewhat relieved that I won't have to go through whatever it is that Rose is about to do, though.

"Hey!" Killian is about to pass us, but he stops, instantly stealing my attention. His smile falters when his eyes drift over my shoulder, obviously landing on Kyrin.

"Going to bed early for once?" Kyrin asks him skeptically, standing right beside me. I try to draw some heat from Kyrin without actually touching him but fail miserably.

Killian rolls his eyes. Something I would have missed had it not been for the bright garden lights that lead paths toward every RV and trailer, as well as one that goes straight to the big tent at the end. "No."

Killian shoves past Kyrin. "Wait here." He disappears into the RV and returns with a hoodie in his arms. "Here." He shoves the warm garment into my chest. "My cock is shriveling up just watching you shake like that."

"Ah." I ignore him. "Thanks." Without looking, I slip my arms into the hoodie, instantly sighing at the warmth it provides.

Kyrin doesn't say anything, so I look at him, finding him staring back at me.

"What?" I ask, curling the hood around my neck. It hangs to my mid-thigh, and I couldn't be more appreciative.

"Nothing," he grumbles. "Let's go."

Killian points to each trailer as we pass, mentioning who is in each one.

"Midnight?" I ask, just as we're passing a pastel purple RV that looks a smidge smaller than The Brothers' RV.

"Yeah," Killian says. "They're the acrobats and dancers. Maya is a contortionist, too, and Val does the aerial straps. D has been trying to get—"

"You're rather chatty tonight, bro. Maybe I should start calling you Chatty Kathy with a K."

Killian replies, but I'm not sure what he says, because as I re-enter the tent, I'm taken aback by fact that it's a completely different world. It's as though they manipulate your mind, re-placing all of what you see during the day and changing it with everything your dreams are made from.

"Wow," I gasp, taking in the droplets of neon purple lights that dip around the ceiling.

"You ain't seen nothing yet. This is just the practice tent. It isn't the one we perform in. Come on. Sit in the front."

I don't reply. I just let both of them lead me to the front seats. As I sit down and the plush cushions sink beneath me, I'm awestruck by everything around me.

The lights are all cut out when a single spotlight beams onto the middle of the stage.

"What's going on?" I ask Killian, since I already know that Kyrin won't tell me anything.

I can feel heat prickling up the back of my neck, and my spine stiffens: King is obviously here somewhere.

Killian leans into me, and I inch closer, so I can hear what he's about to say. My fingers tingle to move, my limbs aching to be on that stage. Why, I don't know.

"If you're scouted into a family that isn't The Brothers,

you have to be initiated by performing their act without knowing what's going on. If you pass, then congratulations, you're a part of the notoriously famous and wealthiest show known to mankind. If you fail, well, you die."

I pause, my head snapping to his just as soft music begins playing through the speakers. "Wait, you what?"

Killian's eyes search mine, a smirk on his mouth. His eyes drop to my lips and his tongue sneaks out to wet his bottom lip. It's then that I catch the silver ball in the middle of his tongue. He has his fucking tongue pierced. "They die."

I instantly look at the stage and see Rose smiling from the center. Crazy bitch is smiling. "Midnight are acrobats as their main act...but not their only act."

Rose stands in the center of the stage, her arms stretched wide. There's nothing but silence and the cool midnight air surrounding us. I lean into Killian when the soft melody picks up and an electric guitar starts playing in the background.

"Why midnight?"

Killian's phone lights up in his hand, and he looks down at it. The light from his phone displays his face. I watch as he slowly smirks as he taps something back. Turning over his shoulder, he sends a wink to someone behind us and then shoves his phone back into his pocket and leans into my ear. "A long time ago, and I mean a long fucking time ago, it was said that when the clock struck twelve, that was when the portal of hell would open and let all the ghosts, that were wanting to come to earth, out. But every night at twelve, they'd get sucked back in, and then more would be allowed through. Like a cycle. They got twenty-four hours here and so on. These ghosts were said to come from a small town in Romania."

I look out at Rose and watch as she wraps one of the aerial

ribbons around her wrist, trying to pull herself up. She's failing, but she's determined. I have no doubt at all that she can do this.

"That's a bit weird. Is this small town still alive?"

Killian smirks. Something he does a lot. "It's just folklore, but yeah, it is. They say that if a woman dances in front of a fire after midnight, she's offering her body up as a vessel for one of her ancestors to jump into."

"That's...creepy," I whisper, the set finishing in the background. I watch as the blonde girl, I think they said her name was Val, grabs onto a large ring that's hanging from the roof, turning it around. She's wearing short spandex and a sports bra. Nothing glamorous, but I'm guessing they save the costumes for the actual performances.

Rose searches me out in the crowd, knowing I'm here, but it's too late because Val is running circles around her, the ring secured in her hand. She swings up, hooking her legs around the ring and hangs upside down as the ring goes higher. On her circling, the ring drops, and she grabs onto Rose's ankles, yanking her upside down. All that's stopping Rose from falling onto her head is Val. She pulls Rose up, and I watch as her arms and triceps contract from the movement. Rose finally figures out what's going on and grabs onto the ring, swinging herself up. They sit side by side as Val performs multiple moves around Rose. I watch as Rose's head turns from left to right. When Val splits right in front of her face, one ankle to one side and the other to the other, Rose falls backward, but at the last minute, Val grabs onto Rose's arm, yanking her back as the ring lowers back to the ground. My heart is thrashing in my chest, and it's not until they're back on the ground when I realize I'm on my feet, my hands fisted and sweating. The music cuts, and the lights flick on.

"What the fuck, Val?" Kyrin yells out from beside Killian. "It was just getting good. Why would you save her?"

Val glares at Kyrin. "Because I happen to maybe like this one. And," Val looks Rose up and down, "she has potential, but not enough to be better than me."

Rose sneers at her, getting to her feet while sweeping her hair up into a high ponytail. "Fuck you."

Val beams a smile at her, wicked enough to match Maleficent. "You're so welcome, precious." She tosses a bottle of water at Rose's chest, who catches it instantly. "You're in. Don't piss me off." Then she turns to leave. I take this moment to head straight for Rose, checking her over.

"Are you okay?" I whisper, noticing the purple and red bruises all over her body.

"I'm fine." She offers me a gentle smile. One that doesn't reach her eyes. One that illustrates just how not okay she is.

"Well, at least you're with girls and not four males who may or may not murder you..." I murmur.

Rose's eyes flick over my shoulder, and I follow. My jaw clenches when I see King seated a few rows behind where I was, his eyes lazy and his lips in a flat line. I hate that my stomach and chest feel as though they've been punched every time I find him watching me. Why does he have to be so infuriatingly handsome?

"I don't know." Rose bumps her shoulder with mine. "Seems like a pretty good way to wake up dead."

I roll my eyes. "Rosé, you don't wake up if you're dead."

She laughs at my nickname for her, picking up her tossed hoodie and slipping it over her slender shoulders. "Always so smart."

I leave her a little bit after that and head back to our RV.

Swinging the door open, I lazily make my way to the back where my bed is, kicking off my shoes and jeans and falling onto my bed, before losing myself in a deep sleep.

Eight

Dove

A jolt jerks me awake as the sun burns my skin through the window, warming me from the outside in. We're moving. I climb from the bed, squeezing some booty shorts on and tiptoe out of my room and down toward the front of the RV, leaning against the walls every time we hit a bump or turn.

"Where are we going?" I ask no one in particular, but as soon as I reach the front, I see the same guy who was in here when I moved in.

"Morning, Birdie. We're headed to New York. You're up early."

I lean against the passenger seat. "I'm not used to sleeping in a moving vehicle."

He chuckles, and it's then that I see the gold tooth in his mouth. He's a big boy. A little short for my taste, and obviously too old, but he's attractive. "There's going to be a lot that you will need to get used to, Little Bird."

I tug my hair out of its ponytail and throw it all back into a high twist bun. "I'm sure there is. Do you drink coffee?"

"Black, please."

"Cool." I turn around to head into the kitchen as Kingston walks down the stairs, wearing only grey sweat shorts that dangle way too low on his hips.

Focus.

I ignore him and start the coffee. I'm grabbing two mugs when I feel the heat radiating from him. He's right beside me, reaching for something above my head.

I freeze at his proximity. The smell of lathered soap, honey, and ash quickly becoming a heady combination of sin.

Jesus.

I close my eyes and exhale, rolling up the sleeves of the hoodie I'm still wearing. I reach for the pot of coffee and pour two cups. I need to get the fuck—The side of his midsection brushes against my arm, and I involuntarily flinch away from him, unwilling to acknowledge the zap that coursed through him to me.

"Sorry," I mutter, stepping away.

King doesn't answer. He doesn't so much as pay me any attention as he pours granola into his bowl. His proximity is toxic, the invisible grip of his fist around my throat, threatening to choke me. Giving a whole new meaning to *take my breath away*. After pouring black liquid into mugs, I turn for the cutlery drawer when the RV swerves, and I fall into his warm chest.

"I'm sorry." I shove away from him, but then yank my hands back when the feeling of his skin almost electrocutes me.

He shoves me away, glaring at me like I'm an annoying child, and he's the hot babysitter who can't be bothered with my shit. "Stop fucking apologizing." He grabs a spoon for him and then one for me, tossing it across the kitchen counter.

"Thanks." I take the spoon and stir sugar into my mug. He lowers himself onto one of the stools, ignoring me while spooning mouthfuls of granola into his mouth. Deciding to leave it at that, I turn to head back to the front of the RV when his voice stops me in my tracks.

"Oh, and Dove?"

I turn over my shoulder. "Yeah?"

His tongue flicks over his lower lip as he points to my back with his spoon. "Take my fucking hoodie off."

"Sure," I reply sharply, hiding the fact that his words stung and that I didn't know it was his hoodie. He can have it back as soon as I've finished my coffee.

I hand the driver his coffee and take a seat on the passenger seat, blowing into the mug. There's a long silence before he says something.

"I'm Justice."

"Nice to meet you," I say, keeping my eyes fixed on the passing trees and farmland.

"You don't have to lie to me, little girl. I know damn well it's not nice meeting me, considering your circumstances," he grunts, taking a sip of his coffee while keeping one hand on the wheel.

I run my palm over my forehead. "What makes you think I had a life worth losing?"

Justice pauses, and I watch as the corner of his mouth turns into a smile. "Touché, Little Birdie."

"Dove!" Kingston barks from the back. I don't turn. I'm not one of his groupies. I don't like being treated like shit when he barely knows me.

"What?" I call out, my monotone voice a dead giveaway on how much I care about his annoyance.

"Hoodie!"

I take a long sip of coffee, swallowing past the burn that each gulp ignites.

"Little Bird, don't provoke the wolf when you're a sheep," Justice whispers.

I stand, turning to face King. His legs are spread wide, and his glare is dead set on me. He's lounging backward, his head tilted slightly. A couple of the other Brothers begin walking down the stairs.

"Oh, did you mean now?" I ask, reaching for the zipper and sliding it down. I'm well aware that I have nothing but my white lace bra and booty shorts beneath it.

Kingston nods his head. "Yeah, Little Bird, now'd be good. You can come shake your ass around me, too, but you ain't getting paid." He cocks his head in challenge.

I unzip it all the way down and shuffle it off my shoulders.

"Jesus Christ, girl," Justice growls beside me.

I fold the hoodie in my arms, and that's when I see the name printed on the back. AXTON. And then below that is THE BROTHERS OF KIZNITCH. My eyes shoot up to where Killian is standing still, a mug in his hands, but his eyes on my body.

"Asshole," I murmur, walking forward and shoving the hoodie at Kingston's chest in passing.

Killian laughs as I stroll past and head straight for my room.

It was Miami Beach, and I was single, so naturally, I found myself sucking face with a random stranger after a night out with Rich and a couple girls from the club.

I pulled the guy in closer as he reached behind him to unlock the door, swinging it open until it was crashing against the wall.

We both laughed, and it was the first time I noticed he didn't have great teeth. Hell, the tequila must had been wearing off, but fuck it. I was here, drunk. I needed a distraction. Sure, picking up a random dude from the club wasn't classy, but tonight, I wasn't looking for class: I needed to be taken away.

We were fumbling to his bed, and I was falling onto the mattress when he started reaching for a condom. I went with it, because that was why I was here. Once he was naked and rolling on the condom, I yanked him down on top of me and lost my way for all of—five minutes. If that. The song "one-minute man" started playing in the back of my brain when random guy fell asleep beside me, but not before muttering that I could stay the night and go home in the morning, which I was more grateful for than the epic failure of whatever it was that he just fucked me with.

I crawled up his bed and yanked the covers up with me, rolling my eyes when his snores gained volume.

I wanted to go to sleep, but I couldn't. The window in his room was open, allowing the ocean air to drift into the room. After ten minutes, my eyes began to get heavy.

So heavy.

I was chasing the sleep I so desperately wanted, when a rough hand clamped over my mouth, bringing me back to life.

My eyes popped open as fear rippled through me. I could see the outline of his hoodie, but a black rag was wrapped around half of his face, hiding it from his nose down.

He leaned down to the side of my ear, his hand squeezing my mouth. "Let's play heads or tails, Little Bird..." The Shadow teased. I felt his knee come between my legs. Even though I had a light sheet covering me, I could feel everything. "Heads, I suck your pussy until you scream, to show this fool how a real man fucks. Or tails, I cut off each of your fingers and fuck you with them. Both will have you screamin', baby. So, what will it be?"

I kicked and turned, but I knew it was no use. The Shadow would come, and he would go. It was what he did.

He shoved me away, and I swiped the saliva away from my mouth, tears pricking my eyes. The day he started was the day my parents died, and I knew that it had something to do with them, but I wasn't sure how long I could hold on until he finally took the one thing he craved.

Me.

Slowly, he stepped backward, and I watched as he pulled a coin out of his pocket. I turned to check on my random one-night stand, finding that he hadn't moved. He was still snoring on his back.

"Tick, tock, Little Bird, it's a race against the clock..."

The Shadow had always tormented me between the cracks, but never had he threatened me sexually.

I chewed on my bottom lip as he flicked the silver coin up into the air. I watched as it curved, flipping around and around, until it landed in the palm of his hand.

He paused for a second, and then his fingers flexed as he checked what it landed on. He grabbed it between his two fingers and flashed it at me. I squinted my eyes to get a better look, but it was obvious that it was—"heads," I whispered.

He made his way back to me until his body hovered over mine, both fists sinking into either side of me. "A deal is a deal, Little Bird."

"I—" he pulled the sheet off my leg.

"Spread your legs," he growled, and a dangerous concoction of fear and heat began to brew in my belly.

Slowly, I inched my leg wider, flinging my arm over my eyes. I am not about to do this. Not here. Not now. Not with the one man who I have feared for years. Truth is, is that as the years have gone on, I had somewhat become accustomed to his presence. Fear made me do reckless things, but this was by far the worst.

Before I could run from the room and away from the very thing that was chasing me, his warm mouth was on my pussy. My back arched off the bed from the sensation as his tongue flicked around my clit. He sucked, licked, and teased me savagely as whimpers left my body.

"Scream," he demanded.

I fixed my mouth closed, my head thrashing to the side to check on random guy. The Shadow pressed against my clit with the thick part of his tongue and slowly licked up. A finger slipped inside of me, just as his mouth clamped down again, with hard flicks of his tongue.

"Fuck!" I screamed, sweat pouring out from my body as the orgasm I so desperately craved seized my muscles and convulsed around me. I didn't even care if I woke up random guy at this point, I was too sedated. A few minutes later, he crawled back up my body, his mouth now fully covered by the rag again. "Next time you wanna bounce on someone else's dick to get away from me, I'll be right here to remind you why the fuck that isn't a good idea. So unless you wanna flip the coin again, Little Bird, keep your fuckin' legs closed." Then he pushed off the bed, and instead of climbing out the window like I thought he might've done, he headed straight out the front door like he owned the place, slamming the door behind himself.

I turned around to check random guy, who was still snoring beside me.

Nine

King

"Don't fucking pull that shit again." I empty my bowl into the sink.

"Oh, come on. It was funny." Killian grins from the other side of the room. "We all know how much you *can't stand* her."

I turn to face them, squeezing the counter. "Figured out what we're going to start with tonight?"

"I feel like throwing some shit," Keaton says casually, drinking his shake.

Killian takes a seat beside Keaton, grinning from behind his mug.

I flip him off and head back upstairs to shower. Fucker.

Kicking my door closed, I stretch out my neck and head straight for my phone that's ringing on my bed.

Sliding it open, I push it to my ear. "Mom."

"Son, I haven't heard from you in a few days. How's everything going?"

I head for my closet and take out a pair of jeans and a beat-up Harley Davidson shirt, tossing them onto my bed. "It's going."

Silence. "Your father wants an update." I hear her click her fingers in the background. Probably at our maid. "*Sapore tuae ne obliviscaris,* son." *Don't forget your task.*

I still, my muscles flexing from the tension. "I haven't."

"Son..."

"Mom, I gotta go."

I hang up my phone, tossing it across the room. Have you ever heard of that mom who drove all of her kids off of the cliff, killing her entire family? Yeah, well, pretty sure that bitch re-incarnated into my mom. If you think I'm bad, which I very much fucking am, then you need to meet my mom.

I head for the shower, leaving any and all of the conversation I just had behind. Stepping under the hot water, I rest my head against the marble wall. She can't fucking know who we are. I mean, who we really fucking are. I smirk as the water drips down my face. Revenge isn't always sweet; sometimes, it's a bitter reminder of the demons you missed, so you need to cock back, aim, reload, and...*bang.*

Ten

Dove

"Okay, okay." I laugh, resting my legs up on the dashboard. It's mid-afternoon, and we've been driving for what feels like days. We have around four more hours to go before we get to New York. "You might be right about that." I chuckle at Justice's poor attempt at thinking up conspiracy theories. "But I think the Avril Lavigne clone thing is a little far-fetched. I mean, you're giving the human race way too much credit. We are not a species made to last."

Justice chokes on his drink. "Why do you say that?"

"Easy," I say, nudging my sunglasses down my nose and looking at him from over the rim. "We live in an economy that thrives on the underprivileged staying under, and the rich getting richer. We have wars happening all over the world, and now, people are so damn sensitive. Everyone is offended by being offended and then get offended that they're offended."

"Okay, you lost me, sugar, but I see your point."

I shrug, pushing my glasses back up. "So tell me something about you."

Justice laughs. "Nope. Not going there."

"Little Bird, come here!" Killian calls out from behind me. I've been purposely ignoring them the entire trip, making small talk with Justice, but this is the first time any of them have actually called for me.

I turn around. "I'm good. Thanks."

"Yeah, that wasn't a question," Kyrin bites, pouring vodka into a glass. He looks at me over the rim as he tosses it back. "You act like you're not a prisoner. Maybe I should remind you and tie you to my bed."

Killian laughs, throwing down his hand of cards. "You're scaring her, Ky."

Kyrin glares at me. "Good. I like them scared. It gets my dick hard."

King's walking down the stairs interrupts our back and forth—thankfully. I really want to go up there to see what it looks like, but it was made clear, at the very beginning, that up there was out of bounds for me, and right now, I don't feel like testing their restraint.

King goes to the fridge, pulling out deli meat and mustard and getting busy on a sandwich. I know that he's the leader of them all, but it's a weird dynamic. They all move fluidly, even though King doesn't really hang with them. From what I've seen. Or maybe he's just not social. Just as that thought breezes through my brain, King drops down on the stool beside Kyrin, taking a massive bite out of his sandwich with his eyes on me. It's creepy. As though he can hear the thoughts inside my head.

Kyrin slides over a glass of what looks like some mix of alcohol. Or Coke, maybe.

King's eyes stay on mine as he picks it up and takes a long drink.

"Little Bird, come play," Killian taunts, snapping me out of my Kingston trance.

"Play what?" I ask, watching them all with suspicion.

Killian raises a perfectly arched eyebrow. "Well, if I get to choose…"

If I play a game with them, cards by the looks of it, what could be the worst that could happen?

"Go on, Little Bird. They don't bite," Justice adds faintly.

"Oh, don't we?" Killian teases, sending me a wink.

King kicks out the chair opposite his, nodding his head toward it. "Well, come on, Little Dove." He leans forward, resting his elbows on his knees, while pinning me with his icy glare. "Don't you want to see if we bite?"

My legs shake beneath my weight, and my breath catches in my throat, but I find myself heading straight for the chair. *One step. Two step. Three…* I sit, noticing the cards laid out on the table.

"What are we playing?"

King leans back in his chair and grins. "You."

I clear my throat. I've never seen his smirk, and now I wish I hadn't. It's deadly, like something you'd imagine in your nightmares. The only difference between him and the monster that awaits you in those nightmares when you close your eyes is that Kingston comes dressed as everything you've ever wanted.

"He's kidding." Keaton stares at me blankly.

"Or is he?" Killian teases.

Kyrin rolls his eyes, dealing my hand. "The game is called sixers." Kyrin hands me six cards and continues. "The object of the game is to read people. Can you do that?"

"Honestly?" I answer, scooping up my cards. "No."

Kyrin pauses his dealing, his eyes going around the table. He keeps talking. "Well, you might learn, or you might not. I guess we're about to find out. So the object is for all of us to pick up the cards. The dealer, who is me for this hand, has three questions. You start with the left and go around the circle. Use your three questions wisely, because that's all you get before you have to guess the one card they pick out of the six they have. You get it right, you get that card. The player with the most cards at the end of the game has one dare to use. So, say if I won, I could choose one of you to do anything that I wanted, and you'd have to do it."

I raise a challenging eyebrow. "And if we don't?"

Kyrin flicks the deck of cards between his fingers. "We've never had someone tap out before, so who knows, Little Dove. I guess it would put you in an awfully fragile situation."

I gulp quietly so I don't exhibit my fear. "What are the rules?" I ask, peeking at my cards. This was an awful idea.

Kyrin pours another glass of vodka, sliding it toward me. "You can't ask the color, the family, or whether it's an odd number."

"What?" I gasp, ignoring the drink. "How am I supposed to figure out the card?"

"I guess you're about to figure that out," Keaton murmurs.

Kyrin places the rest of the cards into the middle of the table and turns to Keaton. He searches his eyes for a few seconds. "What's your favorite color?"

"Black."

"Really? I thought it was red."

Keaton glares.

Kyrin chuckles. "King of hearts."

Keaton flicks the card around, revealing the king of hearts.

"What? That's impossible!" I don't understand the dynamic of many card games, but I'm almost certain I have never seen one played like this.

Killian leans into me. "This will be hard for you because you're new and we're intimidating, but I'll tell you a secret." He leans in farther, close enough for me to feel his lips over my earlobe. "People usually display what they hold."

I have no idea what that means.

"Stop fucking cheating, Kill," King mutters, shaking his head.

"Hey! I mean, we've never had a girl in our group before. I'm just making sure she has a fair go. And man, we've thrown her into the deep end by playing sixers."

"Bullshit." Killian chuckles, glaring at me. "We've been playing this game since we we're two years old."

The silence spills out between the group.

"Two?" I ask, shocked. How could a two-year-old know how to play a game that I can't play?

Keaton answers, "He's kidding." He says the words, but I don't feel their truth.

They continue to go around the circle, and I watch as one after the other gets them right. King has the most cards stacked against him when it's my turn to deal. I put the cards in the middle of the table.

"You gonna drink your drink?" Kyrin asks, nudging his head toward the glass.

"I don't take drinks from strangers."

"Huh." Kyrin smiles. "Maybe that's something we could learn. You know, don't take humans who don't belong to you."

I wince, but not enough for any of them to notice.

My eyes flick to Killian who is on my left. He holds up his card, tapping it against his mouth. "Come on, Little Bird. You know you've got this."

I have no idea what I've got, and this game is weird. I don't know where to start or what I should ask.

"Ever kissed a stranger?" Not sure why that came out of my mouth, but I'll go with it, because it's Killian. What's the worst that could happen?

"Take me to dinner before you fuck me, Little Bird." He chuckles, hiding behind his card.

His left eye twitches.

I have no idea what the hell I'm doing. "I don't know. Six of diamonds?"

"Wrong!" Killian flashes a ten of hearts.

"This game sucks," I murmur, before realizing who is next.

Kingston stares at me flatly, his thick eyelashes fanning across his high cheekbones every time he blinks. His lips are the perfect size. Not too plump but not too thin. His face is in flawless symmetry, every feature perfect and aligned.

He holds my stare, the card tucked between his thumb and his pointer finger. He holds his drink in the other hand. I notice the leather bracelet on his wrist and the black ring on his finger.

Silence fills the space around us, and I swear I'm breathing loudly.

I blink slowly. "Ever been in love?"

He holds my stare, not so much as flinching. "Never."

"Ever plan to?"

His jaw clenches. "Never."

"Some might say you have a black heart."

He cocks his head as the corner of his mouth kicks up an inch. It's subtle, but I caught it. I carry on, my tongue swiping across my bottom lip. His eyes fall from mine to catch the movement before they come back up. Again, subtly. "Some might say…" I whisper. *What the fuck am I doing?* "That you're an ace of spades."

He stills. His eyes narrow on me, and everything around me ceases to exist. In this moment, it's just him and me and our silent tug-of-war.

He tenses his jaw a few times and then flips the card around to face me.

Everything comes back into real time when the rest of the boys erupt into a fit of disbelief. There, between King's fingers, is the ace of spades.

I blink a few times to pull myself out of the daze I was in. "Wait, you swapped that!" I point to the card.

King flings the card into the middle of the table. "I didn't, and I don't cheat."

"That's fucked up." Killian shakes his head in disbelief. He stands from the table, pulling out his phone. He snaps a random photo of us all around the table. "That is going down in history."

I shake myself off and try it on the other two. Keaton was an epic fail. I don't even know why I tried. I can't pull anything out of him, and to be honest, I wasn't even trying, because I don't know how I did it to begin with, and I was too distracted by whatever it was that just happened.

Same with Kyrin. Fail. Fail. Fail. All but goddamn Kingston Axton. Why couldn't he be my fail? Why did he have to hold my ace of spades?

"All right! We don't have to count to know that King won," Killian announces, tossing his cards into the middle and downing the rest of his drink.

"Surprise, surprise." Keaton chuckles, kicking King from beneath the table.

"What will it be, your majesty? Come on. Hand it to us!" Killian teases, tossing potato chips into his mouth.

Kingston smirks, looking around the table.

I freeze when his eyes land on me, and instead of going to Killian, they stay on me.

Oh no.

Oh shit.

I shake my head. "I'm new. You can't include me in this."

His eyebrows raise. "Oh, but I can." He grins, his index finger working his upper lip.

"Yo!" Justice calls out from the driver's seat, saving me from whatever King was about to say. Thank God. "We're here!" I look down at the time that's on the dashboard: 7:37.

Crap, that time went fast.

I stand from the table, taking my glass to the sink as the rest of them disappear left, right, and center to do the things they probably do, which I know nothing about.

I spin around to find King still in his chair. I'm partially annoyed because I have to pretty much brush past him to get to my room. I could sit up with Justice a bit longer, but I think our chitchat has successfully died out.

I begin heading for my room while holding my breath. When I reach King, his hand finds my inner thigh, stopping my movement—and my fucking heart.

I pause, my breathing ragged. As I look down at him, he smirks up at me. His fingers flex around my thigh and I have to internally talk myself down from combusting. "I'll be cashing in on that dare later tonight, Little Bird."

He releases me, and I manage to successfully make my way to my bed without falling flat on my face.

My phone vibrates just as I catch my breath in my pillow; I reach for it, opening the text.

I'm going to kill Val before tonight's over.

Give me girl drama over this any day. I remember being in high school and freaking out over the smallest bit of drama. Now, up against this, it feels miniscule. Even the fact that before I had been taken into Midnight Mayhem, I was starving, broke, and paying my way in life via dancing on a pole every night seems so diminutive, considering my now drama.

Killian interrupts my reply by pulling the curtain open. "Can I come in?"

"Sure." I swallow, keeping my eyes locked on the ceiling and placing my phone to my side.

Killian drops down onto my bed, kicking off his shoes and climbing up farther. I turn my head to face him. He's leaning back on one elbow, his smirk hiding behind his hoodie slightly. "Wanna know what's weird?" His blue eyes dance in mischief. He pushes the ball of his tongue ring out, and I watch as he drags it across his bottom lip.

"What?" I ask, momentarily hypnotized by his tongue.

He pops it back into his mouth, his hand coming to my chin to tilt my face up to his. "You're fair game right now, so I wouldn't be looking at me like that."

I yank myself out of his grip. "I don't know what you mean."

"Anyway." His charm is back in full effect. "The funny thing."

I roll my eyes, tucking my hand under my head to hear what he has to say.

"We've been playing that game since we were two. That's twenty-two years of sixers, and never in those twenty-two years has anyone ever been able to call on King."

I blink a couple of times.

A few inhales of breath later.

"And?" I ask, wanting more. Needing more.

"And?" Killian parrots, flashing his straight teeth from behind a smile. "And that's fucking weird." He narrows his eyes, searching mine. "You're an alien. From Area 51."

I push off the bed, picking up my phone and quickly typing out the text I was supposed to send Rose before Killian walked his smug ass into my Area 51.

Can we swap?

"What is your deal, anyway, Little Bird?" Killian asks, slowly coming off the bed and leaning his elbows onto his knees. "Why are you here?"

I'm about to say *you fucking stole me* when the curtain that separates me and the rest of the RV is ripped open.

"Get out." Kingston hikes his thumb over his shoulder, glaring at Killian.

I shoot up from my position, as if I've been caught doing something wrong.

Killian doesn't move; he remains silent, and it's not until I look at him that I find his smirk fixed on Kingston.

"Really?" Killian laughs, shuffling off my bed and leaning into Kingston to whisper into his ear. I don't even want to know what they're talking about. I'm too busy stressing about what King might have me do for my dare. Maybe I should counter it with a game of poker and see if he still wins.

Killian leaves, and the RV comes to a stop. The silence that fills the distance between King and me is loud enough to wake the dead.

"So, this dare…" I joke, squeezing the blanket under my fist.

"Do I need to lay out some rules? I mean, some pretty fucking obvious ones?" he counters, throwing me off course.

"What do you mean?" My cheeks heat. I don't know why I assumed that he would be back here specifically for his dare.

He comes closer, leaning down onto the bed with his fists, caging me between two large arms. His proximity reminds me of a song I danced to one time. "Breathe" by Mako. "The power of distraction when you're in a vulnerable position could be the immediate decider between life or death, Little Bird." I close my eyes, mainly to shut out the voice that haunts me even when my eyes are open.

"You're not to fuck, kiss, or so much as touch any of The Brothers. Do I need to put that in writing for you to get that through your pretty little head?" His voice is low, his breath warm against my lips. Slowly, I open my eyes and notice he's right there. Face-to-face. Nose-to-nose. He searches my eyes and then drops to my mouth. "Answer me, Dove."

"No, you don't need to put that in writing. I won't go near any of you."

"You seem so sure," Kingston argues, his head tilting as if he's studying every inch of me, but he's not. He's merely bored and playing God, making sure his pawns are moving across the board sufficiently. I know his type. The broody alpha male who likes his soldiers in a line, ready for battle. I've just got to figure out whether I'm one of his soldiers or an enemy.

I clear my throat, my lips curling between my teeth. "I am. Somewhat."

"What makes you second-guess that?" I need him to back up from me.

I want to say *you! You fucking make me second-guess that*, but instead, I shake my head.

He pushes back, squaring his shoulders. "We'll see about that." He leaves, and I watch as he disappears into the darkness of the RV. The only light illuminating the area is the bulb on the roof.

Justice stretches his arms above his head, yawning. He catches me staring and cuts his yawn short. "Little Bird, you all right?" He has an accent, and I have no idea what it is. Scottish, maybe? It seems almost gypsy-like. Maybe it's just some weird hybrid accent from traveling so much.

"Yeah." I stand from my bed, grabbing my phone and shoving it into my back pocket. I make my way down the RV. "What usually happens from here?"

He rolls his shoulders. "Well, we drink while the construction crew sets up."

"The construction crew?"

"Yep!" He moves into the kitchen and takes a bottle of water out of the fridge. "We don't do any of the labor. We all have to…" He pauses, takes a sip, and momentarily thinks over what he's about to say next. "Reserve our energy for the show." He disappears behind me without saying goodbye. What even is this show? Everyone has made it clear that it's not a circus because they don't have animals, but I can't call it a carnival either because they don't have rides. What is Midnight Mayhem? Aside from the midnight folklore myth that Killian shared with me?

After throwing on warmer clothes, tight skinny jeans, Uggs, and an army green utility jacket with warm fur—fake, I hope— around the collar, I make my way outside to find Rose. The RVs are lined up beside each other, with just enough space to give some privacy, but ours is more to the back, hidden behind a large honey locust tree. Its branches float over the RV, curving around it as a form of shade. There are a few guys who are setting up the small solar lights, lining each RV's walkway, and I find myself watching them *watch* me. I offer a small smile, but they all quickly look away, as if they've been caught doing something that is forbidden.

"Hey!" I call out to a young girl who is bending over to shove a light into the grass near ours. She stands and turns toward me slowly, her eyes lighting up briefly. "Do you know where I can find Midnight's RV?"

The girl tilts her head, eyes searching mine. Her mouth opens, but just as she's about to say something, another man is behind her, his hand securely placed on her arm.

His eyes remain on mine as he says, "Ariana, go and help with the tent." His lip is curled, his face harsh, but his words are soft, the tension reduced for the small girl.

She gazes up at me pleadingly, and then her head falls between her shoulders, and she dashes off down the already lit pathway.

I bring my attention back to the man. "Well, do you know where I can find them?"

His arms fold in front of his chest, taking an intimidating stance. "You have no place here, *witch*."

Just as I'm about to ask him what the shit he's talking about, my phone vibrates in my back pocket.

I pull it out, ignoring him and turning back to find my own way. It's a text from Rose, explaining how to get to their RV.

I follow her instructions, finding the large tent not far away, deflated and spread across the grass. I wonder how long they go on the road for, and why I've never heard of them before. I need to make sure I do some research on Google the second I'm away from everyone and in my bed.

"Dove!" Rose calls out, and I turn to face her. She's waving near Midnight's purple RV. There's a small fire pit set up outside of it and chairs circled around it. I can see that all of the Midnight girls are there and a big part of me wishes I didn't come. I should have stayed in bed, away from people. Before I can think of a valid excuse to leave, Rose is bouncing toward me, her arm hooking into mine.

"They're not so bad. I mean, the other three. Val is a fucking bitch, and I wouldn't test her, if you know what I mean," she whispers in my ear right before we reach them.

I smile at all of them as I approach, every bit uncomfortable.

"Hey!" A brunette girl stands, handing me a drink. "I'm Mischa!" She points to the dark-haired girl who is seated beside her. "And that is Maya." She brushes her hand toward the blonde, who is seated on the other side of the fire, staring at me with her head tilted and her legs crossed. I mean, she's beautiful, but they're all contrastingly beautiful. "And that's Val, but she's a bitch, so you don't need to know her. Come sit!"

Maya watches me from her seat, her eyes wary. She's quiet. I think I like her.

"So, how are you finding it?" Mischa sparks the conversation. I'm thankful for that.

"Ah, let's see. I was kidnapped, and then—"

"What she means is that she'll settle in," Rose interrupts, squeezing my arm.

I tilt my head at her, before dropping down in the chair beside Maya.

Mischa and Rose continue talking, and I pretend to suck down my sour drink. Fucking margaritas. In this weather? No, thanks. Placing the cup back onto my lap, I watch as Mischa goes off about some guy she was seeing and she and Rose continue an easy conversation.

Maya is relaxed beside me, and it's not until I smell the sweet smoke of marijuana that I know why. Maya is half African American with long dark hair. She has almond eyes and thick eyelashes. Eyelashes that I would honestly kill for. She's wearing boyfriend jeans and a hoodie with the hood over her head.

"You know, it's rude to stare." Maya flicks the ash off her joint.

"Yeah," I say, looking back to a now silent Rose. "I know."

Maya is different. I see that. I can't exactly imagine her in skimpy clothes and doing the splits on stage.

"You're not drinking your drink, Dove," Val interrupts. She tilts her head to the side, and I watch as the flames from the fire flicker, creating shadows over her jaw. "Why is that?"

I shrug. "I—"

"Just don't drink." Kingston snatches the glass from me. My heart pounds in my chest, but rage burns in my belly. All of the feelings of seeing King eventually end like an angry rapid gushing at the bottom of my stomach.

I ignore him and the other three who make themselves comfortable around the fire. King sits on the grass opposite me, bringing the glass to his mouth while keeping his eyes on mine. I watch as he slowly tilts my margarita up and swallows it in one gulp. I expected something. Maybe some disgust. Since when could guys stomach a margarita?

Killian pulls over a chair and takes a seat beside Val,

propping a boombox on the ground. He flicks through his phone and hits play on an R&B song I recognize. "Antisocial" by Ed Sheeran and a rapper. The beat kicks in, and Killian winks at Maya. "Your song, aye, boo?"

Maya flips him off, blazing up another joint. "Be nice, or you can get your own ganja."

I'm a big people-watcher. I've never been a talker, and a lot of people have said that they assumed I was a snob. I'm not. I'm just quiet. Too many people are quick to spew words and don't take enough time to think before doing it. I'd rather watch people. How they speak, hold themselves, and what they say and the manner in which they say it. I guess some think that's creepy. Maya and Killian, though, I could cut their sexual connection with a blunt knife. They're saying a lot, by not saying anything at all.

My fingers flex on my lap, and now I wish I had something to at least take the edge off. I'm not a big drinker. I drink when I feel like it, and it just so happens that I don't feel like it often. I'm also not a very nice drunk. I get sloppy, weird, and say things I don't mean--the exact reason why I people watch, so I try to avoid it or keep it to minimal sips at best.

"And why don't you drink, Dove?" Val further asks, studying me. Why does she keep looking at me like I've kicked her puppy?

I shrug. "It's not that I don't." My eyes flick to King briefly, who is still watching me. Did he realize that I didn't touch my drink during our game of sixers? No. Surely not. That would mean that he was paying close enough attention to me. "It's just that I don't *often*."

Val seems to think over her next words, but when our little party turns into a rager, with more people piling in, she yanks her eyes away from me and zones in on Kingston. She pushes up from her chair, and even though there's a swarm of people walking around and grabbing drinks now, I can't help but force myself to watch her climb onto King's lap as if she belongs there. My throat goes dry, so I look away quickly, not wanting to get caught stalking. I never would have thought they were something. King seems so unattainable. He's like top shelf alcohol, nice to look at and dream about, but you just know that one taste will knock you on your ass. I find Rose watching me. She offers a soft smile, and then passes me her cup, moving her chair directly beside mine, on the other side of Maya.

"If I'm right," Rose says, pointing to the glass, "you need that."

I raise the glass and take a small sip. The beer rests on my lips before I swallow it.

"Actually, I might go take a walk. I'll see you a bit later?" I say to Rose, who is now taking the joint off Maya.

"Do you want me to come with you?" She wraps her lips around the end and inhales.

I shake my head. "No. I just need some air."

I look to Maya, who's ignoring me. "Bye, Maya."

Her eyes come lazily to mine. She has the worst resting bitch face I think I've ever seen. "Bye," she answers flatly, before looking out into the distance. As I turn on my steps and make my way to God knows where, I try to figure out whether Maya is weird, disturbed, or just a recluse. I had a plan to walk around until I ended up back at our RV, but the tent is already set up, and it instantly catches my eye.

Neon lilacs, obscure blacks, and dusty greys illuminate the dark night, like a warning on what's to come. Midnight Mayhem is an evident reminder that the myths were true. Monsters really do come out at night.

"Little Bird, are you lost?" Delila interrupts my stalking.

I spin around to face her and watch as she puts the end of a cigarette into her mouth. She inhales and then exhales softly.

"No. I was heading back to my—the RV."

Delila comes forward, taking my hand in hers. "Follow me, lost one."

I don't have a chance to refuse because she's dragging me toward the opening of the tent. It's much larger than the one that was set up at her house and bigger than the average circus style one. Instead of red and white stripes, it's lilac and black, and there are little fairy lights embedded into the material. A big sign hangs over the entrance, and in messy black writing outlined in lilac reads *Midnight Mayhem*.

Delila pauses at the threshold, waving her hand inside. "Come on. It's not all set up yet, but the floor is open."

I am about to say that I'm impressed with the fact that this monstrous tent is already set up so quickly when I realize what she had just said.

"What do you mean 'the floor is open'" I ask, falling into step behind her. As soon as I enter, I almost trip on my own feet. There are no chairs right now, but the floor is set up. There's a makeshift stage that sits behind one large circus patch, which lies empty.

"I mean," Delila stomps on her smoke, putting it out, "I want to see you lose yourself." Her eyes drop to my feet. "Let me guess, ballet?"

My eyes snap to hers after hungrily eating up the space. "Yes. How'd you know?"

"The way you walk." She snaps her fingers, and a boy around my age comes rushing forward, swiping sweat off his forehead. I don't pay him much attention because Delila is still talking. "Fetch me a chair and some scotch. Is the sound ready?"

The young guy nods submissively. "Enough to run some music through, but not all the way set up."

Delila nods, and he disappears, running off to grab her royal highness her items.

She watches me carefully, as if intrigued. "You're not drinking with the rest of them. Why?" She lights up another smoke, and I seriously wonder what this woman's act is and how she keeps so fit while smoking so many cigarettes.

"Drinking isn't really my scene."

"Hmmm," she answers, sitting down on the chair the young man brought back. He also places a small table beside her that holds a bottle of scotch and a clear tumbler glass. "Interesting for a girl of your age."

I want to remind her that I'm not a teenager. I don't need to party like one either, but instead, I say, "When life has taken control of you in the form of tragic incidents, it's hard to allow something so hollow to fill the empty parts of your life."

She flicks the smoke between her thumb and her index finger. "Huh. You're smart. Lucky me." She exhales, flicking her wrist to the stage. "Sorry to say I don't have a leotard, but there are some slippers there and shorts and a hoodie. I want free, Dove. I don't want a dance that you have to work for. I want Dove Noctem Hendry flying across my stage."

"Okay." I turn, making my way to the makeshift stage. I have no idea what I'm doing in regards to whatever it is that she expects, but I'll do what she advised I do—dance.

As soon as I've ducked onto the stage, I hide behind a red curtain and strip off my skinny jeans and shoes, squeezing on the white shorts she left me—that are more like booty shorts—and then throw on the grey hoodie. I prefer to dance in tight clothes when it's constricted movements that I want to accentuate.

Pink silk slippers catch my eye, and my heart slows in my chest. I haven't worn them in so long. Since before my parents died. I tug at my hair, pulling it down from the high ponytail. I run my fingers through it as I weigh my options. I want to see if I still have it, but another part of me thinks I'm not ready. The part that thinks I'm not ready is usually the same part that keeps me awake every night from overthinking.

"Sorry," the guy from earlier interrupts my pacing. "Do you have a song request?"

"'Breathe from Mako, please."

The young guy disappears back the way he came, and I go back to stressing about the slippers. Slowly, I reach down to touch the soft silk. *"Your arabesque is so much better, Dove. Keep at it."* Sharon, my tutor, looked down at her phone and answered it. *"Hello? Yes, no, Dove is here. She's doing great, Mrs. Hendry. Much better. Okay, thank you."* She hung up the phone and smiled sweetly at me. *"Your mother is proud of you. You are very lucky."*

I yank my hand away as if I've touched a raw memory.

Which I had.

Deciding to leave the slippers for another night, I make my way out to the center of the stage.

"Ready when you are, Dovey!" Delila yells out from somewhere in front of me. I can't see anything because she dimmed the lights. "I want your all."

I can't give her my all because I lost crucial parts of myself years ago, but I close my eyes and breathe softly. The guitar to the song starts, and I curl my body around in a circle, slowly sinking to the splits with both feet facing outward. I drag myself out, letting the music float through my limbs, and possess my movements. I haven't danced this style since I lost them. Since that night. It's not traditional ballet, but it's somewhere in the middle of gymnastics, hip-hop, and ballet. With every beat, I swing my leg up to standing splits and roll my body over in fluid movements. *God, I love this song.* It's not until the music stops that my breathing and tears catch me off guard. I quickly swipe them away as I come to my feet.

Clapping sounds in the audience, and the lights flash on. Not only is Delila sitting there watching, but so are The Brothers.

"King?" Delila calls out, but her eyes remain on mine. "Try not to break her, because she's going to have her own act as well as be in yours."

I subtly clear my throat, so I don't give away that I let the music take over my emotions. "And what is it exactly that they do?"

Delila seems to ponder over her thoughts and I silently plead with her to give me something. Anything that can prepare for what is in store for me tomorrow.

"A lot." She flicks off the loose ash at the end of her cigarette. "The cage? That's part of their act. The Triple Wheel of Death? Also theirs. If you see knives, they're theirs, too, but my favorite?" Delila grins, standing. "Is what they do to your mind. Nothing can help you prepare for that." She flicks her hand up and down my body. "Have an ice bath to cure whatever muscles might be spasming and get good rest tonight." She flashes a grin. "You're going to need it." She spins around and leaves me here, alone with all four of them.

"Little Bird," Killian interrupts my panicking.

"Hmm?" I give him my full attention, mainly because I don't want to risk looking at Kingston.

Killian's eyes lock onto mine. Dark blue swirls in a pool of dark water, entrancing me to swim into the deep end. He quirks an eyebrow. "Come here."

AMO JONES

I start walking toward him. I don't know why, and I can't stop it, but I do. I'm directly in front of him, standing between his legs, when I feel his palms touch the back of my thighs, his knees spreading wider.

"What are you doing?" I ask. My mouth is moving and words are coming out, but I don't know where they're coming from.

Killian smirks as his hands continue up the backs of my thighs. I clench them together to get him to stop touching me, and he chuckles. "Does Little Bird wanna play?"

No. No, I don't want to play. "Yes."

Killian looks up at me from beneath his eyelashes, a grin on his mouth. "Touch King."

What. Why would I touch King? *No. No.* I sidestep out of Killian's legs and find myself right between King's. My heart thunders in my chest as sweat trickles down the side of my temples. King is laid back farther into the seat, his ripped designer jeans hanging leisurely off his hips and his military boots tied loosely at his feet. He's leaning to the side on his elbow, and his T-shirt is slightly up, showing off his V and the Tommy Hilfiger briefs.

Oh God.

He sucks a smoke into his mouth and blazes the tip, his eyes closing in as he concentrates before bringing them back to mine.

He blows out a cloud of smoke. *"Perserva."*

"Put your hands on his knees." Killian's eyes darken, flying between King and me.

I do as I'm told, bringing my hands to his knees. I squeeze roughly as the scent of burning nicotine drifts up my nose.

"Remove his shirt."

Oh my God. No. What the fuck. My hands come to the end

88

of King's shirt, and I try my best to ignore the electricity that passes through his hot skin and into my knuckles.

Gripping onto the edge of his shirt, I slowly lift it further up. My lips curl beneath my teeth as I fight the urge to obey my body. It's as though Killian's words are the strings, and I'm the puppet. King leans forward just enough for his neck to skim over my mouth. Hot skin brushes over my swollen lips.

I suck in a breath, and just as I yank his shirt over his head, he pauses at my inhale. I flick his shirt to the side, stepping backward.

Killian leans into his seat, his cigarette burning between his fingers. His other finger is running over the top of his upper lip, his eyes never leaving mine. The atmosphere kicks up to ardently high levels. "Climb onto his lap, Little Bird." Killian continues. My eyes shoot to him as panic seizes me. I don't want to. I know what happens when he's close to me or touching me. I don't like it. I don't like anything that makes me feel things I don't want to feel, and right now, Killian is making me do things I don't want to do. Feel things I don't want to feel.

I look back at King, but he hasn't moved. His eyes are bleak, his expression bored. I bore him.

Slowly, I step forward and sink my knees into the hard chair that he's sitting on. Biting down on my lip, I slowly lower myself onto his crotch. My cheeks heat, and my thighs clench.

King is still in the same position, unfazed. Only now, he's staring up at me, and I'm closer. I don't like him this close to me. Kingston this close is not a good thing.

Everyone else slowly ceases to exist, disappearing into white noise. I can hear "Love is Madness" by Thirty Seconds to Mars playing in the background. King's eyes are still on mine, the cigarette burning between his lips. Before he can inhale again, I remove it from his lips and bring it to my own. Inhaling softly, I roll my body in his lap to the music. His hands come to my hips as I blow the smoke out from between my lips. His fingers trace up my side until they're buried in my hair, before he's yanking out my hair tie. I swing my hair around as I flick the smoke behind me and bring both hands to the back of his neck. When the chorus drops, I brush my chest against his. My face is so close that I can feel his lips against mine and the words stop. Everything slows and the music fades into the background, my breathing thickening. Just as I'm about to pull away, he locks his arms around my back and pulls me in harder. I can feel him between my legs. He raises his hips up and grinds against me. His lips are hovering dangerously close to mine, and just as he opens them, he ducks to the side and bites down on my earlobe. "If you want me to fuck you like a groupie, keep doing that, but I don't pay for my pussy."

I don't blink, unfazed with his cruelty. Leaning backward, I bring my hands to his cheeks. He thinks I'm a whore. As in, he thinks I wasn't a stripper—I was a whore. "You probably couldn't afford me anyway." I swing my legs off his lap, shoving him away. Everything comes back into real time as the cackles of laughter erupt from around us. I forgot all about the rest of The Brothers who were here, and Killian, the little shit.

Before anyone can say anything, or worse, Killian gets inside my head again, I run out the door until the hot congestion of the tent is replaced with the cold night air. How did I get here? I had a family who loved me. My future was bright. That's changed now.

I run to our RV and swing the door open, angry with myself for getting into this situation—even though it's not exactly like I planned it. Tearing all of my clothes off, I slip in and out of the shower and shimmy into a long shirt before any of them get back. Opening the back curtains, I sink into my pillow and gaze out at the stars. It's always been therapeutic for me to watch space. You don't know what's up there just as much as you don't know what's in the ocean. We think that what we see is all we know, but that's not true at all. My eyes close slowly as I drift into sleep.

Eleven

Dove

I wake before the sun comes up and throw some sweats on. I need to exercise before The Brothers wake up. If that's what Killian is capable of, then I don't want to know what the rest of the boys can do—particularly King. Pushing my wireless earbuds into my ears, I push play on "So Far Away" from Martin Garrix and manage to sneak out of the RV undetected. I don't know where I'm going per se, but I know a little about New York and the surrounding suburbs. My legs carry me toward a track that has a dirt path, which leads God knows where. I sweat it out and run until I can't feel my limbs and my legs burn. By the time I come back to camp, I'm drenched in sweat, and Delila is marching straight toward me.

I tear out my earbuds.

"What the hell do you think you're doing, Dove?"

"What?" I squeeze the pods into the palms of my hands. "I went for a run."

Delila glares at me. "Well, we will see how much that was a good idea later tonight when it comes to your act. You only train excessively when you have a rest day the day after, which is why most of the crew work out before we come and before we leave. The rest you gain from the show." She clicks her fingers together, and that same young man comes rushing to her side. "Get the stands ready, please. Aeron and Beat are joining us tonight, and I want to make sure they're taken care of." She looks back at me. "Your lack of caring is beginning to get a little unnerving, Dove. Are you a liability?"

"No," I answer, even though I want to say that I don't care what she thinks.

Once Delila has disappeared as quickly as she appeared, I find myself walking aimlessly back to the RV. How the hell was I supposed to know that we weren't allowed to train on the day of a show?

I pause as I come up to the RV, finding King and Killian talking with a few guys I've never seen before. They mustn't be in the show either, or I'm sure I would have noticed them.

Killian hands them a few tickets, before turning his eyes to me. "Where'd you fly off to, Little Bird?"

I scan the new guys with careful eyes. One is absolutely inked, with a pretty enough face to feature on every cover of *GQ* magazine, one is dark and broody, and reminds me way too much of a certain male I've come to know, and the other one I feel uncomfortable even looking at because he's that scary—but I can't look away because he's *fucking hot.*

93

Killian catches me staring. "Little Bird." He gestures to the guys. "Meet Nate, Bishop, and Brantley. A few of my oldest friends. They're coming to the show tonight."

King puts a smoke in his mouth and dismisses me. "You can leave now."

My mouth slams closed as I give the boys a wave. "Nice to meet you."

Quickly turning back to the RV, I pick up my steps, desperate for a shower. If only the water could wash away the dirty look King just gave me.

The crowd is quiet. I can hear Delila's voice expand through the speakers, summoning everyone's attention. *If only I could see.* I yank on my arms and legs, but I'm tied spread eagle while standing.

"Ladies and gentlemen, welcome to Midnight Mayhem." *Welcome to Midnight Mayhem?* People should run. "This is neither a circus nor a carnival. This is what happens when the clock strikes twelve and all of the monsters you thought never existed expose themselves."

Suddenly, there's a shocked inhale from the audience, and the blindfold, that's covering my eyes, has light fighting through. I tug on my hands again.

"Sit back, relax, and keep your mind closed. Because if you open it, you don't know what will creep in." She ain't lying.

I hear the loud rumble of a bike. Multiple bikes. I don't have to hear them to know they're here. I can feel them, their presence and their power. The crowd cheers, only enticing my fear.

I clench my fingers around the rope that's tied around my wrist, using it as a way to keep myself together. The bikes grow louder and louder until I'm squeezing my eyes shut. Some strangeness washes over me from their deep rumble, but I can't quite put my finger on why. They're close now, so close. I can no longer hear the crowd or the heavy metal music. An engine is revved, and then another, and another and another, until I hear them zip forward into what sounds like circles around me. I wonder in the back of my head if they're on the Harley Davidsons I saw earlier. They were the smaller kind, obviously not road bikes but not pit bikes either. Dust slaps my legs as they continue to go in circles around and around, until suddenly, they stop. The bikes idle in the background, and I feel the palm of who I know is King brush my upper thigh.

"This is Little Bird's first show," he calls out through the mic.

I swallow.

His hand moves up past my thigh and over my exposed belly. Delila had me change into black leather shorts and a short leather crop top. My hair is dead straight, and I have enough makeup on my face to make a drag queen envious.

The blindfold is gone, and I'm looking straight toward a spotlight that's beaming on me. I notice I'm hanging on a wooden board with my arms and feet spread. Before I can think of what it is that I'm doing here, something whips past my belly, sticking to the wall that I'm in front of.

What. The. Fuck.

Another on my other side. It's then that I notice the black handle of knives.

I yank and pull on the cuffs when the crowd goes silent. My heart beats in my chest.

Another one that lands right near my cheek. I can feel the cool metal of the blade press against it. Fear ripples through my bones, and just when I think I'm going to pass out, Killian is beside me, his hands traveling up my leg. Only his face is completely camouflaged by distorted clown makeup. Blood drips around his eyes, his pupils covered by white wolf contacts. He bares his teeth, and my eyes catch the fangs extended on either side.

"Jesus Christ." He's terrifying.

"Enjoy it." He walks around me, and I can feel his lips smirk against my earlobe. "Make those panties wet."

My eyes close, and my breathing hardens, just as another knife is flying between my legs, pressing against my pussy.

Who the hell is throwing the knives? My thighs clench.

I sit there for another five minutes as four more knives are thrown, and the crowd erupts into cheers.

Do they not realize that I almost died?

That I haven't trained?

King comes forward, exposing his face. His makeup is almost the same as Killian's. All similar, but I don't have time to compare notes right now. He's wearing no shirt with blood smeared all over his rippled chest, hands, and neck. *This is an act. This is their act. Or one of them.* He tugs on the binds that are around my wrists, unclasping them. The curtain is drawn across, and in the background, I can see people quickly moving around, removing the wooden plank and replacing it with the triple ring of death.

Kingston yanks off the ties that are around my wrists. I stretch them out, massaging where the rope indented my flesh.

"What's that?" I ask King, just as his hand comes to the large metal ring. There are three. Three large metal wheels with no sides. They're connected to multiple long metal poles. They look as though they go round and round in circles.

"You'll see." He grabs my hand and pulls me into him. "You're good at reading people. That game sixers? Teaches you how to explore the expression of others, which will help you in this scene, amongst others." My eyes drift over his shoulder, my focus waning.

His fingers come to my chin, forcing my eyes back to his creepy ones. "This is when you need to focus. You need to watch my cues and what I'm doing."

"Why?" Everything is such a riddle when it comes to these acts. I don't understand it, but I have felt what they're capable of. The thing with riddles is that people underestimate their underlying meaning. Some people aren't smart enough for them and the others? Wish they weren't. I know what Killian can do, and what I'm pretty sure Kingston just did. Throwing knives at me was risky, and I'm almost certain it would have been a lot better had they given me a warning before to…I don't know…keep still?

When he doesn't answer me, I gaze up at him, only to find him still watching me. "Because you're going in that ring with me."

"Oh."

"With my bike."

Gulp. "What?"

"While I ride circles around you."

"Wait."

"While you hang on the swing."

"Nope." I turn around to leave, making peace with the fact that I will face the repercussions of whatever Delila sees fit as my punishment. Fuck the crowd, too. They can settle for an average circus. I am not a fucking trained monkey.

His hand connects with mine, and he forces me back around. I come crashing into his chest. "First of all, you don't have a fucking option. Second of all, I haven't had anyone in my wheel since—ever. I'd appreciate if you took this seriously for a second."

"Why would you care?"

King collects himself and chuckles. "I didn't say I cared. I'd just rather not wipe your blood off my bike." He leans in, his lips brushing over my ear. "I won't hurt you in there, but that's not because I care. It's because I have a colorful imagination of other ways I'd rather do it."

The curtains open again, and I'm, once again, blinded by a spotlight. Kingston is still glaring at me as he walks back toward his bike. He jumps back on and starts it up, just as Delila's voice booms through the speakers. "As some of you may have heard, our Sons of Kiznitch have a few tricks that they keep up their sleeve. Their infamous act is the tricks they play with you, their clownage and stunts…" She pauses, and I realize that that pause is obviously in regard to my play in this whole act. "And, of course, our next one, The Triple Wheel of Death. Tonight, we have Little Bird stepping inside the wheel with our favorite, King. The pleasure is all hers, because our King doesn't share his spaces with anyone." My fists clench together tightly, enough for sweat to spill from my flesh. The loud roar of his bike drowns out the crowds gasping, and I watch as he revs it a few times, tossing on a cap and flipping it backwards before driving the bike up a metal ramp and into the wheel.

Oh God.

My stomach swims in nerves as all of the women in the audience lose their minds. He's wearing destroyed jeans with his shirt tucked into the back of them. I notice the actual wheel isn't moving with him inside. I have roughly three seconds to back out. I bring my palm to my stomach as King glares at me, his feet on either side of the rings. I see the platform I'm supposed to sit on, floating in the middle of the ring, as if it's attached to nothing.

"Get on, Little Bird," Killian yells from behind me. "Ride on the fucking merry-go-round." He's delusional—this is no merry-go-round. That is exactly what the name says. The Triple Wheel of Death.

I'm stuck momentarily battling with myself on whether or not I want to get into it with him. King revs his engine loudly, and I find myself walking toward the wheel beyond my better judgment.

Before I place my foot onto the metal, I hear Keaton holler, "Good girl!"

Instantly, I turn to face Killian, who I know is watching me on the opposite side, sitting on his bike. He nods his head, as if I should trust Kingston, though I don't want to. I don't want to trust him, and I don't trust him, but I step inside anyway. The scent of gasoline hovers around me with the underlying scent of his cologne. King's hands come to my waist, as he lifts me onto the metal platform, that I now see is attached to two metal poles that dangle down each side of the wheel, which are also attached to the small platform. *It's a goddamn swing!* Only one that doesn't move.

As soon as I'm on the platform, I take a seat, my eyes dropping to his hands. He curls his finger, urging me to come closer, so I do, wanting his approval, needing his embrace. I couldn't tell you why, and just as quickly as those feelings rose, they disappeared before I could analyze them.

The ring starts swinging back and forth as his fingers lock against mine. He pulls me in closer, hauling me into his body as

I swing back and forth slightly. "I won't ask this anytime outside of our scenes, but I need you to trust me."

I pause, not wanting to give him anything. Trust is earned; it's not given just because someone has a pretty smile. Pretty smiles are the way trust is broken. Pretty smiles are the pavements that crack.

"Trust you?" I shout into his face because "Closer" by Kings of Leon is playing loudly in the background, and his bike is pulsing just as loudly. I've come to realize that the music is played to distract the audience from hearing us talk. "How can I trust you, King, when I barely know you?"

He seems to ponder over my words as we rock back and forth, the wheels moving faster, harder, and higher. He rocks his bike up and down at the same rhythm as we begin to swing higher and higher. *Great.* Each wheel hangs to each point. Keaton is flipping around outside of the wheels, doing all sorts of tricks to make the audience crazy. He tears his shirt off and begins tying it around his eyes. *Crazy. Mother. Fucker.*

"Because you don't need to know someone to trust them."

"Oh, really?" I counter.

He nods. "You just have to take my fucking hand and know that I won't hurt you right now."

I laugh sarcastically. "Ah. Right now. See, that's the thing I have a problem with."

The song powers up as Delila introduces the next scene. I almost feel like I should have had a shot of something. Anything to get me through this. "Are you going to keep talking shit about trust, or are you going to leave your tight little ass on that swing while I ride circles around you?"

This is probably the longest we've ever spoken together, and it's not something to be proud of.

I move to the middle. The space is large. Bigger than what it looks like from the outside. Big enough for him to—I look above my head and gulp—ride above my head.

"Good girl," he murmurs.

I want to say that I'm scared. Because, of course, I am. I don't know these boys, and I don't know King. But all of a sudden, I'm to trust him? Trust that he knows what he's doing on that bike, enough not to kill me? He pulls a T-shirt out of his jeans pocket and throws it at my face.

I take it, guessing he wants me to put it on. I want to give it back to him since he's the one who isn't wearing it, but I find myself shoving my arms through the sleeves and slipping it over my head.

The music cranks up, and the swing goes higher and higher. If I were religious, this would be the part where I start praying. Closing my eyes doesn't help; it makes me feel off-balance, so I open them, finding a spot in front of me. It's a black shadow that looks like an ace of spades engraved into the metal side of the ring. I keep my eyes locked on that spot. His bike zaps over me, zooming around and around in circles. Eventually, after I have no idea how many minutes, the swing slowly calms down and comes to a stop. I think we're back on the ground, until I look down and see we're actually high up and the next wheel is on the ground. Kyrin revs his engine, driving it up into the wheel. I notice his doesn't have a swing attached to it. *Interesting.*

I look to Kingston quickly, panic in my eyes. He does nothing but stare, his bike rumbling beneath him. Moments pass between us when Kyrin's engine breaks our contact.

The swing starts again, and my eyes go back to the ace. King rocks his bike back and forth as the swing gains momentum. It begins again, going around in circles as the loud bikes drown out my thoughts, then we stop again. I look down to see the third wheel there, and Killian riding his bike in it. The audience is losing their mind by this point, and when Delila brings out Maya, everyone silences. My heart is thrashing in my chest from adrenaline. I can feel myself latch to the feeling, bubbling beneath my skin, like a concoction of poison. Thank fuck the wheels themselves don't move.

Maya steps into Killian's wheel as she shifts her long legs over the swing and hikes herself up.

She looks up at me when she's seated and winks, blowing me a kiss.

"Jesus," I whisper, even though no one else can hear me. Killian starts rocking his bike again, and once again, my eyes find the spade to focus on. The swing picks up momentum, faster this time. I ball my fists, my toes curling. Sweat slips down my temple as the swing continues higher until we're eventually going in full circles. I can see Keaton from the corner of my eye, dancing and throwing himself around the planks and cages. He's ripped off his shirt now, tossing it away. He jumps onto our wheel, and I briefly look up at him. His fingers are clenched around the bars of the bike, his clown face makeup smirking back down at me, and then he's jumping somewhere else and my eyes find the ace again. The crowd is roaring with praise, so loud that I can hear them over the bikes and the heavy metal music. Slowly, and many minutes later, the ring reduces finally, and I break my focus from the ace of spades. I don't even realize that we're back on the ground until King grabs my hand and pulls me to the back of his bike. I swing my leg over and squeeze him with my thighs as he drives us out of the wheel and down the ramp. He stops in the middle and revs his engine again, swinging us around and around in circles until the dust from the ground has kicked up all around us and no one can see in.

His hand finds my outer thigh, and I pause at the connection. He goes higher and higher until his hand has slipped under my leather shorts.

I suck in a sharp breath, one I'm sure he caught, because he squeezes my thigh and then releases me, going back to his handlebar and driving us out toward the back of the tent. The cool air whips across my face as I climb off his bike. He switches it off just as Killian and Keaton come up behind us, kicking down their stands and switching off their bikes.

"Where's Maya?" I ask Killian, searching behind him.

Killian chuckles. "She doesn't ride, bitch, and that's not from a lack of me trying."

"There's a thirty-minute intermission before we open again," Keaton says, staring at me.

"Okay?"

"And you need to know that the next act is going to be like what Killian did." Keaton and I haven't spoken many words to each other since meeting. He is about as unapproachable as King, only he's dripping with tattoos and almost always has a scowl etched onto his face.

I look straight to Killian, who's smirking at me.

"What are you going to make me do?"

His grin deepens. "Whatever I want."

"Killian."

He chuckles, pushing off his bike and lighting his smoke. "This is Midnight Mayhem, sweetheart. You can fight it, but it'll only make the show better."

My eyes fly to King, who is watching me carefully with a blank expression. "I don't understand why I'm here. You stole me, I get that, and you steal people in general—I'm guessing, which I don't understand, but it clears up the how I got here part, but—"

King steps into my space, his hand coming to my throat. He squeezes hard enough for me to wheeze out a cough. "Stop digging and asking yourself questions, because you won't like the answers. You think that you being in that cell was a coincidence?" His head tilts. He studies me carefully. From my lips to my eyes to my neck. "You're wrong." He leans down to my ear. "And I think you know that."

I pull away, or rather he lets me go. Stepping backward, my hand comes to my throat, massaging where his hand was just a second ago.

Kyrin comes around the corner, his eyes swinging around the group. "What'd I miss?"

We all make our way back into the tent when Delila pulls me behind a curtain and shoves a new outfit in my hands. "Change."

I take them from her, yanking off my clothes and King's shirt. "What is he going to make me do?"

I peek my head out of the hole and catch Delila watching me. "Anything he wants. Killian is a show all on his own, but he's also fascinated by you."

"Why me?"

Delila smirks, tossing me her lipstick. I pull it open and swipe the bright red balm over my lips. "I'm sure you'll find out soon enough, but for now, just go with it."

"What's after Killian's show?"

"The girls have theirs. The acrobats, the aerials, and the hoops with the bikes, and then Kyrin plays fire. The next time you'll be up is the closing act."

"Closing act?" I ask, eyebrow raised as I watch her in the mirror.

She smiles, but it's not a nice smile. It's a smile that you give someone when you know something they don't. Which she does. "Yes." She looks over her shoulder and grins, just before she disappears. "Did I mention that this show is rated R?"

Fuck.

Twelve

King
Past

ad locked his door when he got home from work later that night, a cigar hanging from between his teeth. He was agitated more than usual. My father was a sinner, and he did it well, but something was annoying him even more. Enough for me to pick it up as he stumbled through the house. He never stumbled. Ever the calm and collected muse for any mobster, his steps were always calculated and were never taken without him knowing the next twenty he was going to take after that. For all of my sixteen years, I had known that this day was coming. I sensed it in the water like a shark would blood, because that's how I was trained. With my senses and not so much my words.

I padded through the hallway of our mansion, passing the perfectly *painted family portraits of us. They always said that one kid was enough for them and that they never needed three... Whatever the fuck that meant. My hand came to the golden handle of his office, and I pressed it down, shoving the door open. It was dark, as dark as his mahogany office desk that sat perfectly in the middle. Bookcases filled the walls, from the floor to the ceiling, and the only form of light that was pouring in came from the full moon, beaconing through the floor-to-ceiling window that overlooked the front of our plantation-style home.*

"Dad..."

"Sit." *His voice was low, sounding as though he had swallowed a handful of gravel before saying it. Unlike me, Father was good with his words. He had to be.*

I took a few more steps in until I was dropping down onto the chair that was tucked underneath his desk.

"Este timpul, son." *It's time, son.*

I shook my head. "I'm not ready."

His head, that was bowed between his shoulder blades, raised, his eyes connecting with mine. "You're ready, son. The only reason why you think you're not is because I'm here."

I scratched over my heart, where my Sons of Kiznitch tattoo was stamped. His eyes followed the movement, a smirk touching the corners of his mouth. My father spoke fluent English, but Romanian was his first language, because it's the land of our family. We moved between Greek and Latin, but Latin was the language we mostly used, with it being the original language of our country. Of us. "You need to rise. You need to gather your brothers and begin your journey."

"I'm sixteen," *I blurted out through my amateur mouth. Of all the things I could've thought of, 'I'm sixteen' was the first thing that came spewing out. Like it mattered. Like the fact I was sixteen had stopped me from committing the most heinous crimes. Like the fact just a few months ago, I killed for the first time. Or the fact when I was but a child, I* became so obsessed with someone who would later become a pawn on my chessboard. That I would eventually do anything to be near her—even if that meant breaking her in the process, because breaking her only meant that I was close enough to her to do it.

Dad sank back in his chair, opening a drawer and slapping down a manila folder. "Delila needs you. All of you. Whether you think you're ready or not, King, it's time for you to do what you've been training your whole life to do. We've done our rounds. It's time for you to start yours."

"But you, Uncle Kratos, and—"

"They all agree." He brought his eyes to mine, pinning me with his stare. "It is time, Kingston. You need to reign. You need to fulfill all that I have left for you to do."

I paused, thinking over his words. I knew who he was talking about before he even had to say her name. Her. The girl who had a broken smile and bright eyes. The one I hadn't spoken to, but I knew exactly the way her tongue would move around each alphabetical syllable. I'd never touched her teenage skin, but I knew how she would feel beneath the palm of my hand. I was engineered to hate her, but my humanity wanted her. I couldn't fucking want her. My cock swelled in my pants, and I coughed, shuffling in my seat.

A moment passed between us before I opened my mouth. "Are you sure you can trust me with that?" My father, Kauis, the great terror of them all, stared me right in the eye. A man who was intimidating to most but had been nothing but a comfort to me. The edges of his eyes crinkled as he smiled. "Yes, son. I trust that you are well-equipped with enough power and sense to take it now."

I slouched in my seat, bringing my hands to my mouth. "She reminds me of her."

Dad chuckled. It's the type of chuckle that put the fear of God into every single person who had met the receiving end of his blade. "A bit weak, don't you think?" His eyes darkened. "Push her harder."

Thirteen

Dove

I learned that between Midnights scenes, there are also others who have small acts. I don't learn too much about theirs, mainly because it goes for so long. Every show is for three hours, with a forty-minute intermission for people to go to the bar, grab a snack, and get entertained by everyone walking around. I caught Killian chatting to the same three dudes as before, only they had a girl with pink hair with them now. I dashed away from them all before they saw me, afraid that King would think I was stalking his friends now. After watching some of the show from backstage, I dip back into the cubicle. The next scene is Killian's before the final, and I'd be lying if I said I wasn't worried. I am. Very. I know what Killian is capable of and I know I can't trust them.

I swipe my sweaty palms down the side of my thighs when Delila interrupts me, swiping the curtain to the side. "Killian is going to introduce what will be your act. We've had a change. Though he can persuade you to do whatever he wants, they all can, what he wants is going to be your act."

"Wait!" I whisper-yell. "What do you mean?" I'm confused. Yet again. I have to wonder whether they do this with all of their new acts, though I'm pretty sure Rose knew at least a little bit of what was going on during hers, since she had to actually perform.

Delila exhales, massaging her temples. "Pay attention, Little Bird. You need your own act, but Killian is going to introduce you. That's all you need to know."

If that was all I needed to know, then why am I asking more questions?

The curtain spreads open, and Delila is suddenly on the other side of the tent, walking down the stairs with the mic in her hand. "Our next act is by one of our very favorite Brothers."

She lands on the bottom step and makes her way toward us. By this point, the crowd is so drunk that everyone is losing their shit by the sound of it. Thanks to the open bar they provide each person. "Sic 'em, boy."

Killian smirks, his clown grin teasing me. He brings his mic up to his lips. "Come here."

Again, my legs move without me entrusting them to do so. I don't know what it is that Killian does, and I'm not sure I really want to know, but I'm intrigued. Intrigued because I've never felt so completely out of control before.

I'm face-to-face with him, the audience quiet while the spotlight beams on both of us. He licks his soft lips before I feel his arm wrap around my back, pulling me into his body.

He moves the mic away from his mouth and whispers into my ear, "Do you trust me?"

"No," I answer instantly.

He comes back to standing, his grin deepening. "Good. You shouldn't." The mic is back at his mouth. "Play 'Two Weeks' by FKA Twigs." I want to break eye contact to find the sound booth that I know he's talking with on top of the audience. But he grins at me, yanking me back into his body. "Dance." He releases me, pushing me onto the center stage. I curve my body around the sounds that are coming out, losing myself in the movements. My mouth curls around the lyrics, my arms flying up to entice the audience. The song ends, and when I turn around, Killian is perched on a chair, smirking. Beside him are Kingston and Kyrin. They're all wearing no shirts and a skull bandana tied around their neck. That mixed with the sick clown makeup is too much.

The crowd laughs as Killian stands from his chair and circles me like a shark. I suddenly feel exposed, raw, here for everyone's entertainment. Is Killian the equivalent to a crazy clown? If the clown was ridiculously hot, of course. He would fit the suit, though. The jokester, the funny one.

He continues to circle me, and when the mic comes to his mouth, I know I'm in trouble. "Who wants to see just what this little bird can do?" The crowd erupts, but before I can see, Killian's next words throw me off. "I know King does." I fight against my impulse to check to see what King is doing. Killian tilts his head. "Play Marilyn Manson." Oh no. Killian smirks. "'Third Day of a Seven Day Binge'" He drops the mic, and I feel his arm wrap around me again as he pulls me into his chest, his lips brushing against my ears. "I don't even have to pretend to the audience that you're doing as I tell you, do I?" My brain is a haze as he shoves me onto Kingston's lap.

Kingston's hand sprawls out over my lower stomach, his lips now touching my neck. "Strip, Little Bird. Show us what you've got," King whispers, just as he shoves me back to my feet. "Dance like you fuck. *Like exactly how you taste.*" Does King have this power, too?

My hands go up above my head, my eyelids heavy. I roll my body against Killian, dropping to my knees in front of him. He glares down at me, his hand coming to the back of my hair where he wraps it in his fist. Just as he yanks my neck back, King's hand comes to my throat from behind, and he's pulling me backward until my head is in his lap, and I'm looking up at him from a bent, and very fucking uncomfortable position. "Don't push me, Little Bird."

His words spark a fire inside of me. Something I didn't know I had, or maybe something that someone has never had the power to ignite before.

I stand back to my feet, just as "Coming Undone" by Korn mixes in. I slowly unzip the front of my crop top, flinging it at King as I turn back to face him. The chorus starts, and I drop down, with Killian behind me, flinging my hair and twisting my body around, grinding my ass into Kingston's lap. I feel him against my ass, and it only intensifies the power I think I have. Killian grabs my hand and shoves me into his chest, turning me around to face the audience—not that I can notice anything right now—as he bends me over, his hands on my hips. Just as I'm about to continue dancing, Killian's gone and Kingston is in front of me with Kyrin right beside him. Before I can understand what's going on, "Toxicity" by System of a Down has started playing and a cage is being dropped around us. This one is square. Locked. Nowhere to run. What the fuck do they do for the final act?

"This show is rated R ..."

I look around at all three of them, wondering where the fuck Keaton is. Of course, only I would wonder where Keaton is, not why the hell I'm being locked in a cage with three possible undiagnosed psychopaths.

Killian brings the mic to his mouth. "Now, I don't know if you know this, but Little Bird is new. This is the first time she'll be participating in the final act. If you've been to one of our shows before, you know what is about to happen." He pauses, and it's right then that I realize I'm probably going to get fucked by all of them—bar Keaton.

Right now.

In this cage.

In front of an audience. I don't know why I assume that right away. Maybe it's the setting, or maybe it's because I'm locked in a damn cage with all of them. And they look hungry. *Starving.*

The crowd is roaring with praise. Oh good. They totally support this.

I try not to look panicked. I don't want to give them any more power than they already have, and something tells me that if they knew they had my fear, they'd only use it as a snack.

I don't want to look anywhere, so I straighten my shoulders, close my eyes, and take my mind back to the place where it always goes when I need to be surrounded by something dark. To remind myself why I'm so lucky to be bathing in this light. *The Shadow.*

Killian's voice comes through my ear. "Do you want this? Or are we all wrong to think you can handle it?"

I lick my lips, bringing my hand to the back of his neck. Right now, I still have the power. I can feel it. He hasn't told me what to do; he's merely asked me a question. I can do this, but only if it's on my terms. I yank his head into my space, whispering into his hair, "Play 'Breathe' by Mako, and don't fucking use your juju on me. I'll do whatever the fuck I'm supposed to do without it."

He pauses, and then leans back, bringing the mic to his mouth, repeating my song choice. It starts, and I begin slowly dancing around them, focusing on Killian. I force his face to mine. When I feel his lips close, he pushes me backward until I'm falling onto a lap. The electricity that explodes around me is a dead giveaway that it's King's lap I'm on.

I moan softly, not wanting to be here right now. Killian is easy because there's no big bang. No feelings. No... *King*.

He doesn't touch me, so I turn in his lap, straddling him. Running my fingers through my hair, I roll my body over him, reaching behind his head to untie the bandana that's covering his mouth. What's with the bandanas? His eyes drift to the crowd slightly before coming back to mine.

King is still not touching me, so I turn in his lap, ready to go to Kyrin, when he grips onto the back of my shorts and tugs me back down.

Kyrin, who has stayed in the background throughout the whole thing, hooks his finger around the belt loop of my shorts and yanks me into him. He leans down and whispers into my ear, "Is that all you've got? Gotta say, I'm pretty disappointed."

My stomach sinks. I hate disappointing people, and I'm well aware that this feeling probably stems from feeling as though I've always failed my parents.

Angry and annoyed, I turn in his grasp, reach up on my tippy toes, and bring my mouth to his. I stare right through him. "You don't know the first thing about me."

"Pretty sure we know everything about you."

"Carousel" by Melanie Martinez stars playing loudly, igniting my reckless soul.

Fine.

Another arm grips around my waist, and I turn in King's grasp. I don't know what's going on, but it's almost like there's a battle happening on the floor, and I don't know if it has anything to do with me or not.

Kingston squeezes me into his chest. I grind my ass against his crotch, dropping to the floor. When Kyrin goes to step backward, I reach for the waistband of his pants and yank him forward. Kyrin is strong, but he doesn't fight me, stepping so close that my face is directly in front of his crotch.

To the beat of the song, I wave my torso around as my fingers inch up to his zipper. I reach for it, just as King yanks my head back by my long hair. I'm staring up at him upside down when his jaw clenches.

"What?" I smirk. "I thought this was Midnight Mayhem?" I'm bluffing. I had no idea prior to tonight what the fuck this group did.

King bares his teeth, hissing, before shoving my face away from him and into Kyrin's crotch.

Asshole.

I yank Kyrin's pants down and his cock springs free. I don't have any want or need, just anger. I grip his long, thick shaft in my hand and tug on it lightly. I lick my lips, and Kyrin steps backward, his face coming to mine. "You really want to suck my dick, Little Bird?"

I smile up at him sweetly. "Yes." I have no idea.

He shoves his thumb into my mouth, pressing it down onto my tongue. "My cock is worth dying over?"

I shrug. "Don't care." The song changes, but I'm lost. I turn my head around to see Maya walking in with no shirt on and holding a plate of what looks like weed. She's wearing no bra—her tits out—and has on tiny basketball shorts. A red bandana is tied around the front of her head, her long straight hair falling down to her butt.

She winks at me again and then blazes a joint, sucking on it. I watch as she lowers herself to Val, who is waiting. Maya blows a cloud of smoke into Val's mouth, and then slowly licks her from her chin to the tip of her nose.

Jesus fuck!

I shake off my nerves and stand, gaining false confidence from Maya and Val and whoever else is in here now. I get it. This crew is fucked up. I have to learn how to swim, or I'm going to drown.

The cage slowly lifts, and Maya slips down behind me, her hand going to King. I squash the jealousy that roars in my chest as best I can, but when he touches the back of her thigh, the jealousy knocks the breath out of me. I feel as though I'm choking on air.

Maya turns over her shoulder, her lips touching my ear. "Go with it, Dove. Would you rather me or Val?"

She has a good point.

King grabs her by the hair and yanks her to her feet, just as Kyrin spins me around by my hips, his fingers digging into my bones.

King's eyes are on mine, his makeup taunting me, and his smirk testing the restraint of my anger. I don't know why. It's not like we're anywhere near being able to call dibs on each other. My jealousy is arbitrary. Unwarranted.

He yanks the zipper of his pants down and I watch as his palm grips the length of his cock. He pulls on it softly.

"Girl," Maya whispers from behind me. "This isn't my first rodeo, so I apologize now." Then her attention is on his cock, and I have to stop my chest from exploding and killing everyone in this fucking room.

I flash a smile at King that says *I take your dirty blowjob and raise you a fucking pounding.* I grip onto Kyrin from behind me, my fingers latching around the back of his neck. I drop to my hands and knees, leaning over my shoulder and smirking at him. "Fuck me."

Kyrin's eyes flash with fire, just as Killian steps up beside him, his head tilting.

"Dawg, if you don't, I will." Kill whistles, shaking his head.

Kyrin's eyes fly over me, and I don't have to guess to know where he's looking. I turn around and face him, yanking his pants down instead. Okay, so he won't fuck me for whatever reason, but I'll still play, and if he doesn't participate, I'll go to Killian or Keaton. I grab his dick, and before he can say anything, I wrap my lips around his tip and. Fucking. Suck.

Drawing him in deeper until I feel his pre-cum latch to the back of my throat, I twirl my tongue around him.

The crowd is quiet as I suck, every single person in that audience disappearing. Kyrin pulls out of my mouth and smirks, gripping my chin and yanking me up to standing. I know he almost came twice because his cock was pulsing in my mouth.

"You play dirty, Little Bird, but can you keep it up?" His eyebrow cocks before he disappears and grabs onto Mischa, yanking her onto his exposed dick. She moans, rolling her head and sliding herself down over him.

Oh my God. Is this even legal?

Maya leaves King, and I'm left gasping, the song switching to "Nightmare" by Halsey.

Everything fades as King stares at me through his makeup.

"Little Bird, do me a favor," Killian whispers into my ear.

117

My attention doesn't move from King. "See if he'll kiss you." He hands me a shot glass filled with white liquid, and I take it, throwing it back.

I take one step, and King's eyes narrow.

Another step closer, and I can almost feel him around me, suffocating me without contact.

Quickly, I throw my hand around the back of his neck and pull his face to mine. My lips graze over his. "Why am I the only one not naked?" I lick his lips softly.

Just when I think he's not going to take the bait, he leans forward and bites down on my bottom lip. "Because you're not for them."

What the fuck does that mean?

I grind into him, reaching down. I grip onto his cock and tug on it. Either he can get hard really fucking fast or Maya didn't finish him off.

He hisses, biting my earlobe between his teeth and yanking on it. His fingers dig into my thighs as he lifts me off the ground. My legs wrap around his waist. "Who am I for?" I can't believe I said that out loud.

"Not for them, but most importantly." He sucks on my neck as his fingers slip beneath my panties. He slips between my folds, and I tremble in his grasp, my pussy clenching around him like a vise. I don't care what's going on out there, even though I know what is. I just hope everyone is too busy watching someone else to catch King and me.

He circles me while his thumb presses against my clit. "Not for me either." His finger continues bashing inside of me, his thumb on my clit. My stomach clenches as familiar waves crash over me, my release gushing over his hand.

"Remember that next time you want to try to make me

jealous." He shoves me away, bringing his fingers to his mouth and sucking me off.

Everything disappears into the background again, like it always does when he's around me. I panic, my heart thundering in my chest. Have I failed? Made things worse? I can't believe I fell into Killian's trap. After what feels like hours, the curtains slowly close with the audience going crazy, and I quickly zap out of the tent, my heart speeding in my chest at whatever the hell that show was. I know why they call them Mayhem now, and they fit it to a damn T. Just as I'm running back to the RV, I slam into a hard chest, bumping me backward until I fall straight on my ass.

"Ouch," I groan, massaging my temples. I think I would rather they kill me than put me through all of this. This is a special kind of torture. One I will never survive.

"Jesus, Aeron!" A girl's voice breaks through my haze before hands are reaching underneath my arms. "Are you okay?"

I'm on my feet when my brain registers what—or rather who—is in front of me right now. Aeron Romanov Reed—as in the famous rapper and mafia prince, Manik. I almost want to yell his name because that's pretty much how everyone else says it.

"Yes," I mutter, looking at the girl who helped me up. She's beautiful. I think I know who she is, though. I'd seen her on TV whenever Rich would have E! playing in the bar—which was never, but that's saying how often she's in the media.

"You were amazing up there," she says, and then wipes her hand on her jeans, bringing it out to me. "I'm Beatrice, but you can call me Beat, and this is my husband Aeron." First impression of her is that I like her instantly for the mere fact that she hasn't introduced her husband as "this is my famous husband, Manik." It's an instant turn-on for a lady friendship if the other woman isn't constantly stroking her own ego.

"Thanks." I can't help but stare at her. He's handsome, but everyone already knows that. Beat is something else. Long raven black hair and olive skin, she's everything every model wishes she was made from.

"Are you doing anything right now? My grumpy husband is on his way home because, well..." She grins at Manik, who rolls his eyes at her. "He's grumpy, but I'd love to have a chat with you? Are you free?"

I open my mouth to answer. To say no and that I'm tired, when Delila's voice interrupts me. "Beatrice, how lovely for you both to show up."

Beat's smile instantly falls as she spins around to greet Delila. "Delila."

"I hope you're talking to my favorite lead girl to see if you can dance for us again and not because you're trying to poach her."

Instantly, that makes me smile. Delila and Beat don't get along? Maybe I will take her up on her offer.

"Actually," I interrupt Delila before Beat can say anything. "Neither. We were just about to go for a drink. You know, to celebrate my first successful act." I try to keep the sarcasm out of my tone but fail miserably when I notice the twitch in Delila's eye.

"Great!" Beat claps her hands. "We'll meet you at the limo when you're ready. We're parked on the curb."

I nod, offering her a small smile, as she and her entourage disappear into the darkness.

It's not until Delila clears her throat that I realize she's still standing there. "Be careful, Little Bird. Not all that glitters is gold."

I roll my eyes, heading back to the RV and quickly

changing out of my scandalous clothes. I ignore my phone vibrating in my hand and I quickly grab my fur coat and dash back out the door, before any of The Brothers come back. I don't want to see any of them right now, and to be honest, I feel like a drink.

fourteen

King

The music hums around me, as my thoughts remain fixed on a certain red-haired girl who won't stay the fuck out of my mind. *You can't have her.* No matter how many times I replay that same sentence over in my head, it seems the dots just won't connect in my brain. I know why I'm drawn to her, and I made peace with that a long time ago. It's part of the deal. Some sick game I like to play with myself, like a damn masochist.

Most of the Midnight Mayhem crew is buzzed as fuck from all of the alcohol being passed around. It's the after party, but we have one after each damn show. It gets old pretty fast when you've been on the road since you were fifteen fucking years old.

My phone pulses in my pocket, and I reach in, thinking over whether or not I want to answer it. My mom calling at this time of the night should be worrying—had my mom been a normal mom, which she's not. I hit ignore just as Val drops her bony ass into my lap.

"Awww, where's your cute little toy gone?" Her hand runs over my cheek, the scent of expensive champagne tainting her plump lips.

I whack her hand away. "You of all people should know how my toys are treated."

Her eyes darken as she brings the bottle of Moët to her mouth. "Don't I ever."

I glare at her. "I'm not interested."

She wiggles in my lap. I clench my jaw and spread my knees out, so she drops between them, landing on the dirt ground. A few people around us stop to look, but not for long, when she snaps at all of them to mind their own fucking business.

Her eyes cut back to mine. "Jeez, King. When did you get extra moody?"

Keaton kicks my chair. "About the time someone decided to sleep in our RV."

Val stands, dusting off her pants and picking up whatever self-respect I've left her with. "You're such an asshole."

I look over her shoulder, dismissing her, just as Keaton takes the seat beside me, chuckling. "Any idea where the little bird has flown off to?"

I take a sip of my whiskey, allowing the liquid to burn in my mouth before swallowing. "She's gone with Beat."

"Beat as in Manik? She's hanging around again?"

I shake my head, reaching for the pack of smokes on the ground and banging the end onto my thigh. "Naw. They just come to the New York shows when we're here. Seems this time, Beatrice has found a liking to Dove."

Keaton doesn't answer, so I look over at him just as I blow out a cloud of smoke.

He smirks.

"Don't fucking say it, Keats. Unless you want me to rear-range that pretty little face, I wouldn't fucking say it."

Keaton chuckles, resting his head back against the back of his chair. "I wouldn't, but I would get a handle on that before it gets out of control. You're losing focus."

"The fuck I am," I snap, flicking the ash off my smoke. "She's not the fucking one."

Kyrin must have sunk into the chair on the other side of me because his voice cracks through next. "They come in twos."

fifteen

Dove

Beat orders two vodkas and then rests her eyes on me. Her two bodyguards are probably outside waiting for us, but Aeron went home. "Where did you learn to dance like that?" she asks, stirring the olives around in her martini.

"Ah," I lean back in my chair, "my mom ruled her expectations with a heavy foot, and that foot usually had a ballerina slipper attached to it, so…"

Beat laughs, flicking some peanuts into her mouth. "I get it. I mean, I don't really get it. I—my mom and—"

"Oh!" I shake my head, thankful for the drink when it finally arrives. I take a sip before answering. "No, I mean, it was great, but they died when I was young."

"Oh." Beat softens her tone, her shoulders sagging. "I'm sorry to hear that."

I wave her off, not because I'm unaffected by their death anymore, but because after all these years of having to explain or say the same thing, almost like a rehearsed script, it's easier now. "It was a long time ago." Lie, you're still affected by it. Shutting out bad memories doesn't help you cope. It's the easy lie that we blanket ourselves with for a false sense of security.

"So how has Delila been?" Beat changes the subject.

I shrug. "A total bitch at the best of times." The alcohol is warming my blood and fueling my confidence to speak.

"So, still the same then." Beat rolls her eyes.

"You used to be in Midnight Mayhem?" I ask.

Her shoulders sag. "Yes. A long time ago, but essentially, yes. For a couple shows anyway."

"How'd you find it?" I'm intrigued by her on a level that I'm not sure I can quite grasp yet. Fascinated. I want to know her in a way.

"Well." She exhales. "I was running away from my husband because he kidnapped me. Then there was this whole 'he might kill me thing' and I didn't feel like dying."

I laugh, throwing my head back. I laugh so hard my belly tightens. When I finally come down from my fit of giggles, she's watching me with surprise. "You're not freaked out by what I just said?"

I swipe at my eyes. "No. I mean, if you knew how I came about my current position."

Beat searches my eyes. "Oh, I think I have an idea. Maybe. Though I'm not sure."

I shake my head, sighing. I feel relaxed for the first time in a long time. Being around so much testosterone has taken its toll on me. "I swear you could write a really creepy book about my life."

Beat snorts, leaning into her bag that's near her ankles and dropping a book onto the table. She points. "Join the club." My eyes fall on the cover, the bright green title catching my eyes first. The title is simple. *MANIK*. The cover image is of Aeron's chest, but where his face is supposed to be, there are ravens flying out.

"Wow! You have a book?"

She waves me off. "I didn't write it, but yes. It's the story of how Aeron and I met. I'm all for creepy stories. I wouldn't recommend this author, though. She drinks too much, procrastinates a lot, and is easily distracted."

I laugh, running my hand over the book while sliding it back to her. "So why did you want to have a drink with me tonight? Or this morning?"

Her focus drifts. "Well, I was really just hoping to pick your brain on how you dance. I run Aeron's backup dancers now, and they're driving me crazy. That's saying a lot, because my crazy threshold is high due to who I'm married to."

"Ask away!" I gesture with my hands as she peppers me with questions about my technique. I tell her that I not only have been dancing since I was able to walk, but I had lessons growing up, too, which she understood. Once we're finished going back and forth, an hour has passed easily, and empty glasses are sitting in front of us.

"Wow." She leans back in her chair. "I wish I could poach you."

I'm barely keeping my eyes open. "I wish, too. Oh, how I do."

"Where are you based?" she asks. "Your home base. Do you have one yet?"

"I don't have one yet, but I think Delila likes us all to stay very close."

"Yes, she does, so you'll be close to the mansion. I wouldn't be surprised if she was sorting your own house to be built on the property." Beat pauses, emptying the rest of her drink into her mouth. "Tell me. Do you want to do this?"

I think over her question, wanting to give her an honest answer. "I want to stay alive."

After a couple more drinks, we swap numbers, and Beat drops me back at the grounds, also called a "compound," when Midnight Mayhem are on the road. My head is dizzy, and my thoughts are wavering. The vodka has long since left its claws inside me. I swing open the RV door, stumbling to the back of it toward my room. After wrangling my clothes off, I pull my phone up and grab my earbuds, hitting play on my playlist in hopes that music will make my head stop spinning. "Far Away" by Nickelback starts playing. I softly sing the words, tying my hair into a high ponytail and slipping beneath the sheets. I need to go out and grab some more supplies and do some laundry if I don't want to start wearing the same clothes. I'm singing the chorus when my curtain is pulled open, and Keaton is watching me carefully, a drink hanging between his fingers. He pulls out his phone, so I remove my earbuds.

"What?" I don't mean to be snappy to Keaton. It's not like he's been exactly rude to me, if you don't count acting like I don't exist as rude.

He presses play on the song again, pointing to me with his drink. "Sing it again." When I don't budge and the opening starts, he rolls his eyes and starts singing it lazily. Even lazy, he's nailing it. I had no idea Keaton could sing at all. He doesn't look like a singer, even if that does sound like a shit judgment for me to make. When the chorus comes in, I power it out, and our voices merge together in perfect harmony. As the guitar plays, he drops down onto my bed, dropping his drink on the floor in the process. He continues the song, and I come in again on the chorus, hitting the high notes with him merging through the rough notes.

He tilts his head, watching me with a new fascination. "Who taught you how to sing like that, Little Bird?"

"I was born with it, and then my mom had me take singing lessons every day after my ballet classes."

"She sounds like a bitch," he bites out, stumbling up from my bed and reaching for his bottle.

I lean over, snatching it out of his reach. "She wasn't. She was just...driven, and I think you've had enough."

Lying backward on my bed, he lets the bottle slip to my fingers. I catch it just in time. My head spins, but I curl my lip beneath my teeth to stop my laugh.

"What's funny, Little Bird?" he murmurs, shading his eyes with his forearm. He kicks off his shoes and removes his shirt, before climbing up my bed and dropping down into a comfortable position.

"Yeah, you're not staying in here, Keaton," I say, shaking his arm. But it's too late. It's like shaking a corpse. He won't move.

I sigh, climbing off my bed. I make my way into the kitchen when I pause in my steps at Kingston perched on one of the chairs, a drink just short of his lips. I ignore him, moving further into the kitchen. I pull open the fridge, pausing when I see it's fully stocked again, reaching for a bottle of water.

"What'd you think of the show, Little B?" Kingston's voice is cold, bitter. It leaves his mouth sharp and swallows down mine like a bitter shot of tequila. My hand comes to my mouth briefly at the thought of tequila.

"About as bad as I thought it'd be." I screw off the lid and take a sip.

He laughs, standing from his chair. That's when I notice he's not wearing a shirt, only loose jeans. He looks dirty, deranged, and not someone I should trust to be around me right now. He's obviously drunk.

"You haven't seen anything yet."

"Because I haven't seen all of your acts?" I ask, squeezing the bottle in my hand. I'm well aware of their stunts and what they can do physically, and Keaton can sing, and I mean the man can sing like Lewis Capaldi, and that's drunk, but I haven't seen a show from start to finish.

He pauses a few short steps away from me and tilts his head. I try to fight myself and not look too closely at what he's doing or how he's looking. I fail, though, because his hair is floppy and messy, his cheeks slightly flushed from the alcohol, and his body. *His damn body.* It's not fair. I catch the two roses that are inked over his left hip, ducking beneath his briefs. One sits just above the other. The other over the edge. It looks to have less detail, less love. The one that slightly dips underneath has clarity and precision. It has passion.

"Getting a good look?" he asks, shoving past me to put his glass in the sink. "I'm getting tired of you eye-fucking me, Little Bird. I might just see if those eyes can match the promises they're giving out." He turns to face me, and I can feel his breath over my flesh.

I close my eyes and shove away from him, needing to be away. Away from him. From the fire that threatens to burn me to a crisp.

He brushes his chest against mine, and I back up, slamming against the kitchen counter. Each hand comes to the counter, caging me in. "Just to be clear, I hate you."

"You don't know me," I snap, bringing my eyes up to his.

He searches mine and smirks. It sends chills down my spine. "I know more than you will *ever* know."

I shiver, taking my attention away from him, only his hand comes to the back of my hair, and he yanks on it, pulling my eyes to his. "I don't have to like you to want to fuck you, so just in case you get bored one night, my room is the one at the end of the hallway upstairs. Before you even think of wrapping these pretty little lips around anyone else's cock again, I'd advise against it."

"Why?" I yank my hair out of his grip.

His eyes slant in suspicion before he collects himself again and steps backward. "Because you'd go to waste on anyone else."

He turns, and I watch the stupid muscles on his back contract as he retreats upstairs.

Storming back to my room, I'm even more annoyed when I see Keaton is still on my bed, now snoring.

I exhale, dropping down beside him. I turn to face his back, studying all of the tattoos that go up the back of his neck. They're almost demonic. I've heard people say that some use tattoos as a way to express how they feel inside. If that's the case with Keaton, I wouldn't want to know who he is inside. It's a form of art, and there's no right or wrong way to art. No one can tell you what is wrong art or what is right art. If you don't see what the artist wants you to see, then that art is simply not for you—that doesn't make it wrong. It makes it wrong for you. My eyes drift closed and I'm pulled into a deep sleep.

I'd made a lot of mistakes growing up, but I've never thought of them that way. I never regretted the decisions I made because, essentially, who was to say that those decisions weren't what saved me from another.

That night with The Shadow ate away at my insides and turned me rotten at my core.

Not because I hated it or regretted it.

Not because I felt dirty or disgusting.

It turned me rotten because I found myself drawn to him even more. Like a moth to a flame, uncaring by the fact that I could die if I flew too close to the very thing that I'm attracted to. But that feeling became worn as time went on. The Shadow became more violent with his presence. He never touched me again like he did that night.

He never teased me or drew me in.

He took back the fear that he had installed in me when my parents died and threw it back in my face at supersonic speed.

Sixteen

King
Fifteen years old

"Are you on your way?" My father asked through the phone.

I brought my eyes up to Killian, Keaton, and Kryin, who were all opposite me in the back of the limo.

"Yes. How long will you be?"

There was a long stretch of silence before he answered. "Twenty minutes."

I pushed up my bandana, hanging up the phone and tossing it onto the seat beside me.

"What'd he say?" Killian asked, watching me as he pulled his up to cover his mouth.

"He'll be there in twenty minutes."

"*King,*" *Kyrin murmured, but I ignored him. I knew what he was going to say.* "*They won't initiate the kill on her. They can't.*"

I cranked my neck. "*She doesn't deserve to live.*"

"*She can't even…*" *Kill shook his head, exhausted.* "*Never mind.*" *I knew what he was going to say, though, and although he was right, it still didn't trump the fact that Dove was the reason why so much tragedy had happened.*

Present

My hand rests on my stomach as my other shades my eyes. I'm trying to fucking sleep, but all I can think about is her. And it's fucking annoying. I don't want to have anything to do with her any more than what I'm here to do. She's waning on my restraint, teasing it. I hate her with a fire so hot I want to dip her in gasoline and use it to detonate her. But I can't. I have to stick to the fucking plan, even if the plan kills me.

Seventeen

Dove

I'wake up the next morning, my limbs sore, and my head pounding. An arm tightens around me, and I freeze, the recollection of last night coming back to me at one hundred miles an hour. Picking up the thick, muscled arm, I fling it off me and curl off my bed.

I groan again, my hair falling to the front of my face. I didn't think I drank that much.

Padding my way into the kitchen, I clamber for a glass of water.

"Have a good night's sleep?"

I spin around to catch Killian walking in, sweat pouring down his bare chest. I notice that the star that King has on his chest, Killian has over his lower left hip.

He catches me staring because he clears his throat. "You're a little pervy."

I snort, turning back around to empty the water out of my glass. "Not at what you think."

He chuckles, his hand coming to my hip. I freeze at his contact, when his lips touch the side of my shoulder. "Chill," he whispers, sending goosebumps over my flesh. "I'm not King. I'm not like the rest of them."

My eyes close as I relish in his untrustworthy words, before shaking him off and spinning around in his grasp. "It doesn't matter, Killian. You're all bad."

He seems to think over my words, because his eyes search mine. I take a moment to admire his bright blue eyes and tanned skin, and the way his dark hair flops over his forehead slightly.

"Yeah, so what if we are?"

I pause. "That's your answer? You're not even going to pretend that you're not bad guys?"

Killian smirks, and for a second, I want to step backward, but I can't. The damn kitchen counter is, once again, pressing against my ass. "If that's what you want, Little Bird, to have us reassure you that we're not bad people, then you're tripping."

"Oh really?"

His eyes narrow, his mouth opening. Just when he's about to say something, I notice another shadow behind him. I feel him before I see him, and as cliché as that may sound to most people, it's the only way I can describe the attraction I have to Kingston right now. Or the only way I want to describe him right now.

King steps into the space that Killian left. His eyes drop to my mouth. "We're not good people, Dovey." His eyes come to mine, the dark green depths enticing me to test him. Just push him a little further. His eyes narrow. "But I think you know that."

I swallow, just as his hand comes to my chin, tipping my face up to him. "Have a good sleep?"

"Yes."

"Did Keaton fuck you good?"

"What?" I yank my face out of his grip. "No."

Just when I think he's serious, his lip curls. But it's not a smirk. It's more of a satanic smile. One I don't really want to test today.

I step around him, only for his hand to come to my arm. "We're on the road today. The next show, you'll be rehearsing."

"Okay," I answer, wanting his hand to release me, but not wanting him to release me. Oh, what a mindfuck.

He cages me back into the corner, both hands resting on either side of my body. "And you won't go off on your own again."

I shove him away, dipping out of the kitchen and making my way back to the end room. Keaton is bent over the bed, his elbows resting on his knees and his face in his hands.

"Hurt that bad, huh?" I tease, feeling strangely comfortable in his presence.

His hands move out of the way, his head tilting to the side. "Something like that."

Annoyed with the ever-growing cryptic messages I get thrown at me by everyone except Kyrin, I pull open my closet door and take out some comfortable clothes that I can wear today, since we're back on the road.

"Dove." Keaton's voice is so low I almost miss it.

"Yeah?" I answer, slamming the closet door closed.

His eyes come to mine, and for a brief second, I think I see something pass between us. Feel something pass between us. "Do as he says." He stammers off my bed and disappears through the curtain, leaving me standing there speechless. Again.

I move through the RV and into the small bathroom as soon as I know none of them are out there and scrub up in record time. I'm tying my hair into a top knot and slipping my spandex shorts on when there's a knock on the door.

"Dove, it's me!" Rose's voice soothes me instantly, and I yank the door open, my arms flying around her neck.

"I feel like I haven't seen you in forever!" I exhale. I snatch my toothbrush and squeeze some paste on. "How was last night?"

Rose is dressed in loose sweatpants and a hoodie, her hair casual. She rolls her eyes and kicks the toilet cover down, taking a seat. "I drank way too much. I think everyone did, though. Everyone but Maya, of course."

Rose massages her temples. "What is going on between her and Killian? They're driving everyone insane."

I pause my brushing, then spit and rinse and repeat. "I don't know. I sensed something, too."

Rose opens her mouth, but then closes it, when her eyes go over my shoulder. Her eyes turn distant, and her body tenses.

"What's wrong?" I murmur around my toothbrush.

King walks in, snatches my toothbrush from my mouth, and pops it into his own. He licks the edge of his lip as his eyes drop to mine. "Get your friend out of my fucking space."

"King!" I instantly snap. I don't really answer back, mainly because I know what he and they are capable of, and I happen to enjoy being alive, even if my life isn't in stellar form right now.

His eyebrows raise in challenge, his white teeth clenching down on the shaft of my toothbrush. "Wanna fight me on that, because I can do with some cardio this morning."

Rose's hand comes to my arm. She smiles weakly at me. "It's okay. We're all heading off soon anyway. I just wanted to see you."

I can hear King brushing his teeth—with my toothbrush.

I let out a breath of air. "I'll see you at the next stop, which is…"

"Texas," Rose answers.

"Texas. Right." How and why do I not know this? Why do I feel that even though Rose and I were both "captured" at the same time, I'm not being shown the same courtesy she has been shown by Midnight?

Rose leaves after another hug and after I promise her that I'll have a drink with her after our next show—or before.

My eyes find King's in the mirror, only he's already watching me. He gargles the water in his mouth, his eyes still on mine, before he spits into the sink. "What?"

"Can you try to be nice to her?"

"Why?" he asks, tilting his head.

"I don't know… because she hasn't done anything to warrant your wrath?"

"No. But you have, and when I'm rude to her, it affects you." He wipes his mouth and steps closer to me. "You're making this game way too easy for me."

"Why?" I yell, just as his hand touches the door handle.

He pauses.

I carry on. "Why do you hate me so damn much?"

He inches his head over his shoulder. "Because you took something from me."

"I didn't take anything from you! I only just met you!" It's a shame that I have to point out the obvious, but I don't think he's getting it through his head.

"You don't have to know someone to take something from them." He leaves, and I'm, once again, standing like an idiot and left with a disarray of thoughts.

139

Eighteen

King

"How long?" Killian asks, his foot on the dash as I drive us out. Because the drive is twenty-six hours, and Justice has to drive Keaton's Ford Raptor with our bikes and trailer on the back to the next stop. We're all switching drivers as we go.

"When it's done." I already know that Kill is going to hammer me about Dove. We all know that. It's in his DNA to be a fucking pain in the ass.

"You're acting like it was her fault," he whispers, and I have to fight the urge to elbow him in the face.

Dove's laugh breaks out from the back, and my eyes fly to the rearview mirror, catching her laughing with Keaton.

"That's just fucking weird," Kill adds. "Seeing Keaton smile is about as rare as seeing you smile. Pair of serious bastards."

"It's not as weird as you'd think." I focus on the road, wanting this long ass trip to be over.

A few hours later, we pull into a gas station. I kick Killian's leg, waking him up.

"What? Already?"

I ignore him and make my way out of the RV to gas up. Killian is already in the store, grabbing every single piece of junk food he can find like a starved toddler. Twenty minutes later, we're back on the road; only this time, I'm in the kitchen, flicking through Facebook on my phone.

Keaton is still talking with Dove, only he has his guitar out now.

Dove shakes her head, smiling again. I hate how much she reminds me of *her*. Just when I think she's different on the inside, she goes and does something that *she* would do.

Her eyes come to mine, catching me watching her. Her cheeks flash red as she quickly looks away from me. Pussy. She can never hold eye contact for long.

Keaton starts playing Jo Satriani on his guitar when I start to drown them out and search her up on Facebook. I dodge past Val's passive-aggressive status. **You think you don't need me. We'll see…** She gives herself way too much credit as far as my cock is concerned. Opening the search tab, I type in *Dove Hendry* and watch as the results come up. I find her instantly and click on her profile photo. My eyes go up to where she's sitting with

Keaton, before going back to my phone. Her profile photo is of her on a snowboard, wearing the entire getup. The board is flipped to the camera, and she's making the hang loose sign. Holiday photo maybe? Fucking weird, considering her life as I knew it and as it was, wasn't luxurious at all.

I scroll down to see she hasn't been online much since she's been here, only enough to be tagged in one of Rose's statuses. Some guy Richard has put a post on her wall asking when she's coming back. *Never, motherfucker.* I click on her photos and flick through them. Photos of her dancing, one with her friends at what looks like a club. Not her club, though. Another one with her and the same guy Richard. And another with Richard.

Keaton disappears upstairs, and now it's just Dove and I and the silence that stretches out between us. Just as I'm watching her, my phone vibrates in my hand.

I need to kick this up.

Nineteen

Dove

My first real boyfriend was Lionel O'Connor; he was two years older than me and street raced as a side hobby. His parents were rich as sin from old oil money, and he had a slight Southern twang to end each sentence. I have to admit, it was partially what made me fall in love with him. That and the fact he enticed my rebellious nature to come out and play every Saturday night when there was a race. I would always be sitting shotgun, and other girls hated it. They were envious that Lion chose me. He had a square jaw and prominent cheekbones, and he smoked cigarettes like they were an oxygen source. We dated for almost a year through high school, and he was my first everything. Lionel turned out to be one big mistake because he got bored and cheated on me with my best friend at the time, which was also around the time that my parents died. I would give anything to have King bored of me and move on to the next person to terrorize, because right now, he's staring at me like a starved bear, and I'm the freshest fish in the ocean. It would make this whole experience and life change a little easier to swallow.

When he doesn't look to be moving from the chair he's on in the kitchen, his phone in his hand, I end up asking the question that has been burning my throat since he made me come in the middle of a show. Literally. "Why touch me like that at the show?" The words fall out of my mouth without any thought of catching them and shoving them back inside.

He tilts his head. "Because I fucking wanted to." The longer he stares at me, the harder it is for me to look away. "Come here."

I pull my eyes off him.

"Stop fucking doing that, Dove."

"Doing what?" I ask, allowing myself to get lost in him again.

"Looking away from me. Come. Here."

"Come where?" I counter, looking around the table. King is bad for every girl walking this planet. He has a face that is crafted to perfection, with a body built from steel, but that's not why he's poison. He's everything you were instilled to fear as a little girl. He's your father's worst nightmare and your mother's wet dream. He carries himself with confidence and danger. His felonious smirk is one thing, but the way his eyes dismiss you is another. King is exactly like Lion, only worse. So, so, so much worse. Because even after two years of dating Lion, I never felt with him the way I feel while being around King. Because even if Lion was a cold bastard, he would never have done anything to truly hurt me. And that scares me, that King already makes me feel vulnerable. You can't have feelings for a corpse. They don't feel back.

King shuffles in his seat, spreading his knees wide. His eyes, again, remain cool, but his mouth twitches on the corner.

I look down to his lap, and then look back up to his face. I don't trust him or the game he's playing, but I find my feet moving anyway. And it's not because of some creepy mind game they all like to do; it's because underneath the cement of trust issues I have, especially when it comes to The Brothers, I want to know what he wants. And maybe that makes me dumb as fuck.

I'm standing directly in front of him when he tilts his head and stares back up at me. Killian is blasting "Deuces" from Chris Brown, which I'm thankful for because it drowns out the bad decisions I'm thinking about making.

His fingers come to mine, and he yanks me down until I'm on his lap.

I turn in his grip until his face is directly in front of mine. "What are you doing?"

"Does it matter?"

"Ah. Yes?"

His lips come to mine. His tongue dips into my mouth and fills the pit of my belly with lava, using my organs as a mixer. Deadly, but warm. Slowly, I open wider for him, running the tip of my tongue across his bottom lip. Well, Killian did ask to see if he would kiss me...

A chuckle breaks out behind me, and I go to pull away, knowing that we've been caught. Only King's hand flies to the back of my neck to hold me there. He deepens the kiss, so I wrap my arms around his neck.

Kyrin is sitting at the table, texting on his phone, like what just happened didn't surprise him. I'm guessing not much does.

"King!" Keaton calls out from the top of the stairs behind me.

Kingston takes his eyes away from me as they go up to where Keaton is. He taps my leg, and I swing off him, brushing my hair out of my face. I try to ignore how the blood rushing around my insides is making my ears throb, but it's a little hard when his kisses are like heroin, taking hold of my control and smashing it to itty bitty pieces. King says nothing as he disappears upstairs, taking my pride with him.

I can't believe I kissed him. I can't blame it on the hype of the environment either. I was stone-cold sober and normal.

"Don't get too excited," Kyrin says. His tone is bored, his eyes never moving up from his phone. It's probably the most Kyrin has ever said to me.

"I'm not."

Finally, he lifts his eyes to mine. Kyrin's features are as sharp as a samurai sword. He's almost too pretty to be human. His eyelashes are so black and thick that it looks like he's always wearing eyeliner and mascara. But he's scary. "King never does anything without a reason, much less a girl. Like you. And no offense," his eyes go up and down my body, making me squirm in self-consciousness, "but you're not his usual type."

"Correction," Killian calls out from the front. "He doesn't have a type."

I shuffle away from Kyrin. He goes back to doing whatever it was that he was doing, and I make my way to the front of the RV, sitting in the passenger seat.

"Don't take anything that Ky says personally. He doesn't have good people skills."

"I figured that out. Are you the outcast Brother?" I joke, putting my feet onto the dash and embracing the afternoon sun that's warming my skin.

Killian laughs. "I've been told that many times."

"So, what's the deal with the whole Brothers of Kiznitch thing?" I finally ask the question that's been poking around in my brain since finding out.

Killian doesn't answer, and for a second, I don't think he's going to, until he simply says, "It's a long story."

I let the silence settle around us. I like silence. I need to be able to sit in silence with people, and if I can't, then I can't be around those people. Silence is the most underrated sound. "What Kyrin meant to say was that King doesn't do the whole exclusivity thing. If you're with him, you have to know that he's never fully yours."

My eyebrows shoot up. "We kissed." I play it off as if it's nothing, ignoring my heart beating in my chest and my stomach curling.

"Yeah, it shocked me because King doesn't kiss. Ever." Killian snorts. "And that was a kiss that was hot enough to be turned into porn." My eyes fly up to the rearview mirror and then go back to the road. "Just know that he's never had a girlfriend. Ever. There will never be a girlfriend as far as King goes. As long as you're cool with that, then you're good."

"Why are you telling me this?" I swallow past the boulder in my throat. I'm a damn masochist because the pain that comes with this knowledge doesn't stop me from asking questions, knowing that the answers are going to hurt me.

He shrugs. "Is it hard to believe that I don't want you to get hurt?"

"Yes," I answer instantly. "Because you guys had me locked in a cell for a whole week. So yeah, it does."

Killian laughs. "Well, you remember that next time you have your tongue down the devil's throat." He chuckles. "All things sinister taste like honey."

I sigh, resting my head on the back of the chair. I silently vow to myself that I won't kiss King again.

Twenty

Dove

We're in Texas and the location crew has already started setting up the equipment. We got in late last night, and, somehow, between us arriving, sleeping, and waking, the crew has already partially set up the monstrous tent. Texas is hot. So hot that I can barely damn well breathe, so I'm making my way through the RV in my sports bra and little shorts. Sweat is pouring out of my flesh everywhere, and if something doesn't cool me down fast, I think I might die. The front door swings open, and King is standing there shirtless with cotton shorts on that hang nicely off his hips. His hair is in disarray all over his head and sweat slicks over his muscled torso.

Focus.

"Why is it so hot?"

King's eyes go up and down my body before coming back to my eyes. "Because Texas."

"No, I mean, do we have air-con in here? I might die."

"If only," he mumbles, climbing up the steps that bring him into the RV. "Get your bikini. We're going to the waterhole while we wait for the crew to set up the generator."

I dash into my room and grab the first bikini I can find, slipping it on. Nothing fancy. Just a yellow and white two-piece. I take a couple of bottled waters out of the fridge before slipping on some little white ripped shorts and a tank. I'm taking a sip of water and waiting for King outside when he finally emerges. I fall into step beside him.

The silence that hangs between us is comfortable as we pass everyone's RVs. Just as we come up to Midnight's, Maya and Rose are exiting, but Val and Mischa are already sitting outside, rubbing oil onto their bodies. Killian, Kyrin, and Keaton show up next with a few people I haven't met yet. I make eye contact with a few of them, but they make it obvious when they pointedly avoid me.

Val pauses while rubbing oil onto her leg, her eyes fixed on me. She pushes off her chair and bounces her way to King. "Can you oil my back?"

King pays her no attention. "No." He shoves past her and goes straight for Maya. He leans into her ear and whispers something, her eyes coming to mine.

"Don't get comfortable on that seat. You're only keeping it warm until he comes back to me," Val announces as I'm passing her.

"I don't know what you're talking about," I throw back over my shoulder, mainly because I don't. Unless she's picking up something that I haven't yet. Or maybe she's just insecure because I'm staying with them.

Rose comes over to me, wearing a little red bikini and nothing else, her arm hooking with mine. "I need a swim before I melt."

"Ditto."

"Hey." She tugs on my arm, just as we all start walking toward God knows where. "Are you okay in there? You can ask Delila for your own trailer. I heard her speaking with Justice the other day, and they both agree that you're going to have your own show on top of the SOK scenes."

"SOK?" I ask, before I connect the dots. "Right. I don't know what she would want me to do."

"Um…" Rose rolls her eyes. "Dance, of course."

I drop my sunglasses over my eyes. "I'm nothing special."

"You are so wrong." Rose turns her head over her shoulder slightly, before coming back to me. "When you dance, Dove, you create a new world. You captivate the entire audience. There's peace in your movements."

King's arm wraps around my torso, pulling me into him as he walks behind me. "Yeah, but always remember that in peace always lies havoc."

I try to wiggle out of his grip to no avail. Once we're in the parking lot, King pulls out a set of keys and pushes the unlock button on his keyring. A black Ford Raptor lights up. He points to it. "Get in the car."

"Can she ride with us?" Rose pleads. "I haven't seen her in so long!"

King pauses, cutting her with his corpse eyes. "No."

At least he's not an asshole just to me. It's an overall personality defect. "I'll see you when I get there," I tell Rose, making my way to the truck. I go to slip into the back when someone picks me up from behind and puts me in front of the passenger's side door. I turn around to find Killian smirking. "Little Bird rides shotgun."

Sighing, I open the door just in time to see Val glaring at me from the other side of the parking lot. She's about to slip into a white Range Rover, but paused her movements to make it known to me that she hates me.

"Don't worry about her," Killian catches me off guard by whispering into my ear. "She's just jealous because King has never paid her any attention that goes past the bedroom."

"What?" I say, turning to face him.

Killian shrugs. "King fucks her and disregards her. When I say fuck, I mean just fuck. He never touches her. Never kisses her. Everything they do is in the bedroom, and nothing past that door, and it's her door, not his door."

"Are you both done gossiping?" King starts up the loud truck, and I pull myself up by the running board, sinking into the leather seat. I can feel him watching me out of the corner of my eye, but I ignore him. I'm confused by the sudden back and forth. At what point did he and I establish something? I missed it. That's what worries me. It was organic. The knots and bonds were knitted without me noticing. Now I don't know how to untie all the knots because I missed how they were woven together.

"Stop thinking too much into whatever the fuck Kill is filling your head with." King drives us out of the parking lot, following behind the Range Rover and another car.

"I'm not."

He chuckles. "Yeah, you are."

"And you can read my mind now?" I tease, chancing a look at him.

His jaw tenses, and for a second, I want to hit myself for joking with him. It's bad enough that I can't stop kissing him or being on his lap, let alone joking with him. And anyway, he probably can read my mind. I wouldn't put it past him. Or any of them.

He hits the stereo, and we let the music fill the empty space around us. Which is a lot because this truck is massive. "Hail to the King" by Avenged Sevenfold starts playing. I roll my eyes at the irony of the song and distract myself with all of the passing trees and buildings. The road turns into gravel, and we're bouncing down a bumpy road.

I spin around and look at Killian, Kyrin, and Keaton, who are in the back.

Killian's already smirking at me from the middle. "What? Scared we're taking you somewhere to kill you?"

"Actually, that thought didn't cross my mind, surprisingly, but where did the rest of them go?"

"Lost them on the trip." Keaton catches my attention. Talking with Keaton on the way here was probably one of the highlights of my trip. He's not someone who looks like he makes a lot of friends, but for whatever reason, he's chosen to make one out of me.

I turn back around, just as King pulls up to a clearing. "Wow!" There's a long waterfall that's pouring over a cliff, crashing into the clear water below. "Wait, how do we know there aren't gators or anything in this water?"

King shrugs, climbing out of the truck. As soon as his door is opened, the humidity slaps me across the face, and suddenly, I no longer care. Anything to take away this sticky heat. Just as I'm closing the door, the Range Rover and other truck pull in, parking beside us. I'm instantly annoyed that Val is here.

They all stammer out, and Rose yanks at my towel. "Take your clothes off, Dovey!" She hands me a wine cooler, and we clash our bottles together in a cheers.

I take a sip and watch the rest of the girls strip half naked and all go diving into the water after The Brothers.

"You all right?" a voice says from behind me. "Why aren't you in the water?"

I turn around to find a guy I haven't met yet. He's tall and slender with kind brown eyes. He's attractive, at first glance.

"I'm getting there." I chuckle.

He laughs, and I notice his white teeth instantly against his tanned skin. His eyes fall on me. He has a friendly face. "I'm Jackson, but people call me Jack."

My hand meets his. "Dove."

"I know who you are." He winks, removing his shirt. No ink. Not even the star that The Brothers have. Interesting.

He dives into the water, just as I slip out of my sandals.

"Oh, come on, Little Bird. Get in the water!" Killian yells.

"What are you scared about?" Val snaps, climbing up one of the rocks, shaking the water from her toned body. The Brothers don't pay her any attention.

Shrugging off my towel, I toss it to the ground, placing my wine cooler on top. I pad my way to the rock that Jack dived off of.

"Dovey! Holy shit!" Mischa is laughing from the water. "That dancer body, though!"

"What?" I look down at my soft curves, but athletic frame. I have a tight six-pack and more muscles than bone, but essentially, I still wiggle in places. I like it that way, because I love food. "You're insane. You're all fit."

"And you're not?" Rose challenges me with a sneaky eyebrow lift.

154

I roll my eyes and dive into the water, instantly releasing all of my stress that the heat had brought upon me. My head breaks through the water, and I swipe the excess off my face, laughing.

"Feel better?" King whispers from behind me, just as his arm locks around my torso.

I spin around, wetting my hair back, so it's not all over my face. "Much better." I'm still laughing when I lean forward and kiss him softly on the lips. I freeze when I pull back. "Sorry—"

His lips are on mine again, his arm tightening around my waist. He releases me after a few seconds, and his eyes are searching mine.

"What are we doing?"

"Don't do that," he murmurs against my lips.

"Do what?" I want to know what he means. Suddenly, everyone and everything has disappeared behind me, and it's just King and me.

"Don't ask questions that you're not ready to hear the answers for."

"And you think I'm not ready?" I probe, wanting something. Anything. "You said that you hated me."

"Yeah, and what did I say after I admitted that?" The words come out of his mouth, but his arms are still holding me beneath the water.

I think over my very brief memories, before his words come back to me in a violent echo. *"I don't need to like you to fuck you."*

"Okay." I flutter my arms to keep me afloat, but fail miserably when I sink back under water. His hands come to the back of my ass, and he lifts me up out of the water again, forcing my legs around his waist. I'm chuckling with my arms around his neck. "We didn't finish that conversation. Why do you hate me?"

His eyes narrow, and for a very brief second, I'm lost in his blatant masculinity. His dark hair and lashes. His very prominent jaw that always looks as though he's tensing it—that's how cut it is, and the way his eyes can express almost every human emotion while not exuding any at all. "All in good time."

"Dovey! Want your drink?" Rose hollers, snapping me out of King's trance. I push away from him and start swimming to the shoreline until my feet touch the sandy bottom. Once I'm out of the water, I take my drink and set my towel up beside her as she flicks through her phone and turns some music on.

"Are you okay?" she asks without looking at me. I get the feeling she's trying to be secretive in her questions.

"Why wouldn't I be?" I answer, running my fingers through my hair before it tangles.

She exhales, turning her full attention to me. "Please be careful, Dove. They're not what you think they are. They're—"

"Hey!" Mischa, the brunette girl who seems to have way too much energy for her little body, flicks her towel down on the other side of Rose. "You and King?"

"Ah…"

Maya drops her towel beside mine, complaining about wearing a bikini, even though she's wearing sport shorts over her bottoms. "Fucking hate this Texas heat."

"So?" Mischa further forces.

"Oh, for fuck's sake, Mischa. Shut up and leave her alone." Maya puts a joint between her lips and lights the tip, inhaling. She passes it to me, but I decline.

"Oh, come on." Maya smirks. "I just put her in her place. The least you can do is have a puff on me."

"Trouble," Killian teases, and instantly Maya's face drops. "Leave Dove alone. You know how King likes his toys untarnished."

I laugh this time, flipping onto my back and relishing in the sun. "Well, then he better find a new toy, because I'm definitely a shade darker than tarnished." I wiggle my fingers toward myself without even looking at Maya, gesturing to the joint. I want to say that it's partly because of what happened in the cell, but I don't. I don't want them to know anything about what happened, because that'll probably just give them more satisfaction to my pain. My chest tightens with that knowledge. My crush on Kingston Axton is poison, but apparently, I'm willing to die for it.

I feel the smoke between my fingers and bring it to my lips, inhaling deeply. I hold it in my lungs for a beat longer before blowing out. Once I give it back to Maya, Rose has finally stopped fighting with Mischa about the music before a song starts playing. One I don't recognize.

"I'm serious, Dovey," Rose whispers. She's on her stomach now, her head resting in her arms and her face toward me.

I exhale, turning onto my stomach and turning my face to hers. No one can hear us because the music is loud, and we're so close we don't have to yell. "Why?"

"Me being here?" she whispers. "It was part of their initiation. Everything that Delila had explained—was why I was here."

"Okay." I search her eyes. "And me?" The heat is not helping my buzz. In fact, it's intensifying it. A lot.

"You were not a normal recruit, Dove. That's why you were there for so long. Why you're with *them* and not on your own or with another family."

"And what is it that I should be worried about?" My heart pounds in my chest. I'm not naïve. I know there's something else. It's why King likes to tell me that I've done something to warrant his wrath. It's why he apparently hates me and that I took something from him.

"Do not fall for King—"

"Am I interrupting something here?" Val drops down in front of us, the sand kicking up and flicking me in the face. I actually want to kill her.

I sit up, shading the sun from my eyes. I'm feeling a range of emotions, but one that trumps them all is the lack of control that I have. I've lost my life to four men, and they haven't even killed me yet.

I groan, standing, and make my way back to the water. King and the rest of The Brothers are up by the truck, but Jack is still in the water with the people he came with.

"So…" he starts, his head bobbing in the water.

"Nope." I laugh, shaking my head while sinking in. "If you're going to ask me about King, the answer is no."

Jack laughs, which makes me want to laugh. I realize I genuinely enjoy his presence. I've known him for all of twenty minutes, but I feel at ease around him. Like I know him or have met him before. I know that I haven't, though. I'd remember his face. I haven't met such kindness since Richard.

"I've known King for a while, and I've never seen him like that before," Jack further says, swimming closer to me.

"Oh really," I dig, kicking out to the deep. He follows closely behind me, while still keeping a safe distance. I appreciate that.

When I'm far enough out, I turn around, and he's a few steps in front of me. My eyes go over his shoulder and to the truck, where the boys are now all watching us. "How well do you know him?"

Jack runs his hand through his hair. "Well, since I was nine. His family is close with my family. You know, that sort of thing."

"Ah, right." I don't want to sound nosey, so I change the subject. "And what is your act or role in Midnight Mayhem?"

He pauses. "You mean aside from the final act?"

I tilt my head. "I don't think I've fully experienced the final act."

He chuckles. "No, you haven't, and the way things are looking," he turns his head over his shoulder, "you may never."

"Can you tell me a bit about it all?"

He swipes his hair again. "Well, it's for us as much as it's for the audience."

"It's live sex."

He laughs, his head tilting back. "Yes and no."

I shake my head. "Is all the crazy crap that you guys do not enough?"

"It's more of a reenactment. You'll see tomorrow. Whether you're involved wholly or partly like before, I'm sure you'll see."

"And who is all in the final act?"

He smirks. "Everyone."

A whistle breaks through the air, interrupting our chat. King waves us to the shore.

I grumble, "We've been summoned." We both start swimming back.

"Is he always moody?" I ask, just as my feet touch the sand again.

"Nah," Jack says. "He usually has a coping mechanism."

Before I can ask what that means, Jack is heading over to the other guys he came with, throwing a towel around his back. His friend slaps the back of his head, and Jack laughs, turning around to face me and sending me a wink.

These people are strange. Not the kind of strange that's enticing either. They're the kind of strange that you don't want to be a part of, or even admire from a distance.

Maya is heading my way wearing a cap flipped backwards.

"You got a death wish, Dovey?" I know what she's implying. What with King right there.

"No. Just making friends."

"Hey!" Maya calls out as I pass her. I turn around. "You should come drink with us tonight. We're having a fire pit lit and all the rest. Since, you know, you haven't yet, and you went drinking with Beat first…"

I smile. "Sure."

"Dove!" King bellows from across the grass.

"Oh, girl." Maya chuckles. "You're in trouble."

I turn around to face him and see the rest of the boys climbing into the truck. "Get in the truck!"

Rose tosses my towel at me, and I catch it, glaring at her. "I mean it, Dove. Be careful."

"She's not lying," Val mutters, flipping onto her back.

I slowly make my way to the truck, and King climbs into the driver's seat as I get into the passenger's side. He slams his door before I'm putting my belt on and floors the truck forward.

"Really, Dove. You just had to poke the bear."

"What?" I turn to face Killian, who shakes his head.

Figuring we're all in one car, I turn to face Kingston, leaning my back against the door. "What did I do wrong?"

"What gave you the impression that you did anything wrong?" he answers, but his voice is detached. Distant.

"Well, I don't know. Maybe the fact that you yelled at me from across the damn field."

He laughs sarcastically. "Because I yelled at you?" He takes his eyes off the road for a second to pin me with a stare. "If that's what has you shaken up, then you're weaker than I thought."

I grit my teeth and remain quiet the whole way home. I realize the longer I'm with them, the more comfortable I get to speak my mind. It's like the longer I'm here, the more I forget everything that they have put me through to this point.

King opens the glove compartment and grabs out an envelope. He points to it. "That's yours. Everything that's inside is yours. Use it as you need."

I open the envelope and a single black card drops onto my lap. "Why?"

"Because you're one of us," Keaton adds.

I flick the black card between my fingers, thinking of what to do.

"Press check account for your pay, or savings for the trust account. They're linked."

I want to fight it. I want to know why he's flipped all of a sudden, and he's not as mad at me as everyone thought back at the lake, but I leave it. Because I'll choose my fights with King, and I don't think this is one to exert energy on right now. At least for now.

We pull back into the compound, and I take a few seconds to climb out of the truck. Everyone leaves, and it's just Killian and I inside. I turn around to face him. "For some reason, I trust you."

Killian freezes. "Well, don't."

"Why do you say that?" I ask, genuinely wanting to know.

"Because as much as I like you, Little Bird, The Brothers are my family. This family is deeper than your mind could even imagine. There are secrets and bonds and all kinds of crazy ass shit that you can never know. That's why you shouldn't trust me. Because if I was ordered to put a bullet between your eyes, I wouldn't flinch when doing it. I may be nice to you,

Little Bird, but don't mistake it for loyalty. Someone like me, like them, we can never be happy with a girl because of it." He climbs out of the truck, slamming the door in his retreat.

I remain seated. Frustrated and angry, and most of all, lost. I feel lost. Like I don't know who I am anymore or even where I fit in. I'm not delusional enough to think that with The Brothers of Kiznitch is where I would fit in, but I thought I trusted Kill.

Pushing open the door, I drop to the ground just as Delila comes heading straight for me.

"Little Bird. Where have you been? Come, I have something I want to show you."

I close the door and do as she says. Delila is probably a lot of things—judging by what Beat has said also—but as far as I stand, she's not threatened my life yet, so that's saying something.

I follow her to the tent and inside. She waves her hand toward the stage. "You will have your own act."

My palms sweat, and I rub them down my thighs. "Dancing?"

She nods, her black bob bouncing with the movement. "Yes. I'll leave it up to you. Different dances would be preferred, but it's up to you. You get five minutes. You may use any of the props. There's a pole there, too, if you need it."

I tilt my head. "You do know that pole fitness is a sport, right? Not just for stripping."

Delila exhales. "Yes, Dove, and I'm hoping that you use it. Practice some today, and we will have you ready for tomorrow night." She disappears down one of the aisles. I'd be happy to actually have my own act. I know I'd have to still take part in at least King's act, too, and the final one, but to have my own gives me a sense of individuality and makes me feel as though I have some sort of purpose here. Something that doesn't involve The Brothers.

In record time, I run back to the RV to change. I pause when I find shopping bags lined out on my bed. I take a peek inside one and find they're all filled with new clothes. Shrugging, I slip into some tight Nike shorts and a sports bra, throwing over a Valentino crop jersey. Grabbing some leg warmers, I quickly run my brush through my hair and make my way back to the tent. I don't want to see any of The Brothers right now, and especially not King. One second he's kissing me, and then the next, he's yelling at me, and then he's telling me he hates me and that I took something from him. There has been no bigger mind fuck than being on the receiving end of Kingston Axton's attention. I'm not sure I want it.

I order a couple of the boys who are wandering around to bring the pole out to the center stage. I can see out of the corner of my eye that Val is stretching on a beam. Ignoring her, I focus on my practice.

"Val?" I yell, and she turns to face me, her golden hair looking every bit Serena van der Woodson. "Do you care if I put music on?"

Val rolls her eyes. "No, Little Bird, I don't."

Tim, I think Delila said his name is, points to my phone. "Hook your phone up to the Bluetooth system, and you'll have free reign. The Brothers will be practicing in a couple hours, so it's all yours until then."

I smile. "Thank you." Flicking through my playlist, I drop my phone onto the ground after leaving "Mother's Daughter" by Miley Cyrus playing. I need to warm up and stretch, since I haven't done much of that for a while. Bending over, I stretch out my hamstrings, before sliding to the ground and spreading my legs wide, leaning forward onto the ground and finishing in a front split. The music is warming me up as much as my stretches are. When I'm ready, I flick through my phone again. I know I want to have a different song for every town. Depending on my mood, I want to express it through my dance. I've always been good at channeling my emotions into my limbs. I'm feeling angry and reckless, and somewhat, warped. I push play on "Carousel" by Melanie Martinez and smirk. "So fitting." When the beat kicks in, I grab ahold of the pole and swing around it. I'm lost for three minutes and fifty seconds. I hit repeat, deciding this will definitely be the song I'm dancing to tonight, and work on my routine.

Twenty-One

King

"We need to talk about her." Killian's persistence to talk about Dove is wearing on my patience. He puts on a good front, he's the best at it, but we all know that she is also wearing on his restraint.

"We don't."

"What are you doing, King? Kissing her and rubbing up on her like a dog in heat. Since when was that part of the plan?" Keaton questions, this time, his eyes trained on me. I shuffle off the couch, tearing my shirt off. "I get it. She's hot as sin, but we knew that. *You* knew that."

Flopping back down, I place a smoke in my mouth and light it up. "I'm playing with my food, so what?"

AMO JONES

"King," Killian warns. "Not a good idea. What happens when we have to do the delivery?"

I glare at him, bored. "What the fuck are you talking about, Chatty Kathy? I've seen the way you look at her."

"Because you wanna get your dick wet all of a sudden?" Keaton argues. He wants my attention, and now he has it.

I get off the couch and make my way to where he's leaning against the doorframe. "What are you afraid of, Keats? Scared that if we play some games with her that she'll break?" I tilt my head and search his eyes. "Her finish line is rather fucking close, so why not?"

"She's not what I was expecting." Keaton's shoulders are straight, his eyes lighting in defiance.

"What part of her? The part where she was always the pawn in our game to end a long-time beef?"

Keaton growls. "I don't fucking know. She's just not what I expected."

I lick my lip and smirk. "Yeah, I could have an idea why that is."

Keaton's eyes narrow, his suspicion growing. "And why is that?"

I make my way back to the couch and drop down, blowing out a cloud of smoke. I have two options here: I can tell this idiot exactly what he needs to know. To put him out of his misery, or I can add it to my bag of tricks and save it for later.

My phone vibrates in my pocket and I pull it out, answering instantly. "Mother."

"Kingston. I need an update." I can already imagine what she's doing. Sitting behind her long table, a smoke in one hand and a glass of vodka in the other.

I lean back. "Where are you?"

"Italy. I'll be back in the US in a couple weeks. Tell Killian his father is calling a meeting too, which we will need you all to attend."

I smirk. Into my bag of tricks it goes.

Twenty-Two

Dove

One of my earliest memories was of my mom dropping me off at my ballet class with tears strolling down her face. I never knew why she was crying. I would have been all of six, or maybe just turning seven. I can't remember anything prior to this memory, and any time I would ask my mom about it, she would say that I suffered from PTSD as a small child and part of my condition was that I blocked out memories prior to that. I would counter what she said and say that usually people would at least have black spots. Or flashes of events that happened early, but I had nothing. Zilch. It was a strange feeling, not having any early memories. Not even some monumental thing that had happened. It's something I have always thought about while not really thinking about it. Hovering in the back of my brain like a bad memory. I never did find out why she was crying that day. My mother never cried. Shedding such raw emotion is not in her nature. *Was* not in her nature, so seeing her cry moved me enough to make it stick in my brain. Even now, as I make my way back to the RV, after practicing a solid two hours on my act, I'm here thinking about something that happened over a decade ago.

"Dove!" Maya calls out, just as I reach the RV.

I turn to face her. "Hey!"

She's slightly out of breath, huffing and puffing. "Sorry. God, I hate exercise."

"You hate exercise?" I giggle. "Your act?"

She waves me off, rolling her eyes. "I sing on a swing and let the boys drive their bikes through hula hoops. I don't—no. I do not do what Midnight does. I'm not even in Midnight. I just stay with them because…" She shakes her head. "Anyway, that's not why I'm here. Hand me your phone!"

I give it to her and watch as she pushes buttons. "I've programmed my number into your phone and now I have yours. So, you can't skip out on our drink tonight." She hands it back to me.

"I wasn't planning to."

She tucks her unruly curly hair behind her ear. "Good. See you later!" And she's off again, as quickly as she showed.

I make my way into the RV and head straight for my room. I need to put away all my new clothes and wash my laundry, but when I open the closet in my room, my dirty clothes that were in my basket have been washed and folded and are sitting inside of it tidily.

I step back outside of my room, looking around to see who is here, when a lady starts making her way down the stairs.

"Oh! You must be Miss Hendry. Your clean washing is folded and put away, and I've refurnished the cupboards and fridge."

"Ah." Obviously based on her very cliché maid attire, I know who and why she's here, but I just didn't know we had one.

"Sorry," she apologizes, wiping her hands with the rag she has hanging out of her front pocket, and puts her hand out to me. "I'm Rhonda. The maid. Each RV has one, and I'm yours."

"Nice to meet you, Rhonda." My hand meets hers, and she squeezes it gently. "Have you been The Brothers maid for long?"

"Long enough," Rhonda jokes. "Well, if you need anything, just text triple seven, and you'll get my cell phone." She makes her way through the kitchen again before leaving me in the RV alone, which is peaceful.

I pad my way back into my room and take a quick shower. I promised the girls a drink tonight, so a drink I will have.

Gun shots ring out. Bang. Bang. Bang. One after another. They pierce through the air and ricochet into me, leaving fragments of blood spattered all over my sundress...

Shaking myself out of my flashback, the Texas heat leaves me drowning in sweat and not wanting to put any clothes on at all, so after my shower, I settle on white shorts that cut off around the curve of my ass cheek and a tight tank that rides up and shows my belly. I couldn't care less. It's hot, I'm uncomfortable, so if wearing next to nothing is what's going to make me feel just a smidge better in this heat, then I'm going with it. I try to straighten my hair dead straight and let it flow down to my tailbone, but the humidity has it frizzing back almost instantly. My skin has a natural tan glistening since our time at the lake today and my cheeks are flushed. I usually wear makeup. Not much, but some, but tonight, I kept it lowkey natural. Bronzer, blush, and some mascara. Really, I'm looking forward to spending some time with girls instead of four very intense boys.

"Hey!" I wave to Rose as I walk up. There are chairs scattered around their small fire pit. I almost want to say it's way too fucking hot to have that blazing, but I sit down anyway.

Maya hands me a glass of something and clinks her glass against mine. "Bottoms up, *Little Bird.*" Her tone is docile and bored, but I've learned over the time that I've been here that that's just Maya.

We clink glasses, just as the crowd thickens. I can feel their presence before I can see them, but I ignore everything going on around me and keep my eyes locked on the flames that flicker through the darkness. Music is blaring loudly, so loudly. it's a wonder anyone can sleep through it—or maybe no one is, and they're all here; there's that many people here.

"You actually came." Jack sinks down in the chair beside mine.

"Hey, yeah, I did. Though I don't know how long I'll last. I was rehearsing all day, and my muscles are tired."

Jack laughs. "I understand that." I take a second to watch all of the people who are here. I'm starting to learn that there are more people than I know who are in Midnight Mayhem.

"So we're going to play a game!" Killian calls out, shutting off the music and interfering with my people-watching.

"Oh no," Jack mutters, kicking back in his chair.

"Why, oh no?" I ask, leaning into Jack.

Jack leans back into me. "The last time Killian wanted to play a game, someone died."

I gulp, sitting up straight. "You're joking, right?" I whisper into him.

"Wish I was." Jack takes a swig of his drink and then tosses his cup into the fire. I watch as the flames burst higher, lost in my own thoughts. Someone died? These people are crazy. "It's a shame," Jack muses out loud, interrupting my thinking.

"What's a shame?" I ask, looking straight into his eyes.

"That you've gained King's attention."

I laugh, shaking my head. "No, I haven't."

Jack's eyes narrow, making me squirm in my seat. It's a weird twitch for such kind eyes. "I've known him a long time, so trust me when I say, you've gained his attention."

Killian's voice comes back into the zone, pushing Jack's ridiculous rambles to the side. I know I have, but it's not for the reasons that people are implying.

"You'll take a bandana and wrap it around your mouth."

Kyrin starts going around, handing everyone a bandana. The white patterns burn into my brain, like a reminder of that one night so many years ago.

My eyes close, and I don't open them until a rag is being waved against my face.

Kyrin is watching me closely. He kneels down to eye level, his eyes searching mine. "What's the matter? Don't like bandanas?" The corner of his mouth tick into a smirk, but his eyes remain passive.

I snatch it out of his grip, ignoring him. He stands and continues around the crowd.

"The game is simple."

People scoff and shuffle in the distance.

Killian chuckles and then continues. "It is simple. Remember when you'd play hide-and-seek as a kid?" Killian wraps his bandana around his mouth and it's then that I see his has a skull on it. My eyes find King, who is already watching me, his tied around his mouth, and, again, another skull. All four of The Brothers have skulls on theirs, but when I look around at the other guys and girls, theirs are normal. "Well, this is much like that, only you hide and we seek."

"And?" Val answers, wrapping hers around her mouth. Finally, I take mine and tie it around my own.

"And what?" Killian raises an eyebrow.

"And what happens when you catch us?" Val places a hand on her slim hip.

"Guess you'll have to see." Killian winks at her.

Val's back straightens.

Kyrin chuckles at her, shaking his head. "As easy as ever, Val."

Val's eyes snap to his. "Really? Because you're wanting me to have another threesome?"

Kyrin's smirk deepens. "No one invited you in. You walked your ass into our room because your clit throbbed for Travis."

I'm lost, my head going back and forth between them. I lean into Jack. "Is Kyrin gay? I never would have pegged that."

Jack's head tilts back in laughter. "Naw. Not gay."

"Bi?" I ask, studying Kyrin. I know he's pretty, but his energy is also very dark.

"Nope again." Jack chuckles, before correcting me when he sees how confused I am. "He doesn't have a sexual preference, but he doesn't identify himself as bi either. He hates labels. His motto is 'he'll fuck who he wants.'"

"Makes sense." I drag my eyes away from Kyrin and watch as Killian continues to stare at me.

"You finished talking, Little Bird?"

I nod.

"You'll get a two-minute head start. If you're caught, it's

your seeker's decision on what he wants to do with you. Will it be slave for the night? Will it be a dare? It's up to the seeker." Kingston stands from his chair, his eyes on me. They're like laser beams shooting right through me. It makes me queasy and uneasy, but I can't look away.

"Three, two, one…" Killian smirks. "Run, run, run…"

I pause, trapped in King's trance. People are scrambling around me, running into the forest that backs up to the field, but I'm imprisoned.

Slowly, I watch as King's mouth opens, before he mouths, "Run."

Just like that, I spin around and zap toward the forest, my heart thundering in my chest. The adrenaline that spikes through my blood gives me a much-needed energy boost because my legs shoot forward through a clearing. I jump and dodge fallen tree branches. I run for a solid minute until I stop, expecting to see or hear someone. Anyone. There were so many people who are here hiding—where have they all gone?

I step backward, the leaves beneath my shoe crunching. *Where the fuck is everyone?*

I walk this time, not wanting to make any unnecessary noise. The bright moonlight battles against the dead of the night, paving the way for me through the mass of fallen branches. I must walk for twenty minutes before I figure I should turn around and start heading back, only when I do, the forest caves around me like an endless maze, enveloping me in its natural form.

I hear rustling from the left. "Jack?"

"Wrong," King whispers, just as my back crashes into his chest.

I screech, spinning around to face him. "That was hardly fair."

174

He steps closer, and I step back, until I'm colliding into a tree trunk.

His chest brushes up against mine, all six-foot-something of him towering over me. "What's your name?"

I hold my breath, afraid that if I catch too much of his scent, his venom will seep into my bones and remain. His hand comes to my chin, tilting my face up to his. King doesn't need to demand an answer from anyone. His presence speaks in volumes that no frequency can calculate.

"Dove." I swallow past my nerves.

He yanks my bandana down and slowly slips his thumb between my lips. I take him, sucking his thumb into my mouth. It's not until the strong flick of metal hits my sensitive taste buds that I rear back, whacking his hand out of my way. "Ew! What is that?"

"What's your name?" he repeats, his knee pressing between my legs, separating them.

"Dove!" I yell, using the back of my hand to wipe whatever it was—please don't be blood—off my lips. "What was on your hand, King?"

He leans down and runs his tongue over my lips. "My revenge."

He kisses me, just in time for Killian to run up behind us with Maya in tow. My eyes fall to her wrists, and I see they're bound together by Killian's bandana. "Killian!"

He shrugs, and Maya rolls her eyes, bored.

Killian searches King. "You ready?"

King grabs my hand, stepping out of my vicinity and pulling me behind him. "We'll meet you back at the RV." I follow his steps, the silence stretching out, as Maya and Killian disappear into the distance.

"Are you going to tell me if that was blood?"

"Does it matter?" He picks up his stride, tucking his bandana into his back jeans pocket.

"Do you ever wear shirts? And yes, since you shoved your thumb into my mouth." When he doesn't answer, I reach out to his hand. It's like an electric voltage passes between us, and he spins around, pinning me with his glare.

"What, Dove?"

Suddenly, the air is thicker, and my chest is heavy. "Why do you keep touching me and then hating me?" Sounds juvenile, but it's the one thing I want to know. Even more than whose damn blood I just sucked down.

He reaches forward, hooking his hand behind my neck, and pulls me into him. His lips crash onto mine, and I open, wanting more of him. Needing him to feed me with the fuel I so desperately want. Only, it's never enough, because every single time our kiss is finished, I'm only left more famished.

He stops, pulls back, but rests his forehead against mine. "I don't fucking know." He shoves me away and disappears behind one of the RVs.

"Dove!" Rose bounces toward me, a drink in her hand. I'm still left flabbergasted by King's words that I haven't even registered that she's still speaking to me. "Here!" She shoves a drink into my chest. "Did King get you?"

I swallow the entire contents whole, swiping my mouth. "Yes."

"Are you being careful?" she asks, hooking her arm in mine and leading me back to their RV where everyone is drinking.

"As careful as I can be." I head straight for the fridge they have outside, taking out an entire bottle of wine and dropping down onto one of the seats. A few people are scattered around, but I notice Val is missing. My eyes land on Maya, who is sitting next to Killian. I pop the bottle and take a long swig, my eyes staying on Kill.

"What's with you two?" I ask, gesturing to both of them with my wine bottle.

Maya stares at me blankly as if I've interrupted her space and I should apologize. She's hard to read, I've gathered that, but I've also found that she somewhat tolerates me. I hope I don't test that when I ask my next question. "Are you sleeping together?"

Killian freezes, his eyes coming to mine. "No, Little Bird. We're not. Why don't you just worry about who will be in, or under, your bed tonight." His eyes darken. A few seconds pass between us. In the corner of my eye, I can see more people coming in, having been found.

I drink more wine.

"Listen," Rose says, leaning into me. "I found this in our RV. I feel like it might have something to do with you, since it's a dove, but I don't know if it means anything." I feel her hand slip beneath my shorts, tucking what feels like a piece of paper into my underwear. "Just don't look until you're alone. I don't think I was supposed to find it, if you know what I mean."

I shrug. "I'm confused."

"About what?" Rose asks, taking the bottle of wine off me and having many sips herself.

I look directly at her, the flames from the fire warming the right side of my cheek. "Kingston."

She pauses, and then slowly lowers the bottle down onto her lap. "I can understand why you might be confused, what with how he's been acting around you. Maya said that he's never been like that around or about any girl—ever."

177

"I don't know," I answer, taking back the bottle. I sip on it, even though, deep down, I know that I shouldn't and that I've probably had enough. I inhale deeply and exhale, the sweet tang of wine simmering behind my throat. "I got the feeling there may have been someone else. At the very least, another friend."

Rose's hand rests on my thigh, and my eyes instantly snap to the connection. "Have you fucked him?"

"What?" I should be shocked by her crass outburst, but instead I find myself laughing and drinking more. "No. That is—no. Well, he made me come, but he hasn't fucked me."

She shrugs. "I mean, I'm just saying, it would be hard not to."

I sigh, resting back into my chair. I know what she means, but I've seen many good-looking men in my days, so I've somehow built a restraint against them. I'm more interested in how someone makes me feel, as opposed to what they look like.

I'm losing that battle with King, though, since he makes me horny most of the time. Or angry. Or a combination of both.

We sit there for a few minutes, and I watch as I think almost everyone is back, except I haven't seen Jack come in yet. My mind is swimming from the alcohol, my head buzzing. I feel good. Warm and good. The song switches to "Company" by Tinashe. My head starts swaying from left to right. Maya starts dancing with a joint hanging out of her mouth, gesturing for me to come to her. I obey, dancing toward her, and laughing. The beat is intoxicating, and I already know I have my next song to dance to. Every thud of the beat, I move my body to it. Maya starts singing and swaying when Rose joins us.

Spinning around, I see King is back in his chair, his legs spread wide and his finger tracing his upper lip. Now I can't move my eyes from him.

He leans up from his sitting position and hooks his hand

in mine, tugging me back onto his lap before he carries on the conversation he was having with Keaton.

Being this close to him is both calming and frightening. It's a concoction that should never be stirred, let alone felt.

His hand comes to my belly, and his fingers spread out, securing me to his lap. Bored and a little drunk, I turn to the side until I'm facing the other person beside him. I was expecting Killian, but instead, I get Delila.

"Delila." I nod my head with a small smile.

Her face remains passive, her smirk wide. "Little Bird, you look rather comfortable on the King's lap."

I snort, and then I want to kick myself because I freaking snorted, and then I'm mad that I thought of the word "freaking." I'm a cheap drunk. "I have an idea," I mumble, watching her. It's true, I do, but I only got this idea about two seconds before I found myself on King's lap.

She waves her hands, bringing her glass to her mouth. "Well, go on."

I wriggle. "Okay."

A hand tightens around my hip, sending a shockwave through my muscles and over my limbs. Just when I'm about to open my mouth, I feel King's lips on my earlobe. "Move like that again and I'll fuck you right here and right now, and Dove, it's nothing that these people haven't witnessed or done before, so don't fucking test me when it comes to your ass on my cock." Before I can answer him, he's already leaning back in his chair and continuing his conversation with Keaton.

My cheeks flush as I look back to Delila, who's laughing behind her drink.

"Interesting," she mutters, her eyes flicking toward King briefly, before going over my shoulder. "Before you tell me what your idea is." She waves her hand ahead of her, and I spin around to see what she's gesturing to.

Six men have entered from—I don't know where—because everything is sort of blurry, but I also notice that there are seven girls with them. They're all blonde and older. They have to be in their thirties. The men are interesting. One has long hair and a long beard, and one has a shaved scalp and a long beard. If I had to say which one is attractive, I'd go with the long hair and long beard. They're all intriguing in different ways, not lucidly good-looking like The Brothers.

"That is The Six and The Seven." Delila's voice carries through as they all pull out seats and get comfortable. "They're one of the acts, but in short, they're the Six Demons of Hell and the girls are the Seven Angels of God."

I pull my eyes away from the new crew and train them on Delila. "How come I haven't seen them before?"

Delila chuckles, lighting her smoke and leaning back in her chair. "Because one, you haven't been here long and two, they don't make themselves known outside of acts. They've been here a long time, and people still travel and pay from all over the place to see their act."

"Which is?" I ask, intrigued. I find myself looking back at the better looking one. "Just out of curiosity."

Delila flicks the end of her smoke out, and I watch as the ash falls to the ground. "Sex, mainly. What happens when demons meet angels?" Delila's eyes flick between King and me. "What happens when innocence collides with corruption?"

I lick my lips. "So they all have sex. In front of everyone?"

Delila must find me amusing when I'm drunk because she's laughing again. "Yes, Little Bird. Each act is different. Think of it as live porn, I guess."

"Isn't that what the last scene is?" I ask before I can stop myself.

Delila's eyes narrow. "No. That is for The Brothers, and it can be whatever they want. Though I should warn you, everyone here has been with everyone here." Her eyes flick to Kingston before she chuckles again. "Well, almost everyone."

My shoulders slouch, my hand running over my belly.

"So anyway, what did you want to talk to me about?" she asks. "Before I leave?"

I think about how I can possibly give her a proposition of me having my own show—with a twist of something else to offer this strange crew—when she just told me that they have a group of good-looking people who give the crowd live freaking devil-angel porn. I just said "freaking" again.

I think I need water.

"I'll talk about it with you tomorrow."

She throws down her smoke and shrugs. "Or maybe I'll be too busy. Goodnight, Little Bird. Don't hurt yourself tonight." She walks away, carrying the echo of her cackles behind her tight ass.

King's fingers dig into my hips before I can so much as think of anything else, and he turns me, so I'm straddling his lap. He looks up at me, his eyes searching mine. "Like what you see?"

"Somewhat." I'm meaning him, but I don't think he's meaning him, and again, I could really do with a glass or ten of water.

His eyes narrow, and I instantly know that I've done something wrong.

He stands off the chair and is flipping me upside down over his shoulder. My hand flies to my mouth to stop a scream from escaping. Now I'm staring right at the destroyed Dolce & Gabbana jeans that are strapped nicely around his tight ass. The little solar lights that lead the way are slowly disappearing with every step he takes.

"Really not necessary, King. I could have walked."

He stops outside our RV and opens the door, carrying me inside and upstairs to his room. I don't get a second to admire the kingdom because he's tossing me onto his bed. My hair is everywhere, and I'm almost certain that the makeup I put on earlier is smudged all over my face, but thanks to liquid courage, I think I look like a ten. Okay, a six at best. *Water.*

"What are we doing, King?" He loosens his belt buckle and undoes his button. His hair is a mess all over his head, and his tanned cheeks are slightly flushed. Probably from carrying me. But then when I look over his muscles, I know that can't be it. He obviously trains as a side hustle. I reach forward before I can stop myself, and my fingertip is connecting with the roses over his hip.

His hand instantly flies out and stops me as his other comes under my chin, tilting my face up to his. "Don't."

"Well, what are we doing?" I ask again, licking my lips.

His eyes drop to my mouth, and he turns around, tugging on his hair. He turns back to face me, his eyes wild. "Fuck if I know, Dove. I don't know anymore. You—you're."

The red streaks around his wrist catch my eye, and I shoot up off the bed, catching his wrist before he can move it. "Blood."

He yanks it out of my hand, and before I can say anything, his mouth is on me, and he's pushing me back onto the bed, his body falling on top of mine. I no longer care what we are doing because whatever this is feels right. At least it does right now.

My legs widen and he sinks into me further, his head moving to the side to gain more access on my mouth. He's heavy, and his breath is brushing over my collarbone. All of these factors contribute to the flight of butterflies that are roaring in my belly. I think of that Halsey song, where she's saying that sometimes the warning signs feel like butterflies, but those thoughts evaporate when he grinds against me. I'm sticky from the Texas heat and from running through the forest, but on top of that, we have the alcohol and the sexual tension that has been about to snap for far too long.

My hips raise up to meet his, rubbing against his swollen crotch.

He groans, and the deep sound vibrates over my mouth, sending shockwaves all the way down to my core. Reaching for the band of his jeans, I yank them down until I can run my nails over his ass cheeks. He bites down on my lip, so hard that I can taste the familiar tang of blood taint my mouth. "You wanna do this?" he asks, though his hands are gripping for my tank. "Speak now or forever hold your fucking peace, Little Bird."

I do what any girl would do with Kingston Axton half naked on top of them, wanting to eat you alive.

I hold my fucking peace.

He tears off my tank top with his bare hands and cups one of my breasts in his hand. His mouth lowers, and he sucks my nipple into his mouth. Warmth satiates throughout my body, tingles snarling all over my flesh.

I moan, pushing my chest into him, wanting more. Needing more. Something more. I reach down and unbutton my shorts, yanking them off and kicking them off the bed.

King stops, his breathing heavy, and his chest heaving. He slowly crawls off the bed, his eyes never moving from my body until he's standing back where he started.

He pulls his bottom lip into his mouth as his hand dips beneath his jeans. Now the bulge that was there has doubled as he slowly moves up and down.

"Touch yourself."

"What?" I whisper out, not wanting to touch myself. "Why, when you could do it?"

His jaw clenches. "Because I can't have you, so I want to watch *you* have you." He pulls his jeans down, and his cock springs free. My mouth waters at the sight. Tight skin around a thick shaft. There's a piercing on the tip of his crown that goes from the top to the bottom. *How did I miss that before?*

"God." My back arches off the bed like a hungry fucking lunatic.

"Touch yourself, Dovey. Show me what you do when you're all alone."

I chew on my bottom lip, and my eyes widen as I watch him slowly pump himself. The sight is traumatic. It's like everything you've ever wanted, but being told you can't have it.

Instead of doing what I usually do, ask too many questions, I go with it. I slide my palm over my nipples before slowly dragging them down my tight stomach. Everything is slick from both of our bodily fluids, so my hands slip and slide all over the place. When I find a spot below my belly button that's a little more wet than others, I lean up on one elbow and see the smudge of blood.

His eyes turn to fire as they catch mine, and he watches with aching pain as I swipe my thumb through it and bring it to my mouth, sucking the blood off my thumb and making an extra effort to roll my lips over with the movement. It isn't exactly hard, since my lips are one of the larger assets on my body.

He turns feral, and a deep growl vibrates through him. The

atmosphere thickens around us, and I know I've hit something dark within him. Something untamed and violent. I don't care. I want it. *I want all of him.* I run my hand back down my body until I'm cupping myself. I slowly sink my index finger inside of me, turning slightly, so he has the best view. Using my thumb, I rub my clit in circles and watch as he squeezes the tip of his dick.

"King," I whisper, wanting him inside me. "I need you."

"Fuck." He exhales, stopping his movements. He leans forward and grabs my hand, bringing my fingers to his mouth.

He sucks me off my fingers. "Finish yourself off." Then he pulls up his jeans and leaves me lying there, on his damn bed, unsatisfied and frustrated. He stops by his door, turning over his shoulder. "Stay the fuck there tonight." The door slams in his retreat, and I take this time to examine his room. I'm irritated, so my eyes flash around the room quickly, taking everything in. Obscure walls, one large window, a *King*-sized bed, a couple dressers, and a large TV.

That's it. The décor is simple but masculine. His heady scent of leather, spice, and honey resonates through his black cotton sheets.

I stroll to the other side of the room, snatching up the first shirt I see on the ground and pulling it over my head. I'm wondering whether I should stay here or go back to my room. Squeezing the doorframe, my frustration gets the better of me, and I back up, hitting his light switch off and sneaking back down to my little area. I notice that no one is in the RV, but I don't care to think more of it. Right now, I just want to sleep. I can smell King all around me as I drop face-first onto my bed, and before I can register that I'm about to sleep in his shirt, my eyes are drifting closed, slipping into a deep sleep.

Twenty-Three

Dove

The next morning, I wake feeling a lot better than I deserve. Yawning, I spread my arms wide, my agitation only growing between my legs. I remember everything from last night, which doesn't help. I'd rather I not remember him turning me down mid—whatever that was—with me spread eagle on his bed, playing with myself.

I fumble into the kitchen, finding Killian already sipping coffee with his hair ragged everywhere.

"Have a good night?" I tease, scrubbing my eyes.

"Not as good as yours apparently." He grins from behind his mug, a smug smile on his face.

"Could have ended better," I mumble, pouring the black java

into my coffee mug, before sliding into one of the kitchen chairs. I blow into the hot liquid, enjoying the warmth that the steam provides, falling on the tip of my nose.

"You ready for tonight?" Keaton comes down next, falling beside me.

"Yes and no," I answer honestly, taking my first sip and instantly feeling my muscles relax.

"You'll be fine," Keaton assures me warmly, squeezing my shoulder blades before disappearing out the front door.

"It's so fucked up to see him be an actual human to someone who is not himself or us."

"What do you mean?" I spin around to face Killian.

"I mean, he's...Keaton." Killian's eyes then drop to my shirt, and his eyes shoot up in surprise before being replaced by his menacing smirk. "You two are fucking weird."

I look down at my shirt to see I'm wearing King's from last night. It has a few tears in random places, but the material feels quality. It's obvious that it has been destroyed for vanity and from age.

I groan, standing from my chair and emptying my mug into the sink. "Don't get me started, please."

Killian's smug smirk falls when his eyes go over my shoulder. His jaw sets and his grip tightens around his mug. I start to turn around to see what warranted his change of mood, but his hand comes out to stop me. I shove him away, continuing to turn, when my eyes connect with Val's smug face walking down the stairs.

"Really." I shake my head, fighting the urge to fly across the room and tear her eyeballs out of their sockets.

She shrugs. "I did try to warn you, Little Bird. You're a seat warmer, and I'm the trophy." She continues out the door, slamming it in her retreat.

"I hate her," I answer out loud.

Killian's arm wraps around my torso, pulling me into his warm chest. His lips caress the back of my earlobe as my eyes remain upstairs. The very same fucking bed I was just in. Where he turned me down and simply replaced me with Val within the same fucking night. "Don't take it to heart, Little Bird. Sex is a weapon in this world, and we have no problem loading it up to utilize it."

I crane my neck to give him more access. I feel reckless and hurt. "He left me."

"Mmmm," Killian murmurs against the soft spot between my shoulder and my neck.

"Naked."

He freezes.

"With my finger inside myself."

Killian's fingers spread out over my belly and slowly lower. My eyes close as I inhale the possibility of doing this. I'm worked up and under fucked thanks to Kingston. But apparently, Val was good enough for his royal penis.

Killian's hand slips lower, pressing against my pelvic bone. "Wanna show me what you were doing? I promise I will fuck you as hard as he hates you."

A door slams from upstairs, and I jump out of Killian's grip. Then I'm annoyed that I jumped out of his grasp. My cheeks flush in embarrassment, and I quickly dash back into my room to change. I need to exert this energy somehow, and if I can't fuck it out of my system, I'll have to dance it out.

I change into some appropriate clothes—yoga pants and a sports bra—and make my way to the tent, swearing under my breath.

I need sex. I've never needed sex so bad in my life, although, getting it before was never hard. I had my regular guys. By guys I mean two—one was Richard (yes, the very same) and the other was Ollie. Ollie was complicated and always wanted more than I could emotionally give, so he wasn't my preference. Richard was. Somehow, we managed to keep our lives balanced and not let our sexual activities interfere with our work or home life. Maybe that was because he and I were rubbing on each other since before he took ownership or maybe it's because Rich and I were just compatible in bed. By compatible I mean boring, but enough to scratch the itch. It's like scratching your itch while wearing acrylic nails. It grazes it, but nothing gives you the full pleasure like using your bare, raw nails.

"Morning, Little Bird. How was your night?" Delila asks, falling into step beside me as we make our way through the entrance of the tent.

I ignore her and ask a question I've always wanted to know. "Why don't you guys offer, like, carnival rides?"

Delila answers quickly. "Quite simple, really. What do carnival rides attract?"

Realization crashes into me, and for a second, I feel miniscule.

Idiot.

"Right."

I take a seat on the center stage and begin warming up my body.

"What did you want to ask me last night?"

"Would you rather me ask you or show you?"

Delila grins, lighting the unlit cigarette that sits in her mouth. "I'm a showgirl, Dovey. Thought you'd know that by now."

I did. I do. But I don't know how I'm going to show her

without having all of my plan with me. I've come to the conclusion that I enjoy being on the road with Midnight Mayhem, as much as I'm still confused with how they go about recruiting their showrunners. I didn't have a fabulous life before. In fact, one thing has stopped since I've been here, and that's The Shadow. He hasn't lurked in the club or been waiting for me in the parking lot. He hasn't shown up in my dreams when I close my eyes at night, and he hasn't whispered sweet nothings into my ear when I've been sitting in silence.

It's been quiet. Too quiet.

After stretching, I make my way behind the main curtain and stand still at the congestion of all the props there. The triple ring of death, the cage, the bikes, bars, and ramps. There are copious amounts of prop equipment and a whole lot of anxious workers running around like bumble bees. I would hate to be behind here during a show. It must be hectic.

"Looks like you survived last night, D?" Maya comes up beside me wearing oversized sunglasses, an Adidas hat, jumpsuit pants pushed up her legs, and a Fluro pink loose shirt that looks one size too large. She's got a coffee in one hand and a joint in the other.

"Good. You?" I ask, eyeing her up and down.

"Don't run your judgy eyes up and down me, little miss thang. I'm doing what I do." She spins around and disappears through the curtain. Seeing Maya only reminds me that I still need to see King. After last night and seeing Val leave his room this morning, and me deciding that I quite like being here, only solidifies the fact that I need Delila to agree to what I'm going to propose to her. She's not all that disagreeable, and she can be approachable, but I've learned in the very short space that I've been here that that is very selective with Delila. One minute she's sunshine and then next she's the storm.

There's no telling.

Movement catches the corner of my eye, and before I can stop my wandering eyes, I'm looking right at King. My heart jumps to life in my chest and almost rears up my throat when I find him looking right at me. He's walking closer and closer, coming closer and closer, and just when I think he's about to talk to me, I figure out his eyes are actually over my shoulder, and he walks straight past me, as if I'm not there.

As if I don't exist.

I used to think that having Kingston Axton's attention was the worst feeling in the world, but I was wrong. Not having his attention is. Especially because now, he's seen me naked.

I squeeze my eyes shut and mentally count to five.

One.

Two.

Three.

Four.

Five.

Then I spin back around and enter through the way I came, knowing full well that I need to do what I'm here to do.

Work.

I had talked myself up so hard during those five seconds. Which is ironic because five seconds was exactly how long it took for that hype to come crashing down.

Which was exactly when I was walking toward the stage and dipping behind one of the chairs.

"Dove?" Keaton calls out when he enters. "We're going to practice on the Triple Wheel of Death. You good with that?"

I gulp. "Okay." I hate that one. I wish we could practice on something else, but I quickly realize that it actually doesn't matter, because King wants me dead.

"Is your act planned out, Dove?" Delila asks, staring at me from down the aisle.

I nod. "Yes. I think. As much as it will be. I'll need a few things, though."

Delila curls her finger, so I head to her and rattle off everything I'll need. Nothing major. A couple wine bottles, a waiter's plate. You know, because I have no idea how I'm going to sell this idea that I not only want my own show, but I want to recruit a few people to join me.

"Dove!" King barks from behind me, just as I hear the loud rumble of his bike vibrate around the large area.

I spin around, knowing how awkward and annoying this is going to be.

"I'll get your things ready, Little Bird!" Delila yells over the bikes. Her eyes flick between King and me. "Good luck."

Stepping into the wheel, I fling myself up on the swing, and King drives the bike in next. He starts rocking it back and forth. He stops rocking once we're partially in the air with Killian starting his bike down below. They're waiting for Maya, so there are a few seconds when it's just him, me, and his bike, and the seconds that seem to freeze time when your feet aren't placed securely on the literal ground.

I want to yell at him.

I want to ask what the fuck Val was doing in his room.

I want to ask what he meant last night when he said that he couldn't have me.

I want to know what he meant when he said I took something from him.

I want to know all of these things, but instead, my mouth is glued shut, and the words are latched around my throat, squeezing tightly with no desire to move.

He starts rocking again, and we're up, doing what I remembered. I keep my eyes locked on the ace of spades again. I take myself out of the wheel while keeping myself aware of what's happening around me. Once that's done and we swing back down, I quickly climb out of the wheel and wait for what to do next. When I'm out, I'm watching as Keaton continues doing flips on the outside of the wheels and the metal planks that connect them as they continue to spin.

Wow.

Slowly, they all get off the Triple Wheel of Death and line their bikes up on the other side of the tent, which I have only just realized, must be five or six times the size of the average circus tent. The roof is pulled up in four different spikes, reaching for the midnight sky every night and the neon lights that dangle from each seam, flashing a glowing white and lilac.

"I don't think you need to practice anything else," Delila assures. "The knife throwing you have, and you're well acquainted with The Brothers' telekinetic and illusionist mind tricks."

"Killian. I'm acquainted with Killian because he's the only one who does it, right?" I want clarification.

Delila pauses, looking between me and Keaton, who is now standing beside me. "Tell me she's kidding. She's kidding, right?"

Keaton smirks. "She's kidding."

Delila rushes off to do whatever it is that Delila does, and I spin around to face Keaton. "Wait, so you're all telekinetic? I thought that was a myth?"

Keaton's eyes narrow, his head tilting. "The thing about myths, Little Bird, is that they're usually true, but humans like to blanket it with the word 'myth' in hopes that people don't find out the truth." He disappears, and I'm left standing near the center stage, thinking over what I've just found out. Delila assumed that I would be acquainted with The Brothers' skills, but I thought Killian was the only one who had that ability.

"She can't be here right now, Amber. Not right now." My father's voice drifted down our empty corridor and slipped beneath my bedroom door.

"What do you mean?" My mom's voice was hushed, but panicked.

"This is what we have to do for her. It's what's right for her to save what little she has left."

My mom was silent. That said something when Mom was silent because she always had something to say.

"What did I do wrong?"

My father was the one who was silent now, before growling softly, "Everything."

I shake my head out of the memory fuzz that I just dived into, confused.

"You okay?" Killian asks, his eyes searching mine. I'm still standing in the center stage, my eyes glassing over in unshed tears. I wish I could roll around in a memory and grasp onto everything I don't have anymore, bringing it back to the present.

"Yeah," I smile. "Fine."

"You sure?" he repeats, and I'm not sure if he wants me to say yes or no.

"I'm sure. Just a memory. Not sure what triggered it."

Killian stands straight, his tongue dragging over his lower lip. "Maybe a scent? I've heard that certain smells can trigger even the most buried secrets inside of your brain."

"Hmmm." I offer a somber smile. "Maybe."

I'm back in my black leather shorts and a black crop top. I already know that this is what I wear during the bike scene and even the knife throwing scene, but I haven't actually successfully made it through an entire show without something happening.

I hope to change that tonight. Right now, with our first Texas show.

The act goes like clockwork, the bikes start, and I step into the Triple Wheel of Death. It swings, the crowd cheers, and then the scene is over. I duck behind the curtain, and we wait for the Six Demons of Hell and the Seven Angels of God to do their first skit, before we head out again for the knife scene.

King seems more on edge. The knife actually grazes my outer thigh this time. I flinch, my eyes shooting straight to him. Was it intentional, or was it an accident? That was my main question. Only I know that King isn't the type to make that kind of mistake, so my question was already answered.

After the knife show, Midnight did their part. Val and Rose on the aerial, and then Maya singing while swinging on a large swing. It's a creepy song. Hauntingly familiar lyrics but with a warped, distorted tune. She must sing covers of songs but turn them into some weird Tim Burton-style nightmare.

Now it's my turn, and I'm not sure if I'm ready.

I run my palms down my thighs as I hear Delila introduce me outside.

"Dove?" a young guy says, a wine bottle in one hand and a waiter's tray in the other. "Would you like me to take these out?"

I nod, again running my sweaty palms down my fishnet tights. I decided to leave the pole out, knowing I could do more damage without it, and I need to drive my intention home to Delila.

"What are you doing out there?" Kyrin asks from behind me, his eyes going up and down my body.

"Dancing," I answer, short and clipped. I can't have him throwing my vibe off.

"Careful, Little Bird. *He's always watching.*"

He shoves me through the curtain before I can ask who the hell he's talking about, and the spotlight is on me. It's dim, burying my body in the shadows. "Carnival" starts playing, and I automatically slip into position. I slide up and down and allow my body to take over the lyrics and beat of the song before moving to the front seats in the VIP section. I mean, these people pay from $1400 onward for a VIP ticket. The least I could do is give them a show, right?

The man whose lap I find is decent. He's already semi drunk as I grind into him to the music, paying special attention to him before moving to his wife. Her frown flips upside down when she sees me going for her as well.

I wink at her before dancing back to the stage, picking up the waiter's plate and dancing onto my ass before spreading my legs wide and using the shield to cover my middle. The crowd roars over the music, hyping me up, and I find my next victim, taking the bottle of wine with me. I dance around them both, pouring wine into their glasses, before taking a sip of my own, swiping the residue off my mouth. It was over too fast because after my second victim, the song finishes, and I'm being led away with the curtains closing as everyone scrambles to get ready for the next act.

"What the fuck was that?" King is seething, waiting for me on the other side of the curtain.

"What?" I ask, panting. "It was what I want to do."

King shakes his head. "Nah. You don't need your own fucking show."

"Excuse me?" My head tilts back. "How about you go tell Val what she can and can't do and leave me the hell alone?" I go to shove him to the side, when he steps forward, and I'm well aware of all the whispers that are going on around us. "Dove, you're not doing that fuckin' act again. Period."

"But she is," Delila says from behind me, her hand coming to my arm. "And better yet," her eyes come to mine, "I'm going to allow her to recruit extra dancers."

My face breaks out into a cheesy smile. "Seriously?"

She rolls her eyes. "Don't act like that isn't what you wanted to ask me, Little Bird. You're too transparent."

"Delila," King growls. "Do I need to remind you of your place?"

"Well, no, but you have to remember that you didn't want Dove in your act, King. So, it's settled. After the meeting you all have with Killian's father in New Orleans, you will go through a recruitment process." Her eyes cut back to mine. "New Orleans is where we have a four-week break. After those four weeks, I expect you to have your team of—" She waits for me to answer.

"Three. I want two girls and one guy."

"Team of three to be in line, but there's a catch, Little Bird." Delila runs her bright red nails down my bra. "You have to follow the recruitment process."

My mouth opens, and then closes, before opening again. "Which is exactly how I was recruited?" I confirm with myself.

Delila pats my shoulder. "Precisely." Before I can get her to elaborate, she's being pulled away by Val, who is having a mid-show meltdown.

"This isn't over." King glares at me before disappearing through the curtain. I don't know what his problem is. Delila is right. He never wanted me in the first place.

Killian's arm hooks around my torso from behind, pulling me into his chest. "Have you come yet?" he whispers from behind me.

"Killian, put her down," Keaton grumbles, dropping down onto the ground to remove his biker boots.

"Oh, you don't know?" Killian's looking at Keaton now.

"Know what?" Keaton tosses the boots across the ground before getting back to his feet and undressing.

Killian chuckles, shaking his head. "Oh, this is great." He looks back to me. "Go get ready for the final act, Little Bird." He brushes up closer to me, running his hand down my ass. "And wear something that shows your tits."

I shove him away playfully, but his face doesn't wave. "I'm not kidding. You owe me after this, though." He winks before walking off.

Owing Killian isn't something I want to do.

Dressed in black straps that crisscross by covering my nipples—and only my nipples—and my private parts, I'm bound with my arms tied above my head and my ankles tied together on the ground. Darkness cloaks around me like a safety barrier, the knot in the bandana that's tied around my eyes secured around my head. Earbuds are in my ears, because Killian said he doesn't want me to hear anything. I don't know who has control over the music, but I want to thank them for putting on something good enough to distract me.

It switches to "You Can Cry" by Marshmello just as I feel a soft breeze of wind brush over my bare stomach. My eyes roll to the back of my head as the breeze turns more forceful. I don't know what it is, but I want it harder and lower. Harder. My back

arches off whatever it is that I'm strapped to as the feeling intensifies. Like ice being grazed over my hot flesh. My lips part, and
my hips roll slightly. Blood red strobe lights flash inside my head,
as if I'm in the middle of a club dance floor. The song remixes
into "Play" by Alan Walker. My mind is an empty vortex, with
nothing but the flashing of the red light and the deep pounding
from the addictive base line of the song. The feeling is in tune
to the song, and then from the far distance in the red, I see a
shadow. He's wearing a hoodie. The song slows for a second. He
gets closer and closer, the song coming back in full force as the
light flickers faster and faster and the feeling is coming harder
and harder—until everything stops. Dead silence. Slowly, the red
light comes alive again, only slower, and standing right in front
of me is the man in the hoodie with half of his face showing. I
can see by the profile that it's King. The sharp edges of his jaw
and his sunken cheekbones. *What.* The feeling hits me right in
my core, just as his mouth slowly kicks up in a wicked smirk.

He comes closer, and my body is pulsing, reacting to whatever is going on outside without seeing it. I reach up, curving the
hoodie around my fingers, and flicking it off his face.

He hisses, baring his teeth like a wild animal. His eyes are
feral, but his hand comes between my thighs. "Mine," he growls,
his teeth scraping against my collarbone. The song is still thud-
ding in the background as his knee separates my legs and his lips
are on mine. My chest is humming, everything throbbing with
need. It's a cruel kind of torture. My eyes open, seeking him out,
but the room is empty again with nothing but the red light.

The ties around my wrists are loosened, and I reach up, ripping the earbuds out of my ears. The curtains are already closed,
and I don't care enough to figure out what is going on around
me because tears are clouding my vision. I push away from all

of them and run toward our RV, bypassing all of the people who are spilling out from the show.

Tearing open the door, I head straight for my room and drop down onto my bed. My head pounds from whatever it was that just happened.

"Little Bird," Killian says from the threshold of my room minutes later. Did he chase me? Why couldn't it be King who chases me? Why is it always Killian?

"Go away, Killian. What the hell was that?"

He pauses, searching my eyes. "There's a lot you don't know about me. About us. But whatever you think of during an episode is on you—not me. I don't force you to see what you see. I just shuffle things to the surface."

I flop onto my back, counting the dots on the roof above. "Why am I here?"

There's shuffling that moves around the room, and when I turn my head to the side to see why he hasn't answered me, my eyes connect to King's.

"What'd you see?" he whispers, his eyes falling down my body.

"I don't want to talk about it." I turn onto my side, ignoring him.

My bed dips, and I have to fight the urge to see what he's doing.

"Dove."

"Go away, King."

"I'm not fuckin' going anywhere!" His tone is like acid, threatening to spill over the edges and burn everyone in its path. He's angry, obviously, only I'm not sure why.

I spin around, annoyed with him being back in my space after what he did last night. And what I imagined tonight. I refuse to believe Killian about him not having anything to do with what I saw. It was too vivid. Too familiar. Too—*King*. "Why are you so confusing? Why didn't you just kill me in that fucking cell instead of dragging me through all of this?"

His eyes narrow. "Oh, you don't think I wanted to?"

That wasn't the answer I was hoping for, and my flinch was a dead giveaway for that. "What do you mean?"

His eyes search mine, and for a second, nothing else exists outside of us. Everything melts away into a smudged painting, a swirl of irrelevant colors surrounding us. "You don't think I wanted to kill you?"

"You're not making sense." I exhale, tired. Drained from the push and pull that's been going on between us both. Tired from him drawing the life directly from my soul.

I turn to face the wall, when his voice interrupts me. "Dove."

"What, King?" I ask, flipping to face him. "I'm trying to understand why people keep telling me that you're a certain way around me, but when you're around me, you're confusing, moody, and a pain in my ass."

His eyebrows lift slightly, and then slowly, I watch as the corner of his mouth slips into a smirk.

"Did you just smile?"

His face falls. "No."

I sigh—*loudly*—and turn onto my back. "I'm tired of fighting."

"Then tell me your name isn't Dove Hendry."

"Why would I do that?"

"So I can stop fighting the feeling of wanting to bury my cock so deep inside your pussy, you'll be screaming my name into the night. Tell me your name isn't Dove Hendry."

I lick my lips, my eyes searching his. "Why does it matter if I am Dove? We don't know each other."

He chuckles, shaking his head. There's something disconcertingly dark about two people who have volatile chemistry, sitting in a dark room.

"God, King!" My tone levels louder. "What the fuck is going on?"

In a flash, I'm being pressed into the mattress, and his body is on top of mine. Everything south is pulsing with need. I slowly spread my legs wide, allowing him to slip between.

"If I told you, you wouldn't believe me." His voice is rough, but his lips are soft, plush against mine. I hold my breath, overwhelmed with his proximity, but addicted to his touch. I like him like this. I need him like this. His danger has always drawn me in. There's power that comes with being touched and caressed by a dangerous man.

"Try me," I finally whisper, leaning up and pressing a kiss to his mouth.

He groans, before dropping down, his lips crashing on mine. I hook my arm around his neck, opening my mouth wider. Needing to be closer to him, wanting his kiss.

He tears off my shirt and stands back, kicking off his shoes. "If you don't want this, you have three seconds to tell me because I'm about to give even less of a fuck."

Slowly, I bring my hand to my jeans button and flick it off.

His chuckle vibrates through the silent bedroom, hitting all the corners of my soul on its way out. Before he can answer, or I can say anything, his hands are latched around my ankles, and he's dragging me down the bed. He tears off my shorts while I remove my bra, tossing them to the side.

I hold my breath, waiting for whatever he's going to do, but well aware that he could quite possibly walk away from me like he did last time and end up screwing Val.

His finger glides down my clit. "How many men have you fucked?"

"What?" I ask, panting. "Why would you ask that right now?"

"I need to know how many you've fucked." His fingertip meets my entrance. He turns it softly, hitting every nerve.

"I don't know."

"That many?" he scolds.

"Five?"

"Five, huh." He slaps my pussy—the motherfucker spanked my pussy—before he shoves his finger inside of me. I cry out, my back lifting off the bed. "Five men?" He's almost whispering it to himself. "Hope they fucked you rough." His finger massages me inside while his thumb presses against my clit. My stomach clenches, and my insides spin around and around, constantly trying to catch the high my orgasm threatens to give me. His mouth covers my clit, and his slick tongue slides over me, circling and pressing. I cry out as my orgasm rolls through me, wave after wave, slowly getting smaller and smaller.

He crawls up my body, grabs me by the waist and lifts me half in the air, his cock pushing inside of me. I clench around him like a vise, not willing to let him go.

"Fuck," he groans, dropping my hips back down onto the bed and covering my body with his. "So fucking tight, and so *fucking mine.*" He caresses my throat softly as he extracts and enters. Slowly pumping inside, stretching me with every thrust. I feel the coolness of his silver piercing scrape against my wall as I contract around him. I cry out again, my legs wrapping around his waist.

He chuckles, his grip tightening around my throat, as he picks up his pace. "So fucking wet for me."

My mouth opens, but he's thrashing into me so hard that my words jerk and swallow.

His fingers dig into my thigh as his other hand comes to my wrists and pins them above my head. I cry out in pain. It's too much. The overwhelming sensations are drowning me, not one part of my body numb.

"Who—" he growls, biting the flesh on my neck hard and pulling it between his teeth, "—owns you." He dives inside of me again, slowing his thrust. The rhythm is powerful. With ever thrust of his hips, he fills me to the brink, until our bodies are slapping together in sweat.

I scream—*fucking scream*—as another orgasm slashes me open and has me bleeding out my cries in raw hunger. I throb around him, and he chuckles.

"King," I plead, wrapping my arm around the back of his neck.

"That's right, baby." He leans up, flipping me onto my stomach. He slaps my ass cheek, the heavy sting biting my flesh. I yelp as he grips onto my hips and pulls me up on all fours. Wrapping my hair around his wrist, he yanks my head back, his lips on my ear. He enters me again from behind, his thick length sliding inside of me. I wince at the pain, but when he hisses and his hand comes to my throat, I know I want to go again, even if it might kill me. "That's exactly who the fuck owns you." Tugging on my hair, he yanks my head back with one hand and locks onto the back of my neck with the other as he slams into me relentlessly. Over and over again. I feel my stomach curl, my pussy throb, and my clit swell, just as I release, another scream splitting through the walls.

He pulls out, and I feel hot liquid shoot onto my back. I can barely keep my eyes open as I drop back down onto my belly, my eyes drifting closed. I don't even have enough energy to care about the cum dripping down my back.

I feel the bed lift from his weight. "King?" I whisper, so softly and using what little energy I have left. "Will you tell me why you're so confusing?"

He chuckles softly. "One day."

Twenty-four

Dove

I'remember my obsession with birds. My mom said I wanted to own a big bird enclosure and keep as many as I could. Of course, that never happened, but I remember the feeling I had. *The want.* The *obsession* that overrode my common sense.

That same feeling has somewhat come back.

I fucked King last night.

I groan, rolling onto my side, while flinching from the bruises over my hips and collarbone.

Deep chuckling reverberates from the entryway, and I snap up to see Killian standing there with a cheesy grin on his face, spooning granola into his smug mouth.

"What?" I swing my legs over the bed, hiding my flinch. I look around the room and wince at the mess. It looks like a stampede of angry animals had run through it. Clothes are everywhere, and the small dresser has been moved to the middle of the room, almost tipping over. *He picked me up and slammed me against the dresser, placing me on top and sinking back inside of me...*

"Well, I can't say I'm surprised. I mean, that was the longest foreplay in history." Killian nods his head. "Get changed. We're going to crash a party."

"A party?"

Killian nods.

"In Texas?"

He nods again, before realizing how lost I am. "You think we don't know people after visiting the same places almost every couple years?"

I think over what he's saying. Obviously. "But I don't really want to go to a house party."

Killian laughs. "Well, you have no choice."

He leaves, and I'm left sitting on my bed, with aching muscles and a confused brain. Why would we be attending a party in Texas? For some reason, I don't think these boys make friends with just anybody.

Once I've thrown on a discarded shirt, I stumble outside of my room and head straight for the coffee pot, pouring the black java into my mug.

"You're up early," Kyrin purrs from behind me, shocking me into turning around.

"I'm not—*no.*" Keaton shakes his head while walking down the stairs. "I didn't want to hear what I heard last night." Keaton, this scary, heavily tattooed and muscled man, looks like he has seen a ghost.

"Oh, soooo, you guys are allowed to, but I'm not?" I ask, one eyebrow quirked.

"First of all, we don't bring girls back here—*period*," Keaton clarifies. "Second of all, we're not fucking each other either."

"I mean, not from a lack of me trying." Kyrin grins at Keaton.

Keaton flips him off and drops down onto the chair beside me.

"Ah." I scoff. "Ya do. It was just a few nights ago I witnessed it myself." Before I can stop myself, the words are spilling out of my mouth.

"What are you talking about?" Keaton answers, shaking his protein shake. "We don't bring girls here. It's against our house rules."

"She's talking about Val," King chimes in, waltzing into the kitchen with no shirt on and with freshly fucked hair. He cuts me with a stare that pretty much translates into *who the fuck are you?* Which, again, confuses me. Or maybe he's mad at me for bringing up Val.

"You brought Val into your bed? I thought you didn't hit that anymore." Keaton glares at King as Killian finally enters.

King stares at me. When I say stare, I mean, he's looking directly into my soul. It's as though he's reaching through my body and grabbing it by his bare hands. Like he damn well owns it. "And I don't."

His words should relax me, but the intensity of his eyes and the tone of his voice flip my belly upside down.

I switch gears, wanting to change the subject, and take some heat off myself. "So, this party?"

Killian smirks, leaning back in his chair. His dark hair

dances in the soft wind that blows through the RV as someone opens the main door. "Well, it's a little more than a party."

"Dude, I'm going to need all of you to stop talking until at least midday." Maya walks in, massaging her temples while wearing oversized glasses and her hair in a mane all over her face. "Tell me that I'm not the only one who drank until the early hours of the morning."

Silence falls around us when I push back from my chair. "What time are we leaving?" I ask no one in particular.

Maya interrupts me, "Where are we going?"

"Nowhere," Killian cuts her off.

Her eyes connect up at his from behind her glasses, and I watch as his hand curls around her chin, his thumb caressing it. "We're just taking Dove for a ride."

"That's all you needed to say, Kill. You don't need to be all *nowhere*." I offer her a polite smile before I make my way into my room, pulling open my closet. I have no idea what I should wear, so I settle on something I would wear if I was at home. My comfort clothing. The clothes I'd like to die in. *Wait. I shouldn't say that where these boys are concerned.* High-waisted ripped jean shorts and a loose white Givenchy tee. I tie it in a knot in the middle, so it rides above my lower belly. Showing enough, but not too much. Like a sliver of skin. Squeezing on my maroon Chucks, I run my brush through my long waves and powder up my face a bit before picking up my sunglasses and wallet and making my way out to the kitchen to wait on the boys. I haven't had to use the card King gave me yet—mainly because I haven't been anywhere—but it's good to know that if I need to, I have money there that I've somewhat worked for. I downloaded the app yesterday, too, so it's easy enough for me to access when needed.

King is still on the table eating when I reappear. "You're not changed?" I ask, cocking my head.

He licks his lip, shaking his head. "Nope. You goin' like that?" I look down at what I'm wearing, feeling thrown off.

My eyes connect back to his. "Yeah, why?"

He shrugs. "No reason." Standing from his chair, I watch as he empties the rest of his food into the trash and then rinses his plate. "If I was a good man, Dove, I'd warn you about today." His tone is smooth, like ice, right before it cracks and creates an avalanche.

"And are you?" I ponder aloud, my eyes never shifting from him. His back muscles tense, and I have to fight the urge to go toward him and run my fingertips over every edge. Every dip and curve that's indented into his skin. Vivid images flash through my head of what happened last night. My mouth waters with what I still want to do to him... *My tongue tracing his V, down, sucking on his skin all the way until I lick the edges of his pierced cock.*

My thighs clench. I'm definitely needing to do that...

"Little Bird," King interrupts my happy daydream. I find him staring directly at me now, leaning against the counter. "If you keep looking at me like that, we will both end up dead."

I chuckle, the depth of his words not yet sunken in. "I wasn't."

His perfect eyebrows shoot up.

"Fine, maybe I was." I'm not going to pretend that I don't find him attractive or that I don't feel something for him. I wouldn't have slept with him last night had I not. I'm about as open about my feelings as my legs were last night.

He pushes off the counter, and every step he takes closer to me, he steals one hundred breaths. "Don't."

"Don't what?" I answer, searching his eyes. I see the fire in his. The way they hood with every stride.

I go to step back when one of his arms reaches out and wraps around my back, pulling me into his chest. His chest that I'm getting well acquainted with. "We can't do that again."

"What?" I ask, swimming in the pool of his eyes, but well aware that an anchor is strapped around my ankles, and if I don't swim hard enough, I'll sink to the bottom of the ocean.

"We. Can't. Do. That. Again."

His words power through me like a frenzied preacher at Sunday service. I rear my head back, yearning for some distance. "Okay, but why?"

He releases me, just as someone patters down the stairs. I don't look at who it is. I don't care. I want to know why we can't do that again. There's obviously a reason. If there wasn't, King isn't the type of man to tiptoe around anyone's feelings. He'd flat out say he didn't want me.

"King, what the fuck, man? Why are you not ready?" Killian scolds him.

King releases me and steps back, before I get an answer, and slowly disappears up the small stairwell.

"Little Bird," Killian interferes, and I snap my attention to him. "It's for the best. Trust me."

I scoff. "I remember one day not long ago, you told me not to trust you."

Killian's carefree smile falls. "I know, but on this, you can."

The drive to the "party" is long. All of us are piled into a black souped-up Rolls Royce SUV. Wheels, windows, even the grill at the front is black. King is driving, I'm in the passenger seat—not sure why—and Kyrin, Kill, and Keaton are in the back. I've tried asking about this party, but none of them have much to say about it. We drive for another fifteen minutes, swerving between cars on the highway and drifting against the ruthless humidity of the South. The sun has set, leaving a burnt orange residue smudged through the sky. We finally pull into a small, gated community. The fence line is hardwired, with the peaks of each curve reaching for the sky. King turns the music down and lowers his window. He leans over, and I watch as he reaches for a small pin box and punches in a long sequence of numbers.

Weird, I think to myself, but otherwise, ignore it. He shifts back into his seat just as the wired gates squeak as they open, allowing us to enter.

"What is this place?" I ask. An air of familiarity brushes over my fickle flesh, but before I grasp onto it, maybe squeeze it a little to see if any recognition drips out, it's gone.

"Just stay close to us," King announces, his eyes flying to the rearview mirror.

"What? Why? I thought this was a party?" I watch as we drive down a dark street, with homes as large as the White House. Large, white old plantation homes with manicured lawns pass one by one. Each house has a streetlight hanging near the front, claws of metal grasping onto the bulbs. They look medieval, wrong, in this type of exclusive setting.

King drives us up a driveaway at the very end of the street. It's long, and has manicured hedges that line it all the way to the front of the house where a fountain is awaiting the center of it. Four monstrous-sized pillars hold up the structure of the home at the front, all glistening white with clean windowsills and a heavy front entrance door that makes you want to run away, rather than knock on it.

"Dove," King interferes my gawking.

"Yeah?" I look right at him, searching his eyes.

"You don't take anything from anyone that is not us four. Do you understand?" I do, yet I don't. But I understand. I mean, it's a party.

"I know not to take drinks from strangers, King."

"That's not my point, Dove," he throws my tone back in my face. "It's not your drink you should be worried about." Then his eyes savagely drop down my body, landing straight between my thighs.

"Okay!" I snap. "I get your point." I sigh, reaching for my door handle as the rest of them start to climb out. The warm air whisks through my red strands, flicking them all over my face.

"Come on," Killian murmurs, nudging his head.

I start following behind him, searching around the house for other clues on what this party could be about when I realize that Kill, Keaton, and Kyrin are all walking in front of me and King is walking directly behind me. I feel like a caged wild creature, either desperate to break free or terrified to be unleashed. Either way, some weird, twisted part of me knew that even though these men have done things to me. Horrible, at times questionable things, in this very moment, I feel like their protected prey. They can feast on me, but if anyone else tried, they'd be torn apart.

I don't know how that makes me feel. Scared? Yes. Confused? Definitely. But do I feel empowered? I'm not sure. I should feel that way, but I don't.

We reach the front door, and Kill pushes it open, exposing a vast, pristine white foyer. A glass chandelier hangs from the ceiling, and I instantly smell sweet lavender mixed with ash.

"Where are we going, and why are there no people here?"

I turn to watch as King shuts the front door with his back, his eyes on me. "Let me guess. You guys brought me here to kill me."

"Quite the contrary, Little Bird." King smirks, waving me to continue walking. I follow his silent instructions and follow the three merry men as we all move through the house and pass the sitting room. It has two dark leather chairs that face a large U-shaped sofa. The chairs twist and turn high at the back, inviting yet cold.

"Stop looking, Little Bird. You might end up in trouble," King whispers from behind me, his hand on my ass. I suck in a breath at his connection.

Killian opens a glass door, and we step through, out onto a large patio that dips into a field. I hear people chatting when I find around a dozen standing around a large fire pit. This is more like a bonfire, as the flames assault the night. It's as though everyone stops as we enter, all eyes on us. I drift around to each of them. Some wearing suits, some wearing casual clothes, and that's when I realize they're all men.

"Welcome, Kiznitch. So nice of you to—" A woman's voice is cut when her eyes land on mine. Her hair is long and black, dropping to her butt, and her eyes are slit in perfect almonds, but shaped with black liner. So black I can barely make out her eyeshadow. She's tall and lean, with a golden tan and sharp collarbones, and it's not until she starts speaking again that I notice what she's wearing. A lace red gown that's completely see-through, with her cleavage pouring out of her dress. "What is this?" she asks, her words faltering as a smile about as fake as her hair plasters over her face. I can't decide how to peg her. What to categorize her as.

"Oh, I'm sorry." Killian's tone is playful, and I just know

he's going to hit her with a smart-ass comment. "I wasn't aware that it was invite only, *Mother.*"

His mom? No fucking way is this woman his mother. She looks to be in her mid-thirties, if that, and I know all about Botox and all the type of shit you can get filled into your face, but there's no way this woman has anything to do with that. Furthermore, why the hell am I here?

"Killian," she grates through her teeth. "A word." She sashays past us and heads straight for the house, Killian smirking from behind her.

"Okay, someone has to fill me in here," I say, loud enough for them to hear me but not for the strangers. "What is this party, and is she really his mother?"

King ignores me, moving straight past me and heading for a group of men who are around the bonfire. They're older men, all classically handsome from what I can see, and wearing sharp, excellently tailored suits.

One in particular catches me eye, mainly because he's already watching me. He has graying hair that's cut short on the sides and slicked back on the top. He's wearing a dark suit with no tie, the collar loosened around his neck. A cigar dangles from between his two fingers, with a red pocket square folded into his front pocket. It's not until King is standing directly in front of him when he finally pulls his attention away from me.

"Who's that?" I ask, nudging my head toward the man, or men, who King is talking to.

Keaton follows my line of sight, and then looks back at me. "It's no one."

Twenty-five

King

"Son." My dad grins. He's aged since the last time I saw him. Wrinkles sink into the corners of his eyes, his skin as worn as his Desert Eagle. "Didn't realize you were bringing company."

My head tilts over my shoulder. "Didn't realize I had to ask?" I don't have to, but they are The Four Fathers, and we are The Four Brothers. Our time will come when we take their place, and the next will take ours, but he knows damn well that if I wanted someone to be here, they would be here.

"You don't." He brings his cigar to his mouth, biting down on the edge. "But are you doing as you're to do, son, or are you getting distracted from the task at hand?" His words evaporate into the air, my shoulders straightening.

"I know who comes first, old man. I learned from the best."

"Son." My father leaned down to face me, flicking his cigar between his fingers. "There's going to come a time where I will need you to do things that you won't want to do."

I sucked down on my ice cream, tilting my head. My eyes squinted against the harsh afternoon sun. "Like what?" I'd always known how my family operated. When you were born, raised, and bred into a community that ran by their own laws and had their own punishments, you learned that way before the way of the world. I always preferred our way, but then again, I was only ten years old and Mum and Dad had always made it clear that I was trained like a machine. To know the loyalty of the brotherhood before anything and anyone else.

Dad's eyes narrowed into slits as he brought the cigar to his mouth. "Like live and fight with the same monsters that haunt you in your nightmares."

I stopped my licking, my fingers flexing around the cone. "I don't have nightmares."

He stood tall, his shoulders squaring. "You're about to."

His eyes pierce through mine, pulling me out of my memory. "Good. You have one place for love, and that place is not for little Dove Noctem Hendry."

"No one said shit about love," I quip, one eyebrow cocked. I pat his shoulder in assurance. "We're still playing the game, only we've changed a few of our moves." My eyes fall around the three of them. *Lie.*

Twenty-Six

Dove

King is still talking with the three men when Killian finally returns, with his mother behind him.

"Hello," she answers, placing her hand out to me. It's the first time I notice her bright eyes. Blue teal, rimmed by black rings. "I'm Drayar. Killian's mom." Her eyes slowly drift to him before coming back to me. Her smile is in half, not authentic. I already know she hates me; I just don't know why. It's not like I'm dating her son.

My hand finds hers, and she squeezes stiffly. "Dove." Suddenly, my words are tangled in a jumble word scrabble in my head, and I'm back on the yacht, unable to form the right letters to construct a single word. I don't want to speak, because my mouth is closed shut.

"Hmm," Drayar murmurs. "Stick around if you want, child. Though I wouldn't advise it." She starts walking away, her back turned to me, when I follow the trim line of her spine and land on her tailbone. I notice the same star tattoo that the boys have is over her lower back. I stand in silence, wanting to ask the question I've had at the edge of my brain since meeting them. The night moves along, and Killian takes me under his arm, walking me near the fire. He takes a seat on the ground and looks up at me. "Are you going to sit or stand? Because it might be a long night."

My eyes find King who is watching me from the other side. They're actually all watching me. I instantly sit beside Killian, wanting to hide from the attention I've so effortlessly attracted.

"Why am I here?" I lean into Killian, searching his features for any telltale lies. It's no use, though. These men are armed with the talent to lie. Being illusionists, telekinetic, and whatever else it is that they do—Killian, I'm almost certain, has some sort of hypnotic powers—but I try to find the lie between his truths.

"Would you believe me if I said we had been planning to have you here for years?" His voice is dipped low, and I'm drawn to the way his bottom lip's dimple sinks in.

"No," I answer through a whisper. "Because that would mean you all knew me before I was picked up and put in that cell, which goes against everything I know, which in essence, makes me uncomfortable."

"We don't care about your comfort, Little Bird." Kyrin takes a seat on the other side of me. I instantly shuffle closer to Killian. Kyrin makes me uncomfortable. His eyes are untrustworthy. I can almost judge all four of them by their eyes.

Kingston: *Strong, assertive, broody, intense. Liar.*
Killian: *Playful, devious, trickster. Liar.*
Keaton: *Confident, skeptical, careful. Liar.*

219

Kyrin: *Manic, Rage, anger, resentment. Liar.*

See, I may not know these boys as well as I want to, but I'm beginning to think that they may know me. And maybe I'm wrong and I'm seeing what they choose for me to see, but I look between the truths and lies, and I've noticed that even through all of their faces, the one thing that does not change outfits is their eyes.

Kyrin stirs something inside of me that shouldn't be tampered with, which is why I trust him the least out of all of The Brothers, which is also why I find myself moving away from him just as fast as he sat down.

"I've figured as much," I answer as music starts playing. The rest of the night goes uneventful. People stare, and I watch them back. I notice the atmosphere shift the later it gets. The more the fire burns, the more people drink, the more people start to open up.

Music is playing like a trance when Drayer begins to dance in front of the fire. I'm in awe, trapped in her performance, as her body moves like fluid waves against angry flames, licking through the dark night. I'm unable to move away from her as her back arches backward, and her hands flail out beside her. King must have sat down at some point because his voice is behind me in an instant.

"Want to talk?" he whispers, his lips softly touching the nape of my neck. *Yes*, I want to say, but the stubborn part of me—the bigger part of all my five-foot-four—wants to fight him. My attitude is as hot as my hair. I never got picked on as a child for having red hair. I remember my dad always saying, *"The world can't handle redheads. That's why God only created a small amount."* I understood. Sometimes, but otherwise, I was a fairly chilled out child.

Until I wasn't.

Right now, I want to be the child who isn't.

"Sure," I answer, standing. I follow him as he leads me away from the crowds of people and up the porch steps of the house. I turn around to have one more look at Killian's mom when I notice everyone watching me—sans Kill's mom. Chills break over my spine from the uncertainty of the atmosphere, but I follow Kingston anyway. I always go back to the fact that if he wanted me dead, I would be.

We continue inside and then out the front door again. Aside from the valet driver, who is standing far away from us, it's just King and I.

He drops down onto the step and looks up at me. I try to ignore the way his muscles flex when he leans on one arm, or the way his eyes speak to my soul without any words being spoken. Or the fact he's scary as shit, but I can't help but be drawn to the beast.

Slowly, I take a seat on the same step, folding my arms over my stomach and pulling my knees up. "So, what did you want to talk about?"

"What happened the other night." He kicks out his leg. Military boots. *Why them?* I wonder to myself.

"You already made it clear where that all stands." I don't waver, semi-proud of myself for keeping my composure.

"And if I told you that I changed my mind?" This time I turn to face him. He truly is magnificent to look at, but just as frightening. There's an emptiness behind his eyes that I haven't been able to see into.

"I would say why?"

He keeps his eyes on me, pinning me with the same stare he gave me this morning when he said he didn't sleep with Val.

His tongue sneaks out and slips over his bottom lip. "Is it not obvious?" The corner of his mouth slants up slightly, before his eyes drag up and down my body.

"Right, and what are your terms?" I'm not dumb. I know that someone like King doesn't do exclusive. "And what if I've changed my mind?"

He chuckles, shifting and leaning up onto his elbows. He searches my eyes, only closer this time. He's every bit intimidating, and even more so up close. Now he's close enough to bite. "I'd say you're a fucking liar."

"Maybe," I whisper, my eyes on his bottom lip. "But I'm also stubborn."

He smirks this time, and on all things holy, it almost knocks the wind right out of me. Someone so sinfully beautiful should never wear the devil's smile.

The door slams from behind us, and Killian walks out. "We're fucking leaving. I'm not watching my mom fuck any of them."

King rolls his eyes and stands. "Where are Keaton and Kyrin?"

Killian glares at King. "Where do you think?"

"Fucking your mom." King shakes his head. "Meet you in the car."

Killian storms off, and I watch as the valet driver quickly grabs the keys from beneath the stand and scurries off.

"Killian!" I yell out, jogging to catch up to him. "What do you mean your mom is getting fucked?"

Killian doesn't stop. He continues walking until the valet parks the SUV up against the curb. I thank him because Killian clearly isn't going to, and I jump into the passenger seat, turning to face him. His head is turned out the window, his features marred with anger.

"Kill?" I question.

"What, Dove?" he snaps, glaring right at me. "Why do you fucking care so much?"

"Because I just do. It's what the fuck I do!" I snap back.

"Well, you shouldn't." His eyes glass over, and suddenly, I don't feel as though I'm having a conversation with Killian. I'm having a conversation with the shell of him.

"Why?" I ask, reaching for his leg. "You've always been the nicest one to me."

He scoffs, and then leans forward, until his lips are brushing against mine. "If you knew half of the shit that we have done, not just to others, but to *you,* you wouldn't be so nice. Nor would you be bouncing on King's dick either." He sits back, as though he didn't just raze me with his words.

"What do you mean?" I ask, tapping his leg. "Killian!"

He ignores me now, keeping his eyes outside. "Nothing, Little Bird. I'm just playing."

I twist back in my seat and sigh, leaning my head against the headrest. The car fills with the scent of marijuana, and I turn slightly to see Killian smoking a joint. I smile weakly at him, before the front door slamming cuts me off.

Keaton and Kyrin are laughing, throwing their shirts over their head as King is scolding them from behind. I never did find out what Killian meant about them fucking his mom. He can't be serious.

They all climb back into the car, Kyrin sliding in next to Killian. "Oh, come on. You know she can't have King, so she goes for us. You could have mine, but she's, ya know, old and shit."

Killian flips Kyrin off. "Why can't you keep your dick out of her for three seconds?"

Keaton slams the door closed. "In my defense, I think she used her juju on me."

Kyrin laughs again, and my eyes catch King, who shakes his head and pulls out of the driveway as he drives us back to the tent.

I almost forgot all about Midnight Mayhem because tonight was so bizarre.

Twenty-Seven

Dove

The Texas show goes smoothly, and I dance my set perfectly. I did more ballet movements with my solo acts, but when I finally recruit my new members, I will have that scene be fresh and raunchy—purely for entertainment. Delila agreed to fly me out to the boat next week, which works perfectly because, right now, we've just got into New Orleans for our month break. I didn't ask why here, but I have a feeling that maybe New Orleans is where one of The Brother's family is. Or maybe they just prefer it here.

King has been cryptic since that night, and aside from always having a hand or something on me when we're in public, he's not been around me much, which has been ideal, because I wanted to be able to think about what he was offering. Which is something I still don't know.

"Dove!" King swipes open the curtain of my room, just as I'm reaching for my clothes. I'm standing in my bra and panties and nothing else.

"Wow, couldn't you knock?"

He cuts his glare to me, running his eyes up and down my body. "It's nothing I haven't seen before."

My chest rises and falls. The more time I spend with King, the more I see him open. He has a hard shell, one that, as far as I'm concerned, no one has been able to so much as scratch the surface of, but there are times, small times, where I see him struggle with something internally.

"Thanks," I mumble, rolling my eyes. "Why is it that when you're not yelling at me, you're scolding me."

His hands come to the back of my thighs, and I squeal out in shock as he picks me up from the ground. "I yell a lot," he grunts out, biting my lip. "But you scream a lot more." His smirk presses against my mouth.

"What are we doing, King?" I ask, searching his eyes.

He groans, rolling his head back, before coming back to me. "Why does there have to be a thing? Why can't we just go with it?" Maybe because when people 'just go with it' that's how they get hurt...

I shrug. "I guess what I'm trying to say is that I don't know where we draw the line between yelling at each other and sleeping together."

He seems to ponder my words, his fingers flexing around my thighs. The edges of his sharp jaw tense. "Alright," he answers, hiking me up higher. I squeeze my legs around his waist. "How about this. No strings and no label."

I groan, my head tilting back. Gripping onto his hair, my eyes narrow. "So, this thing. You can sleep with other people?"

He pauses, his eyes slanting. "I don't fuck girls easily."

"What's that supposed to mean?" I release his hair, and then I wish I didn't, because now it's standing messily over his head like a "just fucked" monster. *My just fucked monster. Why am I considering this? I need my head checked. This man is dangerous. But he's also very good in bed. And he hasn't hurt me. Yet.* I sound dumb.

He throws me onto my bed. "It means that I don't fuck just anyone. I'm in control of myself. Are you?" he asks, his head tilting to the side.

"What? Of course I am. And what about Val?" I couldn't stop the words from spewing out of my mouth.

He chuckles, his hands coming to my ankles to drag me down the bed until I'm half hanging off. Both his fists sink into either side of my head. He presses himself against me. "Why do you care about Val and me?"

"There's a you and Val?" I tilt my head.

"Fuck no," he answers. "She's the least of your worries."

"Oh, that's reassuring, King. Please do go on."

His eyes narrow, his head shaking. "You're insane."

I shrug, coming up to my elbows. "Maybe." I wrap my legs around his waist and push him down on top of me. "But you're the exact same."

His lips crash onto mine, and he's tearing my clothes off again.

"Wait!" I push on his chest.

He growls. Straight up growls like I've interrupted his feast. "What?"

"You came in here for something. What was it?"

"To tell you that we're here." He shrugs, before he's biting down on my skin again, and I'm moaning his name.

He stands from the bed, removing his shirt and his jeans, pushing them down to his feet. His cock is heavy in his hand as he pumps it softly. "I need those lips around my cock, Little Bird, and I need them on there now."

I shuffle to the edge of the bed and wrap my fingers around his thickness. Peering up at him from beneath my lashes, I roll my tongue over his tip, flicking his piercing softly.

He groans, his head tipping back as he buries his fingers in my thick mane. I can feel him down my throat as I struggle for air, desperate intakes after time. I pump him hard as he slams into my mouth. The salt from his pre-cum clings to my taste buds as I lick around him, sucking up every bit that he gives me. His pace picks up, the grip on my hair tightening. My fingers flex around his heavy thighs as he tenses, right before hot cum shoots down the back of my throat and I swallow each load like a thirsty hooker who needs to make rent.

"I'm obsessed with you," I whisper up at him, still licking his cock.

He chuckles, gripping onto my waist and picking me up from the ground. My legs wrap around his hard waist as he slams me against the wall, his mouth sucking on my nipples. One of his arms is wrapped around my waist while his other is holding me by my thigh. His hand reaches behind as his thumb slips inside my pussy, circling it.

"Always so fucking wet for me, Little Bird. So fucking wet." I groan as he grinds into me with his thumb, his mouth on my neck, licking me and biting me everywhere. Suddenly, his thumb is gone, and that hand is on the front of my throat. "Ever been fucked in the ass?" His grip tightens around my throat, and I know this is a warning.

I freeze. "No."

He releases. "Good." Shoving his thumb into my mouth, he growls, "Suck." I do as I'm told, my tongue curling around his finger, licking off the sweetness from my body. His hand disappears again, and I feel it back between my legs as he hikes me up the wall.

His eyes search mine, a devious smirk plastered on his mouth. "Gonna have to kiss me, Little Bird, might make this easier." His thumb dips inside me again, swirling against my walls, before he pulls it out and slips it into my ass. I tense, not sold on the foreign feeling.

"King," I warn.

"Relax, or it'll hurt."

"It's going to hurt anyway," I muse, frantically looking around my room. I gesture for my makeup bag that's beside my bed. "Grab the little red tube that's in my bag."

He glares at me.

"I'm serious, King. You are very large, and," my eyes drop down between us. "Very pierced. You will do some serious damage. Get the tube."

He drops me back to the floor and does as he's told, rustling through all of my makeup before he flashes the red tube. "What's this shit?"

I take it from him and squeeze some onto the palm of my hand as his go back under my ass and he lifts me in the air, shoving me against the wall.

"It's Coconut oil. It has many purposes, but tonight…"

King chuckles against the corner of my neck. "Tonight, it's going in your ass." He lifts me further and swipes the balm off my hand. "Chill."

I do as I'm told and feel myself loosen around his thumb.

He bites my lower lip and sucks it into his mouth, the friction from his lower belly against my clit and his thumb in my ass, opening a new portal of pleasure. I start to grind against him, his mouth on my neck again, right below my ear. "Ready?" he growls heavily into my ear.

I nod frantically, wanting this. Any way that I can have him. His thumb extracts, and then he's slipping two fingers in, stretching me further, and then three fingers. I whimper in the confusing sensations that are seizing me, holding me hostage.

I can feel his fingers back inside of me, curling before he rubs some of my wetness onto his cock. He brings the palm of his hand up to his mouth, his eyes remaining on mine as he spits on it and rubs his saliva over himself and at the entrance of my ass.

His lips come to mine, and he grins. "Always was going to be the first." His cock forces itself inside of my ass, and I scream, my nails clawing into his shoulders.

"Jesus, fuck," he whispers, but not stopping until it's all the way in. "You good?"

I nod, swiping the tears that have pinched out of my eyes.

He starts pumping in and out, and after some time, I find myself convulsing around him. His finger comes to my clit as his cock thrashes inside of me relentlessly. I can feel myself chasing that high, like a junkie to the climb and a slave to the fall. I wrap my arms around him as King bounces me up against the wall, my head smashing against it. He lowers his head and sucks one of my nipples into his mouth, pulling it between his teeth and grazing it. A guttural scream rips out of me as I finally catch my orgasm and ride it to the end. I feel his cock throb inside, but he drops me back to the ground and pulls me closer to the bed.

He hooks his fingers into mine as he lies back. "Ride me."

"What?" I exhale, trying to hide the fact that I'm tired as shit, and my limbs are weak. "As in with my pussy?"

He rolls his eyes and brings his finger to my slit. His finger slips inside and swirls. "Really wish I could give you a double penetration experience, Little Bird, but the thought of another cock anywhere near you damn near makes me violent."

I freeze, crawling up the bed as he lies back down. I'm throwing my leg over him and sinking onto his dick when I lean over and brush my lips over his. "I don't want any other cock near me, so I'll pass." I ride him slowly as he groans, his hands coming to my waist.

"Speed up." It's not a question; it's an order.

I don't. I need a second to catch up because he just made me orgasm, and I need a damn minute. When I don't listen, he takes charge again, lifting me off his dick and smashing me back down. His other hand snakes up my back as he yanks me down on top of him, his lips coming to mine.

He growls and flips me over until he's on top of me now, hiking my leg up to his hip. He circles into me slowly, his thrust every bit powerful. His lips never move, his tongue on mine like a hungry category five hurricane, threatening to kill everyone in its path. He rides me until my legs shake. I can barely lift them higher. The only time he breaks the kiss is to drop his forehead onto mine, eyes directly on mine, his sweat dripping from the tip of his nose and onto my mouth. I lick it up, bringing my hands to his face. Before I can analyze what the hell it is that we're doing, I'm squeezing around his cock again, my constraint on how much I can physically handle slowly snapping as I ride through my second orgasm and then come down.

This time he's losing the fight against his control. "Fuck," he moans into my mouth. It's brutally soft and could well be my undoing. I clench around him again as he picks up speed, his mouth back on mine. Whimpers fall from my mouth as I feel my clit swell.

"Let go, baby. For me," he whispers, his voice strained. As if on cue, I release around him, this time when I come, I don't scream. I weep into his neck, damn fucking tears almost stinging my eyes. His cock jerks inside of me as he growls through his release. "Fuck!" He pulls out softly after, rolling onto his back with one arm shading his eyes. "Yeah, I'm nowhere near done with you."

I giggle, but it's fake. What happened between the two of us toward the end was intense, strong enough to weave the strings we both agreed we wouldn't have.

After getting rid of King, I'm wincing and running to the tent to meet Delila. My ass and pussy hurt, but it has nothing on the confusion I feel inside my head. My running stops when my eyes land on that little girl again. I can't remember her name.

I look to the left and right, wondering where her father is, or whoever it was that scared her away from me the last time.

"Hi." I wave.

It's coming up to Thanksgiving weekend and then it's Christmas, and although it's not as cold here as it is farther up North, it's cold if you've just come from Texas heat. The little girl is wearing a light jumper and little gumboots with her dress.

"Hi." She swings her arms back and forth. "My daddy said that you're a witch."

I flinch, just as King's hand comes to my arm. "Go home, Jessie."

Jessie shrugs, and then turns and runs through the clearing of the forest. It's the first time I have really taken a look as to where we are, and it doesn't look like our usual spot.

I turn to King, whose arm is hooked around my back. "What was that about?"

King's eyes are still following the young girl before he looks down at me. "She's just a kid."

I raise my eyebrows. "Sounds like a pretty convincing kid."

He releases me. "She has convincing parents."

I let it go, looking around at where we are. "Where are we?"

He gestures in front of me. "At Delila's other mansion. We come here for Thanksgiving and Christmas."

"You guys have traditions?" I ask, falling into step beside him. "I'm shocked."

"I didn't say a tradition, just something we do."

I want to say that that makes it a tradition, but I get the feeling Kingston has two different moods. One when we're in bed—by far my favorite—and the second when we're out in civilization. It's intense and rocky, and quite honestly, it gives me whiplash.

We step through the forest clearing, and the first thing I see is the large tent set up in the backyard. Behind the tent, I can see the sides of an old-style brick home. Delila and these people obviously have too much money.

"She leaves the tent up for practice."

I turn around to face King. "Why did you keep me for a week in that cell?"

He doesn't flinch. Doesn't so much as blink. "Because you weren't ready." His eyes drift over my shoulder.

"Is that what you guys do? Steal people off the street and

then force them to work for you? Is that the way everyone got here?"

King looks down at me, somewhat annoyed. "Yes, Dove. Everyone who works here who isn't in a founding family is recruited. No, we don't have to force anyone to join. Usually it's a pretty easy decision, but none of them are civilians."

"And if they say no?" I ask, searching his eyes. I'm guessing by founding family he means the creators of Midnight Mayhem, so I don't question that.

"Then they say no," he adds, without saying anything else. I get the feeling they won't let people walk away from this. They're loose ends. Maybe Delila wasn't joking when she said that she saved my life.

"And how do you choose them?" I further ask as we make our way toward the tent. I'm dressed to dance. I need to dance.

"You're awfully nosey tonight, Little Bird," he jokes, and then his hand comes to mine and he pulls me through the opening doors. "Did I not fuck the questions out of you?"

Killian, Keaton, and Kyrin are inside talking. The conversation looks heated, and when we enter, they quickly turn to face us, their angry faces morphing.

"What's up?" Killian nods his head at us both.

King stares at him, his lips slowly curving up as his arm snakes around my waist. "Dove is going to practice. On me. Wanna watch?" Why is he tormenting them? "What about you, Keats? Bet you do."

I suddenly feel like the rose in a garden of thorns. "King," I whisper. "What is going on?"

"Nothing," he answers loudly, his eyes still on The Brothers. "Just a disagreement. Go set up."

I head to the center and drop my ballet slippers onto the

ground. I need something hot and fast to warm up my body, so I fiddle with the sound deck while I stretch. I tie my shirt up at the front and flex the band of my Nike shorts, snapping them against my skin. I close my eyes and then open them, hitting play on "Dark Times" by The Weeknd featuring Ed Sheeran. The beat infiltrates my mind, and my body follows its lead. My hair trails down my back as my eyes close when the hook kicks up. I drift around delicately, my body hitting every beat in fluid, strict movements. The chorus sneaks in, and I flick my head over, my hands coming to my ankles. Hands grip my hips from behind, momentarily shocking me. I flip my hair back and turn over my shoulder, smirking when I see King shirtless behind me. *Damn.* He spins me around roughly as the chorus plays. I go flying across the floor before he yanks me back into his chest, and we move fluidly together. I run every beat, and he chases it.

I never *ever* would have thought that King could dance. He's way too serious, too scary to be so blessed with so many talents. If you ever wondered if God played favorites, just look at King. Then again, wasn't Lucifer also a favorite? When the beat slows, I rub my body against his, and then just as the closing chorus starts again, I smirk from over my shoulder, grinding into him. He pulls me in again, and I lean back, my hair sashaying across the ground. The dance is intimate, our movements igniting fire beneath our feet.

The song finishes and the next one starts playing, but I bounce away and hit pause, spinning back around to face him. "What the fuck! I had no idea you could dance!"

King shrugs, wrapping his lips around a bottle, his eyes still on mine.

"It's no secret that he can, Little Bird." Val slithers in, and I spin around to see a whole lot of people in the tent, obviously watching our little—*thing*. "It's just that he doesn't want to."

"Fuck off, Val," King bites, tossing the bottle across the ground. I try to search out the rest of The Brothers but only find Kyrin. Keaton and Killian long since left.

Kyrin leisurely walks onto the stage, and King starts laughing, shoving him back by his shoulder. "You can fuck right off."

Kyrin's eyes slide off me and onto King. "Why? At least let me in."

King pauses.

Kyrin chuckles. "Or don't you trust her?"

"I don't have to trust her. We're just fucking."

Val winces, as do I, deep down. Val quickly composes herself and walks off.

"Well, then if we're just fucking, sure, Kyrin. Take a seat." I glare at King and grab one of the chairs from the audience.

"Oh, I'm here for this." I hear one of the Demon actors say from the seating area.

Kyrin shakes his head, finally bringing his eyes to mine. "You know where my room is when the time comes." He turns to head out of the tent, and I spin around to face King, my hands on my hips.

"Don't go bitch on me, Little Bird. You know damn well that's all we're doing." He leaves behind Kyrin, obviously going to do damage control. I'm confused with what's going on, and I can feel the tension between them all. All I know is I don't know why. I know how I felt when we had sex earlier today. Multiple times. But there were times that were *more*. I don't know if he noticed it, but when he's lost inside of me, a small part of his wall cracks, and I see flashes into his soul.

"Hey, chica!" Rose hits my hip with hers. "You and King finally there."

"Yeah," I say, bringing my eyes to hers. "Though I'm not sure if it's something I should be talking about."

"Hey," she says, looking around skeptically. "Did you open that note I gave you?"

"Oh shit!" I whisper. "I forgot all about it. It will still be in my room. Come on, let's go."

"I'm coming!" Maya yells out, leaving Val and Mischa behind, dumbfounded.

"She's different, Dove. You can trust Maya." I'm not sure why she felt the need to tell me that, but I thank her anyway. We start on our way back to the RV, and while Maya and Rose talk about some guy who's missing, I'm lost in my head trying to figure out what The Brothers could be fighting about. Is it about me, or is it still about Killian and his mom being some weird sex addict? And what about all those strange men? Killian's mom had the same tattoo. My eyes close for a brief second, but it's enough for a flashback to come over me.

Red hair fell over the girl's shoulders as she ran toward a field. I stopped; my hands tightly secured in my father's. I pulled on him. "Where is she going?"

Father looked ahead and smiled. "Probably to watch the hot air balloons. It's your favorite part of carnival weekend."

"I know." I rolled my eyes at my father's obvious fact. "But why is she excited?"

"Well, you're not the only one who loves hot air balloons, Little Bird. Your sister does, too."

I freeze, my footing falling. We're a few footsteps away from the RV when Rose and Maya both turn to see what's stopping me.

"Now what's wrong?" Maya asks.

I think over what I just saw inside my head. The clean, crisp blades of grass underneath the soles of my shoes. The early sunset off in the distance burns against an orange sky. The girl with red hair, who looked like a replica of me. "Nothing." I keep walking, my brain fuzzy in confusion. I've never seen that before, never had a memory that dated that far back. Maybe I fabricated it somehow. I squeeze my eyes shut and count to three before swinging the door open.

"What's wrong?" King asks, his eyes searching mine.

"Nothing." I shove past him as the girls follow behind me.

King lets them through before yelling, "Bullshit."

I glance out the side of the window on my way to my room when I see Killian standing outside, staring right at me as I move through the RV. This is a depth I've never seen in Killian, and it frightens me. Enough for my footsteps to pick up.

"Dove!" King blocks me inside my room, both of his bare arms stretched on either side of the exit. I try not to look closely at his chest, but every time I do, I find myself drawn to his tattoos, especially the two red roses over his hip. "What's wrong?"

"It's nothing. I think. I just had a weird flashback." I take a seat on my bed, looking behind him to see Rose watching me from the kitchen. Maya is making herself something to eat, but my eyes lock on Rose like *don't leave me here*. It's the same silence we used when we were both locked on the boat.

She nods, and I know she understands.

I exhale.

King tenses. "You don't have them often?"

I shake my head, my eyes landing on the clothes I was wearing that night when I was with Rose, and she tucked the note inside my shorts. I can see the edge of the paper sticking out from beneath my bikini. "No. Not usually. I actually can't remember anything from before my father and mother were killed."

The air shifts, and for the first time since I first met Kingston, I feel unsafe with his proximity. The air thickens, and darkness caves in around me. I swing around, with an eerie feeling that something, or someone is watching me. I haven't felt this feeling since they stole me.

I haven't felt this feeling since that night.

I know what this feeling is. It's like an old friend has walked into the house for the first time in a long time, carrying his aura with him.

"The Shadow," I whisper, standing. I almost trip over myself and land back on my ass when King reaches out and catches me.

"Thanks," I say, my eyes traveling up to his. When I land on them, they're bleak, black, and send chills down my spine. Suddenly, I don't feel comfortable with his hands being around me.

"King," I whisper. "Why did something just change?"

His jaw clenches and then his eyes soften. "What? It didn't. Get changed," he announces, turning back around to exit the room. "We're going to another party. This time, it's with my parents."

Twenty-Eight

Dove

As soon as King leaves my room, Rose is there, glaring at me. "What was that?" The presence of The Shadow has gone, as if it was never there, and it's left me feeling a merge of emotions, mainly confusion.

"I honestly don't know." I stumble to the ground and pick up the piece of paper from beneath my clothes, unraveling it. The image is a sketch of a dove. It's juvenile, as if a kid drew it, but not terrible.

"Weird," I say, turning my head to the side. "What does this mean?"

Rose takes a seat on my bed and draws her knees up to her chest. "I don't know. I was hoping you would. I mean, it's a little strange that it's a dove."

I examine it again. "Yes. It's weird."

Rose stands from my bed and kneels in front of me, her hands on top of mine. "Something doesn't feel right about King, Dove." Her voice is a whisper, but her eyes are a glare. "And with Jack missing, I don't think—"

"Wait," I interrupt her. "What do you mean Jack is missing?"

"What, you didn't know?" she asks, one eyebrow quirked. "He's been missing since we all played Killian's hide-and-seek game." She exhales. "What I'm trying to say is that we can't forget how we came in here. Maya? She was born into a founding family. I was a recruit."

I pause. "Wait, what does that mean?"

Rose waves me off. "That my family had ties to Kiznitch, making me instantly a part of the families. Delila explained it all to me on my first night here, but Dove," pain flashes over her face as she takes her next breath. "My mom isn't actually dead. She just doesn't want me."

Anger roars to the surface. "Then fuck her. You don't need her."

Rose giggles, swiping her eyes. "We're supposed to be talking about you and this picture, not me." She takes a deep breath. "So that's why I'm here, but why are you here, Dovey? That's what scares me." She has a point. It's something I have been thinking about since meeting Delila. When I woke up in the cell, I figured I would be sold or something cliché like that, not be pulled into this strange world. Aside from that, if Jack has been missing since that night, why has no one said anything? Why didn't I notice him not being around? There are a lot of people here who I see, but Jack made an impact on me, so I should have realized that he wasn't around.

"Rose," I murmur. "I know. Something isn't right, but I

need to get ready for this party, and I don't want King coming in and catching us talking about this. When I get home, I'll come find you. Okay?"

She stands, her slender body towering over me. "Okay, Dove, but be careful. I've heard King's family is royalty."

"Wait." My hand catches her arm. "What do you mean?"

"The Brothers of Kiznitch family *is* the royal family, but the Axtons are like, next level. His father is like Don Vito, the motherfucking Godfather. They have their..." She pauses. "You don't know anything, do you?" I shake my head. "I'll tell you what I know later, but it isn't much."

"Wait!' I repeat myself, just as she's about to leave. "You have to come to this party."

"She can't," Maya interrupts, standing behind Rose. "It's against the law."

"Law?" I ask, standing. "I'm confused."

"Likely, and make no mistake, that's how they would want you." Maya stares at me until it makes me shuffle uncomfortably. "I would come with you." She sighs. "But Kaius scares the shit out of me, and Dahlia, King's mom? I swear she's the worst."

"Thanks," I mutter, running my fingers through my hair. "You're really helping."

Maya rolls her eyes. "You should be lucky. There's obviously a reason why you're still alive."

"I don't know if that's such a good thing anymore."

Maya pauses. "You have real feelings for him?"

I freeze, my eyes flying to her. "What?"

"Oh, holy shit, you do." She enters my space, her hands coming to either side of my cheeks. "You can't, Dove. You have to protect yourself. Whatever he's saying, you can't trust." I want to tell her that she doesn't know what she's talking about.

But she's right. I may have grown something for him over the weeks that we've been around each other, but it's hard not to when I know what he feels like between my thighs. And I know what he tastes like.

"Maya," King interrupts from behind her and she pauses, but doesn't flinch. He doesn't scare her, which is interesting considering he scares everyone else I've met. "Get out."

Maya's eyes turn lazy. "Come see me after the party." Then she turns around and glares at King. "Because she will return."

"Maybe," King answers flatly. "Or maybe not."

As soon as Rose and Maya leave, I look to King. "What do I wear?"

Twenty-Nine

Dove

I remember my mom loving candles. Not just the normal light-a-candle-after-a-big- cleanup type—I mean, really loving them. I think she had more candles around our house than she did electrical lighting. I remember the smell of burning leather surging with sweet lavender. The smell was somewhat comforting, to a point.

I hadn't seen this many candles since my childhood, but stepping through the front doors of King's parents' house felt just like that. To the left, a young man was shirtless, playing a soft melody on the piano. He had smudged black eyeliner under his eyes and a straight square jaw. His hooded eyes came up to mine, his cheeks sunken in. When they connected with mine, a slow smirk crept on the corner of his mouth. I shivered, running my hands up and down my arms.

"King!" Killian snaps at King's retreating back as he enters farther into the house.

King turns around and pins Killian with a feral snarl. "Shut the fuck up and remember where the fuck you land on the scale, brother." His eyes drop to mine, before going back to Killian. "And watch her."

"Didn't think you gave a fuck," Keaton addresses from beside me.

King's eyes whip to his. "I don't answer to you." He turns back around and disappears around a corner. He has been agitated all the way here, more than usual. I don't know much about New Orleans or the state of Louisiana in general, but the area where his parents live is very country. It's about a thirty-minute drive from the city, where Delila lives. I think I heard Killian say the town's name is Destrehan. Their home is a giant modern mansion in the middle of an aged field. I feel as though the house itself stands out from the rest of the old plantation-style homes. Everything is glass and licked in rich deep reds. The setting in the house is smooth and mellow, much like an intimate restaurant.

Keaton's hand comes to my arm. "Stick by me, Dove."

I rest into his embrace, but not long enough because Killian is pulling me out. I suddenly feel like a used toy that people don't get to play with enough, bringing my thoughts back to the drawing of the dove that's burning inside my bra. "Actually, she needs to be with someone who can make an unbiased decision."

"That would be me," Kyrin's arm wraps around my torso, tugging me into his chest from behind.

"Ah, no," Killian says. "We said an unbiased. Not someone who will kill her."

"What about me?" a voice says from behind us, and we all turn to see who it is. The guy who was playing the piano is now standing, glaring down at all of his. He's got to be around the same height as King, and has an uncanny resemblance to him.

"Ah." Killian shuffles. "I don't know, Kohen."

Kohen brings a glass filled with white alcohol to his lips and smirks. "Why not?" My eyes run down his torso. He's almost identical to King, only no tattoos. I can't make out much of his face because he's wearing stage makeup and eyeliner, but he's definitely got to be related to King. A waiter walks past us, and he swings around, snatching another glass. When he turns, I face the same tattoo the boys and Killian's mom have, only Kohen's is massive and fills his entire back. Each tip reaches the edge of his body.

Kohen spins back around and hands me a glass. My eyes go from it to him. "For me?"

Kohen smiles, waving his other hand. "Of course. Rude of these fuckers to not offer you one as soon as you walked through the door."

I lick my lips and his eyes follow the movement. Slowly, I reach for the glass, my eyes on his. "I'll stay with Kohen. You boys can leave."

That seems to satisfy Kohen, who grins proudly, standing back to his full length.

"Little Bird," Killian murmurs, and in an instant, I watch as Kohen's face changes. Shock, recognition washes over his beautifully stained features.

"Little Bird?" he asks, only he's not angry. At least he's not showing it. He's... intrigued.

"Fuck," Killian curses. "Kohen, she needs to stay near us. I'm sure you understand now." A silent conversation passes between them and I'm left standing in the middle, dumbfounded.

I take a long swig of my drink. "I'll be fine. I've been here for five minutes."

Kohen reaches for my hand. I find myself allowing my fingers to separate, allowing his to fork between mine. "Come on, Little Bird. Do come meet my parents."

"Your parents?" I ask, looking up at him as we move through the main foyer and to the sitting room. He reaches out a long-stretched hand to a woman and man who are sitting in chairs that are designed for a king and queen. There are other people in the room, but I'm so distracted by the power that's radiating off them both that I'm trapped in a trance.

Lost.

In danger, maybe.

"Yes," Kohen announces. "Mom and Pops!"

Fuck. That must be King's parents, which means Kohen and King are brothers. Double fuck! I thought King said he was an only child? Or did I imagine that? I must have.

Kohen's fingers tighten in mine and he turns me around to face him. I can't breathe. My chest is heaving, his eyes searching deep in mine. "Little Bird," he whispers like he's screamed that name one too many times, and I continue to lose myself in his gaze. Where King's eyes are a burning green, Kohen's are pitch black. They're frightening, but there's a simmer to his fire that I find myself drawn to, like a dumb little bird.

"Do I know you?" I whisper, searching his eyes.

He exhales, running the cushion of his thumb over my bottom lip. "You—"

"Kohen!" King growls from somewhere in the room and I instantly pull away from him, like he's a flame that's licked my skin.

I find King instantly and hate myself for needing him to touch me where Kohen had just touched me. Replace what wasn't someone else's to touch. *Goddammit. When did I become so fucking whipped?*

Silence cuts through the air. All of the yapping is silenced. I drag my eyes back to King's parents. Dahlia is staring right at me. Dark eyes like Kohen's and long brown hair that looks like she's put a hair straightener through it one too many times. She's flawlessly intimidating, and she's not even spoken a word yet.

"Kingston." She turns to look at King. "Do I need to ask?"

Kohen shuffles his feet, standing in front of me. "A promise is a promise, Mother."

What the fuck is going on? I turn around to seek out Killian. When I find he's watching me closely from behind with Keaton and Kyrin beside him, I calm slightly.

"Hmmm, maybe." She flicks her nails around. "Dove Noctem. Come forward, please. I would like to get a good look at you."

I freeze, and then run my hands down my white skinny jeans. Sidestepping away from Kohen, I begin to make my way toward her when Kohen catches my arm. "Dove." He looks at me, confused, his eyebrows crossed and his forehead marred in confusion. I'd like to see what he looks like without all of the stage makeup, but I'd be lying if I said he didn't pull it off, looking like a hot deranged pirate.

I try to pull my arm out of his grip, but he doesn't budge. Then I see it. The cool, candid guy I met earlier has slipped and now something else has come over. It's eerie to watch. Kohen's eyes go straight to his parents. "She's not Dove."

"Pardon?" I ask, searching his eyes. "What—"

"Yes. She is," King says, his eyes on Kohen. "I've been around her. She *is*."

Kohen yanks me into his chest and I throw my hands out, stopping him from coming any farther. "Really, brother? Mind if I test that theory?" Kohen doesn't wait for King to answer because his lips are on mine. I keep mine closed, along with my eyes and count to ten.

One. A river flashes over my eyes with the same little girl with red hair.

Two. She slightly turns her face, and I try to grasp more of it. Instead, my hand goes to the back of Kohen's neck, and my head turns, giving him more access.

Three. The girl finally turns around, only it's not me. She looks like me, exactly like me, only different. My tongue slips into his mouth and he pulls me into his chest tighter.

Four. The girl waves, a big smile on her face. Two dimples pop from her cheeks, only she's not waving at me.

Five. I slowly turn around to see who it is that she's waving to, when I see two little boys, a little older than us.

Six. One is wearing a baseball cap backwards and the other is wearing a small fedora.

Seven. Kohen picks me up from my legs and I wrap them around his waist, holding on and deepening the kiss. The boy wearing the cap that's flipped backwards comes toward me. Closer and closer. He's familiar. So fucking familiar.

Eight. He smiles, so bright that his straight white teeth gleam against the sun. The one wearing the fedora strolls straight past me and goes for the other redheaded girl who looks like me.

Nine. Who is the girl who looks like me? I don't know. But this boy is almost right in front of me now. His fingers stretch around my chin as he tilts my head to his.

Ten. "Kohen fucked around and Mom and Dad are fighting again."

I jump away from Kohen, shoving him off me. "What just happened?" I swipe at my mouth and search for King. "What the fuck was that?"

King is glaring at me, seething, but something else sits behind his eyes. "Told you," King announces, his face dead and his eyes emotionless. "It's Dove."

I turn back to face Kohen, who is searching my eyes.

"How do I know you? And you!" I turn, pointing to King. "I fucking know you!"

"No, you don't," King says, picking up a glass of whiskey and shooting it back. He runs his fingers through his hair and points at Kohen. "You know *him.*" I've seen King like this, but not for a while. Even when he was standoffish in the RV, he was never cold. The way he is now is similar to how he was when I first met him in the cage.

I spin around, tears blurring my eyes.

I hear his mom sigh, before she makes her way toward me. When she stands, she towers over my short frame. She has to be over six foot. "You are Dove Noctem, and you, my sweet little witch," she presses her fingernail underneath my chin, "are not welcome here."

"I did what you asked," King says, looking at his dad. "I chased this bitch for the better half of her fucking life, made her fall in love with me enough for her to trust me to bring her here, managed to not let Kyrin kill her." My eyes flick to Kyrin, who shrugs, as King continues to dig the knife deeper and deeper into my chest. "And let's not forget about her fucking parents."

I swipe the stray tears that fall down my cheeks. "This was a setup," I whisper, squeezing my eyes closed. I want to scream and kick and shout and ask what the fuck is going on. Why I know these boys from my memories and where the rest of my memories have gone. When my parents were killed, I was traumatized for years. My foster career put me into therapy, extensively in order to help me speak. I didn't talk for years after. *"I'll hear you when you speak, Dovey. I will always be there."* It was enough to silence me at times. When I started working at the bar, I met people. I felt somewhat safe around them. They became my family, which became my security. I still to this day can withdraw my speech under duress, but it hasn't happened.

"I was sure that you would be triggered with her, son." King's father stands from his chair as everyone continues to remain silent. "But you've once again proven to be stronger than I give you credit for."

"Wait." Keaton slides in front of me. "You can't kill her."

King's eyes fly straight to Keaton. *Was he really going to fucking kill me?* Everything I thought I knew about King was a lie. A motherfucking *LIE*.

"You're a liar," I whisper before I can choke on the words. I search the prim marble floor for answers I know I'll never get, but anger bubbles beneath my skin anyway. "Everything you ever told me was a lie!" I yell toward King, who stares right at me.

He smirks. "Was it?"

"Fuck you!" I scream and fall to the ground. My hands cover my face as I begin to rock back and forth.

"You can't kill her," Keaton presses, but I'm still momentarily lost in my own turmoil. "I know you want to because of an old beef, but you actually *can't*." I knew King was a hard man. I knew he was savage, but I never knew he was soulless.

"And why is that, Keaton? Please, do tell me why I cannot

kill someone who belongs to a family that carelessly tried to destroy and expose the brotherhood. A family whose mother was a deranged psychopath and broke multiple laws, and then who further birthed a little girl who recklessly tried to kill my child in his sleep? The deal was that he put her in a home, not run off with them both and hide! Now, my wrath is long since tipped." King's father spits sarcastically. "I don't want to hurt that girl, but what I want and what I stand for are two different things. She has done wrong. She was the *wrong child*. Nothing like her sister."

"What happened with Dove and Kohen when they were children wasn't in Dove's control. She was not normal. They always played sick little games, wanting to test each other to see how far one can go. Dove was toxic for Kohen, sure, but she didn't mean to hurt him when she pushed him into the lake. She was still a child, and aside from that, you can't kill her be- cause—" Keaton mumbles. He must kneel beside me because I can feel his hand come to my arm.

"Since when did the darkest of them all have a heart?" King's mom says, but it's too late. I'm dead inside. I'm flat. Numb. Coolness brushes over me and my mouth is slammed shut.

I don't want to fight. When all you do is fight in life, fight to live, to breathe, to exist, you get tired. I'm tired. Drained. I don't know why it is that I know King and Kohen, but I'm tired. I wish I could be back at Midnight Mayhem, but then would Delila really help me? Or was she in on this whole thing? I can't trust anyone.

No one.

"Dove?" Keaton whispers into my ear. "I need you to pay attention."

I don't answer. My mouth is sealed closed by my

unwillingness to obey. What's the point of speaking if every-thing around me is false?

"Keaton," another man's voice booms from behind him, but I'm trapped in my thoughts, swimming in my pity.

"Keres," Kingston's dad interferes. "Please, let us hear what your son has to say."

Keaton stands tall, keeping one protective hand on my shoulder.

Inhale the pain, exhale the agony, live another day.

There's a long pause before his finger squeezes over my shoulder. "She's my sister."

"What?" I think that was King's dad.

"I'm sorry, Dad." Keaton mutters under his breath. "They have to know about her, or they will *kill* her." He must be lying, wanting me to follow his lead in a desperate attempt to save my life. Not sure why. I don't know why Keaton has been so nice to me, I just bought it down to him not being as dark as he looks. Or maybe I was wrong. Maybe this is all part of their plan. *I can't trust anyone.*

"Keres, care to explain this?" Dahlia interferes, and I finally bring my eyes up to her. She'd be beautiful if she wasn't so hate-ful. Her long dark hair and almond green eyes. She looks so much like her sons it's almost frightening. But then you see their dad, and it all makes sense. They get their beauty from her and their manhood from him.

"Stand." Killian's hands come around my arm, pulling me up. I obey, leaning into him and not wanting to bring my eyes to anyone. I trust Kill.

"It's true," Keaton's father says, and I turn to face him, want-ing to know who this man is who owns such a smooth voice. Like warm hot chocolate on a cold day. He has brown hair that has greys scattering through it and bright blue eyes. His face is muscular, just like Keaton's.

Nothing like me.

"Her mother hated her," Keres says to them, but his eyes are addressing me. "They were Klaus and Ash's love children."

"Wait!" King's mom snaps her fingers. "Are you telling me that she's a Kiznitch, not a little witch?" She exhales. "That still doesn't defeat the fact that she's clinically insane and wants to destroy us. She's a liability. We will make an exception for this once."

Keres shakes his head, his eyes going to her. "You know good and well how this world spins, Dahlia. Her father who wasn't Kiznitch blood..." He pauses, and I notice a drastic shift in the room. Why do they keep saying *they*? "She died, but this one didn't."

"This one *who*?" King demands, but I don't look at him. I don't want to. I don't want to so much as pay him any of my attention. I'm broke, as far as currency spent on Kingston Axton goes.

"Dove, I'm sorry for what happened to you and your father." Keres walks up to me, shoving his hands into his slacks. "Ash loves you and your sister." The lines around his eyes deepen.

"'Kay," I say, but it comes out broken, through cracked dry cement. I can't wait to meet this Ash, only so I can ask questions. I feel nothing for her emotionally right now.

"Dove," Kohen murmurs from behind me, and I turn to face him, ignoring everyone in here, especially King.

His eyes laser into mine, and the world slows for a few seconds. He opens his mouth. "Do you still have that burn mark over your hipbone?"

"What?" I ask, confused.

Kohen's eyes darken as obvious triumph comes over him. "Do you still have that burn mark over your hipbone?"

I lift my shirt, as if I didn't already know the answer. "No?" I run my thumb over my bare, smooth skin.

The room silences.

Keaton sucks in a breath.

Killian yells, "Fuck!"

"Jesus Christ." Dahlia massages her temple and takes a seat back on her throne. People are still watching, and the room is caving in. "That could have ended tragically."

"Why would you ask me that?" My eyes go back to Kohen, who is smirking like a Cheshire Cat.

"Because Dove Hendry was burned Christmas 1998 after she fell against an iron fire pit."

"No, I wasn't," I argue. "I mean, not that I remember. I don't remember much."

"You don't fucking say," Dahlia groans. "We're about to lose him," she whispers, but I don't miss it.

"No," Kohen murmurs. "You weren't burnt. *You're not my wildcat.*"

"I don't follow." His footsteps come closer, the room smaller.

"Because you're not Dove Hendry."

"*What!*" I snap, annoyed. "Of course I am!"

Kohen shakes his head, his eyes flying over my shoulder and landing on someone else. "No, you ain't. I would know, because Dove was *my* girl. You are not her."

I swing around, finding King standing still, motionless with all of the color drained from his face.

"Elaborate!" I search Kohen's deceitful eyes.

255

"You're Persephone Noctem Hendry, not Dove Noctem Hendry, and you're not my girl." Kohen's eyes flash back over my shoulder, and he points to King. "You're his."

Thirty

King

I pace back and forth in my father's office after telling everyone to get the fuck out. Dove—*fuck*—Persephone is still sitting in the sitting room, this time talking with Keaton and Keres. Her name has always been weird as fuck, but it's pronounced *per-SEF-un-nee*. I always called her P.

"There's no way that's her," I mutter, my hands running through my hair. "P is fucking dead. The reason why she's dead is exactly why I killed her fucking parents!" I glare at my dad. Keres, Kratos, and Kallisto are all in here, as well as Kyrin and Killian.

He exhales, placing a cigar in his mouth. "She doesn't have that burn mark, son. You were there when Dove got that. It was

AMO JONES

lethal. She was in the hospital with first-degree burns. That type of scar doesn't disappear. There's no other explanation, and besides that," he tests out, his eyes coming to mine, "your brother knew."

"And I fucking didn't?" I argue, my anger bubbling to the surface, because if Kohen knew, why the fuck didn't I?

"Did you fuck her?" Dad asks, throwing me off slightly.

"Yes," I seethe.

"So, you fucked her when you thought she was Dove?" He's judging me now, the smug fuck.

"What can I say?" I add dryly. "I was starving."

He watches me carefully. "I'm going to pretend you didn't say that, and Kohen won't know, but that girl is not Dove Hendry. She is Persephone. Your brother will now have to mourn the fact that Dove has been dead all along, and it was Persephone that was alive."

My fist flies into the wall, and I feel myself slowly start to lose control, everything crumbling around me. "How can we give her back her memories that Keres took?" I ask, my lip curling as I watch him. I glare at my father. "And Kohen is barely sane. He didn't even recognize her when she walked in until one of them barked off *Little Bird.*" Little Bird was what they were both called by everyone. Confusing, but convenient, when no one could tell them apart.

Keres looks at me, his rough edges smoothing over him. "It was simple hypnosis. As if dealing with addiction, I didn't take her memories away. I simply made her feel like she didn't need them after the incident." He stands, going straight for the whiskey stand and pouring himself a glass. "If she gains them back, she will know everything, King. *Everything.* Are you sure you want that?" He turns to face me, his eyes going to my father.

"It would make her a liability. She's not known this life. Ever. She doesn't know the code we live by nor has she been acquainted with her duty as a Kournikova. Her father was weak against her, and her mother was merely a civilian whore."

"You can't do that, P. Our parents will know." P shrugged her small shoulders, a smirk that raged mischief dangling off the edge of her soft lips.

"So what?" she said. "As long as I stay top in my class, Momma doesn't care what I do during the day."

I looked at her closely. P was always mischief. She liked to tease people, torment them, and enrage them all at once, right before she'd charm their pants off. Hoping when she's old enough, it won't be literally. You see, Persephone Hendry was handcrafted for an Axton. Not just any Axton—me. She was named after a great Greek Goddess who was married to Hades, where they both ruled the underworld. She was born to be a pain in the ass. But my ass, that is.

"P, please stop doing that!" Dove whispered, her small frame coming into the room. Dove and Persephone Hendry were identical twins in every sense of the word, but their looks was where their similarities ended. Dove was demure. She was the peace to which P was the havoc. In peace there would always lie havoc with these two.

P kept swinging higher and higher on the aged swing that hung by rusted nails in the old tree at their house.

"P!" I barked when she only kicked up higher. I shuffled around the front of her swing, anger simmering below the surface. I glared at her. "Fucking slow down."

She laughed so loudly that her giggles reverberated around the small forest that surrounded us, and probably over the beach at the front. "You're both too careful."

"The fuck I am!" I yelled. She knew damn well how not careful

I was, but being reckless with myself was different than being reckless with her, which I would not be.

P rolled her eyes and slowed the swing until it finally came to a stop. She took three steps forward until her little hand clasped over my clenched fist.

"King, you can't always be angry at the world." For a nine-year-old, she was too smart. Smarter than my eleven.

I brought my calloused knuckles up to her soft cheeks. "As long as you're walking in it vulnerable, I fucking will."

She leaned into my hand, just as her mom came rushing out onto the porch. "King, your mom and dad want you home for dinner."

I left after that, and that was the final time I ever saw Persephone Hendry. It was the day I began to mourn her, only I was mourning the wrong sister. My world ended that day, my mind caving in, shutting everyone out. I'm fuckin' reeling that she's alive, but I know I've fucked up, and once she gains her memories back, I'm even more fucked, because she's going to remember everything about us and be even more hurt by the shit I've put her through lately.

Thirty-One

P

"I need to know what happened, Keaton," I whisper softly. "I understand why you would lie and say that—"

"It wasn't a lie." He takes a seat beside me on the sofa, handing me a glass of something brown. "I'm your half-brother, Persephone." I wince at that name. "Sorry, would you rather I call you Dove? Just feels weird calling you that now that I know you're not her." I pause, tilting my head and examining his features. I don't think we look anything alike, but then again, he looks a lot like his father. Maybe our mother was like me. *What a mess.* Everything I thought I knew about my heritage, my family, was all an illusion. My mother wasn't my real mother. It made sense with her detachment from me.

"What did she look like?" I ask, my eyes zeroing in on the lights that are illuminating near the pool outside.

"She's still alive."

My heart sinks.

"Listen, Persephone. Shit, is it okay to call you that?"

I shake my head, tipping my head back to take a sip. "No, it's okay. It will take some getting used to, and I still don't understand, but I think deep down, I always felt a disconnect to the name Dove. The name felt so—"

"—Placid?" Keaton chuckles, running his hand over his tattooed neck.

I snort. "Yeah, placid."

"I'll tell you everything." He slams his whole drink in one go. "What do you remember about the day you moved?"

"I don't remember anything about that day," I whisper, shivering.

"That's because they didn't want you to remember," Killian murmurs from the entry.

I stand, staring at him. "Why?"

His eyes stay on mine, but for the first time since I've known Killian and been caught up in this clusterfuck of a life, Kill looks normal. There's no ulterior motive to his words or even a hidden smirk behind the easy smile.

Killian points to the sofa after looking over his shoulder briefly. "Sit down."

I do.

Killian walks closer to me, running his hand through his dark hair. "You've been getting flashbacks, right?"

"Yeah," I say, twisting my fingers together on my lap. "I mean, they're not flashbacks. They're more feelings and images. Like I remember feeling a certain way and a shed near an ocean. Stuff like that."

262

"Good." Killian's fingers come to my chin. "When you kissed King, did you get anything else?"

I shake my head. "I don't know. I remember dreaming, I think, after he left. Mainly, my flashbacks came whenever you were around."

Killian smirks. "I figured."

"You fucking knew?" King's voice shocks me. I refuse to look at where he's standing, not wanting to give him the satisfaction of my attention. "You knew who she was?"

Killian's hand stills on my chin. I keep my eyes on Killian.

"Yes," he answers, glaring over his shoulder. "But not right away. I saw it."

"Saw fucking what?" King yells, though I still don't understand his rage. He was about ready to dish me up to his father and mother as a fucking six-course meal.

Killian chuckles, shaking his head. "Saw it between the two of *you*, fucker. The fucked-up thing is that you didn't, King. You're that fucking detached from feeling any kind of emotion that you couldn't even *feel* the reason why you switched off those feelings in the first place is standing right in front of you. In the flesh."

My eyes begin to water, but I swallow them down angrily, not wanting them to spill over my cheeks and expose my vulnerability. *Did I feel it with King?* I don't know. I felt something, but I always brought it down to hormones and me being a girl and him being *him*.

"Give them back to her. Now." King slides down the wall, landing on his ass.

I finally bring my eyes to his. I wish I didn't, because I feel my heart split open in my chest and a sob leave my body. His usually somber and stoic expression is filled with turmoil and

263

pain. Regret, maybe? "I'm sorry," he whispers, reaching for a bottle of scotch and downing it.

I bring my eyes to Killian, ignoring his silent apology. "Give them back to me."

"Well, I can't guarantee anything, but I'll try. One thing you have to understand, Perse." King sucks in a hiss on the other side of the room. Killian continues. "Is that along with those memories will come the pain and anguish that was taken from you. My father didn't remove the memories from your head because that would be some sort of vampire shit. He merely hypnotized you into thinking you did not need them. He put them into a box in the corner of your brain and trained your mind to not open it. But hear this, Little Bird," Killian's fingers wrap around my chin, bringing my attention to him, "once this box is opened, everything could come back to you tenfold. You will know, feel, sense things that were put into that box. You may not feel like yourself after." I want to say that I haven't felt like myself for a long time, but that would mean I know who I am. Which I don't.

"I don't care," I whisper, swallowing past the pain. "I want it opened."

"Lie back," Killian murmurs, and I do, lying on the sofa. Someone enters the room just as Killian's fingers come to my temple.

"Let me, son. She'll have a better chance if I do it."

Killian steps backward, and Keres takes his place. We lock eyes for a second, but before I can say anything, my eyes are rolling to the back of my head, my back arching off the sofa. Images flash before my eyes.

"King! You can't do that! It's cheating!" I scolded, reaching for his deck of cards.

"Nah-uh, Little Bird. Kohen is the cheater."

264

My eyes flick, my head thrashing from left to right. Keres continues to whisper an ancient language, his tongue wrapping around the dead syllables softly.

"Persephone, you can't go to the beach house today. I need you to stay home."

My breathing deepens.

"She can go, Klaus. Stop being so overbearing." My mom walked toward me, kneeling in front of my face. Her long blonde hair was like a curtain, shadowing over half of her face. "You want to go to the beach house, don't you, Persephone?" I nodded, excitement shaking inside of me.

"Can I see King?" I asked, tilting my head. My father was a Kiznitch, only not like King, Kohen, Killian, Kyrin, and Keaton's parents, but my sister Dove and I weren't allowed around them sometimes. The Brothers of Kiznitch were originally from a small town called Kiznitch in Romania. Essentially, my father was a civilian, so I didn't actually know how he became involved in this world. But the Kiznitch brothers were all part of a founding family. The Axton family, Cicero, Nero, Cornelii, Kournikova—all founding families who created Kiznitch. Back in the 1600s, a show called Midnight Mayhem was created by the Patrovas to entertain the people of Kiznitch. Well, that's what Daddy told me, but King told me the shows covered up all kinds of evil. The Kiznitch families were all branded as babies and now wear their patch with pride in the art of a tattoo. Cartier was getting hers soon, and she's two years younger than Dove and me. She's just lucky she had Kyrin as a brother. He always protected her, and Kyrin didn't care about anyone, but we all knew she had a big crush on Keaton. Kyrin once tried to drown me when I was four years old. That was the first time King broke his nose.

My mom clipped my chin with the tip of her finger, edging my attention back to her. "Yes. King and Kohen will both be there."

"Yay!" Dove said, running down the staircase. "I didn't see Kohen last night." I rolled my eyes, not because I didn't understand her and Kohen's bond, because, of course, I did. If anything, King's and mine was stronger. We shared a crib together as babies, shared everything together. But the older King got, the more I witnessed him shift. As time passed, he was turning more into his father. I figured, as long as he had me, he would always keep the part of himself that I loved open.

Something was off with Mom today, though. She never wanted us to see Kohen and King. In fact, she despised the entire family of Kiznitch, even the branched-off families. I'd hear whispers and people called Mom a witch. An evil witch. I could see where they were coming from, but in all of my nine years, she was still my mom. She would say that it was because she was an outsider, and they didn't allow outsiders into the cult. She called it a cult too, but Daddy said it was more like a family.

I was on the fence. I knew King, Kohen, Kyrin, Keaton, Killian, and Cartier were my family, but that's about as far as I got.

We made our way out to the car. When Mom pulled out of our driveway, I turned back in my seat to watch as my father grew smaller and smaller the more we pulled away.

I couldn't help the ball that sat in my throat.

Something was wrong. Off. Mom never drove us to the beach house, and Father never let us out of his sight with her for too long. I turned to face Dove, who was watching the trees pass, but I could see it on her too—the uncertainty. She faced me just as I thought it and her eyes glassed over.

"Dove," I whispered, my hand coming to hers. Dove was troubled. Papa had said that she sometimes wouldn't be "all there" in the head. That she had a different personality sometimes, and that, at times, she could even be dangerous. I had seen those sides to my sister

266

many times, but not once had I ever been afraid. I thought she was more misunderstood than she was insane.

She squeezed my hand as my eyes went to the rearview mirror. Mother was already watching me, her dark eyes turned to slits. My heart thundered in my chest as she continued to drive us. She took a turn that wasn't in the direction of the beach house and continued to drive just as she reached into her brown handbag that was in the passenger seat of the car.

"Mom?" I asked, because I was always the inquisitive one and Dove the demure. "Where are we going?"

She didn't answer. Her fingers flexed around the steering wheel of our Aston Martin as she drove.

"No, no, no!" I scream, tossing and turning. "I don't want to! I don't want to remember!" My voice is hoarse, ripping out from my dry throat and shredding my voice box.

"I have to keep going, King. She's almost there. As soon as she remembers that day, everything else should be unlocked. Trust me, son."

Mom pulled onto a long gravel road, and I swiped my tears away to finally see where we were. It was the beach house, only from a different access. Maybe she was bringing us here and I was wrong. Maybe she had a surprise for us since we were only a couple days away from Halloween.

She didn't speak when she climbed out.

Not when she opened Dove's door and pulled her out. Everything slowed as she raised her left arm and pointed a gun at Dove, who was scrambling across the dirt ground.

"Mom?" Dove whimpered.

She flicked off the safety and cocked the gun. My mouth couldn't move. I couldn't scream or yell. Everything went into slow motion. *Bang! Bang! Bang-Bang!* I screamed so loud my chest squeezed as blood *splattered all over my mother's white dress. Tears poured out of me as my heart broke, but I was already reaching for the door handle to run. The door swung open as I sprinted forward toward the house that I once called home. Past the swing that King and I played on. King. I burst into tears as my battered soul craved his presence. I needed him to latch onto for safety. Bang! Bang! Shots fired from behind me as bullets flew past me into the fence in front. I decided to run for the driveway at the front of the house, as it's not that far until you hit the main road or a neighbor's house. The fires stopped and my ears started ringing as pain ripped through me. I didn't know if I had been shot or if the fact I just lost my twin sister had affected me so severely, but I kept running. My mouth wouldn't move, the words lodged in my throat at what I just saw. My father's Range Rover skidded to a stop in front of me. He ripped open the passenger door and came to me, his face falling as he dropped to his knees in front of me. "Perse, what happened?"*

The passenger door opened and Ashley, Keaton's mom, came sprinting out. When she saw me, her lips trembled. "What's happened?" Her eyes flew over my shoulder. She squared her stance and her hand came to mine, pulling me behind her body to shield me.

"What have you done, you crazy fucking bitch!" Ashley screamed. "I'm going to fucking ruin you!"

My father pointed to the SUV. "Ash, put her in the car, please. I need to handle this."

"No, Klaus. I will not leave you here with this creature! Where is Dove?" Ashley directed down the driveway again. She always could tell my sister and me apart.

I couldn't turn around to see who she's talking to.

I couldn't speak.

My body was convulsing. My lips were trembling.

I wanted King.

I needed King.

"De—" I managed to say, a notch above a whisper, but when I tried to force the rest of the words out, my mouth snapped closed. I never wanted to speak again. It would have only reminded me of my sister. We had the same voice, the same cry, and the same scream—"Mom?" The memory gnawed at my brain, stabbing it with a sharp knife and twisting it until everything turned numb.

Everything silenced, and I broke out into sobs, making my way into the car. I slammed the door closed and locked the doors, curling into a ball.

My sister was dead.

My twin sister was dead.

My mother murdered her and then tried to kill me.

A door opened and closed, just as I heard Ashley's voice whisper, "It's going to be okay, Perse. We will fix this and make it better."

I fly off the sofa, my skin drenched in sweat. "She—she—" My legs tremble as I fall to the ground. My hands cover my face as I feel thick arms wrap around my body.

"I'm so fucking sorry." I hear King's voice behind me, his lips on the back of my head. I jump out of his grasp as quickly as he put me there, spinning around and pinning him with a filthy stare.

"Where were you?" I scream so loud everyone silences.

King runs his hand over his mouth, his eyes on me. "We didn't know, P. Mom and Dad didn't know you were going there. Jessika, she set it all up."

I run my hands over my arms. "I've been living a lie. I stole her life."

"Truth," Kohen says, walking into the sitting room with a bottle of whiskey dangling between his fingers.

"I'm sorry, Kohen," I whisper, but he ignores me.

"You're sorry?" Kohen chuckles, shaking his head while he drops down onto the Lazy Boy.

"Kohen," King warns.

"Nah-uh." Kohen chuckles, swiping the dark eyeliner from beneath his eyes. "You lost a sister that day, but I lost my sanity."

I believed him. All of the memories are in vivid detail in my head. Every single Christmas, every single argument King and I had.

"I thought you thought she was alive and I was dead?" I ask softly.

Kohen shuts down, his eyes turning on King. "No. I thought you were both *dead*. Until tonight."

"I took you to see Keres after that," a soft voice says from the entryway, and when I look up to find it, I notice the strawberry-blonde hair naturally around her collarbone. The dark green eyes that glisten with unshed tears. The small face and pixie nose. *Ashley.* She steps forward, closer, but remaining a safe distance away from me. "He worked his voodoo with you and made me swear to not say anything to anyone. We agreed for your safety that we would say you both died." The first tear falls as she swipes it away angrily. "I thought we agreed and had a plan."

"What happened?" I ask. I trust her. I know I can trust her. All those years ago, I still remember the fierce wave of protection she washed over me in that split second she shoved me behind her body.

"Well." She continues, taking out a cigarette and placing it between her lips. She lights it and exhales the thick cloud of smoke. "Your father lied. He was so blinded by that *witch* who he thought he could fix her. He took her with you when he ran, and he ran from Kiznitch ever since."

"Only when we finally caught up to you all," King growls, but again I don't look at him. "We found *you* alive and *you* being called Dove by your father. You were both called Little Bird,

270

so the nickname didn't mean shit." King snatches the bottle off Kohen and takes a long swig. "Figured P was the twin who was killed and you were the survivor. We agreed not to tell Kohen that you were still alive, because of his fragile sanity and his history of violence. We couldn't risk him losing his shit again when he found out that Dove was, in fact, alive." He brought his eyes to mine. "I fucking hated you when I saw you for the first time. When I was given my first task, I just wanted to kill you. Why could Dove live while P died?" He tilts his head, his bleak eyes examining me closely. "I hated you, but I had my task."

"And what was your task?" I ask, and suddenly it feels as though it's just him and me in this room together. No one else.

His eyes darken, and his mouth kicks up in a deathly smirk that sends chills down my spine. "You."

"I don't understand," I murmur, looking around at everyone who is here. If I've done my math correctly, all of the fathers are here, as well as King's mother, Ashley, Kohen.

King steps forward, his head tilting and a cigarette hanging between his perfect lips. Lips I've felt on my body more than I can count. *Oh God. He was always right.* Even as a child, he was right. He always said that I'd be his last. Even if I wasn't his first at everything, I sure as fuck would be his last.

He stops when he's a breath away from me, and I look down at my feet. Converse versus military boots. It couldn't be more accurate for us. He leans down into my ear and whispers, *"We'll be back, Dovey. I'll hear you when you speak, I'll see you where you dance. I'll always be watching you."*

The glass I was holding falls to the ground, and I hear the smash from behind the ringing of my ears. "You're The Shadow."

"You gave me a pet name?" King steps back, assessing me. "That's cute."

My elbow veers back and I swing before I can stop myself. Pain ripples through my hand as it connects with his strong jaw.

He laughs, his face not moving. I go to swing again when he catches my hand and grips it so tightly I flinch. "The first one you get for free. The second one will have your ass laid flat out over my knees."

"Fuck you," I seethe, yanking my hand out of his grip.

He chuckles. "There she is."

"Perse," Keres interrupts. It doesn't go unnoticed how effortlessly everyone is using my old nickname. Everyone called me Perse, except for King. I was simply P. It was his name and fuck if anyone else thought they were using it. "The reason you were King's task wasn't because we wanted to kill you. In fact, the reason why *I* killed your father was because of his lack of ability to keep you safe. King was the one who pulled the trigger on your mother, for obvious reasons. She was his first kill."

"You're the one who killed her?" I ask softly, my eyes connecting with King's. There's no denying the connection now. The bond, the absolute raw emotion that we both share. King is mine and I am his, but that doesn't mean he gets away with every goddamn thing he ever did to me.

Fuck that. I'll hate him for as long as I want to, and he can fucking deal with it.

"Yeah, P. Yeah, I fuckin' did."

I nod, as if thanking him, because I am. The bitch stole my sister. Now her murder that has acted as a nightmare inside my brain suddenly morphs into a dream. *Bitch!*

I remember that night like it's a bad dream. I don't remember seeing who shot her, but I remember the blood. I remember the taste and the loud screams of my mother. Then I remember running. I remember them not chasing me. I thought

I got away, but I was so wrong. Some hunters don't catch you right away; some love to watch you run before they feast on you.

"Why?" I snap, turning toward Keres. "Why was I so special? Because of our talent with dance and singing?" I ask, already knowing his answer.

"Yes and no," Keres murmurs. "Midnight Mayhem is what keeps our name alive. It continues to act as a curtain to The Brothers and The Four Fathers of Kiznitch, but that's not why. It's because of the blood that runs through your veins."

"So you steal us all," I whisper as recognition slowly seeps in. "All of the ones who were on that yacht? They were part of Kiznitch one way or another, weren't they?" I can feel my anger simmering to the surface.

"Yes," Keres agrees. "We're a talented bloodline. One that must remain pure. Not all of them are of direct line like you, but they're in the line, one way or another."

My head spins from everything, my eyelids heavy. I want to sleep for days, hours, and I'm thankful that at least this is happening during our break. I can't imagine dealing with this and then performing the next night.

"You and your sister were special, P. You are Ashley Kournikova's blood daughters. Kournikovas' lineage is one of the highest rankings in Kiznitch. She married me, a brother, had Keaton, and then had the affair and had you and your sister. It's why we always kept you close to the Axton twins. We thought it fate." I wince, the memories so raw and undiluted. King and Kohen are twins, and all four of us went down in history. Keaton must also be some special hybrid breed if he has both a brother and whatever lineage Ashley is.

"But why did I think I was Dove and not Perse?"

273

Kaius steps into the conversation. "That is something we will never know. I tried to get it out of your father that night, but he never budged. He vowed he'd go down with that secret, and he did."

My eyes flutter. "Probably because Dove was always his favorite child. Why not just let me take on her name and it'll almost be as if she never died?"

Kaius shuffles his feet. My eyes connect with his. "I don't think that's it. I have my theories, all of which are far-fetched. We will eventually get to the bottom of it all, but for right now, we've hit a wall as to why he called you Dove and not your real name."

I sigh, my head pounding from all of the information. "So, if I'm so special," I bring my eyes to Keres, who seems to be answering more questions than Kaius, "why'd one of you almost rape me while I was in that cell?"

Keres freezes, his face falling.

Kaius stills, his hand short of his mouth.

Ashley steps forward dangerously.

There are muffled voices behind me, but the loudest is, of course, King's. "What the fuck do you mean?" he sneers.

I ignore him. "I just want to leave."

"I'll take you," Keaton murmurs, tucking my hand in his.

"No!" King steps in front of us, his fingers coming to my chin to tilt my face up to his. "What do you mean one of us almost *raped* you? None of us almost fucking raped you!"

I inhale.

Exhale.

Count to ten. "The man with the neon mask. He did things to me. He didn't go all of the way, but he made it feel like I was the messenger, and he was the one sending the message."

King's hand falls away as his face pales. He takes one step, two steps, three steps back. His face is blank. "Take her home."

I don't argue, slipping under Keaton's arm as he steers me out of the house and into a waiting limo.

Thirty-Two

King

I drop down onto the sofa, my hand coming to my hair. "I'll kill him." My head is spinning.

"Make it clean." Ashley takes a seat opposite me. I've always known that Ashley was P and Dove's birth mother, so I've always seen the resemblance. "She won't forgive you, King. Remember, she's the stubborn one."

"I don't want her forgiveness." My eyes connect with hers. "I want her vengeance." I shake my head, rage burning hot inside of me. "He did this for Patience. It's what they do to check that their girls are virgins. They use their fingers to check the barrier. *I'll fuckin' kill him.*"

"Son," Dad commands my attention, and I bring my eyes

up to his, just as the rim of the bottle touches my lips. "You don't need my permission to kill the man, but be careful with how hard you go for her."

I stand tall, handing the bottle back to Ashley. "I'll go as hard as I want. I'll only ask you this once." I pause, locking my eyes on his. I've come to know when Dad is lying. Only just, and even then, I think some shit still passes over me. "Did you know that she was P?"

Dad doesn't flinch, his eyes staying on mine. "Would I have put anyone else on her if it wasn't?"

"Motherfuck!" I storm out of the house, slamming the front door. I should have known my father knew all along. He wanted the reveal. He got it. I take a seat on the steps, just as the door opens and closes. I already know it's Kohen behind me. Call it twin fucking intuition. We always thought we were in sync with the girls, too, but I'm not so sure anymore since I couldn't pick out that it was P. I didn't even think of the fucking scar because I was too blinded by lust whenever she threw her clothes off.

"You fucked her," Kohen states, leaning behind me.

"Yeah." I swallow, looking out to the dark night. "I did. Should have pegged it when the fuckin' turned into some other deep shit."

"Don't blame you." Kohen sits behind me, and I shuffle around to face him. Kohen's story isn't mine to tell, but when he lost Dove, he lost all parts of himself that could show any emotion. He's dead inside, and not in a way that is a challenge for a new girl to take. I mean he's clinically insane. There's no coming back for Kohen, ever. Some people lose themselves on the path we travel every day, and whether they know the road back or not, they just choose not to take it. That's Kohen. He doesn't want a life without Dove. There will be no one else.

"You don't?" I joke, an eyebrow quirked. "I'd kill you if you fucked Dove while thinking she was P. Fuck brotherhood. I'd straight up cut you." I pull out my pack of smokes, banging the edge on my palm until a fresh one slips out. "You coming back to Mayhem?" I flick open my Zippo and blaze up the end.

"Nah." He turns his head sideways, looking out to the empty paddocks that lead to the street. "I don't know what I want to do yet, but I know I don't want to be around the people of Kiznitch or Mayhem in general."

I blow out the smoke. "Fair, fair."

"So you watched her dance, huh?" Kohen grins, and I know that in his sick, perverted mind that images are flashing behind his eyes. The final act was something else entirely when Kohen was in Mayhem. One day, I hope he comes back.

I throw dust at him jokingly. "Yeah. It was almost fun."

"Almost?" He licks his lips. "Come on. Give me something."

"It would have been all the way fun if I wasn't trying to hate her all of the time. Resenting you for maybe having another shot at being happy, but still being happy for you. I don't know, Koh, it was fucked. I wanted her, but I hated her, because she reminded me of P, and I resented you for having her and hated myself for wanting her, and my head space was ugly. I wanted to fucking kill her, just to take it all away." Silence stretches between us, and I puff on my smoke a few more times. When I think he's not going to answer, I raise my eyes up to his and find him watching me carefully.

"You would have, too." His face is emotionless.

"Would have what?"

"Killed her," he says. "You're trained to do it, King. You took your first kill at sixteen years old for the sake of fuckin' love. Does she know what you were doing the day Dove was killed?"

I shake my head, flicking the ash off the end of my smoke. "I doubt it. P *then* didn't know what I was doing, so P *now* won't." I was training for a kill; I just didn't know that kill would end up being her mother.

"Well, maybe Dad and Mom still have hope on some grand-kids." Kohen smirks.

I flip him off. "Fuck you."

Thirty-Three

*M*emories are a cruel reminder of what you don't have anymore. I thought I wanted to know everything, be opened to all that was taken from me all those years ago, but as I stay rolled in a ball on my bed, squeezing my eyes shut, I watch that day over and over again on repeat. I have to force myself not to seek out Killian and demand he slam that box closed again.

Bang!

Bang!

Bang!

Bang, bang!

There were five shots, and then I was running. I saw the car, and Dad climbed out. I was angry with King before I remembered, and now I'm livid. There's just the small fact that when I opened that box of memories, everything I felt for him rolled in tenfold. Now I'm angry with him, but I'm also other things for him.

Nothing is going to change the fact he wanted me dead.

That he had tormented and stalked me for years. He was The Shadow, the man I feared. Now the man I feared is also supposed to be the man I loved? Fuck. That.

There's a knock on my door, pulling me out of my panic. "Perse?" It's Delila's voice. "Can I come in?"

I don't answer, and she takes that as a cue to enter. "I'm sorry." I want to ask what she's sorry for, but my mouth won't open, and I can't find the urge to ask.

Because I don't care.

Bang!

"I know this might not help you right now, but I want you to know I have your RV here. I bought it before we got here, actually. You can decorate it however you like, and there's enough space in there for five of you. It's actually around the same size as this ridiculously overpriced hell on wheels." I can just imagine her looking around my room. She sighs. "I'm not going to lie to you, Perse. I knew everything. I knew you when you were a little girl, and I knew the ratchet bitch who you thought was your mother. *The witch.*" Her hand comes to rest on top of my leg, pressing through the blanket. I swipe away the tears. "I had a feeling you weren't Dove when I saw you dance. Dove was good at ballet, but you were always better. Your movements were always fluid. Your precision with dance has always been like art. Dove was the same, but there has always been something else about you. An edge to the way you moved. Like you'd take on a role while the song was played. Dove was always a little shy to do

that, silenced by the voices that lived inside her beautiful head."
I remain quiet and still, not wanting to interrupt her obvious
oversharing in case she pulls back. She stands, and a loud clink
sounds out as she drops something onto my bed. "I understand
you'll need your space, so here are the keys. It's all yours. When
you're ready, we can start on your recruits, and the tent is there
for you."

Once Delila leaves, I swing up from my bed and throw on
a loose shirt and some tights and leg warmers. Snatching up my
slippers, I head out of the RV and toward the tent.

I need to vent.

I need to dance until my feet bleed, and my muscles ache,
to remind me why I'm here, alive, and I'll do it finally with my
slippers tied around my ankles.

I make my way into the tent, where I see Jay, one of the men
who handles the DJ booth. "You want me to hit the switches on,
Perse?" News must have traveled fast, and I'm partially thankful
for him easing into calling me Perse.

"Yes, please," I answer, tossing the keys and my hoodie onto
the ground outside of the ring.

I tie my hair up into a high ponytail and push play on "You
Should See Me in a Crown" by Billie Eilish. Lifting my hands
into the second position, I roll my head around, closing my eyes
and allowing my mind to drift into another dimension. Rolling
into an alignment technique, I flick my foot up as the chorus
kicks in, and then twist it out into a turnout technique before
coming into a pirouette. I continue to dance until my feet ache,
and sweat drips off me. Finally, as the song ends, I jump into a
split and then slide into a bravura. The song cuts out, and my
deep breaths take over me, tears pouring down my face. It was
the first time I've danced in slippers since before my parents

died. Now that I've done it, it feels like clarity. Like a dark cloud has cracked open to allow light through. My mind struggled for years to wear my slippers again, and now that I have, I don't want to take them off.

"That was beautiful," a small voice says, and I jump, turning around to face where it came from. The little girl from a couple weeks ago stands there in a long-sleeved cotton sundress and a small leather jacket.

"Hi!" I whisper, unsure on how to approach her. The last time I tried to talk with her, her father had a hernia. "Your name is Ariana, right?"

She nods, bringing her fingers to her front. "Papa says that you were cursed, but that you're free now."

I freeze, swallowing. Kneeling down to her level, I smile. "Well, at least it's lifted now, right?"

Her little face lights up as she nods. "Can we still be friends?"

I chuckle. "I thought you'd never ask." My phone starts vibrating in my hand and I watch as she waves. "I'll see you later, friend!"

"Okay," I whisper. Swiping my phone to answer it, I bring it to my ear. "Hey!"

Richard sighs. "When are you coming home, pumpkin?" His voice shocks me, but I exhale, relieved to have someone familiar and away from this world.

I chuckle. "I'll come home for a visit sooner than you think." A thought pops into my head. "Actually, hopefully sooner than I think."

"To work?" I can hear the question in his tone even though he knows the answer already.

I blow out a breath of air. "Is it too late to hand in my resignation?"

"It's a strip club, Dove. You don't need that." I flinch at that name.

"There's so much I have to tell you, but my name is actually Perse."

Silence.

"So Dove was your stripper name?"

I laugh out loud, my hand coming to my mouth.

"Girl, stop laughing at me. I can't spank your ass when you're all the way over the fuck wherever you are."

"I'm," my chest tightens, "a little bit away. I'll give you a call tonight with more details, 'kay?"

He grunts, which is Richard's way of saying yes. He could write an entire dictionary and translations from grunts to meanings.

Hanging up the phone, I decide to seek out Delila to help me find my recruits. I want to throw myself into dance and my act, and build what I know and what takes away the pain. *Pain.* Picking up my hoodie, I head back to The Brothers' RV and get started on packing up my things. It's funny now that I have my memories back how I know the simplest things that I didn't know before, like The Brothers of Arms emblem, or the "weird star" I once called it. Each point signifies the suburbs in Kiznitch, and the thick lines that make up the star represent the generations of blood. One day I hope to go back there, maybe learn about my heritage, but right now, I need to move into my RV.

"I think that's everything, which isn't much, but you know…"

Rose laughs, picking up one of my boxes and making her way out in front of me. "Have you seen your RV yet? It's fucking red. As in your hair."

"I've seen the outside." And it's hard not to since it's right behind the boys' RV. Too close for my liking, but at least I'm out of their hair. I haven't seen King in days, or any of the boys. It's as though after that night, they've all gone ghost. I feel sick to my stomach about everything that has happened, but at the pit of my stomach holds mine and King's bond. The organic love I have for him. I know I somewhat miss them all to an extent, but I can't get past the taste of betrayal that King has left in my mouth after his final lick of defeat.

The memories are good. I welcome them, but what I don't, and what I wasn't prepared for, was the emotion that came with them. Memories aren't like photographs. You can't just flip over them and admire their vivid detail. You have to inhale the same air, embrace the same feelings, and whiff the same scent.

I push the key into the lock and swing the door open.

"Wow," I whisper, stepping inside as Rose piles in behind me with Maya behind her.

"This is sweet! You know, I can totally slide into your act if you want." Maya shoves me playfully on the arm while blazing up a joint.

I think over what she has just said, obviously playing with the idea in my head.

"I was kidding," Maya says, her eyes flying between Rose and me. "Tell her I was kidding."

"What's wrong with being in my act?" I scold her, dropping the box onto the white marble kitchen counter. "I happen to think my act is going to be pretty fantastic."

Maya chuckles, shaking her head. "I've come to love you, Sef, but I can't be living with someone who uses words like 'fantastic'." I ignore her new nickname for me, bringing it down to Maya and her peculiar personality.

I flip her off as she disappears up the stairs. "Of course she furnished it," Maya calls out. "Sometimes I hate her."

My eyebrows raise at Rose.

Rose shakes her head. "I'll explain later. We are having a housewarming, aren't we?"

I shrug. "I don't see why not." I want to talk with Rose about everything that has happened, but I don't know when or how.

I climb the stairs and examine the bedrooms. Mine being the master room. It's much like the boys' RV, with my room being where King's is. Soft pink covers are on the bed with gloss white posts where the bed sits in the middle.

"I was joking," Maya interrupts my examining. "I mean, as much as it would be an honor to come into whatever you're about to begin—"

"Stop." I bring my hand up, stopping her. "You don't need to say any more, Maya. I know."

She stares at me, her almond eyes coming to mine. "It's not that. It's that I've always had my own act because…" She stops, and for the first time since I've known her, I watch as she cowers slightly. She exhales. "My mother. She's, well, persistent."

I lean against the doorframe, my arms coming to my chest. "Who's your mom?"

Maya blushes, and I almost feel bad for asking. "Well…" Her hand comes up to tuck a stray hair behind her ear. "It's Delila, actually." She rolls her eyes.

I lean back, shocked. "Your mom is Delila?"

"Yup!" Her eyes slant. "Don't judge me for that either. My old man was much cooler."

I chuckle, shaking my head. "I'm not judging you at all."

"Good!" She smirks, nudging her head back downstairs. "Let's have one big party before you bring in your new recruits. I always hate when newbies come in."

"Jeez." I shove her playfully. "Thanks."

She laughs. "Girl, I'm not even sorry." Of course she isn't.

Hours pass as I settle into my room, hanging my clothes on their hangers. I pull out my phone and dial Richard, feeling bad on how I left him on our last call. I need to tell him that I won't be able to make it back when I wanted, and then I need to find something to wear tonight.

Because I need to blow off some steam.

Some ancient, fucked-up, and mentally unstable steam.

After hanging up with Richard, I'm ass deep in my closet with Maya, Rose, Val and Mischa sitting on the bed.

"Just wear a bikini," Val says, smirking from behind her glass. She has already started drinking. Surprise, surprise.

"I'm not wearing a bikini."

Val is someone I have come to tolerate, but not necessarily like. I feel like I want to swap stories with them all. Who they are? Why are they here? *Who are they damn well related to?*

My fingers brush over a short black slinky outfit. "What are the chances of us maybe hitting a club later?"

They all pause before chuckling. "I mean, we can," Maya purrs. "We just never really have."

"What?" I scold, standing and grabbing some shoes that will match this scandalous little getup. "You're in The Big Easy and you're telling me you guys have never hit Bourbon Street?"

Val quirks an eyebrow. "Yes, we have, but not to go out as just the girls. Usually The Brothers are with us, if you know what I mean." She smirks, looking to the side.

My hands drop to the side of me and I step closer to her, my head tilting. "Are we going to always have this problem between us, Val? Because we've both danced on King's dick?"

Val freezes, her eyes slanting as they come to me. She seems to battle with her thoughts inside before finally exhaling, bringing her glass back to her lips. "No. You're right." She stands, swiping her hands on her short little skirt. "Truce?"

I examine her hand. "What were you doing in his room that day anyway?"

She raises a perfectly arched eyebrow again. "Oh, so you care?"

Of course I do. "No," I answer smoothly. "I want to know."

Val exhales. "I went to try to talk to him to see why he wasn't sleeping with me anymore. Nothing happened. I'm sorry for allowing you to think it did."

I sigh, watching as her head bows slightly between her shoulders. "I believe you."

Her hand slips in mine. "You have my word, but Perse, not again."

"Good! I want him to suffer."

I think it's the first time I've ever known her to look serious. "The King never suffers."

I humph, hanging the dress in front of her. "Louis Vuitton anyone?"

Val smirks. "She's catching on."

An hour later, we're all primed to the nines. I'm wearing an LV black dress that clings tight and hangs to my upper thighs. It's see-through at my midriff and my ass, so I'm wearing a G-string and a black lace bra. Grey Goose, Hendricks, and old whiskey line the tables outside the RV, with everyone surrounding them. No fire pit. No relaxed clothes. This party is tasteful, upper class, and I get the feeling this is the theme for the girls. "All I Ever Wanted" by Mase is playing as I dance down the steps, my red-bottomed heels clinking against the metal.

"Yaaaaassss!" Rose slurs, raising her bottle to the air at my entrance. I sing the chorus fluently to Rose, censoring the N-bomb when Rose pauses, eyebrow cocked, to see if I'll say it.

I drop down low, raising my bottle in the air, dancing in circles. Val and Mischa erupt in laughter, with Rose taking my bottle off me, bringing it to her lips.

"Girl, gimme this."

I laugh, dancing and spinning around to face Delila, who raises her champagne glass to me. My laughing simmers as I make my way to her. I want to talk to her.

"Hey, Justice." I smile at Justice who is standing beside her, his arm hooked protectively around her waist.

"Hey, Little Bird. How you doin'?"

"Better now." I wink, before looking back at Delila.

Justice bows, excusing himself and leaving Delila and me to each other as he gets lost in the pool of bodies. The sun is only just setting, leaving a warm hue in the sky.

"You like it?" Delila asks, a genuine smile on her mouth.

I laugh. "Yes. Thank you, Delila. I think I had the wrong impression of you when I started."

"Oh no." She shakes her head, laughing and holding her drink in. "You definitely did not. You're just," she searches my eyes, sighing, "special. You're special, Perse. Very special to not just Kiznitch, but to us, Midnight Mayhem. I hope you find a home with us."

I smile, snatching a glass from a passing waiter. "I think I will." *Regardless of the fact my soul mate has been deceiving me for months on end*, is what I want to say.

"Another thing." Her hand comes to my arm as I turn around. "I found the recruits for you. Listen, can we sit?"

I search her eyes. I somewhat have come to the conclusion that I trust this woman. Through everything that has happened these past months, she has been the only one—not including my psycho friends—that has remained constant. "Sure."

I drop down onto the chair beside her. "So, you found some?"

She nods, sipping on her champagne and draping her red dress over one leg. "Yes. We don't have many to choose from right now, but what I want you to know, Perse, is that we don't want to harm these girls. We keep them there to condition them." I think over her words, but before I can answer her, she's continuing. "The three that I chose are the best that you could ask for anyway. One of them is a delicate subject, one is a male, and the other is so broken I don't think we can save her, so just comfort her when you can." I take another sip of my champagne. Half of me wants to run from this conversation, but I know it's only because I'm afraid of who these people are and what they've endured. I know I need one massive blowout tonight before I take on responsibility for them.

I throw back another drink.

The sun has gone down farther now and fairy lights have come alive everywhere, giving us a brighter view without it being intruding.

"Go on."

Delila takes another sip of her drink. "Okay. That's all." I know it isn't, but I allow her to say it. "Just take care of them.

One is very special. More than the rest." I sigh, sinking the rest of my champagne and craving something stronger. When I look to Delila, I can see she's in pain. The least I can do is put some of this out of her reach.

My hand comes to hers. "I promise I'll take care of them, Delila."

Her eyes fly to mine, glassing over slightly. I watch as her face relaxes. "I know, Perse."

"So!" I stand from my chair, putting my glass on the ground. "Do you want to come out with us tonight, or are you on babysitting duty with my new family?"

Delila chuckles. "You girls go have fun." Her smirk deepens, and I see the Delila I met all those months again. "While you can."

Thirty-four

King

I lost her.

Thirty-five

C ouple hours later, the music is blaring in my ears, the lights
flashing in my eyes. I'm so drunk I can barely walk straight,
let alone think straight and not one single fuck is given.
I've walked through my life caring too much. Caring about how
I'm going to get food. Caring about my weight. Caring about
whether or not my piece of shit mother cared about me, when
in natural fact, I don't care. At least not anymore.

Rose grabs onto my hands, pulling me into her and grinding against me. Maya and Val are around us with Maya beside
her as the music takes over all of us. I'm not sure if Maya and Val
have taken anything else other than weed, but they seem way
too into this dance. "Alive" from Offset and 2Chainz is pulsing

through the oversized speakers, the strobe lights flicking. I bring my glass to my mouth and throw back the rest of my drink. We decided to venture to the clubs about an hour ago, and I'm un-decided whether it was a great idea yet. I've never been against clubbing, but again I've never been hot on drinking. I'd be happy to not drink ever, but since being with Midnight Mayhem, their culture has latched itself into my bones. I twist around to the beat, flicking my hair around the place and losing myself in the intricate beat, booty dropping to the ground and twerking my way up. Tensing my abs, I flick around again until hands are steadying me.

"Whoa!" the guy mutters, his eyes searching mine.

"Sorry." I laugh, shaking my head. "Didn't mean to stand on your foot."

His eyes are green up close, his skin a beautiful soft brown, and his cheeks puffed. He's hard and strong, and not bad to look at.

"You didn't stand on my toes." He yells into my ear. "You come here often?"

I snort, leaning into his neck and inhaling his smell. Like a weirdo. "Does it look like I come here often?"

He pauses, searching my eyes before chuckling. "You're right. You don't look like you come here, but you can dance, so…"

"Really?" I raise an eyebrow in challenge. "You know about dance?"

"I mean." He shrugs, rubbing his palms together. "I know you can do that cute little thing with your ass while I stand here and look good." The song remixes into "Bed" by J. Holiday. A bit slow for my vibe, but whatever.

"Oh, okay!" I grin, turning around and flinging my hands

up, keeping everything still but my torso. I grind to the music as the chorus comes on, my eyes landing on Rose briefly who is shaking her head furiously at me. I wink at her playfully as I lean over and touch my toes, grinding my ass into his crotch. I refuse to turn around, continuing my dancing, rolling my body side to side. I reach for his hands and bring them to my stomach, widening my knees as I drop back down to the ground and rubbing against him, flicking my hair around.

Again my eyes land on Rose, who is giving me serious eyes right now with Val, Mischa, and Maya smirking beside her.

I spin around, laughing and bring my eyes up to Mystery Dancer, and then stop.

Mystery Dancer is no longer there.

King is glaring down at me, his eyes feral.

I step backward, but his hand hooks around my neck, shoving me into his chest. His lips come to my ear. "Stop fuckin' around and get your ass home."

I shove him. "Fuck you." I turn back around to either get another drink or go to the bathroom, but his arm hooks around my stomach, twisting me back into his grip. His fingers wrap around my chin, tilting my face up to his. His eyes glare through me, hitting every single empty corner of my deranged soul and filling it with his presence. "I go for two days and you're already trying to fuck around."

"I don't have to try, King!" I yell, and I'm well aware that my hands are doing that thing when they're flying around everywhere. "I can if I want."

His eyes lift over my shoulder and I turn to follow them, landing on Killian, Kyrin, and Keaton.

I chuckle. "Well, of course."

His finger hooks into my underwear through my dress and

he pulls me back into him, my back crashing against his chest. His lips come to the crook of my neck, sending butterflies and chills all over my flesh. "I'm not playin' this game, baby. You know who the fuck I am now. Don't fucking test me."

I bite down on my lower lip for self-restraint before spinning around to face him. "I'll talk to you."

"The fuck. You'll do more than that!" He catches me around my waist and pulls me into him, pressing two fingers into his mouth and blowing out a whistle to gain attention from the rest of the boys who came with him. I don't ignore the way everyone stares as we walk out the club. The girls drooling and the guys trembling in fear.

When we hit outside, King nods his head at one of the bouncers. "Later, boss man."

A limo pulls up to the curb and King swings the door open. When I don't budge, he glares at me through hooded eyes. *Is he half drunk?* "Get in the fuckin' car, P, before I throw you in there."

I roll my eyes as chuckles sound out behind us. Sliding in, I lean over the console and grab the champagne straight away. Popping off the bottle, I take a swig as everyone else piles in.

"Jeez, King. She can't go to the club?" Maya blazes a joint, knocking on the window that separates us from the driver.

King doesn't say anything, his thigh pressing against mine.

I remain silent, drinking my champagne.

The window rolls down and Maya requests a song.

"You disappear for two days, and then come back and drag me out of a club?" I ask when it begins to be too much.

"Yeah, so?" King answers, brushing me off like I mean nothing. He pulls out his phone and starts flicking through his contacts.

"King!" I yell, clicking my fingers in front of his face.

He ignores me, his eyes staying on his phone.

"Why!" I hit the phone out of his hands, and it goes flying across the car. Everyone quietens.

King looks right at me this time. "Oh, wait, you think this is because I'm pulling some jealous boyfriend act?" He laughs, and then looks at Killian. Just when I think he's going to continue, he shakes his head and leans back in his chair. "I can assure you, P, that's not what this is. You can fuck whoever you want."

"Really?" I say in my drunk state. I call bullshit on his bullshit. Lucky for us, the drive isn't that far away. My eyes drift over all of who is in the car. Obviously, Keaton is out. Incest isn't really my thing, but Kyrin I know for a fact would be down. Killian has loyalties that are probably stronger than his sexual urges.

My eyes lock onto Kyrin.

His narrow.

I smirk.

He chuckles, shaking his head and leaning back in his chair. "Oh boy. Well, all right then, Little Bird." His eyes come to mine, his tongue coming out to whip against his lip. "Come use my cock."

I shake off my seat, leaning forward to flash my ass directly in front of King. I don't know why I'm playing with him right now because I'm still mad. Mad at him, and The Brothers, and everything.

King's hands come to my hips, and he yanks me back into my chair, so hard it could almost pass as domestic fucking abuse. I glare at him, his hands flying to my throat. "You so much as go near his dick, and you won't be able to walk for a fucking week, and trust me, P, it won't be from his."

I whack his hand off my face. I'm too fuming to even realize we have pulled up at the compound. The limo stops and I reach for the handle, flying out of the limo.

"Oh no, you don't get to fucking run away from this!" King comes up fast, interfering my footsteps until I crash into his chest.

I shove him. "Fuck you!" Tears threaten to spill down my face, but I fight them. I fight my misery with anger, because if I let my sadness roll out, I'll drown in my tears. "You lied to me, King! You lied, stalked, stole, and *lied* to me! I feel so fucking betrayed by you! By you, King! Not from anyone else!"

He doesn't say anything, his shoulders rising and falling as he takes in deep breathes. His square jaw is clammed closed, his eyebrows knitted together. He inhales my sharp words and swallows them, because deep down, he knows he deserves them.

I carry on. "On top of it all, you," the tears spill down my face and I swipe at them angrily, "you offered me up as a fucking sacrificial lamb! All for fucking what?"

He winces. "You were Dove then."

"Like that makes it okay!" I yell, my hands doing that thing again. My head thuds from the alcohol.

"You we're my fucking task, P! This is my life! I didn't get to walk away from it like you did and have for the past ten or so years! This is what the fuck I do!" He steps forward and I swallow. "You want me to have emotions, baby? To be soft and that same little boy you knew all those years ago?" He tilts his head, leaning down until his lips come over mine. "I will never be that boy. He died when *you* died." He licks my bottom lip. "*One cannot exist without the other.*"

I shove him away and run toward my RV, pushing open the door. Tears are streaming down my face when I roll into bed and drift off into a deep sleep.

Thirty-Six

P

I'm scrubbing up in my shower the next morning, my head pounding when flashbacks of the night before come pounding through my head. "Oh God." I massage my temples. The fighting with King, him finding us in the club, *the fighting with King*. I'm still angry with him, but he doesn't deserve my words or my wrath.

I turn off the faucet, stepping out in my towel. Dressing in double time, I settle for ripped boyfriend jeans that hang off my waist and show the strip of my G-string and a crop top. Delila called this morning to tell me I have to meet my new recruits and I don't know why, but I'm nervous. What if they're not what I want? I can work with anything, but what about their personalities? I have to *live* with them.

Rushing toward the tent, I ignore the people walking around whispering, probably about mine and King's explosive argument when we got home last night. I run into the tent.

"Sorry I'm late!" I yell before I look. I pause when I see that The Brothers are all sitting in the chairs. King has his foot up on the back of a chair, his hoodie drawn over his head, shading half of his face.

"Good!" Delila claps her hand. "I'm glad you made it."

"Hmm." I smile at her, taking a seat on the ground in front. There are a few people scattered around, but the ones I always find myself drawn to are the four psychos.

I fight it, noticing the three people near Delila.

She points to a small girl with long, dark brown hair, soft, flawless skin, and the brightest blue eyes I have ever seen. She is drop-dead beautiful. "This is Saskia." The girl bows her head between her shoulders, resting her forehead on her arm.

Delila carries on, pointing to another girl with blonde hair. "That's Callan." She's beautiful too, classically. You can see the beauty they hold even beneath whatever darkness each of them is carrying. Looks like Delila already scrubbed them up and put them in clothes too, thank God.

Delila finally points to a young guy, who can't be older than me. He looks to be around eighteen—if that. He's slim, without being skinny, and his facial structure is made for an upper-class fashion magazine. Most of the guys from Kiznitch are good-looking, and when you see The Brothers, that only sells you on that, and this guy is no exception.

He tilts his head up to look me right in the eye, a small smile on his mouth. "And that," Delila points her perfectly manicured finger toward him, "is Kenan."

"Okay." I clear my throat. "Do any of you dance?"

"Yes," the blonde girl says, clearing her throat. "I do, and so does Kenan."

"And you?" I ask to the ridiculously stunning brunette. "Do you dance?"

"Oh, she doesn't talk much."

I chuckle. "I can relate to that." Looking up, I catch King's eyes, and then bring myself to their level. "What about freestyle?"

They all nod, and Kenan stands in front of me, his eyes twinkling with mischief. Oh boy. He's trouble. "Such an honor to meet you, Perse."

I scan his hand that's out to meet me before slipping mine into his. "You too."

He jumps onto the stage and the two others follow behind him. Delila sneaks up beside me, her arms crossed. "They're going to do great, Perse."

I tilt my head, running my fingers over my face. "I hope you're right. Hey, while I have you here." I smirk, turning over my shoulder slightly to catch the boys all staring at me. "For our acts, would it be too much to ask for the same face makeup that the boys wear?"

Delila cocks a brow. "Oh, you're brave."

I laugh, jumping up onto the center stage and ignoring everyone behind me.

"Okay," I say, looking around at all of them. "I get that this might not be ideal for you all to do so quickly."

"Perse?" Kenan interferes and I look straight at him. "We're good, baby girl. You'll see."

I exhale a shaky breath. "Okay, good. I put a lot into this, and I don't want to be an asshole, but it would be a huge relief if I didn't have to train you."

"You don't," Saskia murmurs, and then as if she's surprised she's answered, she looks around at all of us. "Train us, I mean."

I nod, smiling at her. "Good. So, I'll play a song, and I want you all to just do what you feel like you want. This song is pretty mellow, but I feel like it loosens your soul and makes it easy to express yourself. The quicker I see your style, the better."

They all agree, and I spin around, glaring at Delila.

God, I hope she's right.

I ignore the magnetic pull that is coming from the boys, and from King, picking up my phone and hitting play on "Breathe" by Mako. I hope to erase the memories this song gives me of King and me, and I hope to do that now. With this dance.

The song starts playing and I slightly watch them as they slowly form into a dance line, as if choreographed. They are talented. I can see it already.

When the beat kicks in, I roll around and wave my hips to the rhythm. Swinging my hand out, another hand catches onto mine and Kenan pulls me into his chest. I turn in his grip as the verse comes in again. I roll slowly off him, sweat spilling off me already—all of that alcohol—and when the chorus kicks in again, he throws me out while holding on to my fingers and I dance around him, him moving against me perfectly. Holy shit, Kenan is incredible. My eyes find King's and I'm locked in. My breathing harbors and my eyes flutter closed. His finger is running over his upper lip, his eyes somewhat shaded by his hoodie. His knee is jiggling, and I can tell it's agitating him. The song finishes, and I step out of Kenan's grasp.

"Smooth. Very smooth," I joke, shaking my head.

Kenan winks. "Yeah?"

I jump off the stage and pick up my phone again, still

catching my breath. "The song that we will be doing for our first act will be 'Copycat' by Billie Eilish. I have the choreography in my head so I'm going to start laying it out. Though I feel like you all have a good platform of dance so you should catch on quickly." I inhale, taking another breath when King's hand comes to my belly. I stop breathing. He pulls me in closer and I feel him against my back. Ignoring him for now, I keep talking, "We'll play it through. I want you to dance how you want so you can warm up with the song and your body can become warm to it, and then I'll show you the move—Jake! Play the song and thank you!" I spin around in King's grasp. "What are you doing?"

"I need to show you something. Now."

I lick my lips. "Okay, I'll follow you out." I follow behind him after yelling at my new dancers to warm up for a few seconds. Once we hit outside, I reach for his arm. "What do you need to show me?"

"It's in the RV." His tone is clipped, even though his body language is loud.

I follow him to the RV and inside when we reach it.

The smell hits me first. *Blood.* The distinct scent of metal. My eyes come to King who is watching me as I close the door. "What have you done?"

King smirks, pulling out a pack of smokes and putting one between his lips. He flicks open the Zippo, and when the light catches it, I recognize it straight away. *"King!" I scolded him as I continued to chase him through the forest, diving over fallen branches. "You're running too fast."*

"Or are you just too slow?" He grinned as he ran backward.

I growled out as I zipped forward, only my foot clipped an old branch and I was falling, straight for the dirt ground.

"Ouch!" I yelled, pushing my palms off the mud.

"You okay?" King asked, kneeling down beside me and grabbing me by the hand. "I can't trust you for a second, can I?" His smirk was cute, his dimples deeper than ever.

I shoved him playfully just as something flashed on the ground. I bent down and picked it up. "Huh. A lighter!"

"Zippo!" King corrects, taking it from between my fingers.

I shrugged. "Zippo then!" He pockets it and takes my hand. "Hurry up before it gets dark."

I step up beside King. Slowly turning my head, the body on the floor catches my eyes straight away. There's a pool of blood spilling out from his body, his face turned toward me. "Jack?" I rush toward him, dropping to my knees. His eyes are rolling to the back of his head, blood leaking out from between his lips.

"King!" I scream, turning to face him. "What did you do?"

King blinks, his eyes coming to mine. "Revenge, only this time, he's not walking away alive."

"What the fuck are you talking about?" I whisper-yell, taking Jack's hand in mine and squeezing it.

King steps forward and I quickly stand to my feet, putting distance between him and Jack. "Why would you *do this*? The door opens to the side, the light breaking through. Delila steps inside, assesses the current situation and shakes her head. "I hope you deal with that, King."

King continues to look at me, his eyes searching mine. "You won't believe a fucking thing I say anymore, will you?"

"You lied to me! And then you were going to fucking *kill* me, King!"

"Yeah?" He grabs me by the front of my throat, blocking my airways and forcing my lips against his. "I've killed for less, P." He shoves me backward and I fall onto Jack, my hands slipping in the warm goo. "Good luck with your bullshit, P. I'm fucking done." He turns and walks out, slamming the door in his retreat.

"Jesus Christ." I turn quickly, my hands coming to Jack's chest. "It's going to be okay. We'll get you some help." I pick him up, but he coughs, clutching his ribs. His shirt is torn and blood is spilled all over it. I swing his arm over my shoulder and wrap my arm around his waist, pulling him up to stand straight. "I'll get you to a hospital and say someone jumped you." I help him to the door, yanking it open. Thankfully, there are not as many people hanging around because most of them have disappeared for the holiday. I yank him forward, pushing him against the side of the RV. "Wait here. I'm going to get King's keys." I rush back inside and shove papers, keys, and other random crap out of the way to find his keys. Running up the stairs, I head straight for his bedroom, shoving away the memories of the last time I was up here.

Finding the keys on his dresser, I pick them up and quickly rush out, heading back to Jack. Scooping him back in my arms, I direct him to the parking lot. I find King's Rolls Royce as soon as I get there, pushing the alarm on the key to unlock it. Swinging open the door, I put him in the passenger seat and run to the driver's side.

"Drive and I'll show you where to go," he huffs, blood coating his lips.

"To a hospital is where you need to go!" I yell, pushing the engine button to start the car. It roars to life and I skid down the gravel as if I'm being chased by the five-oh.

"No!" Jake coughs, blood spilling out of his mouth. "Please. This isn't the first time King has hit me. Just follow forward and I'll tell you where to go. There's only one person who can help me." I hesitate with myself, but when he pleads again, I agree and begin following his directions.

AMO JONES

Twenty minutes later, we're pulling up into a long drive-way that's lined with shrub bushes. Jack groans beside me, so I quickly floor it forward, pulling up right outside the front door.

A woman comes rushing out, shoving her hair out of her face and panic struck in her eyes. She must be mid-forties.

"Jack?" She hurries down the marble stairs and straight for the door without giving me a second glance. It's not until Jack is out and under her arms when her eyes connect with mine.

She freezes. Something I can't quite piece together flashes over her eyes. "Hello." She looks up to a window that overlooks the driveway before coming back to me. As soon as I look up to what had caught her attention, the curtain has already moved and whoever was standing there is gone.

"This is *Persephone*, Mom. She helped me."

The woman eyes me skeptically before nodding. "Come inside." I follow behind them, closing the doors to King's car. I pat the back of my pocket for my phone before realizing I left it at the compound.

We hit the inside of the foyer and the door slams shut behind me. Chills break out over my skin, like a warning that maybe I shouldn't have come to this house.

"Perse, can you help me?" Jack says, reaching for my hand. My eyes fly from his awaiting hand to his mother, who is beside him. "Perse?"

I step backward, but crash into someone behind me. Before I can scream, a hand is over my mouth and I'm being lifted off the ground.

"What are we doing with her?" the man says from behind me as I kick and shove away from him.

"We don't have much time," Jack says, massaging his head with his bloody hands. "King will come here first."

306

"The Brothers of Kiznitch don't know this house," his mom says. "We can tie her up in the shed outside."

"In the shed for now. Then I'll gather everything I need to deliver her. This bitch. They're crazy about her."

His mom eyes me up and down. "She's the ugly twin obviously."

I scream again and bite down on the palm that's covering my mouth. I want to rip out her hair and chew on her eyeballs, but not because she called me the ugly twin, because she is obviously hiding something I don't know.

I'm being lifted off the ground before I can process anything.

Thirty-Seven

King

The grip that P has around me is as tight as a fucking vise, but her acting up and throwing her tiara across the room because I beat up Jack tugged on my final string. When she was a kid, she always had this idea that she could fix people. Not just hurt people but really fix them. She'd always ask if you're okay and what you were thinking. That's P, always a healer.

The door to P's room swings open and I raise my head from between my shoulders as Killian glares at me from across the room. The room is shit. There's too much pink. "You're both fucking exhausting. You know that, right?"

I chuckle, sitting up straight. "I do."

"And in other news." Killian strolls in, falling onto my bed and leaning against the headboard. "Have you seen the new girl?"

I roll my eyes. "There are two of them, so I'm going to need you to cut it down."

A pillow hits the back of my head. "You know I'm a brunette man."

I snort. "I know you're a *Maya* man."

"Man, fuck that. She knows the deal. We don't touch, kiss, or anything. She's like the little sister that I wanted to fuck for a very brief period of time." He pauses, blows out a breath of air, and then taps me with his foot. "What's up with you? Moodier than usual."

I rub my hands over my face. "Don't know." *I know.* "Ever since finding out that Dove is P, it's fucking with my head."

Silence stretches out. "And what did you do?"

"I almost killed Jack." Images flash over my head.

"Good." Killian stands and rounds the bed, dropping down on the floor opposite me. "He should be dead."

"Oh, he would be." I laugh, shaking my head. "Only I wanted to give *her* the power to do it, instead of taking it all for myself. Man, do you know how hard it was for me to rein in all of my rage and hand it to her on a fuckin' silver platter?" I bring my eyes to Killian below my hoodie. "I tormented this chick for the better part of her life, Kill. I hid in the corners of her bedroom and heard her screams in her nightmares. I'd watch her toss and turn in her sleep. Sweat would pour off her body every night and I watched."

"You actually added to her nightmares." he adds.

I glare at him. "Yeah, so I know she doesn't want me, and that was never the end game. All the shit we were fed as kids, the meal which we fed each other, it's gone stale. We both know that."

"I feel like there's a point to this."

"So I handed Jack to her. Had him in our RV bleeding out. All she needed to do was say the word and I would have snapped his neck."

Killian grins, running his finger over his upper lip. "That's cute. Where is she now?"

I wave him off, leaning back on one elbow. "I left her there with him. He didn't have much life left in him."

Killian doesn't say anything, and then he flies up from the floor. "Our RV?"

My eyes snap to his. "Yeah. Why?"

I watch as his face pales. "Pretty sure the door was open when I passed it." I shoot up off the bed and we both run down the stairs, out the front door, and straight for our RV.

Empty. The blood puddle where Jack was is *empty*. I punch the door until it swings open. "Fuck!"

"Yo, we need to go get her. He'll deliver her to Patience if we don't." *I can't even fucking think of Patience right now.*

"What is going on?" Delila comes rushing toward us, dressed in her costume.

I dash back inside as Killian explains what's happening. Searching around the room, I try to find my keys, knowing I left them on the counter when I dumped his sorry ass on the ground. *She's taken my SUV.*

I run back out to see that all of The Brothers are here now. "We need to go. She has my ride so I can use GPS to find where she is."

Three carloads is all it takes.

Thirty-Eight

P

I shiver in the corner, my fingers flexing around my arms. He hasn't touched me, but now I know who he is. He was the one who wore the mask in the cell. Who came for me. It was Jack. Was that why King had brought him to me? Whose blood it was on his finger when we were in the forest? Jack had disappeared after that.

Banging snatches my attention from above, and I stop breathing. Who is Patience, and what does it mean?

The door swings open and Jack steps forward. He still looks battered, but you can see he has attempted to tidy the wounds that are fresh on his face.

"Persephone fucking Hendry. The perfect little princess.

How much money you are worth?" He tsks, shaking his head. "They'll be very happy."

"Who are they?" I ask, and when he reaches out to touch me, I rear backward and sneer. "Don't fucking touch me!" He swings backward as the back of his hand swipes across my face. My face numbs and thuds with pain, blood filling my mouth.

I spit it out onto the ground. "Fuck you."

He hits me again.

And again. Until I am sure that I'm going to pass out.

I'm curled on the ground, cradling my head. Jack finally pulls me up to my feet. "You're going in the shed. You're going to give me my own show."

I yank my arm out of his grip. "Fuck—" A sharp needle stabs my arm, and I fall backward as fluid pulses through my blood. The ceiling spins as Jack's face fuzzes in front of me. He triples. "Get used to this, Perse. This is how Patience does things." The room spins.

I see grass.

Heavy boots.

Jeans.

His voice sounds deeper, funny, like a broken record or a flat battery. Swirls morph in my vision, everything doubling in effect. My head is slammed against the ground, my body frozen, and my head fuzzy. I don't know. *Where am I? What's happening?*

I'm yanked up to my feet, the smell of sweet marijuana filling the air.

"Dance," Jack says, but his voice is distorted.

I can hear the distinct tune of Tool's "Schism" with smoke clouding my vision. Or maybe that's my brain. Everything hurts as my body sways from side to side. My arm throbs where the sting hit it and I slowly gather what has happened. *Motherfucker drugged me.*

He grips below my shirt and tears it off, and then works on my pants. Tears roll down my face as I fail to stop him.

Fail to fight. Being robbed of my control. I'm going to die here, or, at the very least, wish I did. Jack comes in again, and I watch as he brings the needle to his arm and blows out a cloud of smoke, injecting himself. He pulls my body into him and dances around the barn with me, lost in a drugged haze, before shoving me down onto the hay. The particles fly up around me, my eyes crossing together as I focus on one stick that's floating down over his shoulder, slowly dropping and dropping. My eyelids flutter, my vision being cut black every two seconds as I fight sleep.

Jack bites at my breasts, and just as he swipes my underwear aside, King's face appears over his shoulder, and I know I must be dead. There's a lot of yelling, but I don't know.

In a perfect world, King would save me, not want to kill me.

In a perfect world, I wouldn't be lying here, drugged and vulnerable, all for what? For the mistakes of my parents?

In a perfect world, I wouldn't be a broken girl trying to find her own way.

But this isn't a perfect world. King isn't here to save me, but I go with it. My blinking slows as I lean up on my elbows and watch as King's figure moves fluently in triples. All I see are King and Jack, and then an explosion of blood. My tongue sneaks out, just as Killian and Delila drop down on either side of me. Metal slips over the tip of my tongue. "Revenge?" I whisper to myself, only to myself, because this is a dream. This is not real.

"Yeah, Little Bird," Killian whispers, only it echoes into my head. "Fucking revenge." But then Killian is being torn away and so is Delila.

313

I inhale, recognizing the smell of fresh burnt ash, leather, and honey. King picks me up in his arms and cradles me into his chest. My head tilts back as I finally lose myself in a deep slumber.

I wasn't saved by Prince Charming. I was saved by a villain, and fuck being on his warpath.

Thirty-Nine

M y mouth feels like cotton, my limbs cemented into the mattress. I groan, raising my body off the bed. The smell hits me first, and then I scrub my eyes and open them. The large glass window to the left. The black leather bed, leather dresser, and large TV. The black walls and large white triangle of Kiznitch painted into the wall above the bed.

"Shit."

The door opens, and King walks through, pausing when he sees I'm awake.

"What happened?" I ask, running my hand through my hair. It feels like straw and I smell. Badly.

"You don't remember?" he says, attentively stepping inside the room.

"Not really." I reach for the glass of OJ and take a sip slowly, rejoicing in the cool pulp juice. "God, I smell."

King shakes his head, and when our eyes connect, we do that thing we always do. When our eyes say the words that our mouths cannot, I see the strain on his face. His pupils dilate, and his jaw sets to stone.

"You can go for a shower, P," he whispers, stepping forward. "But I'm not letting you out of my sight."

I squeeze the sheets. "That bad, huh?"

King chuckles. "Yeah, baby. That bad. Come on." He reaches for me, my hand connecting to his. It's a small gesture with so much meaning. That's the thing with King and me. We write our story in invisible ink, so no one else can read it. He tries to carry me to the small steps near his bathroom, but I push him away.

"Stubborn," he murmurs, and for a brief second, I see the old Kingston I knew all those years ago. Once we're in the bathroom, he turns the faucet on and waits for it to heat up, closing the glass door. "I wiped your face down when you were asleep. I mean," he kicks down the toilet cover and takes a seat, "Delila wanted to give you a full-on bath, but I almost killed her, so she didn't try again."

"King," I whisper-scold, my heart clenching in my chest. He looks so...*tormented.*

He shakes his head and gestures to the shower.

I smile, taking a small step inside and undressing while I'm in here. It's stupid because King has seen me naked before, but I'm not feeling very *anything* right now, and I need to sit in here alone. I close the glass door, knowing he hasn't moved from his spot.

"Music," I murmur, knowing he would hear me.

The door opens, and then closes, before opening and closing again. The sound of the sound dock picking up his phone dings through the air as I reach for the soap. Seconds pass before "Evil Angel" by Breaking Benjamin starts playing. My eyes close and I inhale, exhale through the waves of music surrounding me. Music has always and will always be the main part of me and how I express myself and vent my energy. I think that's the same with everyone in Midnight Mayhem. I work on the shampoo and conditioner, rubbing it through my hair. Squeezing soap onto my palm, I scrub my face and then wince when I feel how bruised my cheek is. After I rinse off, I slowly slip to the ground, pulling my knees up to my chest. The door cracks open and King looks down at me. I draw my knees in closer. His eyes don't drop. He doesn't eat me alive with lust. He's tortured and guarded and...*broken.*

Breaking Benjamin continues to fill the silence between us as he kneels down and reaches for my chin. The water cascades over my face, hiding the tears that are free-falling. "I guess that wasn't going to be the last time you kneeled for me." I try to joke about the words he used when I first formally met him on the boat, but hiccup and choke on my words when tears tremble out of me. "I remember everything." I swipe across my cheeks even though I don't need to.

King pauses, his eyes darkening. "I promise you, P. No one will ever come near you again. He wasn't even supposed to be on that fucking yacht. We've got some digging to do, but from where we're standing right now, we think he's been sleeping with the enemy and he killed a guard to get on the yacht." There's so much promise in his words. Can I trust him again? What happened now seems like an ant in an army of soldiers. Jack killing the guard obviously explains why his knife had blood on it.

My shoulders jerk as memories flash through me of Jack drugging me and then trying to rape me again.

King steps into the shower, military boots and all, his arm wrapping around my waist and taking a seat on the floor. He pulls me between his thighs and I rest against his chest, crying.

Yes. *Yes, I can trust this man.*

"Give me your pain, Dove," he whispers into my hair. "Give me all of it."

"Why." I shake, pressing against him harder.

"To numb mine."

I suck in a breath, pushing off his chest and looking into his eyes. Water pours over his hoodie, and I reach up, pushing it off his head to expose his hair. I run my fingers through it, my finger coming down the side of his cheek. "You've grown so much."

He pushes my finger away. "Ditto." He stands, pulling me up with him. When we're both standing again and I'm leaning against the wall, I run my index finger across his lip and he freezes. Have I overstepped? I don't care. Right now, I want to kiss him. Even if we don't go further than this, I want to kiss him.

I lean forward and he remains completely still, unmoving. When my lips touch his, his arm tightens around my waist. My hand comes to his face and my mouth opens as his mimics mine. His tongue sneaks out across my lower lip before he's picking me up with one arm, my legs wrapping around his torso. The song has switched to "Crawl" now, and I'm thankful for the angry tone from Breaking Benjamin drowning out my thoughts.

He shoves me against the wall, his head pulling back and his eyes searching mine. He has one hand pressed against the wall while the other is wrapped around my waist.

"You want to do this again?"

"Fix me," I whisper, leaning into his lips. "I don't care if it's just right now. Just fix me, King. You're the only one who can."

"Why is that?" he asks, and his voice washes over me like silk, turning my limbs to mush.

"I don't know," I whisper, clenching him around me. "Maybe because I've always been and always will be yours."

"Even if I can't have you?" he asks, tilting his head. The light behind the shower door creates a perfect shadow for his sharp jaw.

I swallow down the pain those words cause me. "Even if you can't have me."

His lips fall on mine as he pins me to the wall with his hip. His kissing slows until I'm wriggling and panting for him. Soaking for *him*. And only him.

I reach for the buckle of his jeans to shove his pants down when his kisses go down my collar, down my sternum, and over my belly. His lips come to my inner thighs and his tongue snakes out as he licks me from the crease of where my thigh meets my apex and brings it straight to my clit, pressing against it with his tongue. He grabs my thigh and swings my leg over his shoulder.

"King," I pant. "I want you inside of me. Please," I whimper.

"I can't," he murmurs, flicking my clit with the tip of his tongue.

"Why?" I groan, even though I don't want him to stop doing what he's doing, my hands buried in his hair.

"You know how I fuck, P. I can't be gentle."

His tongue slices me in half down below before slowly circling my clit. I ride against his face, the water dropping down over us. His finger slips between my folds and I come violently, crashing around him. My release drips down my inner thigh, but my muscles release the tension.

Slowly, he stands back to his feet, his eyes solely on me. His focus eating up everything that is me. The intensity in the air shifts around us as we remain locked. I feel his finger swipe up my inner thigh as he stands, bringing his finger to his mouth and sucking off the cum that was obviously on his finger. It is by far the sexiest thing I have ever witnessed, and it being done by King? Deadly.

"Dance with the Devil" is playing now and I start chuckling, breaking the cackle of the intense atmosphere. "I've just figured out that you have a Breaking Benjamin playlist playing."

"What?" he jokes, smirking. "You just figured that out?"

I shove him playfully, my eyes landing on the tattoo over his lower hip. My fingertip glides over it softly. "What does this mean?"

He sucks in a breath. "When I was getting my SOK tattoo, I told the artist to do this one, too. I wanted them done at the same time." He pauses, grabbing my hand and pressing against the rose that doesn't have much detail, bland and dying. "That's Dove's spot." Then he moves his finger to the other one. The detailed rose with bright red petals and the smallest details sketched in. "That's yours."

I lean up and press my lips to his. "I love it. I'm sorry you went through losing me."

He doesn't smile or move. He remains passive. "I'd do it again if I got to have P here and not Dove. Trust me, having you alive is like I've been given a second chance or something."

"Well, don't fuck it up!" I holler jokingly, as I exit the shower.

King wraps a towel around my body from behind me, our eyes connecting in the mirror. It's the first time I've seen the bruises on my face, but they're still not as bad as I had expected. "Thank you, King."

He remains focused on me. "Always, P. Just don't make a habit of defying me."

I smile gently and watch as he disappears into his room, leaving the door open. "The girls brought over some clothes for you. They're on the bed."

"The girls?" I ask, leaning against the vanity.

He nods. "Your girls. Saskia and Callan, and Rose. Kenan tried to get in, but I locked him out."

"King!" I scold him. "Don't be mean to my crew."

King shrugs, ripping off his clothes. Instantly, my libido pings to life. Shameless. I am shameless. King is the cure for my broken and battered soul. *One cannot exist without the other.* Quickly spinning around, I grab the only toothbrush that's in here and squirt toothpaste onto it, brushing my teeth. I sigh before rinsing it off and putting it back.

"Sorry," I murmur, swiping my mouth and entering the room now that he's changed. "That was a bit unhygienic, but I really needed to brush my teeth."

"Considering my mouth has been on your pussy and my cock in your ass, pretty sure I don't care." He throws on new boots and gestures to the clothes. "Get changed and then we need to go have a meeting with Delila, if you're up for it?"

I nod, reaching for the skinny jeans and T-shirt. I drop my towel and change quickly, ignoring the fact that King is probably staring at everything. Once I have my Chucks on my feet, we make our way downstairs. The talking and mumbling silence as I take the final step.

"Wow, you know, you guys are really discreet," I joke, looking around at all of The Brothers.

Keaton is pacing back and forth, and when he sees me, he stops and takes three big steps until I'm wrapped in his burly arms. "This fucker wouldn't let anyone near you for the past twenty-four fucking hours."

King flips him off and heads toward the door. "P."

"I'll be back." My eyes find Killian, who hasn't looked at me. His hands are buried in his hair, his elbows on the table. I find myself beside him, reaching up to touch his hands. "Kill?"

His eyes, red-rimmed and swollen, come to mine. "Worst twenty-four hours of my life."

"Ah, you're not so scary after all, huh?"

He chuckles, shaking his head. "Little Bird, we are not good people. Not even decent. We've all killed, almost been killed, and some of us," his eyes flick to Kyrin, "have been through unmistakably disgusting ordeals, but lemme tell you." His eyes narrow on mine. "Nothing has scared me like walking into that barn did." My heart softens and I pat his head.

"I love you too."

"AYYYY!" Killian jokes, rearing back. "Don't get ahead of yourself. No one said shit about love!" I roll my eyes and make my way toward King, who is still standing with the door open. "Tell her that Kill doesn't love!" I can still hear him protesting when the door closes and we make our way across the field to the tent. Instead of going inside, though, we snake around the back and toward the mansion. I know how Delila lives—hell, I've seen her mansion in New York.

"King." I reach out for his arm, pausing his movements.

"Don't." He shakes his head. "Don't put words in your mouth that I can't follow up with, P." His eyes search mine.

"Why?" I ask the question I've been wanting to ask for way too long.

He pauses, and just when I think he's not going to answer, he does. "Because you're too good for me. Because I break everything that falls on my hands!"

I step up to him, my eyes commanding his as my hand wraps

around the back of his neck. I yank him down to my level so our noses touch. "I've been in your hands since I was one day old, King."

"Yeah," he whispers, his eyes deep in mine. "And look at what good that has done." He pulls away, leaving me standing here alone.

The wind whisks through my hair, and just as he steps through the door, I call out, "I know why you did it!" I tuck my hair behind my ears. "Follow me all those years. I know why."

He steps backward and spins around to face me. "Why. P? Why do you think I stalked you for years?"

"Because I was your task, to watch and wait, to pounce, but the other half of you knew, King. Deep down, you knew I wasn't Dove."

"I didn't," he whispers.

"You're a *liar*," I counter.

He picks me up by the backs of my legs and slams me against the wall on the patio, probably giving everyone inside a show of our own. "I'm many fucking things, P, but a liar is not one of them."

"Then why?"

"Why?" King counters. I can see his anger simmering beneath his cool exterior. "Because you've been wanted, hunted for years before your mother lost her shit." He exhales. "Because even though I knew what I had to do, I knew you were my brother's one true love. The one girl who could bring his sanity back to him, but I still didn't want to give you to him. I still wanted you even though I knew I shouldn't!"

My airways close in. "That's not a bad thing, King."

"No," he mutters, his hand coming to the front of my throat where he massages gently. "But it's a dangerous thing."

He drops me back to the ground. "There's a whole lot you need to hear." Then he disappears into the house, leaving me breathless and twisted in knots.

forty

*D*elila's eyes glisten as I walk in, a glass of vodka on the rocks dangling between her fingers. She exhales. "Goddammit, Perse. Way to freak us out." I lower myself onto the plush white sofa as she stands and pours herself another drink.

Maya, Val, Mischa, Rose, Saskia, Callan, and Kenan are seated around the enormous sitting room. There's a large U-shaped sofa that is facing the floor-to-ceiling window overlooking where King and I just came from.

I was right. We would have given them all a show.

"We need to talk," Delila says, just as Justice walks in with more people behind him.

I notice a few of them. One being Killian's mom, the

sex-crazed addict, and another being King's mom. I wince when I see her. I find Keaton's—well, our mom—Ash, and their fathers, as well as a few older men and women. There was another woman who walked in too, but she came alone. She looked out of place the most, wearing a knit cardigan and a long dress. Her blonde hair was pinned back in a braid, and her eyes looked tired.

"Help yourselves. I don't have time to call the maid." Delila gestures to the small bar that's tucked away in the corner. I watch as some follow and gather drinks and others take a seat in various parts of the room. No one is speaking. The air is suddenly thick, and my anxiety comes in quicker.

I lean into King out of instinct, and his arm wraps around my back, forcing me closer to him. He presses his lips to my head. "You're safe."

I trust his words, but it wouldn't be the first time I have, and he's failed me one way or another. Trust is a learning process. You can completely trust someone, but it will still be a work-in-progress.

"Right." Delila claps her hands, standing in front of her chair. "I would like to take this moment to allow anyone who is looking to harm Perse because of her parents' mistakes to step forward right now, so I know who to kill first." Some chuckles vibrate around as well as gasps of shock. King's shoulders shake beside me, his face burrowing into the back of my neck to hide his laughter.

"No one?" Delila looks around at everyone. "Good, because although I know The Brothers and Four Fathers run this world and we answer to them," her eyes fly straight to King's father, "I have no problem ending anyone if someone else comes after my prized possession. In fact!" She raises a hand, and I wonder if she has slightly lost the plot after all this time. "If you come

325

near any of my prized possessions, I will see to that ending." She exhales peacefully and finally falls to her sofa, takes a sip of her vodka, and then flicks her hair over her shoulder. "Now to the issue at hand, Patience." I've heard that name be passed around a lot lately.

Kaius steps out of King's mom's grasp, a cigar hanging from his mouth. He reminds me of a drug lord. Tony Montana. "Patience wanted Persephone because they knew her linage with Mayhem. They didn't get her. It's settled. We part ways for now."

Delila shakes her head, throwing back more vodka. "Nope. I'm not okay with that. King, are you okay with that?"

King freezes, and then slowly peels himself away from me, his eyes going to his father. "No. I'm not."

Kaius shakes his head. "You're blinded, son."

"Sorry I'm late! You fuckers didn't invite me!" Kohen stumbles into the room wearing suspenders and a tie. His eyeliner is smudged beneath his eyes and his colorful socks are pulled up to his knees. His hair is a jumble of chaos like he hasn't showered in days and his mouth is in a perfect O when his eyes land on mine. "Oh, wow. Looky what we 'ave here." He staggers toward me, snatching a bottle from the bar.

"Jesus, Dahlia, stop your son," Draya murmurs, shaking her head while sipping on her glass.

The woman who looks uncomfortable twists her fingers together, her eyes always coming back to mine.

Kohen drops onto the other side of me, taking a long swig of the bottle. He stares at me blankly, void of all emotion. It's like staring into a machine.

"We share. Did King tell you that?"

"Fuck off, Kohen." King cuts him with a death glare before we all take our attention back to Delila.

"Personally, I think it's time we start fighting back toward Patience. This is the first time they have ever tried to actively step on our toes by using one of our own. Nonetheless..."

"Ahhh, yes, let's talk about little Jack. Where is he?"

King answers quickly, "Dead."

His father's eyes go to him. "And was it cleaned properly? I can't have anything falling back on us. We've lived beneath the shadows, quite literally, for decades. I won't have your dick getting us into trouble."

"It's clean," King clarifies. "He changed teams and went to Patience. Not sure for how long, but I'm gathering it has been a while."

"Actually, Jack did things to Perse while she was in our care, so I would say that he needed to be weeded out. He and his mom were drug addicts. When they saw an opportunity with Perse, they jumped, knowing that Patience would pay big bucks for a Kiznitch, especially one of the Hendry girls." They start bickering in the background, so I look to King, finding him watching me. I focus on his soft lips, the dip from his cheekbone, and his perfectly structured nose.

I want this. You. I say.

The fuck you don't. He replies.

"Where are our brothers anyway?" Delila asks, her eyes flying around the room.

King finally drags his attention away from me and to Delila. "They're not coming. They'll agree to whatever I agree to."

Delila nods. "So it's settled? We will conduct a plan?"

"Son," King's dad interferes. "A word?"

King squeezes my hand and then stands, disappearing with his dad behind the door.

Forty-One

King

As soon as we're out of view, Dad turns toward me. "Do you know what you're doing? Had she not been in the picture, would your decision still be the same?"

I think over his words, though I'm pretty sure I don't have to think long. I will always do what's best for Kiznitch—period. It's why I'm my father's son, why I will take his place when he passes, because I have no problem making decisions for the families, and most of all mine.

"Yes," I answer, fishing out my pack of smokes from my back pocket and biting one out. I flip open my Zippo, grinning that I still own it, before blowing out a cloud of smoke. "Like you even have to ask, Pops."

"Listen." Dad sighs, and I know what's coming. The talk about how I stress my mom out and how there has always been bad juju around the Hendry twins because of their witch mother. When I say "witch," I mean she practiced witchcraft. She called herself a white witch when our parents were younger. People thought they could go to her to be healed, but in actuality, she ended up cursing everyone she touched. I mean, not a real curse, but she let off bad stigma amongst those she touched. It's one of the reasons why a lot of people who are in Midnight Mayhem steered clear from P when they saw her. They thought she'd—I don't know—work voodoo on them without even knowing it. When she found out about Dove and P, she became more violent with her evil. "I know she means a lot to you. You four have this twisted little bond—and I blame that on your mother and her poor choice of friends." My mom was always very close with P's father. It's why we were practically raised together. Whether they fucked or not is a different story. You never know in this world. Very rarely do wives and husbands remain in a completely monogamous relationship. "It puts stress on your mother who thinks you will make the wrong decision."

I roll my eyes, puffing on my smoke. "Mom needs to chill. She's getting old. She needs a new hobby. She wants my Aston Martin. Well, she can take it."

Dad laughs, a full throat chuckle after a while, shaking his head. "Man, you boys really are going to be the death of her."

I shrug. "Is that all?"

"No." Dad clears his throat. "This King and Persephone thing. It full swing?"

I freeze. I don't want to say no, but I don't want to say yes either. "It's where it needs to be right now."

Dad searches my eyes, finding the answer he so desperately

wanted between the words I didn't speak. "Well, bring her home for Christmas anyway. I'm sure we are going to have a full table like every year."

I shrug. "She'd come anyway. Delila has become far too attached."

"Just Delila?" Dad cocks a brow, just as Delila interrupts us from behind.

"If you're both done, we're ready to carry on our discussions."

We both are still chuckling as I make my way back into the room. I'm halted, momentarily, when my eyes come to P, who is sitting on the sofa, laughing with Kohen. The fuck? Kohen isn't funny at all. He's about as funny as The Joker.

I pause, watching as her head tilts back, flashing her teeth and the small dimple in her left cheek. The air shifts between them as P reaches inside of her pocket and pulls out a piece of paper. Kohen's Joker smile vanishes instantly as he slowly reaches out to take the paper. He nods at her appreciatively before carefully putting it into his pocket. I know how I feel about P, but my feelings toward this one girl have never been the issue. It's what I would do for her that scares me, and I don't scare easily.

I slowly sink back onto the sofa beside P, who flops her leg over my lap. I lean back, running my finger over my upper lip and watch her and Kohen talk, moving fluidly through their conversations. When Delila calls for our attention, Kohen turns around and winks at me over his shoulder.

Fucker.

I trust my brother to an extent, but I don't trust anyone with P, much less him.

"So, it's settled." Delila claps her hands. "We will conduct a plan to take back the power they think they have."

"And what's that?" my mom says, ignoring everyone. My mother is like the Dark Queen. No one pushes her boundaries but my brother, my father, and me. Everyone else cowers in her presence, and with good reason. There are some pretty rough stories that float around about my mother and her attaining my father's attention.

Delila grins. "Well, I think we cage all their best acts. How about we start there?"

"So close to Christmas?" Maya asks, her eyebrow cocked. "That's a bit rough. Even for you, Mother."

Delila sneers at her, before addressing us again. "Because it's Christmas. I'm feeling… light."

"I have a better plan," Maya says, leaning forward on her elbows. "We put someone in that they don't know is with us."

I freeze.

Delila snaps at Maya. "They know you're Mayhem, Maya. Stop talking. All that weed is going to your brain."

"Not me." Maya rolls her eyes. "Someone new!"

Oh no.

forty-Two

"Absolutely fucking not." Delila's eyes swing between Maya and me, and I find myself standing and making my way over to Saskia and Callan, further protecting them. "No." After giving the dove drawing to Kohen, I found I was right, and it had something to do with him and my sister. I don't know what, but Kohen's whole vibe dropped when he saw the familiar drawing. He placed it in his pocket with a smile. Had I earned a smile from the one who doesn't possess a soul?

"Okay! Well, how about this?" Delila's voice breaks through. "After New Year's, we'll walk through this again. The fact is, something is happening, and we need to take control." Delila's eyes drift to Maya before coming back to me softly. I see the apology in her eyes. It's already settled. One of my own will be going un-dercover, and there's not a fucking thing I can do about it.

Shit!

"I need to dance." I turn, leaving the room and passing all of the adults. I love Delila—she has taken me under her wing more times than I can count—but I can't agree with this. Not ever. I can't agree to put one of my girls or Kenan into the pit of hell.

I'm pushing out the door when my harem follows behind me.

"Are you okay, Perse?" Saskia asks, stepping beside me.

"Yeah," I answer, walking back toward the compound. "I just need to dance. Let off some steam."

Kenan comes up on the other side with Callan beside him. "You know, we'll be okay if one of us has to go."

"Fuck that!" Kenan scoffs. "Have you heard of Patience?" We're making our way out of the clearing now and I take a sharp turn for the tent, knowing I have some clothes there.

"I haven't," I say, shrugging. "I've heard the name a lot lately, but haven't had the time to ask about her."

"Patience isn't a her, it's a show. They're like us, from Kiznitch, only they don't do shows. I mean, they do, but their shows are underground and for one purpose only," Kenan mutters.

I shove open the door. "And what's that?"

"To sell you."

I freeze. "Holy shit!"

"Yep," Callan murmurs, and I follow her through the en-trance. "It started because a couple of people were offended for not being picked for Midnight Mayhem, and then it grew. It seems selling humans, girls to be exact, is worth more money than what people pay for a Midnight Mayhem show."

"Are you sure?" My eyes narrow. "I mean, twelve-hundred large isn't exactly cheap!"

"That's how much they pay?" Saskia freezes, her eyes wide. "That's a lot of money."

"No shit," Kenan scolds. "But yeah, so once a month, they host a show that's at an undisclosed building. The most powerful people in America, people you couldn't imagine, attend them. They get a text the night of and the rest is history. I mean, if you ask me, that's fucked up. I know Midnight Mayhem is fucked, but they've always stayed in a moral lane."

"Eh." I shrug. "I mean, sure. But not really."

"What, because of the sex?" Kenan grabs his cock and his head tilts back as he bites on his lower lip.

"You are crazy." I shake my head.

He winks at me. "Go get dressed."

I'm still laughing when I move away from them and slip backstage, heading straight for my duffel bag that's hidden beneath a chair. I pull out some ripped boyfriend jeans and a Calvin Klein crop top. The boyfriend jeans are way too big for me but still manage to hang off my hips, courtesy of my ass. I stroll back outside, piling my long hair onto the top of my head, but then change my mind and ruffle it back out again.

Jay hollers from the DJ booth ahead and I raise my hands at him, signaling him to hit me with a mix.

I start snaking my body around the place as The Weeknd's "The Birds Part 2" starts playing softly through the speakers. Rolling my head back until it looks almost inhumane, I roll back to the front of the stage and move my body to the music. *He doesn't want anything like that with you. You're still the annoying little kid he was stuck with all his life.* I swing my hair around in circles, riding the slow beat and bringing my hand down the front of my body, down my tight abs. "Trade It All Part 2" mixes into the song. I change my movements to tight, hip-hop moves. "The Dark of You" by Breaking Benjamin mixes in next. It's slow, throwing me off beat. Literally. My footsteps falter at the change of pace as I take a couple steps backward, waiting to gather enough of the rhythm to be able to use. I start flicking around the place in ballet movements, standing splits and swinging around. When the chorus kicks in, I grab my head and circle it around, entrapped in the song. Sweat pours out of me as the music hydrates me again. *Anything but Breaking Benjamin.* I roll my body back up off the ground, feeling a bit weird doing ballet in inappropriate clothing. The chorus drops again, and I pike up, pressing one foot into my inner thigh and spinning around in circles, dropping to the ground just as "Lalala" starts pumping. I shift into that song, shaking my ass around the dance floor. The rest of my crew piles onto the stage, and we laugh as they all start dancing.

Kenan makes an effort to grab my hips, so I go with it. "In Those Jeans" starts playing and it turns into a Kenan and Perse show. He hooks his fingers into my belt loops, pushing my ass into his crotch. I bend over, rolling my ass and grinding into him.

Okkkuurrrr.

I laugh, biting down on my lower lip, as I raise up slowly, rolling against him. He drops in front of me, his face deep in my crotch. I grab the lower part of his arm, dropping down in front of him and snaking my arms out. I grab his crotch, smirking while rolling sexy circles around him, teasing. I reach for my crotch and pull it softly while rolling my body. The chorus hits again, and he slides into my legs again.

I laugh this time, signaling cut to Jay.

The lights flick back on, and King is sitting in the front row, his hoodie covering his face. Kyrin is beside him, whispering into his ear while his eyes go up and down Kenan, probably sizing him up. Hopefully in a sexual way.

"Hey," I murmur, looking at King.

He gets up from his chair and leaves.

I rush forward, chasing him. "King!" He ignores me. When we get outside, I grab for his arm, laughing what just happened off. "Hey!"

He swings around, cutting me with a glare. "What, P?"

I still. "Wait, why are you mad now?"

He pulls at his hair. "Everything is fucked." He grips me around my arm and yanks me toward his RV. Stepping into it is like taking a step back into the past. The smells, the setting. My small little room in the back. It all feels like lifetimes ago. He starts pacing in the kitchen, and I take a seat tentatively. King is like a ticking time bomb. Only when he explodes, those he loves and keeps close to his heart never get touched.

"Do you know what this life is about, P? I mean, really?" He pauses abruptly in front of me.

"No? I mean, yes but no. I'm hoping I'll learn everything else as it goes on, but King, this is my family. You are my family. The Brothers are my family, and Delila may as well be my mother."

He shakes his head, dropping down onto the sofa while exhaling. His knee jiggles from beneath his elbow as his head hangs between his shoulders. "You were right when you called me a liar." His voice is smooth but thick like cognac. Easy enough to slide down your throat, but with the right amount of dosage, it could kill you.

"What do you mean?" I ask, kneeling in front of him and bringing my hand to his arms.

He looks up at me. "I do fuckin' want you, P. I've wanted you since I was an adolescent child, and as sick as that sounds, I don't give a fuck. I fucking *want* you."

"I'm here," I plead softly, needing him to wrap me in his arms and tell me everything is going to disappear or work out. Our lives will figure themselves out. Only I know that's not going to happen. I know he's not going to tell me that, because truthfully, I know this can't happen.

My heart snaps in my chest. "I can't lose you again, King."

He hisses out a deep breath and leans back in his chair, flinging his hoodie over his head. The night is drifting in, darkening the inside. "I can't fuckin' share you, P. *Ever.* Even when you're not mine officially, you're still mine. That's how it's always going to be. I can't fuckin' function knowing you're walking this earth, and it's not me you're walking it with. I can't fuckin' share you."

"What?" I rear back. "What has that got to do with anything?"

He stands and searches through the cupboards. He takes out a clear bottle of Grey Goose, pouring some into a glass.

He turns, facing me and bringing it to his mouth, shooting it back. "The final act. We always have to participate. You really think I want other men salivating over you and seeing you in questionable positions, even if you're just with me? It turns me into a feral fucking maniac just thinking of that." I stand and walk toward him.

Toe to toe.

Converse to military.

My hand snakes around the back of his neck, and instead of his touch coaxing my pain, it only fuels my empty pit with easily digestible contents. "We can work through it."

He pushes me away.

AMO JONES

I snatch his face back to mine, my fingers around his cheek. "Fuck you if you give up on me again, King. *Fuck. You.*"

He laughs sarcastically. "You think me doing this is giving up on you, P? Quite the fucking opposite."

"How so?"

The door slams open behind us, but neither of us turns to pay it any attention. Music pours through our empty silence. "How, King?"

He steps forward, leaning down until his lips touch mine.

I stop breathing.

"Because you get to live a life without me." Then he walks out of the RV, leaving me breathless on the spot.

"Are you okay, Perse?" Saskia says, and I turn to face her.

She's dressed in a tight crop top and skinny jeans, her makeup done to the nines, making her crazy blue eyes stand out. "Yes." I exhale. "I have to be." Though I'm angry. Like angry as fuck that I feel like we've done a complete one-eighty.

He wants me. I know he does. Not because he says the words, but because of the way the energy in the room crackles anytime we're near. Like an explosion ready to collide. He's ice and I'm fire, and every other element in-between doesn't matter.

She hands me a drink, and I take it, sipping straight away. It tastes good. Like ginger ale only with vodka.

"Come. We're all out in the middle. I think it's called the pit?" Her perfect eyebrow is arched.

"Yes." I chuckle, hooking my arm in hers. "Party pit."

"So, how are you liking your first week with Mayhem?"

"To be honest, I'm not digging it."

I laugh as we head out of The Brothers' RV, making our way to where the loud music is coming from. A fire pit is blazing in the middle with people seated in a circle.

338

I drink the rest of the alcohol and then make Saskia tell me where I can get more.

She takes a seat of her own, away from the crowd. When Killian tries to sit next to her, she moves. I watch and laugh as Killian sits there confused.

"Yo!" He nudges me as I drink my second glass and make my third. "What's her deal? How have I never been able to lay a girl?"

"You won't lay that one," I answer, studying Saskia as she sits on a rock, peacefully okay with being alone and watching the fire.

"But whyyyyyy?" he groans like a child.

"Ew." I slap him. "Stop that right now and go one night without fucking someone."

He drops his lip and I know it's supposed to look ridiculous, but because it's Kill, it only looks slightly adorable. I say "slightly" because he's also annoying. Once I've drunk my third glass and filled my fourth, ignoring the laughter behind me, I take a seat between Maya and Rose.

"Hello, ladies!"

Rose rolls her eyes. "You throwing shade at me since you have new friends?"

I shove her playfully. "Shut up. I am not."

Rose giggles, taking a sip of her drink. "Damn. I so can't wait for Christmas at the Axtons'."

I drink two more and steal Maya's vodka bottle, taking swigs out of that. "Please don't say that. It gives me anxiety."

Maya snatches the bottle back. "I need this more than you."

My eyes go up to what she's looking at. Killian now talking with Callan.

"Oh God..."

Maya shrugs. "It's nothing I'm not used to."

"What is up with you two anyway? I'm confused."

She laughs, looking between my glass and me. "Because you're drunk, or because of Killian and me?"

"Not sure." I sink the rest of my drink. "Both, I think."

"Well." She exhales. "He and I have been best friends since we were babies. Inseparable, that's us. Only we're *just* friends. There was this one time when I was younger that we had sex. He wanted to be my first, and I wanted him to be my first, but after that, he shifted me back into the friendzone, and I him. He scares everyone off me, but I sit there and take him with everyone else."

"Sounds like these boys have a pattern."

Maya smiles, but it doesn't reach her eyes. "Kill doesn't. He just doesn't care."

"Yo! Perse!" Keaton waves me over with his big, burly, inked, demonic arm. I notice a lot of things about Keaton, and one is that he talks to no one. I mean no one. Except for The Brothers and Delila. He sneers at everyone else. I'm thankful I have never seen his feral side, because he's scary enough to look at, and that five o'clock shadow is not helping.

"Yes, brother dearest." I drop down beside him.

He shakes his head. "Wanna sing?"

My eyes go up to King, who's sitting in a chair opposite us with his hoodie drawn. He has a bottle of whiskey dangling between his fingers, his dead eyes drawing all of the energy out of the room and throwing it into my chest.

"Sure!' I answer recklessly.

He starts singing the opening to Billie Eilish's "Ocean Eyes." It throws me off because I wish he would have played something else, something with him singing too, not just me alone. I sing through the lyrics anyway, and when the chorus hits, I can't help but find my eyes on King.

Everyone else disappears around us, and it's just he and I and the crackle of electricity that's passing between us. I don't move, never leaving until the song finishes and Keaton shoves me playfully. "That voice."

I laugh, but then when I find myself disappearing behind my smile, a stab of loneliness beats at my heart.

King nods his head, raising his glass to his mouth.

I stand and make my way to him because I want this. I want him. I've not gone through all that I have all to just give up on him.

I'm standing in front of him when his knees separate and his head tilts back. I see it in his eyes what he wants me to do, so I snake my hand around the back of his neck and lower myself onto his groin.

While I straddle his waist, he buries his face in my neck. "I'm fucking sorry." His voice is mumbled, but that doesn't destroy the fact that every single one of those words had a direct line to my heart.

"It's okay," I whisper, massaging his head.

He tilts his head up to me, and I drop my lips down to his. I kiss him softly, and his tongue sneaks out, licking me in my mouth.

Everyone starts clapping in the background, and I turn my hand around and flip them off behind my back.

He pulls away, searching my eyes. "I can't have you in the final act. Period. We will have to take that up with Delila."

"She's not going to like that," I answer, and King turns around to face everyone.

He pushes his fingers between his lips and blows out a

whistle. The music pauses. "Yo! Anyone else looking at finding a chick, falling in love, and thinking maybe you'll kill a fucker for laying hands on her in the final act?"

Everyone pauses, but my breathing has caught.

What did he just say?

He continues. "So everyone understands that if you find love in Midnight Mayhem, you still have to whip your cock out for shits and giggles at the end of the night? None of you bitches are going to detest it? Use mine and P's relationship as a get out of jail free card?"

They all agree with a round of murmurs.

I want to say that's not fair. Obviously, none of them are in love right now. I turn my head over my shoulder as my eyes fall on Maya, who's glaring at Killian. "Agreed!"

Jesus.

Wait. Back up.

"Good!" King's grip tightens around my waist as his attention comes back solely to me. "Guess we have a selling point."

"But you said *in* love," I whisper, searching his eyes.

He freezes. "What? You think I didn't figure I loved your annoying ass way back when you ate all of my cookies?"

I pull my lip between my teeth and smirk. "You love me?"

His head jerks back, and he brushes me off. "Outta here, girl."

"You heard that, right?" I say to Saskia who is beside us.

She laughs. "Yup!"

I bring my lips to his and rub against his growing cock. "Okay, can we go to bed?"

He lifts me off the ground and starts carrying me to his RV. Everyone starts clapping again with a whole round of "Finally!"

"Yo! You two need your own fucking RV! Fucked if I'm putting up with that noise!" Kill calls out through his laughter.

I don't care. I have King in my arms again, and although our journey wasn't an easy one, it was one that we both needed to take. Every turn, every bump we hit in the road, only helped pave the way to our future. Sometimes it doesn't matter if you know you love someone, or they know you love them. Sometimes, you still have to fight for it, for them. For us. Marriages fail because so many give up without going through the hurdles. Love is a battlefield, and my knight is a villain.

Epilogue

King

I died the day I lost P. Everything inside of me ceased to exist. I didn't want to breathe if she wasn't breathing the same air, exist where she didn't exist. I cut off all of my humanity like a fuckin' cheesy vampire and dove straight into the brotherhood. When she came back to me, the time I spent with her, even thinking she was Dove, slowly turned on all the switches that I had so violently flicked off. She will always be not just my soul mate, but my better half.

"King!" P scolds, walking into the kitchen with my mom in tow behind her. They're trying to get along, but I think it's going to be more a work-in-progress. My mother is a hard woman. "Stop eating all of the cookies before everyone gets here."

I roll my eyes, tossing the cookie back on the table. "Come here." She does, fluidly moving across the room and taking a seat on my lap.

"What if she doesn't like me anymore?" She turns, her hands coming to the back of my neck.

"Who?" She can't be talking about Ash. She and P have been talking on the phone nonstop. Mom is making noises behind us, yelling at the cooks who are trying their hardest to get all of the food cooked for everyone before they get here. We have Thanksgiving and Christmas here; my parents throwing the ultimate bash, and every year, my mom throws a diva fit when something isn't right.

"Cartier!" she scolds, as if I wasn't fucking listening, because I wasn't.

"What? She will love you. Stop tripping." I'm not lying. Cartier and P were tight when they were young, being the same age. Cartier is Kyrin's baby sister and probably the only girl he gives a fuck about and ever will give a fuck about, but she's fucking insane. She's played princess all her damn life and has no problem doing it.

The front door opens down the hallway, and Mom calls to us, "King!"

I tap P's leg, rushing her off. "Ready for some family drama?"

She snorts. "I'm well acquainted with drama." I take her hand and pull her under my arm, exactly where the fuck she belongs.

The door opens, and Kill strolls through with his mom and dad. The Cornelii family, always so fucking strange. Kill slaps my ass in passing before seeking out someone to torment. Behind the Cornelii family is the Nero family—aka Kyrin's family—and the princess herself. Long teal-colored hair, milky white skin, and bright blue eyes look up at P.

Her little tattooed arms fly around P's neck, pulling her in close. "I'm so glad you're alive, P!" Cartier is the only other person I have ever let call P by the nickname I gave her, and that's only because the little shit doesn't scare easily.

"Move, Cartier. You're blocking the way. Ky pushes inside and heads straight for the patio out the back. His parents come in, and before I know it, Cartier and P have whisked off somewhere, as if there was no absence.

Behind the Neros are the Ciceros, aka Keaton's family. Ash still makes Keres use her last name sometimes, though, what with the power struggle between the two of them. Ash and P's family is one of the highest ranking to come from Kiznitch because they owned the entirety of the land. The literal land was her family's; the rest of us just helped find it. There was a war between the Kournikovas and The Brothers way, way back when the settlement happened, and then Ash went and married Keres. Ash jumped into the wheel with him and carved an ace of spades into the metal to help keep her focused and grounded. When we asked her what that ace meant, she just winked and said, *"You'll find yours one day, and you'll know."*

My hand comes out to her as she passes, the memory reminding me that I need to ask her. "Ash!" She pauses, turning back to me. God, she looks so much like P. "Your ace, are you going to tell us what that means yet?"

She shuffles her feet, waiting until Keres disappears into the sea of people. She sighs, folding her arms in front of herself. "I was in love with Klaus, King." Her eyes soften around the edges. "He was my *ace.*"

"As in the game?" I ask, my eyebrow cocked.

She nods. "You know the old legend. Don't pretend that you didn't play a game of Sixers with her." Her eyebrow cocks as though she already knows the answer.

Because she does. Because it's the game we all play with new recruits and/or with each other.

"I did," I answer. "But I didn't know that the ace of spades was a thing?"

Her mouth splits into a half smile. "It's just a myth, Kingston..." She turns and disappears. I'm left speechless. Part of the legend back in Kiznitch started with a specific deck of cards. They were essentially the same kind that you buy everywhere, only these were made for an illusionist. The face of the deck was black, with small little demon babies on them. They were creepy as fuck. The game of Sixers was originally a game that was created by Killian's great-great-great, (and so on), grandfather. During the game, it was fine to be dealt the ace of spades, but if your opponent picked the card from your hand, then that girl or guy, would be either the reason you live or the reason you die. She would either be your blessing or your fuckin' curse. In Ash's view of things, I guess it was more of a curse, because now Klaus is dead. For me, I don't know if I'll ever know whether P will be my blessing or my curse. She'd be my blessing because I fucking need her, but she'd be my curse because I'd fucking die for her. But I mean, shit, it's a myth. Everyone knows that it's basically illusory, because if it was real, that would be magic, right? And magic isn't real...

I sigh, sipping on my cool drink as Cartier prattles on beside me about the next tattoo she's getting. Apparently, on her leg. She's so much more beautiful than I remember, now sporting long, wavy teal-colored hair.

"I heard you and King caused a whole lot of trouble these past couple months." She waggles her eyebrows.

I laugh. "Yes, we did. How about you? Why aren't you in the show?"

She snorts, wiping her mouth. "You think my psycho brother would allow that? Seems he can be a dirty fuck, but I can't." I can't help the laughter that explodes out my chest.

"A dirty fuck?"

She nods. "Yes. A dirty fuck." She leans forward and takes the joint off Maya. "It isn't really something I want to do either, and since my brother is filling the duty for the brotherhood, they don't care too much about what I do."

Maya takes it back. "Only *who* you do."

Kyrin pulls out a seat beside Cartier. "Which is fuckin' no one. *Amiright?*" He glares at his baby sister, and you can see the dark shadow shift slightly, accommodating her.

"Wrong!" She chuckles, taking a swig of her drink.

"I swear to fuck, Cartier, focus on your business."

"I do!" she scolds, and watching their back and forth is amusing, right up until Keaton drops down beside me, his eyes on Cartier. The air shifts around us, and suddenly, I feel like I'm interfering on a very intimate moment.

Cartier's eyes flutter, but then she plasters a fake smile. "Keats! How are you, my monster?"

Keaton's jaw tenses, his eyes coming to mine. "You good?"

I nod, looking around the table. I watch as everyone slips into conversation. Laughter, arguing between siblings, Kill's mom walking around half-naked and sitting out near the fire at the back. "Yeah," I whisper, my eyes going straight for King. "I'm better than good."

Killian jumps up on his chair, pressing his fingers between his lips and whistling out. Once everyone is silent, Killian grins, pulling Callan under his arm. "We're going to play a little game of you hide and we seek!" The parents all roll their eyes, going back to what they were doing, but the younger generation who are here—I've noticed it's not all—remain silent, waiting to hear more.

I groan, massaging my temples. King's arm tightens around my waist, pulling me up from my chair. He bites down on my ear. "You owe me a fuckin' dare."

Shit.

Aftermath

I sat at the back, where the lights were dim, and the audience was quiet. Alone. Away. Behind the spotlight that shone on the cast. This would be my first show, but it would not be my last. Studying every single one of them and what they do.

I picked at my popcorn, the butter slipping down my throat, just as Delila Patrova made her way to the center of the ring. She wore a black and lilac ringmaster outfit and a fedora hat. It was almost as though she had not aged at all.

She brought the mic to her lips and smirked. "Welcome to Midnight Mayhem. We are not a circus, we are not a carnival, and the only thing that you should be afraid of losing tonight, is your sanity..."

A creepy haunting melody started playing in the background as the spotlight dimmed to a deep red. Her smirk deepened as she backed up. Six shirtless men wearing dark denim jeans bared themselves, as seven women wearing white lace underwear and bleached fluffy wings came forward. I knew who they were. The six demons of Hell and the seven angels of Heaven. Seven aerials dropped from the roof and I watched in deep fascination as the angels climbed and twisted and flipped around through the silk. The demons chased them up the ropes as "Threats of Romance" by Marilyn Manson played tragically. We watched as every angel was captured by a demon. Slowly, each demon pulled out a Devil Stick and doused them in gas before lighting them on fire. The crowd gasped when one of the demon's brought the flame to his angel's wings, setting it ablaze. We watched as the wing slowly burned to a crisp, the angel's screaming and howling above the music. One after another, the angels dropped to the ground, hunched over their legs, sobbing. It was almost heartbreaking to watch, if I had a heart. Their demon stood behind them, dripping in sweat. Their faces were painted red, their eyes as black as the midnight sky, and their mouths smudged with dark charcoal. The men danced hypnotically to the music with their Devil Sticks, until the music slowly morphed to "Heaven Upside Down" by Marilyn Manson. The angels slowly rose up, as if from the ashes, now wearing black lace panties and bras, with black leather collars latched around their throats. Each demon had an angel, with one demon having two. They grabbed onto a leash and clipped it to their angel's collar, yanking her back. Each angel is fondled with fire, whips, and chains. The atmosphere is dark and spellbinding. The flashing red lights with the music. The sheer mesmeric feeling of the show already has me on edge. This is the first act, and I know that there are a lot of them throughout the night.

I was here to watch and absorb every single inch of the show Midnight Mayhem... and Kiznitch would never know that I existed in the back of the crowd. Watching. Waiting. Now is not my time, oh, but it will come, and when it does, I'll be raising hell with my presence....

In Fury Lies Mischief

Midnight Mayhem: Book II
Coming soon.

Acknowledgements

To my husband. For being a muggle, but if you weren't, you would definitely be Gryffindor with your kind ass. How'd you end up marrying a Slytherin? (pray for him).

To my kids, for being the best little assholes I could ever ask for.

To my mama, my sisters, my brothers, and my new little nephew, Matai! I am truly blessed to have the most amazing and supportive family.

To Sarah, for being my momager. I don't think she fully understood just what she was signing up for when she became my beta, but now she is my beta, PA, momager, friend, therapist, and my all-round person.

To Chantal, for being the best distraction I could have asked for. For being my rock.
clears throat I'm not drunk enough for this....

To Anne, because you'll always be my sister.

To Lyla, for being my best friend. You're one of the strongest girls I know. We've been through it all. Made mistakes together, made memories together, and cried together. I can't wait to walk behind you as you get married.

To Nichole, for being the best friend a girl could ask for. For drinking my problems away with me, and then curling up in my bed to kick back and Netflix and chill. Drunk. With chocolate wrappers everywhere. You. Are. A. Diamond.

To Leigh, for reminding me who I am when I forget sometimes. You have had my back more times than I can count. I will always have you. ALWAYS! Just don't follow me when we're drunk because I could get us lost again.

To Tijuana! Meeting you for the first time was just like seeing an old friend. Like how Dove explains her and Rose's friendship in this book, our souls knew each other before we knew each other.

To Jacq, you had me read the darkest series I've ever read and distracted me from my writing. But it was worth it and I love you.

SUNNY! Just tell me if I'm the bitch eating crackers.

To my street queens, I love you. Thank you for being everything that I could ever ask for in a loyal bunch of girls.

To my bloggers, thank you for taking the time to read and review my words. I appreciate you more than you could know.

To my readers, if I wrote a 100k novel on how much I love and appreciate all that you are, it still wouldn't be enough. Thank you for riding with me, staying with me, and joining me. You inspire me and keep me strong.

My Wolf Pack, you got the dedication, but again, *howls*

To CrossFit, because without you, I would have committed first degree murder

To my haters, *waves* heeeyyyy, giirrrlll!

To my dog, Raze, for reminding me every single day that owning a Husky is just like raising one-hundred toddlers all at once.

To my other dog, Sarge, for being the toughest little honey bear we could ever had asked for. Also, for making people realize that they shouldn't be scared of Pit Bulls... but those Huskies.... they shady as fuck.

Lastly, to anyone who is trying. The ones who are getting through but kicking off their worn shoes at the end of the day. I see you. I love you. And I acknowledge you. Stay strong.

Xo—Amo.

Other Books

The Elite King's Club
The Silver Swan
The Broken Puppet
Tacet a Mortuis
Malum: Part 1
Malum: Part 2

Razing Grace: Part 1
Razing Grace: Part 2

Perilous Love (Sinful Souls MC, #1)
Intricate Love (Sinful Souls MC, Volume 2)
Tainted Love (Sinful Souls MC, Volume 3)

Crowned by Hate (Crowned, #1)

One Hundred & Thirty-Six Scars (The Devil's Own, #1)
Hellraiser (The Devil's Own, #2)
The Devil's Match (The Devil's Own, #5)

F*ucker

Losing Traction (Westbeach, #1)

Flip Trick

Manik

Made in the USA
Middletown, DE
03 September 2023

37850367R00220